TEAR YOU APART

TEAR YOU APART

SARAH CROSS

carolrhoda LAB

MINNEAPOLIS

First published by Egmont USA in 2015

Book design by Arlene Schiefler Goldberg

Carolrhoda Lab™ is a trademark of Lerner Publishing Group, Inc.

Carolrhoda Lab™
An imprint of Carolrhoda Books
A division of Lerner Publishing Group, Inc.
241 First Avenue North
Minneapolis, MN 55401 USA

For reading levels and more information, look up this title at www.lernerbooks.com.

Library of Congress Cataloging-in-Publication Data

Cross, Sarah.
    Tear You Apart / Sarah Cross.
        pages cm — Sequel to: Kill Me Softly.
    Summary: Teenager Viv, who is constantly escaping her "Snow White" fairy-tale curse, meets the prince who is supposed to save her, but cannot fall out of love with the young man destined to kill her.
    ISBN 978-1-60684-591-2 (hardcover)
    ISBN 978-1-5124-0175-2 (eb pdf)
    [1. Fairy tales. 2. Characters in literature—Fiction. 3. Blessing and cursing—Fiction. 4. Love—Fiction.] I. Title.
PZ8.C8845Te 2015
[Fic]—dc23   2014034324

Manufactured in the United States of America
3-41381-20824-4/1/2016

For my readers

"I want you to bring me her heart.

Her heart—that's what you want, too. . . ."

CHAPTER ONE

VIV STOOD IN FRONT OF THE MIRROR, painstakingly sabotaging her appearance. She needed to look presentable, but not attractive. Plain enough not to upstage her stepmother, neat enough not to embarrass her dad at the party.

She ran her fingers through her shoulder-length black hair instead of brushing it, until she was satisfied that it looked sort of tame, sort of wild. She put on a shapeless white dress that was only slightly more flattering than a hospital gown—then turned to make sure it looked like a sack from every angle. As a bonus, she had red scratches on her arms from getting nicked by thorns in the woods—that had to detract from her so-called beauty.

She looked younger than seventeen: petite and waifish. Her lips were the color of a cherry Popsicle. Her skin was ghost-pale, and when she stared into her own eyes, she felt like she was staring into two dark holes.

"So, Mirror," she said, gazing warily at her reflection, "what's the verdict?"

The glass rippled slightly, considering; and then its oily voice filled her ears:

"Fairer than she is. Like a forest nymph . . . beautiful."

Viv swore and started over.

It never mattered what she did.

The mirror looked at Viv in the same warped way her step-mother, Regina, looked at her.

Viv threw open her closet, startling a chipmunk that was sleeping on a stack of T-shirts, and started rifling through her clothes, pulling dresses off hangers and flinging them onto her bed. Nothing was right. None of her clothes would make Regina forgive her for being herself.

She tried on a boring black cocktail dress, a prissy white lace dress, a slippery red wrap dress that was borderline hideous—and modeled them all for the mirror.

It answered in its typical slick, ingratiating tone: *"Divine . . . so innocent . . . gorgeous. More beautiful than she is."*

Viv sank down into the pile of discarded dresses and called her dad. He was already at the clubhouse at Seven Oaks, where the party was being held. He was rarely home these days. He didn't even bother to lie to them anymore. By now, Viv and Regina understood that he stayed at his girlfriend's place or in a hotel and he wasn't going to talk about it, and they weren't supposed to ask about it, and he just wanted to steer clear of them until the curse was over. At which point, Viv would be out of the house or dead.

"Do I have to go tonight?" she asked when he picked up.

"What?"

She could hear activity in the background. The party

was under way. "Do I have to go to the party? I don't feel good."

"Just make an appearance, Vivian. You sit around all day; I don't ask you to do anything."

"Well, are you coming home first? I don't want to be alone in the car with Regina."

Her dad sighed. "No, I'm not coming home. You two can ride in a car together. Stop being so dramatic."

He hung up.

That was about the extent of the support she could expect from him. He knew how Regina felt about her. He didn't want to be bothered. Sometimes Viv felt like it made no difference to her father whether she ended up poisoned by her stepmother or gutted by a Huntsman. Just as long as he could show her off in the meantime.

A brown mouse climbed onto Viv's knee. It held a wilted daisy in its mouth and made sure that she saw the present before dropping it onto her leg. Viv took the tiny, bitten-off flower in one hand and stroked the mouse's back with the other. "Thanks," she murmured. "Although if you really loved me, you would have given Regina a disease by now."

When Viv was a baby, a fairy had gifted her with animal magnetism—fairy blessings were de rigueur for Royal babies in Beau Rivage. Birds, butterflies, chipmunks, and other woodland creatures were drawn to her, and sometimes they found their way into the house and stayed, like the mouse, and the rabbits in her closet who were always shedding on her clothes.

Finally, she decided on the black cocktail dress, since the loose rabbit hair clinging to the fabric kept it from looking chic, and headed downstairs. Dread filled her, and a sense of helplessness. Usually she opted for being nasty to Regina, but nastiness worked best when she could leave afterward. Tonight they'd be stuck together for hours.

Just before Viv stepped off the staircase and into the front hall, she heard the same oily mirror-voice she'd heard upstairs.

"Your stepdaughter grows more beautiful each day. And each day, your beauty fades."

Viv wondered whether Regina had asked the mirror, or the mirror was offering its unsolicited opinion. All the mirrors in the house were like this. There was one truly magic mirror—the one in Viv's bedroom, which couldn't be broken—but as soon as another mirror was brought into the house, it became part of the network.

Regina capped her lipstick, bared her teeth to check for smudges, then swiveled around to face Viv.

Regina was twice Viv's age, but they could pass for sisters. Regina's hair was the color of black coffee; Viv's was black as ink. Regina's skin was creamy white; Viv's was the stark white of snow. And while Viv's lips were a natural reddish pink, Regina wore berry-red lipstick. Their bodies, however, were completely different. Viv had the slight, boyish figure of a ballerina, without the grace or strength. Regina was toned, voluptuous in a Hollywood way, and had a good four inches on her stepdaughter.

Tonight they were both wearing black dresses. Regina's was flashier, sexier, low-cut, and tight. Diamonds sparkled in her ears and her chest was so shimmery with lotion that Viv couldn't *not* stare at Regina's boobs. She often had that problem. Regina had lived with Viv and her dad for twelve years; Regina's breast implants had been with them for three.

4

Regina was looking Viv over, too. She could examine every inch of her in about three seconds.

"Don't your parents feed you?" Regina said. "I'm kidding." She tipped Viv's chin up to the light before Viv jerked her face away. "I don't think you have any pores at all. You could be a model if it wasn't for those dead eyes."

"Keep your hands off me." Viv hated when Regina touched her. She used to like it when she was a kid—it had felt motherly then, and she'd craved that affection. Now the memory was a reminder of how naïve she'd been.

"So touchy," Regina said. "Shall we get going? I know you're looking forward to this evening as much as I am."

Viv hesitated a moment too long and the mirror caught sight of her.

"Stunning. Perfection. Your stepmother doesn't compare."

Regina's cool dissipated for an instant; something raw took its place. Viv stepped out of the mirror's view so it wouldn't say anything else.

"I'll take my own car," Viv said.

"Oh, please. What do you think—I'm going to run us off the road? I wouldn't crash my car for a chance to break your arm. I'll wait for your boyfriend to do that. Now let's go. We're late."

You're such a bitch, Viv thought. She could have said it— had said it, plenty of times—but saying it would mean dragging out the conversation, and she didn't want to hear anything else about Henley potentially breaking her arm, cheating on her, or killing her. Regina's favorite topics.

So Viv popped her earbuds in and turned up the volume on her iPod until she could see Regina's mouth moving but couldn't hear her voice. She buckled her seat belt in case

5

Regina *did* run the car off the road, and let Curses & Kisses' fiercest songs shield her from her stepmother's commentary.

Viv's friend Jewel, Curses' lead singer, was singing one of her revenge songs. Viv tried to let the bass, the drumming, the screaming push all awareness of Regina from her mind. Tonight, elsewhere in Beau Rivage—in the city, not the green, suburban fringes where Viv lived—Jewel was probably getting ready to go to Stroke of Midnight, the city's evil-fairy-owned nightclub. Wicked stepsisters were forcing their feet into shoes that didn't fit. Villains were angsting; spurned princes plotted revenge. Princesses shook sand out of their bikinis; Match Girls starved in alleys. Wolves spied on girls in red hoodies, and hunters sharpened their knives.

That was Beau Rivage: grime and glitter, magic tucked into shadows and hidden in plain sight. Normal people went about their own dysfunctional lives while the Cursed ran the city, and the strangeness went largely unnoticed. People believed what they wanted to believe.

Once, cursed lives had been turned into fairy tales, repeated, recorded, and passed down. Now, most people thought of the curses as stories—just stories—and even the Cursed of Beau Rivage grew up reading about their destinies in books. There were no new curses anymore, just variations on the same classic roles. Sleeping Beauty's spindle might be swapped out for an earring, Cinderella might ride to the ball in a limo instead of a carriage, but the heart of the curses never changed.

Somewhere, a frog was being kissed, a Rapunzel was detangling her floor-length hair, a thief was sniffing an enchanted rose. At the shore, a mermaid might be crawling out of the sea, her glistening body colored neon by the lights from the casinos. Somewhere, someone's dream was coming true. And someone's was ending. . . .

Viv laid her hand on her arm, feeling how thin the bone got toward the wrist and how easy it would be to snap it. Even with the music filling her ears, the crack Regina had made about Henley breaking her arm was still bothering her. Henley had never physically hurt her . . . but Regina made her feel like it was imminent. Like she knew something Viv didn't.

Viv was full of doubts. Regina was the one who was always sure.

Dark trees bordered the road leading to Seven Oaks. The whole stretch was woodsy and undeveloped, as if to distract from the highly tamed nature of the golf course, and all the poison the country club put into the earth to keep the grounds looking like an emerald paradise. Viv and her dad had argued about it when she was younger, when she first found out from Henley what kind of chemicals Henley's dad's landscaping company used. Back when her dad had been around to listen to her opinions.

"Don't be mad at your dad," Regina had told her. "You should be mad at Henley's father—he's the one putting that stuff in the ground."

"It's not his fault," Viv had insisted, unwilling to be angry at Mr. Silva. That would have been like being angry at Henley, and back then her loyalties were with Henley, always. "It's his job—Dad tells him to do it, so he has to."

Regina had sucked the cherry out of her drink and said, "Interesting argument."

Henley hadn't been cursed then. He'd just been her best friend, her other half. But the conversation must have stayed with Regina, because she brought it up from time to time to get at Viv. She'd say things like, *You shouldn't fight with Henley. Even if he is going to kill you, it's not his fault. It's his job.*

Viv hated that Regina thought that was funny.

She hated most things about Regina.

Jewel's revenge song ground to a halt, then blasted into an angry love song—and Viv heard a muffled explosion, a burst of noise that had never been part of the music. The car started swerving and Viv's head jerked toward her stepmother, whose fingers were locked around the steering wheel. Her red mouth was open; her arms were rigid and the car was shuddering and thumping like they were driving over rocky ground. Viv braced herself, unsure whether Regina had done this on purpose, until the car came to a stop.

Viv ripped her headphones off. Her heart was pounding the way it did when she woke from a nightmare—still alive, two seconds from having her heart cut from her chest.

They got out of the car. Tire scraps littered the road behind them. Regina walked around back to survey the damage and Viv scanned the trees, nervous that she was being set up. There were no other cars on the road. The woods were a black tangle, perfect for hiding someone. Everything was dark, except for the car lights and the moon. Even though she couldn't see anyone, she could imagine someone watching her. Someone who'd been waiting for just this moment.

While Regina lamented the state of her car, Viv dug through her purse for her phone and called Henley.

Henley, who still came to her aid.

Henley, the person she'd be most afraid to see walk out of the woods.

CHAPTER TWO

HENLEY.

She'd known him forever.

He'd found her one day when she was lying in her glass-coffin pose in the woods—a decade ago, when they were both seven—and he'd seemed fascinated by her, as captivated as the animals were. She'd liked him because he liked her so much—it was hard not to like that—and because he knew the forest as well as she did, and never got tired of being there.

They'd spent their days running through the woods, battling imaginary monsters and hanging out in an abandoned cottage they'd found. It had been a hunting cabin once, and they'd cleaned it up, filled the cupboards with books and treasures, and turned it into their secret hideout. It was there that Viv had showed him her dead mother's fairy-tale book, the pages of "Snow White" spotted with bloody fingerprints from the day her mother had cut her finger and wished for a daughter as black as ink, as white as paper, as red as blood.

And it was there that Viv had shared the rest of her secret. *There really is a monster after me, you know. The Huntsman. He's supposed to cut my heart out.*

She'd showed him the märchen mark on her lower back: the pink, apple-shaped mark a fairy had put there as a sign of her Snow White curse. He'd recognized it instantly—she'd known he would; his bloodline had curses in it, too. Henley had made fists and sworn: *If anyone tries to hurt you, I'll kill them. I don't care who it is.*

He was so fierce about it that she'd believed him—messy hair, skinned knees, and all. He'd instantly shot up in her estimation, secure in his spot as her favorite person in the world.

Years had gone by. They'd moved from pretend games in the forest to kissing in that same abandoned cottage, letting the sun slide lower in the sky until at last it was time to go home. She'd fallen in love with him a little on the day he'd vowed to protect her, and as they grew older, that love had become more real. Now it lived in her mind like a story she'd read. The kind of fairy tale that kids saw on a movie screen, filled with hope and happy endings.

The kind of story she didn't believe in anymore.

In Beau Rivage, fairy-tale curses were punishments, rites of passage bestowed by fairies who'd long ago decided that mixed blood was reason enough for a curse. Somewhere in Viv's past, in Henley's past, in Regina's past, was an ancestor who'd been born from a human-fairy union. Once there was magic in your blood, it never left. And it left you wide open to fairy retaliation—or blessings. Gifts from kind fairies. Hardship from cruel ones.

Curses were often terrible, rarely wonderful. The Cursed were marked to be heroes or villains, to triumph or to lose . . .

and while every person had choices to make, fate usually prevailed.

The day Henley turned sixteen, a fairy cursed him to be Snow White's Huntsman. And everything had changed.

It wasn't that he started acting differently. He cried when he told Viv, but aside from that he was the same. And yet the curse divided them. Because there was something inside him—there had to be—that had led a fairy to give him that curse.

Curses weren't random. A girl who was cursed to be Beauty in a Beauty and the Beast curse was almost always compassionate, capable of looking past ugliness to find the good beneath. A boy who was cursed to be Red Riding Hood's Wolf was usually predatory by nature.

A fairy must have noticed that Henley's love for Viv was strong enough to turn into hate. That he had put her on a pedestal—and she could never live up to that ideal. He was destined to lose her to a prince but, as the Huntsman, he wouldn't have to let her go. He could take her heart—physically take it—so that she could never leave.

That was the Huntsman's role: One day Regina would order Henley to kill Viv. And he could do it—kill her, carve the heart from her chest, and bring it to Regina as proof—or he could spare her life, and lose her forever.

Viv didn't know what Henley would choose. She didn't know which loss he'd rather live with.

I would never hurt you, he'd said, *never*—but was it true? Every promise became something she had to doubt, or she'd be that same naïve girl who'd fallen for Regina all those years ago. The one who'd loved wholeheartedly, trusted implicitly—and been betrayed.

CHAPTER THREE

VIV KEPT HER EYES on the woods while the phone trilled in her ear and she waited for Henley to pick up. Four rings, and then a girl answered.

"*Viv*," the girl said—because of course her name had shown up on the screen. "I've heard of you." She said it like it was a dirty secret, and Viv gritted her teeth and walked a few feet up the road for privacy. She had never answered Henley's phone in all the years she'd known him, and she'd been his girlfriend.

"Where's Henley?"

"He's on the court. He's busy. *Sorry*. Can I take a *message?*" The girl's voice dripped with condescension.

Crowd sounds buzzed in the background. Music. Shouts. A basketball game. Probably at Fitcher Park. Viv closed her eyes and pictured the girl getting hit in the face by a basketball. Or maybe a brick.

"*No*," Viv said with equal snottiness. "You can give him his phone. It's an emergency."

"Oh, okay, *Viv*. If it's that *serious*."

There was a sound like the girl was holding her hand over the mouthpiece, and then the phone shifted and Viv heard "No, they definitely broke up" before the girl started calling for Henley, in a voice that was significantly nicer than the one she'd just been using.

"Henley! Hey! Your friend Viv is on the phone. She says it's an emergency."

Viv could hear Henley's friends making rude comments, and Henley telling them to shut up. They hated her because they thought she was a stuck-up Royal bitch. Well, she thought they were lowlifes, so the loathing was mutual.

When Henley picked up he sounded out of breath. "What happened? Are you okay?"

"I'm fine. Just, we were on the way to my dad's party and Regina's tire blew out. Can you come here? Can you change the tire?"

"Viv . . . just call a tow truck. Or call your dad."

"Please don't leave me here with her." She knew she sounded desperate. Her voice was taking on that whine she didn't like. In the background, she heard a guy yelling, "Hang up!" And then some scuffling and laughter like someone was trying to wrestle the phone away.

Finally, Henley said, "Where are you? On the road to Seven Oaks?"

"Yeah."

"All right. I'll be there in a few minutes."

Viv hung up and walked back to the car. Regina was standing by the blown tire, poking at the torn rubber with the pointy toe of her black witch heels. "You called Henley?" Regina asked.

13

Viv gave a curt nod.

"At least we'll have a hot mechanic."

"Please shut up." Viv's jaw was starting to hurt from gritting her teeth, biting her tongue. Sometimes she just wanted to have it out with Regina, but she knew she'd get the worst of it. She'd get emotional, and if she let Regina make her cry, she'd have nothing, not even her attitude to hide behind.

Regina laughed. "You're so sensitive. Why do you care if I think your boyfriend is hot? Or is it ex-boyfriend now?"

Viv ignored her. She paced up the road, keeping her eyes on the woods. A deer peered at her from the trees, but didn't come closer. It must have sensed that she was agitated.

Finally, Henley's truck pulled into view. He parked behind Regina's car, switched on his hazard lights, and got out. Viv was always surprised by how big he was, even after all these years. Part of her still remembered him as a ten-year-old, with a mini scowl and that dirty Saints cap he always wore, but he'd grown up. He had an intimidating silhouette—tall, broad-shouldered, muscular—and a walk like an executioner's. You could put an ax in his hand and it wouldn't look out of place.

Sometimes he *did* have an ax in his hand. He was the one his Jackass-the-Giant-Killer friends called to chop down the beanstalk whenever they had a Stalking party. Henley was the only one who could be trusted to chop the stalk down before the giant got to the bottom and killed everyone.

Henley had come straight from the game. He was wearing basketball shorts and a T-shirt. His dark brown hair was wet, like he'd dumped a bottle of water over his head to cool off, and his T-shirt had damp streaks running down the front where the water had dripped from his hair.

14

"Our hero," Regina said. She twirled her keys around her finger and went to open the trunk, making it look like a burlesque routine.

Henley mouthed, *You okay?* Viv nodded, and he stepped closer to the car. "Did you call your husband?" he asked Regina.

"No," Regina said with a sigh. "My husband wouldn't leave his party for this. He's not dependable—unlike some people. Anyway, I'm sure you're better with your hands."

"Wow," Viv said. "That would be so much less creepy if he was eighteen."

Henley coughed and looked away.

"Ignore her, Henley, she has a dirty mind." Then Regina bent over and half-crawled into the trunk, the fabric of her dress straining against her ass as she felt around for the panel that hid the spare, or tried to get a rise out of Henley, or whatever she was doing. After a minute or two of searching, Regina announced that there was no spare tire. Maybe she'd known that from the start—but she acted like she was frustrated. She took out her phone to call for a tow truck, complaining that it was going to take forever, they were already late, she'd gotten all dressed up and now she was sweating and *Viv* probably wasn't sweating at all. . . .

"I can drive you guys to Seven Oaks," Henley said. "Then come back and wait for the tow."

"Would you really?" Regina said. "You're amazing." She blew him a kiss and turned her attention back to the phone.

Henley slammed the trunk shut, and left his hand resting on top of it. He had nice hands: big, powerful—reassuring or dangerous, depending on the situation. They were a warm, light brown color, alive-looking next to the dead-white pallor of Viv's. He was looking at her, his head cocked to the side, like now that they were sort of alone they could talk. It had been a few days since they'd seen each other. They'd been fighting then. As usual.

There was always that time, when they met again after being apart—when their irritation was exhausted, and their last argument seemed far away—when seeing each other felt like relief. Like whatever they'd thought they'd lost was still there somewhere, if they could just find it and hold on to it.

Viv reached for his hand. "Thanks," she said. "Did you get a lot of shit for leaving?"

He shrugged. That was a *yes*. She knew his friends harassed him about her. It was their way of looking out for him. None of Henley's friends had been in a relationship that had lasted longer than three months. To them, it was simple: if he wasn't happy, he should cut her out of his life. They didn't understand why Henley put up with her. They didn't understand how hard it was to separate yourself from someone who was a part of you.

"Sorry if I ruined your game. I just panicked, and . . ." Her eyes turned toward the woods, still searching.

"I know."

"It seems stupid now."

"Whatever, Viv. It's fine."

"I wish she wasn't here."

"Don't you always wish that?" His half smile was cute. It made her wish, even more, that it was just the two of them on this road, with the whole night stretching out, unfinished.

"Maybe if I whistle, a friendly hungry bear will come out and maul her. As a favor to me."

16

"I'd probably get mauled first."

"That's a risk I'm willing to take." She grinned; he treated her to that smile again.

"Yeah, I bet."

The darkness, now that he was here—smiling, not mad, not hurt by something she'd done—seemed full of promise. They could drive to the city—or better yet, drive to a town where no one knew them. Find an all-night diner, order burgers and Cokes and some monstrous, dead-looking cake from the display case. And then later, they'd park somewhere deserted, spread a blanket across the grass, and stargaze and talk until a predawn chill crept into the air. He'd pull her closer and whisper, *Why do we fight so much? What the hell is wrong with us?* And she'd say, *We're not fighting now.* And they'd kiss, perfectly in tune with each another, the bad days so distant they seemed imaginary.

She was on the verge of asking him if he wanted to go—leave Regina to wait for the tow truck, screw the party—when she noticed a red heart drawn on the back of his hand in felt-tipped marker. A flirty, bubbly heart.

She wanted to smack his hand off.

"That's manly," she said.

"What?" His dark eyes narrowed. They were almost the same shade of brown as hers.

She flicked the heart. "If you need a new girlfriend, do you have to pick a stupid one?"

"Somebody drew something on my hand. Who cares?"

I care, she thought, feeling paranoid, and possessive.

"Hey." He lowered his voice. "Who did I come out here to get? You. What are you freaking out about?"

17

She hugged her arms around her waist. Turned her back on him.

"Ready to go?" Regina called. She sounded perky, like they were a group of friends about to embark on a road trip. Viv started toward the truck and Regina climbed in before she got there, sliding to the middle of the bench seat like she'd scored some kind of coup.

Whatever, Viv thought. *Knock yourself out.*

The three of them squeezed in, bodies too close for comfort. Just the feel of Regina's arm against hers made Viv feel violated. She didn't want to be anywhere near her stepmother. Didn't want to choke on Regina's perfume, or have to brush strands of Regina's hair away from her face whenever Regina whipped her head around to flirt with Henley.

"So what were you up to tonight?" Regina asked him. "Before you showed up to rescue us."

Henley reached to shift gears and his hand brushed Regina's thigh. "Just hanging out. Playing basketball at Fitcher Park."

"Were you shirts or skins?"

Viv rolled her eyes. Now would be a good time to fall into an enchanted coma, so she wouldn't have to listen to this.

When Henley said, "Skins," Regina said, "I'm surprised the girls let you leave," and laughed like she wasn't thirty-five years old. Her knee-length black dress had ridden up to midthigh, and every time Henley reached over to switch gears, Regina's leg nudged his hand and her dress wriggled higher. Regina had a gorgeous body—the mirror never questioned that. The mirror judged beauty—and Viv was beautiful, supposedly—but Regina was sexy. Viv felt like a stunted little girl in comparison.

The wind was rushing in through the open windows, ruffling Viv's messy hair.

Henley was watching the road, not talking much, but not talking to Viv at all.

And Regina was laughing like she was auditioning for the role of *Sexy stepmom who steals her stepdaughter's boyfriend.*

Viv put on her headphones and dialed up the volume until it felt like the bass and the drumming were living in her head. She needed to be pumped full of an emotion she couldn't muster right now—rage, maybe, instead of the panic she felt when she was stuck next to Regina. She closed her eyes and tried to let the music take her away, but there was no real escape.

There never was.

CHAPTER FOUR

SEVEN OAKS WAS A COUNTRY CLUB that mainly admitted Royals—the cursed elite. It was set on a two-hundred-acre golf course, and had a pool, a gym, a restaurant, and banquet rooms for parties. Viv's dad liked Japanese gardens and Louis XIV France, so the landscape was a blend of Kyoto and Versailles. The grounds around the clubhouse were decorated with cherry trees, a topiary garden, five fountains depicting fairy-tale scenes, and the seven large oak trees that gave the club its name.

When Henley's truck pulled up to the entrance, a valet came forward. Henley told him that he was just dropping off. Viv scrambled out as soon as the wheels stopped turning, but Regina stayed in the truck.

"Henley, you have to come to the party!" Regina said. "After all you've done for us tonight, I insist."

Viv tried to give him a *kick her out right now* glare through the windshield, but she didn't think he saw her.

"I have to go back for your car," Henley said.

"Oh, someone else can do that. And you don't have to hang out with Viv if you don't want to. You can be *my* guest."

Viv didn't hear Henley's response, but she didn't see him boot Regina out of the truck, either. She walked as quickly as she could up the pathway to the clubhouse.

She pressed her hands to her cheeks. Angry tears rolled onto her fingers and she wiped them away. If he couldn't say no to little things, what proof was there that he would say no to the most crucial part of the curse?

Viv burst into the party. The atmosphere—jazzy French pop music, preppy waiters, and guests in country club attire—was such a contrast to the stifling vibe in the truck that it was almost surreal.

She'd been there less than a minute when she was intercepted by her dad.

Stephen Deneuve wore an off-white suit and a vibrant green shirt with mint-green pinstripes. His silvery hair looked freshly trimmed. He'd probably gone for a manicure and a facial, too, but he was spoiling the effect by scowling at her.

"It looks like a cat died on your dress," he said.

"It's rabbit fur." Viv plucked a strand and let it fall to the floor.

"Well, whatever it is—don't you own a clean dress? You're my daughter. People notice you." He took a cloth napkin and tried to brush the fur off, then stopped, probably realizing how it looked. He couldn't stand to be publicly embarrassed, to be talked about in anything less than glowing terms, which made their family drama—and the gossip that surrounded the curse—a source of constant irritation to him.

When Regina and Viv presented the pretty picture of lovely wife and fairest princess, he wanted them around. Tonight they were supposed to be on their best behavior and make him look good. Then, after the party, he would vanish from their lives until he had a use for them again. He needed them sometimes, but he didn't like to be needed. He didn't want the stress of trying to keep the peace. He liked easy successes. He liked games he could win.

Viv's father abandoned the napkin. "Where's Regina?"

"I don't know. She's the one who's obsessed with me."

"Yes, I've heard it before: *you're such a victim.* Please. I can name twenty girls who would love to have your curse. And don't take it out on Regina. Your mother wished this on you. Regina didn't ask for this, and neither did I."

In the middle of the lecture, one of the club members came over, and Stephen's irritated expression disappeared, replaced by the jovial everyone's-best-friend pose he put on for society people. "Ted!" he said, clapping the man's arm. "Glad you could make it!"

Ted Grant was a former Beast. He was about sixty. He'd regained his human appearance, but you could still see traces of the curse if you looked. He reminded Viv of the Cowardly Lion from *The Wizard of Oz,* only without the whiskers and the yellow paint.

"What a beauty," Ted said, ogling her. "The cursed beauties—they're so lovely at this age. Lovely," he repeated, like Viv was a canapé he was snapping up. "May I?" He bowed a little, and gestured for her hand.

No, Viv wanted to say.

She gave him her hand.

Ted brought it to his lips and kissed it, his mouth pushing against her skin like a warm, wet slug. He smelled like old age and expensive scotch, and it took every ounce of restraint not to rip her hand away.

Ted straightened, and glanced across the room at his wife, who was chatting with a woman who'd married a Frog Prince. "Not that Helen isn't lovely. She's a beauty, aging much better than most. But nothing compares to the flower that hasn't been plucked."

Viv's dad laughed politely, the two men exchanged a few more words, and Ted went on his way.

"Ugh," Viv's dad said when he was gone. "Does he not know we're related? What a way to talk in front of me."

"He can go pluck himself," Viv said.

"Viv. Watch your mouth."

She sighed, and her dad gave her a shove and told her to go be social.

She didn't want to be cornered by another sketchy elder statesman, so she beelined for the first group of young people she saw. She didn't realize until she was among them that the foursome was composed of happy couples.

They were all about five years older than she was. There was a Cinderella/Prince Charming pairing she knew a little about. They were sort of infamous for their nebulous happily ever after. They'd ended up living together, and it seemed like they were involved, but no one was really sure what to make of them. And there was a prince and princess (easy to identify because the princess was wearing a tiara), but Viv didn't know who they were.

The princess had long, copper-colored hair in tight, fine

curls. The prince was pale and freckled with a pretty, sculpted face. They had their arms around each other and kept tilting their heads to kiss. Viv was both disgusted and envious. They were just so . . . happy.

"Do you remember," the princess said to her prince, "when you needed a bee to land on my lips to figure out who I was?"

"Your sisters had eaten candy, and you'd had a bit of honey, and that was how the bee knew it was you. Now I know your lips so well I wouldn't need any help finding you. And you always taste like honey to me."

The couple took a moment to gaze into each other's eyes, and then the princess turned to explain. "It was a test to break an enchantment. Connor had to identify the youngest princess out of three—that was me. A bee helped him."

"We know the fairy tale," Max said, swigging his beer. Max was the nebulously happy Prince Charming. He was your standard tall, dark, and handsome type, with the added eccentricity of being an exhibitionist—although he'd settled down since he'd gotten together with Dusty (aka Cinderella). The drunken-frat-boy streaking was before Viv's time.

"A bee landed on your face?" Dusty asked in horror. She was barefoot. Supposedly she had a thing against shoes.

"I was in an enchanted sleep at the time," the princess said, "so I didn't even notice. Besides, that bee brought us together."

"And we lived happily ever after," the prince said, hugging his princess close. They looked like a Valentine's Day card. All they needed was a big heart behind them.

Viv kept turning toward the door, hoping to see Regina

make her entrance—alone. Her worries about what her stepmother was doing, and what kind of seeds she might be planting, made a hot-cold feeling run through her limbs.

The feeling got worse when she saw Henley walk in with Regina. Everyone knew Henley was a Huntsman, and there he was with the wicked stepmother who wanted her dead. She tried to stay focused on Regina and Henley so she wouldn't see the scandalized faces that were no doubt turned toward her, waiting to catch her reaction.

Viv's mother had wanted her to have a dramatic life—that was why she'd wished for the curse. But Viv didn't want it—she'd never wanted it. Sure, she'd liked being a princess, liked having that elite status and being special. But the older she got, as the trap started to close, she just felt scared. None of it was in her control.

"Do you want me to get you a drink?" Dusty asked her. "You look nervous."

"*Don't* get anyone anything," Max said. "No serving." He turned to Viv. "It's not personal. We're trying to break her of the habit. I'll get you a drink, if you want."

"No, I'm fine," Viv said, straining to see past him.

Regina was touching Henley's arm, leaning in to murmur something. It looked like she was dying to wrap her fingers around his biceps and squeeze.

"Stepmothers," Dusty said. "They're the worst, aren't they?"

There wasn't any judgment on Dusty's face, just a strained kind of sympathy. "Yeah," Viv said. "In this town, anyway."

Dusty was by herself now. Max had skated off through the crowd to get another beer. Viv noticed that Dusty's eyes went to him periodically. Not searching or worried. Just like she enjoyed looking at him.

"So, you guys are happy?" Viv asked.

"We think so," Dusty said. "I wouldn't say we're a storybook romance, like those two"—she nodded at the Queen Bee prince and princess—"but it *is* different than a normal relationship. Because your curse, the way it plays out . . . it bonds you. Whatever happens, you have this magical time that you shared, that no one else will ever have.

"I know what it's like to feel like you won't have that, but you have to hang in there. And"—Dusty's gaze traveled to where Henley stood with Regina—"be careful. Because that guy's enormous. And it looks like—"

"I know what it looks like," Viv said.

Regina was introducing Henley to some cursed society ladies; not women she was friends with, just women who'd be appalled at seeing her with a Huntsman, and who'd be sure to talk about it later.

Regina had never been so public about their curse. Usually she was nasty in the privacy of their own home, and played the role of happy trophy wife at parties. But tonight it was like she was making a statement, letting everyone know that change was coming.

Viv left the happy couples and cut through the party to get farther away from Regina's little show.

People were looking at her in a manner they probably thought was discreet. A few of the guests greeted her, and she smiled and said hello because this was her dad's club and that was what she was expected to do. But she didn't linger. She only stopped when she reached the floor-to-ceiling windows that overlooked the grounds. Standing before her reflection, ghostly against the backdrop of night, she pressed her forehead to the glass, yearning to be anywhere else. On the green, a few hundred feet away, cell phone screens flickered in the darkness. Probably teenagers. There was always a group who cut out of the party to drink or fool around on the grounds.

Maybe she'd join them. They hadn't seen Henley with Regina. She could go and listen to their inane conversations and drink until they seemed entertaining. It would be better than this.

Next to the window, French doors led to a terrace that was used for outdoor dining. Viv's hand closed around the door handle.

But first she turned back, unable to resist looking again, and saw that Henley was alone. Regina was with Stephen, chatting with Ted and Helen Grant, and Henley was weaving through the crowd, trying not to act like he was looking for someone. An aura of awkwardness surrounded him. She knew he hated places like this. He was an outsider here and no one would pretend that he wasn't.

Viv didn't like the club, either, but she never felt like she didn't belong. She felt like an outsider around Henley's friends. They were a completely different crowd of Cursed. There was Jack Tran—the self-proclaimed king of the Giant Killers (all Giant Killers took the name *Jack*; you had to know their last names to know who anyone was)—and Elliot Nicks, with his stolen tinderbox and the creepy dogs that did his bidding whenever he lit up. There was always a group of Red Riding Hoods; plus hangers-on, kids without curses who wanted to be part of the crowd; a few Bandit Girls; and that jerk with the mirror shard stuck in his eye who could see everyone's flaws and was always calling people on their shit.

Henley finally noticed her, started to come over, and Viv slipped out the door. The way she was feeling, a simple conversation would blow up into an argument, and she didn't want to be a spectacle for the past-their-prime Cursed at the party. Those vultures had enough to talk about already.

As she stepped onto the dark golf course, Viv was hit by a memory from tenth grade: fall formal, a few months before Henley was cursed. They'd gone to the dance because she wanted the snobs at her prep school to see her hot boyfriend all dressed up. Walking in with him while everyone stared— that was the best part. But the music sucked and she didn't like her classmates, so they left early and came to Seven Oaks. Snuck onto the green with a couple of clubs and whacked balls into the darkness—laughing too loudly, shouting at the night. Henley shed his dress shirt and tie to play in his undershirt, and when security showed up, they ran. Viv abandoned her shoes but saved Henley's shirt. She wore it home where she hung it in her closet and periodically pressed her nose to the fabric, smelling cut grass and Henley's woodsy cologne. Like she had a piece of him even when he wasn't there. The scent had long since faded, but she still had the shirt in her closet.

Viv pushed the memory down. They'd had lots of good nights, but that was in the past. Now, when people stared, they looked at her not like she was lucky, but like she had a death wish.

She heard the door open behind her, a sudden rush of party noise until it closed.

Henley called her name. Part of her wanted to turn back—

28

there was no one here she'd rather be with. But she kept going. She knew it would annoy him—it would've annoyed her, if he'd done it.

"How long are you going to pretend I'm not here?"

She stopped then. "I guess I'm taking my cues from you. Did your date get bored of you?"

"You think I want to be at this party? I'm here because you are."

"Sorry, I could've sworn Regina was parading you around. Was it me? Are we here together?"

"Your stepmom and I," he said, "walked in at the same time. You would have been there, too, if you hadn't rushed inside before I could even talk to you."

"Well, I didn't know I was supposed to wait. I thought you were leaving."

"Yeah . . . why is your stepmom the one who invites me, and you jump out of my truck like you're ditching a cab? I'm not your taxi service."

"No, you're her puppet."

"Really, Viv? I'm her puppet now?"

"That's what everyone *thinks*. That's what you let them believe. And why would you, unless it's true? Do you just like the attention? Or do you just like getting a good view of her boobs?"

"What the hell are you talking about?"

She wasn't sure she knew anymore. She was at the point in the argument when she could feel things spiraling out of her control, when she barely knew what was coming out of her mouth. She felt gripped by panic—the need to make him believe her, to understand why she was upset. There was no

29

backpedaling or apologizing. She moved in one direction and that was away. Farther and farther away from the Viv and Henley who'd played midnight golf on the green—the world on one side, the two of them on the other.

"All right. Whatever. Have fun with these assholes. I'm leaving."

That wasn't what she wanted, but she couldn't stop. "Good. 'Cause I'm looking for a new boyfriend and it'll be much easier without you around."

"Yeah? That's what you're going to do tonight?"

"Maybe I can find a guy who'll draw a heart on my hand. That would be a cute, flirty thing to do."

He sighed. "You're still going on about that?"

She posed with her hands over her heart. "I just think it's *so cute*. So charming. I wish I'd thought of that. You know, sometime after fifth grade."

"You sound like you're in fifth grade."

"That's not what my new boyfriend's going to say."

Knowing he was still watching her, she headed toward the group of kids on the green, following the beacon of their cell phones and cigarettes. She didn't know what she would do exactly. Just that she would do something, as long as Henley was there to witness it.

She edged into the circle—twelve guys and girls from her prep school. There were two princes: Danny Mirza, the youngest brother in a Three Princes and Princess Nouronnihar curse, and Ben Arden, who had a Rapunzel curse. There was a princess-and-servant pair, Acacia Vaughan and Ivy West— best friends who shared a Goose Girl curse. The rest got by on the status of their parents' curses. The boys wore bright polo shirts and the girls wore strapless shift dresses patterned with tropical flowers and birds. The Goose Girls were drinking Grey Goose from a lipstick-smeared bottle.

Danny's eyes were glued to Cara Basil, a girl whose claim to fame was her social-climbing dad's enchanted cat. She was showing everyone how she could tie a cherry stem in a knot with her tongue. Danny was making jokes about popping cherries and Cara kept laughing, but not hard enough to choke on the cherry; and when she showed them the knotted stem, Danny said, "Damn. What else can you do with your tongue?" And Viv threw up in her mouth a little but decided he was definitely her target.

Danny had been part of a cursed love quadrangle with his two older brothers and their cousin, and ever since he'd lost the girl to his brother, he'd been drifting closer to playboy territory. Viv didn't have a lot of patience, and she needed someone who'd flirt with her *now,* not in ten minutes.

"I've been looking for you," she said to Danny, stepping up to him and putting her hand on his chest.

"Yeah?" His eyes flicked past her to Henley. Half wary— Huntsmen had bad reputations—and half tempted, because Viv was looking at him in a way that was about as subtle as one of his cherry jokes.

"Yeah." She curled her hand around his collar, pulled him down to her height. "I have to tell you a secret." And then she whispered something dirty in his ear. Her lips brushed his earlobe; her hair tickled his neck. It didn't matter what she said. It didn't have any meaning to her beyond the reaction it got out of him, which was shocked laughter and fingers that dug into the fabric of her dress.

31

She was only half focused on what Danny was doing. She was thinking about Henley, how angry he would be—as angry as she'd been? Angrier? Her breath caught.

She waited for a hand to grab her from behind, for Henley's fingers to close around her throat—and hoped that someone would pull him off her if they did. But the only hand on her was Danny's, and she was getting tired of that. A few more minutes and he might start to believe she'd meant what she'd said.

When she turned to look behind her, Henley was gone. She let go of Danny's collar, and his hand fumbled to grab her before she slipped away. She jerked free and kept going. He shouted after her, "So that's how it is?"

Yeah, that was how it was.

The night seemed darker once she was alone again, and the high she'd gotten, the sense of righteousness she'd felt, was fading. Her steps got awkward and she walked faster, hoping her body would even itself out. She let herself back into the clubhouse, back to the titter of polite laughter, the strong scent of liquor, and Serge Gainsbourg singing "Couleur Café." The Basils' enchanted cat was standing on one of the refreshment tables, licking livery mousse off the tops of a whole tray of canapés.

The Queen Bee prince and princess were wrapped in each other's arms. Dusty and Max were dancing. They looked happy—like being together was fun. Like they were a team, and nothing could drive a wedge between them.

Viv missed feeling like that. Dusty had said that being part of the same curse gave you a special bond. And lots of people had tried to reassure Viv that she'd have her happy ending one day. But there were different kinds of Prince Charmings. Dusty's prince was a hot rich guy who'd danced with her at a ball, found her lost shoe, tracked her down, and changed her life. Viv's Prince Charming was a guy no one had ever met, who was going to show up when she was already in her glass coffin, see her pretty face and her limp body, and decide to take her home. And even that would only happen if the Huntsman spared her.

So the words *someday my prince will come* had never set Viv's heart aflutter. When she thought of her future prince, she thought of the older Snow White prince who already lived in Beau Rivage: a man who was married to a Snow White princess, and who drugged his wife so heavily she might as well have been a zombie. Rumor had it he'd roofied her on their wedding night because he could only get excited by an unresponsive bride.

Miserably ever after? Was that what she had to look forward to?

The Snow White princess curse had so much status . . . Viv could understand why her mother had wished for it. She was instantly recognizable in Beau Rivage—right up there with Cinderella and Sleeping Beauty. But the way Viv saw it, everyone in her curse wanted her dead. Her stepmother wanted her dead, her prince preferred her dead, and Henley . . . he probably wanted to kill her half the time.

Viv wanted to believe that she could be happy, that her curse would end in something magical—but she couldn't. Happily ever after happened to some people. Viv wasn't one of them.

She wandered through the party, but didn't see Henley or

Regina. Their absence made her nervous. Where were they? Had they left together?

Viv headed out to the parking lot. Regina was there, a lit cigarette between her fingers, chatting with one of the valets. Regina didn't normally smoke; she was too concerned about her looks. But there was red lipstick on the filter, and the cigarette had the same odor as the brand Henley smoked. Viv could picture Regina asking for one, leaning close as Henley lit it for her, and asking him how to do it, the way she'd asked Viv's dad how to swing a golf club when she'd first come to Seven Oaks.

"You're just in time," Regina said. A stream of smoke spiraled up from her fingers. "It's about to get good."

"What is?"

"Wait for it . . ."

Regina was posed, chest up, like she was holding her breath. And then somewhere in the parking lot there was a shattering crunch. Followed by the shriek of a car alarm. Viv followed the sound and her eyes found Henley, lit by the flashing headlights of an orange BMW until he smashed them with a shovel. Danny drove an orange BMW. He even had plates that said 3MIRZA; there was no mistaking his car. The alarm wailed on and on over the sound of Henley bashing in the windows, denting the body, busting it up like it was the bonus round of the old *Street Fighter II* arcade machine in the clubhouse. Viv flinched with every thud, crack, crunch—like the damage was reverberating throughout her body.

"All those tools he keeps in his truck," Regina said. "They're useful for things besides gardening. Just think—that could be you if you play your cards right."

"Aren't you going to stop him?" Viv asked the valet.

He shrugged. "I don't get paid enough to get between that guy and his anger issues."

"You should go over there," Regina said to Viv. "You have a calming influence on Henley. Oh wait—no. You make him want to hurt people. Well, that works, too. Go on. Give him something to hit besides that car. I'm sure he'd love to see you right now."

Viv backed away before Regina could grab her and drag her into the parking lot. Paranoid? Maybe. But she didn't want to take any chances. Regina was the perfect example of how drastically someone could change, how quickly they could go from loving you to hating you. Regina had taught her that lesson years ago, long before Viv had known she would need it again.

CHAPTER FIVE

VIV CREPT INTO THE TOPIARY GARDEN and hid beneath a shrub shaped like a deer, trying to figure out which of her friends would drive out and get her if she called. Jewel was probably at a club—she'd never hear her phone. Layla had work in the morning. Mira didn't have a driver's license. Rafe was probably drunk or not wearing any pants. Blue didn't have a car, but he owed her a favor, sort of . . .

She texted him, worried her voice would make it too obvious that she was upset. She didn't have a confessional relationship with Blue. He was more like the irritating friend whose personality you tolerated, but didn't really mind. They didn't have heart-to-heart chats.

Remember when you woke me up at dawn because you needed me to get Henley to chop down the briar around your hotel? I need a ride to the city. Make it happen. Oh I'm at 7Oaks shitty party don't ask.

He called a minute later. "You're interrupting my date."

"Liar," she said.

"Okay, Freddie's here, too, so it's not really a date . . . luckily for you, since I don't have access to the hotel car these days. Next time you need a ride you should just ask Freddie. His princely honor won't let him say no."

"So you guys'll pick me up? Is Mira coming, too?"

"Of course. She's the only one here who likes you."

Viv heard Mira's "Hi, Viv!" in the background. And Freddie's "That's not true!"

"We'll be there in, like, half an hour," Blue said. "Sooner if I can get Freddie to break the law."

The sounds of BMW destruction had ceased, but Viv stayed where she was. Was Regina right? Did Henley hate her? She'd done worse things. But everyone had a breaking point and maybe she'd pushed him to his.

By the time Freddie's car pulled up, the alarm was quiet. Henley was gone, Regina and the valet had disappeared, and a shocked and delighted crowd had gathered around the wreckage while Danny swore and Viv's dad tried to do damage control.

Viv crawled out from under the topiary deer and ran to the car, climbing in before her dad had a chance to notice her.

Freddie Knight was behind the wheel, frowning into the mirror as he tried to guide an adoring ladybug out of his light brown hair and onto his finger—he had the same animal magnetism gift Viv did. Mira Lively, the newest addition to their group, sat in the passenger seat, her long, wavy blonde hair half-covering the logo of her Curses & Kisses T-shirt. Blue Valentine was stretched out in the back, his blue hair spiked straight up, one knee poking out of his ripped jeans. Viv shoved his feet to get him to move over.

"Did a giant fall on Mirza's car?" Blue asked.

"No. But that's what I should tell my dad if he asks me what happened."

"What *did* happen?" Mira asked.

"Henley. With a shovel. In the parking lot." She was surprised at how blasé she sounded.

"Should we even ask why?" Blue said.

Viv shrugged. "You can probably guess."

She knew it was her fault. She'd wanted to make him angry—well, she had. Mission accomplished.

"I would've liked to see that," Blue said. "Just to see how it's done. I'd like to do that to Felix's car."

"I don't think you're really the shovel-wielding type," Mira said.

"Besides, what purpose would that serve?" Freddie reached for his sword, his voice tense now that Blue's older brother was the subject of conversation. "If you want to stop Felix, you don't destroy his car. You cut off his head."

"Whoa, Freddie," Viv said. "You have really changed."

"I'm just being practical."

"Can we talk about something else?" Mira asked.

They went to Mira's new house, because Viv hadn't been there yet. Mira's godmothers—who were her guardians, and also her fairy godmothers—were in the kitchen, and Mira stopped in to say hello. Freddie, who never missed a chance to make a good impression, went with her. Mira's godmothers didn't like Blue, so he slipped down the hall to Mira's room and Viv followed. She usually avoided talking to her friends' parents. Inevitably, if adults weren't asking you about school they were asking about your family, and there was no way for that not to be awkward. *How's your stepmother? Still set on poisoning you? And your father, as useless as always?*

Blue, at least, knew what it was like to have a messed-up family. All the Valentine men had the same murderous hereditary curse. Blue's dad was a Casanova serial killer, his older brother, Felix, followed in their dad's footsteps, and Blue had accidentally killed his crush at his sixteenth birthday party. Viv had been there, dancing, batting blue and green balloons into the air, unaware that in the other room a girl lay dead in Blue's arms. The party had ended abruptly, Blue's father had ushered everyone out, and gradually, people put the pieces together. If you knew curses, you knew what blue hair signified. That was why Mira's godmothers didn't like Blue—no one wanted their daughter dating a villain, no matter how reformed.

"So." Blue flopped down on the bed. "Haven't seen you in a while. Thought maybe you were in your glass coffin already."

"Can you not tonight? I'm not in the mood."

"Sorry. Habit. You okay?"

Viv glanced around the room, wishing Mira and Freddie would join them so they could all start talking about anything but her. The closet was open. A bunch of dance costumes were hanging on one side of the rack. Sequins and ruffles and flamenco madness.

"I'm just hungry," Viv said. "The food at the party was gross. Pâté and caviar licked by a cat."

"That's what happens when you let a boots-wearing cat join your country club."

39

"He wasn't even wearing his boots."

"Scandalous. What happened to *no shirt, no tiny boots, no service?*"

Viv laughed. "I don't know. Standards are really falling at Seven Oaks. I'm going to see if I can find some food. I'll be right back."

She went to the kitchen where Freddie was winning points—or, actually, probably just being nice; he was ridiculously nice—by doing the dishes. Bliss, Mira's blonde godmother, who dressed like a combination of Glinda the Good Witch and a connoisseur of Lolita fashion, was tapping her glass wand against her fingernails, giving herself a magical manicure.

Mira was standing in front of the table, arms crossed. Her mouth opened and one hand went up like, *You've got to be kidding me,* when Elsa, her brunette, jeans-wearing godmother, said, "And leave the door open."

"With Viv here? What do you think is going to happen?"

"We won't have an orgy," Viv said. "Scout's honor. I don't like Freddie like that."

Freddie dropped the plate he was washing. Soapsuds splattered his shirt. "Viv!"

"Well, I don't."

"Don't break my plates, Frederick," Bliss warned.

It was so easy to mess with Freddie.

Mira turned, a half smile breaking through her exasperated expression. "Fine, we'll leave the door open. But I wish you'd trust me."

"You're not the one I don't trust," Elsa said.

"It's that Freddie Knight," Viv said. "He's such a degenerate."

"I am not a—" Freddie started, before he realized no one was taking Viv seriously. He was a Sleeping Beauty prince, and Mira was a Sleeping Beauty princess. And although he'd already broken her curse, and awakened her from an enchanted sleep, *and* Mira was dating Blue, not him, he still behaved as though his honor were somehow in doubt. There were some pretty perverse Sleeping Beauty stories, and he didn't want Mira's godmothers to think he was one of *those* princes.

Viv asked about food and Mira found some leftover pizza in the fridge. "Sorry. We're still getting settled so there's not a lot here. Do you want me to order something? We have some takeout menus"—Mira turned to look behind her—"somewhere. . . ."

"No, this is fine. Thanks."

"Everything's been crazy since my curse was broken. First packing for the move, and then—I finally met my parents." Mira smiled. "Well, for the first time since my christening party. We went on vacation together."

"Was it fun?"

"It was. But also overwhelming. They wanted to make up for sixteen lost years in two weeks, which is kind of . . ."

"Impossible?"

Mira nodded. "But, I don't think they were disappointed or anything. Which I worried about."

"We told her not to worry," Elsa said. "Why would they be disappointed? *They* were worried about disappointing *her.*"

"You're very lovable for two weeks," Bliss said. "That's your limit, though. I don't know how we put up with you for sixteen years."

"*Anyway,*" Mira said. "They're going to move here. So I'll

41

get to see them more, and see what they're like when they're not taking me around sightseeing. Um—do you want to eat that here, or bring it to my room?"

"Room," Viv said. Freddie stayed behind to finish cleaning up.

They found Blue on Mira's bed, shaping a stuffed unicorn's mane into a mohawk. "Can you kick him out for a minute?" Viv asked.

Blue put on an appalled expression. "You want me to exile this innocent unicorn?"

"Um, sure," Mira said. "Blue . . . go help Freddie with the dishes."

"Freddie's doing the dishes?" Blue sighed and got up. "Of course he's doing the dishes."

"Thank you," Mira said, kissing his cheek and shutting the door behind him.

After another moment, Mira said, "So . . . I'm guessing you need to talk about something serious."

"It's kind of personal."

"Okay."

They sat down: Mira on the bed, Viv on a red beanbag on the floor. Mira was the only person Viv knew who had experience with this particular problem, but it wasn't going to be easy to talk about.

Finally, Viv said, "Are there warning signs when a guy wants to kill you? Like, when he's definitely decided to do it?"

Mira froze, lips parted. Then she lowered her eyes and started playing with the charm bracelet on her wrist. Each of the charms was a märchen mark symbol: the Sleeping Beauty spinning wheel, an apple, a heart, the Beast's rose, Rapunzel's braid. "Um. I don't know if this would really be helpful, in your case. Because the circumstances were so different. But . . . yeah. There's definitely a change."

"I hate to even ask you about this. I don't want to stir up any . . ."

"It's okay."

"But I don't know who else to ask."

Mira had been through a lot since she'd come to Beau Rivage at the beginning of summer. She'd gone from not knowing about curses to learning she was a princess, getting tangled up romantically with Blue's brother, Felix, falling into an enchanted sleep, and waking up, all in about a week. After a brief, sketchy courtship, Felix had tried to kill Mira and almost succeeded. It wasn't over between the two of them. Either Felix would finish what he'd started or someone would kill him. Felix was a villain, destined to be slain by a hero, but there was no telling when that would happen. It did explain, though, why Freddie was so gung ho about decapitating the guy.

"He'd get frustrated sometimes. Mad at me," Mira said. "But usually he was really nice. Accommodating. Like, the way he'd treat a VIP guest, except . . . you know. And then, when I went into that room—triggered the murder part of the curse—he . . . was so angry. Like it was all my fault. Because if I hadn't opened that door, he could have gone on pretending. I never would have known who he really was or what he'd done. At that point, I wasn't Mira to him, I was just another girl who prevented him from being happy."

Viv had never really talked to Mira about that day. She felt a little guilty for bringing it up, but it was too late to take it back.

"And he . . . changed. His whole demeanor. He was very—hard? Like, resolved. He was going to kill me, and there was no talking him out of it. You could see it. Like he'd turned a key, and locked us both into that fate."

Mira glanced up, her fingers poised on the heart charm on her bracelet. "Did something happen? Did Henley—do you really think he'll do it?"

"I don't know." Viv told her what had happened at Seven Oaks. "Sometimes I just want it to be over. Sometimes—I feel like the waiting is the worst part. But I'm not looking forward to the ending."

"I could talk to him. See if he'll . . ."

"Confess? That's not going to happen. He might not even believe he'll do it. That doesn't mean he won't."

Viv's gaze drifted to Mira's bookshelves. They were packed with skinny playbooks, novels, DVD cases. Old movies like *Casablanca* and *Now, Voyager*. "I used to watch movies with Regina when I was little. We'd make popcorn and curl up on the couch. It was one of my favorite things we did together because it was just us, and she'd always find a movie I liked. Have you ever seen *The Yearling*?"

"Maybe, a long time ago," Mira said. "It's about a deer, right?"

"Yeah. This boy adopts a young deer. Brings it home, befriends it, takes care of it. It's a really cute movie, at first. The boy even lets the deer sleep in his bed. And there's this scene where the deer sticks his whole head into a pail of milk. Really adorable animal antics. Which I loved. But then the deer gets older and starts causing trouble on the family farm. Destroying crops, messing with their livelihood. They can't control him.

44

So, one day the dad orders the boy to take the deer into the woods and shoot it.

"I cried so hard. I don't know if I'd ever sobbed like that at a movie. And Regina was stroking my hair, and I was wiping my face on her shirt . . . and then she told me that when a wild thing makes trouble, you have to turn it loose. You have to kill it so it never comes back. She told me I was like the little deer. She said, *One day I'll send you into the forest, and send a man after you to make sure you don't come back.* She told me I should like the movie. It was my story."

"God, Viv . . ."

"Before that, I had no idea she felt that way. I thought she loved me as much as she always had. As much as she'd pretended to? I don't know. And even after she said that, I didn't know what to think. The two of us were a family. My dad was so shitty to her after the first year of their marriage—he was such a bastard, a bad father and a worse husband, leaving her to be my only parent, basically. I didn't really mind that he was almost never home—I was glad, because I had Regina all to myself.

"I used to tell the mirror to shut up when it was mean to her. It was like a game to me back then. I didn't understand why it would hurt her, just like I didn't understand why she'd get so upset when my dad didn't come home. I told her—I remember once, I had gone to her room to try to make her feel better. She was lying in the dark, her hair over her face, just . . . shaking, and I put my hand on her shoulder and told her she was still my favorite. No matter who my dad liked better, she was *my* favorite. I was so stupid; I can't believe I said that. And then she started crying and she said, *I love him.* And I told her, *Then don't.* As if it was that easy.

45

"I don't want to be blindsided again. When—*if*—Henley decides to do it . . . I want to know it's coming. He's pissed at me a lot. But I don't know how to tell if he hates me. I wish I knew. I wish it could just . . . be over, so we didn't have to feel this way anymore. . . ."

Viv wiped her eyes, looked around for a mirror. She didn't want Blue and Freddie to see her like this. "Are my eyes as red as blood?"

"They're barely even pink," Mira said.

Viv hung out there until Mira's godmothers said the boys had to go home. Mira invited her to spend the night, but Viv didn't want to leave her animals unattended. So Blue and Freddie drove her home. By the time they dropped her off around midnight, her anxiety had mostly leveled out, and it stayed that way until she went to put her key in the front door and noticed it was already unlocked.

CHAPTER SIX

VIV OPENED THE DOOR as quietly as she could and crept inside the house. She left her shoes on the mat so they wouldn't make noise. Set her purse down on top of them.

The air in the hall smelled like a sweaty animal.

She could hear voices coming from Regina's office—the room where her stepmother kept her yoga gear, her computer, the handwritten recipe books she'd gotten from witches: *Five Delicious Ways to Braise a Heart.*

"It was amazing," Regina said. "The violence that boy is capable of. He's come a long way from being her pet."

"It's about time." A man's voice. Worn, scratchy.

"You think I waited too long."

"Not saying that. Some like the game. The chase. Me, I prided myself on being efficient. No queen should have to live like this as long as you have."

"That's sweet—I think. But we're not all born ready to kill someone. It certainly wasn't my life plan."

"Just your destiny."

"Some of us need time to warm up to our destinies. But, like I said, I think the boy's ready. If you can call him a boy anymore."

"He's a boy, all right. But he'll man up fast once he feels a knife in his hand." The man's low, dry laugh creaked like old leather. "He can have this one. Cuts through anything."

Viv heard the scrape of one blade against another. Her breaths came harder and she skidded back, her bare feet sticking to the floor.

And then a voice crawled out of the wall behind her.

"Gorgeous. Sheer perfection."

The voices in Regina's office went silent. One heavy boot heel cracked down on the wood—and Viv ran.

Down the hall, through the kitchen. She flung open the back door and kept running. She tore through the moonlit yard, past the well, and as she ran through the ring of fruit trees it seemed like every sleeping songbird woke. They took off into the air, the mad beating of their wings pointing her out like a spotlight.

She swung her arm and hissed at them to go away, but they couldn't understand her, just kept flapping after her.

It wasn't supposed to happen like this.

Breathless, she stumbled through the forest, stones gouging her feet, branches grabbing her dress. The trees had scattered the birds, but the leafy canopy blocked out the moonlight and made it impossible to see. Viv was only making it through because she knew these woods so well. She'd played pretend games here with Henley. She'd spent hours just roaming the trails.

48

Henley lived on the other side of the forest. Could she get there? He wouldn't want to see her tonight, but . . .

Her lungs were burning. A deer crashed after her, then seemed to sense her distress and leapt away. She could hear the animals going this way and that, drawn to her but nervous, and the rustling and the footsteps wound her up so tight she might have screamed if she'd had the breath for it. She didn't know how close the man was. She didn't know if she was hearing his footsteps or hers, his breathing or hers, his—

A gloved hand closed around her arm and jerked her off her feet.

She hit the ground and he flipped her onto her back, pinned her leg with his knee so she couldn't get away. He gripped her jaw with one hand and held the knife with the other. There was just enough moonlight for Viv to see the curve of the blade, and the deep lines age had carved into his face.

"Well, well," he said. "The little rabbit can run."

His knee was hurting her leg and she blinked hard, hoping tears would slip out so he'd pity her. But her eyes stayed dry. She was gasping, choking on the smell of him.

"Uh-uh, don't try that trick on me." His thumb pressed the corner of her eye, crushing an imaginary tear. "I've been hunting girls like you since before you were born. Some Huntsmen get swayed by a princess's crying. . . . I'm not one of them."

"You're a Huntsman?"

"Sure am. Maybe you want to offer me something to save you. I hear you've been giving plenty to the other Huntsman."

The fact that he would say that—not just say it but imply that she was whoring herself out to keep Henley from killing her—made her stop caring about earning his pity. She told him where he could stick that knife.

He smacked her full in the face. The leather stung—and the blade would feel worse. But she wouldn't let him talk to her like that.

"You're lucky I'm retired," he said. "Otherwise you'd be in pieces."

"Retired?" She pressed her tongue to the inside of her lip. There was a blood-flavored, tooth-shaped gouge there.

The old Huntsman got up. Her leg was numb where he'd been kneeling on it. She quickly pulled it under her so he couldn't trap her again.

"I'm out of the princess-killing business. I'm here as a consultant. In case Boyfriend doesn't have the proper equipment. The blade—or the balls—to do the job." He laughed and Viv stared daggers at him. He didn't know anything about Henley if he thought Henley was afraid.

"I'm here to make sure he gets it right the first time. And that he doesn't bring back some animal heart in place of yours. I've known your stepmom since she was your age. Back when she thought that apple mark meant she was a princess. She tracked me down and did me a very nice favor so I'd spare her. Of course, she didn't need saving. She had a different fate.

"But I do repay my debts. So you bargain with whatever you got," he said, looking her up and down, "but don't count on it working. Your stepmom's going to have the happy ending she deserves."

The Huntsman didn't bother to sheathe his knife. As he strolled back toward the house, he ran his blade along the outstretched tree branches like a child might run a stick along a fence. Viv stayed huddled on the ground, the feeling returning to her leg in slow pulses, the tears coming more slowly. The smell of the Huntsman's sweat was heavy in her lungs, and she doubled over and breathed in the scent of earth until she felt less like throwing up, less like death had come and laughed in her face.

CHAPTER SEVEN

VIV KNEW THE HUNTSMAN was gone when the animals emerged from their hiding places. Three rabbits approached and she rubbed their velvety ears while tears dripped down her face. All the emotion had gone out of her; she felt numb so she didn't know why she was crying now.

She'd known this day would come—the curse demanded it—but it was still a shock. Part of her, no matter how afraid she'd been, had always been in denial.

Instinct told her to go to Henley. Even though she knew he wouldn't want to see her. Even though he wasn't her hero, wasn't her savior, and never would be. All the times in her life that she'd felt safe, she'd been with him. But those days were gone. She couldn't get them back by crawling into his arms now.

Still . . . he was the one person she wanted to see.

Viv nudged the rabbits away from her and started through the forest. There was a path that would lead her to Henley's house, and once she found it she followed it out of the woods—to the place where the trees opened up and showed her the ranch-style house, the perfectly landscaped yard. The one blight on the scenery was an old swing set, kept around because Henley's cousins liked to play on it when they came over.

She sat down on one of the swings and creaked back and forth on the rusty chains. The lights were on in the house—every so often she saw one of Henley's parents pass by a window. His dad was generally friendly. His mom didn't like Viv and called her "princess."

Eventually the lights went out. A couple of raccoons pawed at Viv's feet, checking between her toes as if she might have hidden a treat there.

She brushed them aside, got up, and tapped at Henley's window. She saw his neatly made bed, his weight set. Photos pinned to the wall, mostly of her or the two of them, including some that had been ripped in half and then taped back together. Sports junk on the floor. But no Henley. His door was shut, which meant he probably wasn't home.

The raccoons had followed her, but their love was fickle, and it wasn't long before they abandoned her to ransack the Silvas' trash cans. Viv left as one of the cans clanged against the driveway—before the noise woke Henley's parents. She didn't want to be caught.

Maybe it was better that Henley wasn't home. She couldn't keep running to him. He was the Huntsman, the person she was supposed to run away from. The fairies had made it that way when they cursed him.

It was just the way things were.

CHAPTER EIGHT

"NOTHING LASTS FOREVER, HENLEY. She doesn't want you anymore. Denying it isn't going to help."

Regina was smiling as if she were simply telling him what he needed to hear, and not being cruel.

It was after midnight. Regina had called and told him Viv was missing, and Henley had gone into the woods to look for her. He'd checked the cottage, and Regina had followed him inside and cornered him.

He didn't want to have this conversation. Not with Regina, not with anyone.

He sat hunched at the edge of the bed—a plastic-coated mattress on a rusted metal frame—his elbows on his knees, his head resting on his fists. The lantern was casting strange shadows and illuminating the decay, the broken things that were better left hidden.

Regina wore a short silk robe over a nightgown he could almost see through. Her robe was loosely tied and she was playing with the belt, slowly undoing the knot, tying it again, sliding the silk strip between her fingers.

"For what it's worth," she said, "I don't know what she sees in Royals. Obnoxious, spoiled boys . . . That doesn't go away as they get older. I should know—I married one."

Her words twisted around him like a snake. Hissing in his ear, making him picture every prince Viv had messed with in the past year. Always when he was there—like she was practicing leaving him every time she did it.

"Maybe in ten years she'll realize what she's missing," Regina said. "But by then it'll be too late. She'll have her prince, a home, maybe children . . . so many ties to her happily ever after that it won't seem worth breaking them for you. You'll never have her. Unless . . ."

"No." The word came out gruff, hard. He knew what she wanted. It wasn't an option.

Regina came and stood too close to him, the toe of her sandal touching the tip of his shoe. The lantern light caught the sheen on her thighs—he didn't look higher.

"Listen to me," she said. "We both know what you want. If you can't have her, you don't want anyone else to have her. Isn't that right? Well, you can live as a shadow of yourself, unable to let go . . . or you can become the man you're meant to be. You can have her heart—forever. Your destiny is telling you what to do."

He was sweating. It was hot inside the cottage and this conversation was making it worse. Usually his exchanges with Regina consisted of her telling him what kind of yard work needed to be done. She'd been nicer to him since he'd been cursed—once she'd decided he was useful to her. But tonight was the first time she'd spoken to him like he was the Huntsman. Like he could murder the girl he loved.

He closed his eyes and Regina touched his shoulder, as if she sensed weakness.

And maybe she did.

A heart in a box was not a substitute for Viv; Regina was crazy if she thought that it was. But . . . it was true that he didn't want to give Viv up. He would do anything not to lose her. That was why he put up with her crap, let her humiliate him, and then, the second she needed him, came running. Because he still had that shred of hope that they could be together.

Or maybe he didn't anymore. Maybe he just remembered that hope. He didn't feel hopeful when he listened to Regina. He felt like everything was over, and he was just clinging to a lie.

"Whatever you two had before, it's gone. And you're the only one who's not okay with that. Because *she* has a happy ending to look forward to. What do you have, Henley?" Regina leaned closer. "You have a choice. You can be laughed at, thrown aside for a boy with a fancier pedigree . . . or you can take what's yours."

CHAPTER NINE

VIV WAS HALFWAY THROUGH THE FOREST when she saw light peeking through the dirty windows of the cottage. The door was open and as she drew closer a woman in a short robe sauntered out. The light swung toward the woman as Henley appeared in the doorway and offered her the lantern.

Regina. The lantern lit her face from below—hollowed out her cheeks and eyes. But her legs were a mile long and her nightgown barely covered her ass, so Henley probably wasn't looking at her face.

Viv bit her torn lip—then winced at the sting, glad for the cover of darkness.

Regina's hand brushed Henley's as she took the lantern. "You sure you won't walk me home?" She smiled, but Henley's eyes were downcast, rooting through the leaves at his feet—watching something? Then the leaves shifted and a chipmunk darted out and scampered toward Viv. The rustling-leaf sound repeated all across the forest floor as one creature after another raced toward her.

Viv crouched lower in her hiding place and let the animals run into her hands, trying to shush their chittering so they wouldn't give her away.

"I'm going to stay here," Henley said. "Think for a while."

"Yes, think about it." Regina trailed her fingers along his forearm, then started away with languorous steps. Henley stayed in the doorway until the lantern light had vanished.

"I know you're there, Viv."

She stepped out of her hiding place. She'd been caught rodent-handed. Chipmunks perched on her shoulders like epaulettes. There was a mouse in her cupped hand, preening its tail like a ribbon. And now the fireflies had woken up and were hovering around her, golden bulbs blinking softly. Lighting the way.

For a moment, there was something magical about it. Dots of gold light filling the air. The soft peace of an undisturbed forest.

Viv had to remind herself that the magic had nothing to do with the two of them. She shooed the animals and they scattered. The fireflies went out one by one until she and Henley were drowning in darkness.

She curled her hands into fists and her heart thumped hard—like a door slamming to keep him out. "I can't believe you brought her to the cottage."

"Viv—"

"This was *our* place! Our secret!"

"I didn't bring her here, she followed me!"

And suddenly they were yelling at each other, their voices ripping up the forest.

"Why don't you tell her everything? Tell her every place

58

I go to hide. Or, better yet, just hunt me down—do the job for her!"

"She said you ran into the forest. She asked me to look for you!"

"Of course she did! That's what she's always going to want! I can't believe you listened! I can't get away from either of you!"

Viv had meant to tell him about the retired Huntsman. But once her anger got going, her mind kept spinning in one direction: Henley would betray her. There was so much hurt and fear in her lungs she was choking on it.

Henley wrapped his arms around her and pulled her against him. She didn't struggle. She was too startled by how good it felt to be there.

"You want me out of your life?" he said. "Say it. Tell me to get out of your life and see if I stay."

Viv closed her eyes. She didn't want him gone—she wanted the Henley of two years ago back, the Henley who wasn't cursed. She wanted to erase the time they'd spent watching their relationship erode, like a bridge crumbling at their feet.

She didn't want what they had. But she didn't want to lose it, either.

She moved so he would let her go, and then stepped into the cottage to see if he would follow.

The air inside was moist and heavy. It smelled like wet earth, rotting wood, and summer decay. It used to smell like cookies and old books. Back when the cottage was their hide-out and they took care of it.

Grass brushed Viv's ankles as she crossed the room—the forest was pushing up through the floorboards. And when she sat down on the bed she sat right in a puddle of rainwater that had collected where the mattress dipped in the middle.

Viv swore. She shot up and slammed into Henley's chest.

"Did you get wet?" he asked.

"Yes," she said sourly.

She heard the *scrick* of Henley lifting the mattress and then the quick rush of water as he flipped it over, dry side up. "You can sit now."

"Thanks," she mumbled. She sat again, but the bottom of her dress was soaked and she couldn't get comfortable. Henley settled in the lone wooden chair. It was too dark to see him, but she'd heard the chair legs scrape the floor.

She sighed and wished he'd come closer.

"Do you remember when we thought we could live here?" she said after a moment.

"Yeah. It seemed like a real house." There was laughter at the edge of his voice, and she felt it, too, rising up in her, remembering how silly they'd been. This rotted little shack—a home. There was something precious about that innocence. That time in their lives when they could overcome anything, because the solution was as simple as grabbing a box of cookies and disappearing into the woods for a few hours.

"I used to think this cottage was a million miles away from everything," Viv said. "That we could hide here and leave the world behind. But if Regina can walk here in her hooker heels . . . it's not much of a sanctuary, is it?"

"I don't know." Henley's low voice dropped lower. "I think it was, for a little while."

The smell of earth and wood seeped from every corner. Murky decay: something old dying so something new could live.

60

"The future was so open then. I never thought . . ." She twisted the hem of her dress to squeeze the water out, then kept twisting, nervousness taking hold. "I never thought you'd do things for her. Help her."

"Viv—I'm polite to her, that's it."

"You shouldn't even be that. She should be your enemy. You should pick a side, and it should be mine."

"Did you pick my side?"

"What?" Her hands went still in her lap.

"When you think about your future, am I in it? Or am I just a roadblock you have to get through?"

"Henley . . ."

"You think you're going to end up with a prince—and I'm the Huntsman. That's all I am to you." His voice was rough. Not the low rumble she was used to—jagged, hurt. "So you don't have room for me in your life. Right?"

"Please don't say that."

"Why not? It's true, isn't it?"

Tears slid down her cheeks. "Maybe. I don't know."

He was quiet then. Maybe he'd expected to feel better. Or maybe he'd expected her to be a better liar.

The hum of insects merged with the throb of blood in her head. It was a mistake to talk about it. They should have learned that by now.

It was too dark to see his expression, so she went over to him and put her hands on his face instead. His skin was hot, damp with sweat but not tears, and she stroked her hands over his cheeks and up into his hair, tenderly. Sometimes she wanted to hurt him but right now it was too much.

"What do you want from me?" she whispered. And then

she pressed her hand to his lips before he could answer. The sounds slipped out between her fingers: *Everything.*

She bent her head to his and kissed him, harder when he tried to ask why, until he didn't have the breath for questions. Explanations were painful. Promises were lies. She didn't want any of that. She wanted his mouth, which was soft and familiar—and hard when she wanted it to be. He always knew. Their hearts were a mystery but they knew each other like this.

His hands found her like he was reliving a memory, and she wrapped her arms around him and gave in to the past.

He couldn't promise he wouldn't kill her. She couldn't promise she would stay with him. They shouldn't be together; she knew that. But she didn't care. Tomorrow she would care, in an hour she might care. But not now.

CHAPTER TEN

THE DAYS MELTED TOGETHER. The nights seethed with sticky heat, and Viv struggled to sleep a whole night through without nightmares. She kept her bedroom door locked, but left the balcony doors open for the animals, and half expected to find the old Huntsman standing there whenever she opened her eyes.

Tonight, she woke not to nightmares, but to a loud animal snort. And the jingling of reins.

A horse?

Viv pushed the satin sleep mask off her eyes to find a brown mouse watching her. She raised a sleepy hand and lightly stroked its back.

"Who's out there?" she whispered. The mouse closed its eyes and gave a little wriggle of pleasure, but didn't answer. They never did.

Moving the mouse onto her pillow, and shooing away the other animals who'd been sleeping around her, Viv went to the balcony, squinting into the dark in search of a horse. None of her friends rode horses. Even the most delusional hero-types had cars.

At first, all she saw was the garden, the fruit trees ringing the well. But then the darkness shifted. Moonlight slid along the glossy black body of a horse, traced the shape of a man holding the reins. Both horse and master were as black as the night they moved through.

Viv shivered with excitement. She knew who the man was—she could recognize a horseman. She just didn't know why he was here.

Horsemen were magical beings, like fairies—except fairies were always female and horsemen were always male. And while fairies attended christenings, and bestowed curses, and otherwise played a role in cursed lives, horsemen were more standoffish. In Russian fairy tales, they served Baba Yaga. There were horsemen representing the red sun, the white day, the black night. This one was clearly Night.

He'd spotted her on the balcony and was watching her, waiting.

He didn't call her name. He didn't have to. It was rare to see a horseman, and there was no way she was letting him leave without finding out why he was here.

Viv hurried downstairs. When she got to the yard Night was standing near the well. The horse was chewing huge mouthfuls of the garden. Flowers disappeared between its teeth and naked patches of earth showed where grass used to grow.

Then Night was in front of her, holding out a black card printed with silver script. The words gleamed with light, so she could read them even in the dark.

You're Invited

A twist of silver branches crawled up either side of the card.

Silver branches meant the underworld. There was a nightclub there where the Twelve Dancing Princesses went to dance, night after night, until someone broke their curse. It was more exclusive than any club she knew. There was no velvet rope, no doorman to persuade—you couldn't even find the underworld unless someone wanted you there.

And now someone wanted her there.

No one she knew had ever been invited.

The underworld wasn't a land of the dead, like in Greek mythology. It was simply a hidden place, a kingdom the fairies had carved out of stone and darkness so long ago that no one remembered who had done it. There, fairies and other inhuman beings could show themselves freely because there was no chance that a normal human would be present. The way there was a secret but most Cursed knew the underworld existed.

More silver words appeared on the card as Viv watched.

Yes
or
No?

She glanced up at Night. His eyes were solid-black pools. "How do I get there?"

"I'll take you." The horseman's voice was deep, and once he'd spoken it seemed to drift away, like she'd imagined the sound.

Viv ran a hand through her messy hair, conscious of her skimpy pajamas and the sweat that coated her skin. "Do I have time to change?"

"We go now, or not at all."

Light glimmered across the words: *Yes or No?*

"Yes," she decided.

At that the message faded. The invitation turned to dust and the branches that had adorned the card appeared on her arms: silver filigree stretching from elbows to wrists. The silver markings gleamed like the words had and were cool to the touch.

"What are these marks?" she asked, holding out her arms so Night could see them.

"This is your way in," he said, taking her right arm. He grasped her left arm. "And this is your way out."

Night stood there a moment, holding her arms at the wrists, his face betraying nothing. And yet, it was clear from the way he hesitated that something was wrong.

"So . . . is there a door?" Viv asked, starting to get nervous.

"There are many doors. This one is . . . inconvenient."

"How inconvenient?"

"Hold your breath," he said.

And then he picked her up and threw her in the well.

CHAPTER ELEVEN

VIV DID NOT HOLD HER BREATH.

She screamed. Her fingers clawed at the slick stone walls, but she couldn't grab on to anything. Night slid in after her and sank like a stone. Disappeared into the dark water, so she couldn't feel him at all.

Until his hand closed around her ankle and he pulled her under.

Her last scream was swallowed by the water that flooded her mouth. She was choking, her head full of darkness. And all she could think was:

This was a plan of Regina's.

A trick.

Regina knew witches—she could commission a magic invitation.

And maybe—

Hire a horseman.

She should have *known.*

This was—

The stupidest—

Way to die.

Viv felt herself being tugged down, down, down—and then someone was dragging her out of the water, across a bed of wet pebbles. Not out of a well. Out of . . . a lake.

She coughed, hacking up water. It all blurred at first—like lights seen through a raindrop-speckled window. Then the underworld came into focus. The silver trees with their knife-gleam branches. The faint, haunting music, like distant bells and snapping icicles. A sky that wasn't sky but a dense mass of shadows.

Night laid her down on the lakeshore. His jet-black face was smooth and expressionless. Not cold, but inhumanly composed.

A man in a silver guard's uniform came rushing over. His tinsel-colored jacket was like something a toy soldier would wear, but the sword he carried was real.

"She has to go through the checkpoint," the guard insisted, sounding nervous—like he was uneasy talking to a horseman.

Viv turned onto her side to hack up more water and Night grabbed her right arm and showed it to the guard. "Check her here. I'm in a hurry."

The guard muttered another protest, but did as he was told. He ran his eyes over Viv's right arm, then touched his ring to the silver swirls on her skin—and the mark disappeared.

"All right," the guard said. "But next time—"

Night vanished before the guard could finish—just kind of disappeared like Batman—which Viv found almost as annoying as the fact that he'd dragged her down a well. He didn't think he had to explain himself? Horsemen were as bad as fairies.

"There won't be a next time," Viv said. Going to a nightclub was not worth almost drowning. She hugged herself and shivered. Her pajamas were sopping wet and it was cool in the underworld. Like an early spring night when the earth was just crawling out of winter.

Silver branches stretched above them, all around the lake, glinting in the lantern light. There was no breeze, but the leaves made a tinkling sound like wind chimes. It was beautiful, still—and a little eerie. Like walking through a dream.

There was a path that looped through the forest behind them where a line of guests in silver party garb waited to show their marked arms to the guards at the checkpoint. They shimmered between the trees like figures made of mercury.

Viv looked down at herself: at the water dribbling down her legs, the wet pajama shorts sagging from her hips.

"I can't go to the club like this," she told the guard. "How do I get home?"

"Traffic's flowing one way right now. Into the underworld, not out. If you want to go to the club, you get in one of those boats." He pointed to a row of gondolas at the shore. "Other than that, you're on your own."

Viv stood and stared at him as he turned his back on her. "So I'm stuck here?"

The guard didn't bother to answer.

Sighing, Viv wandered down to the boathouse. The boatmen wore silver double-breasted jackets like the guards, but they looked like they wore them under duress. They stood together, all slouching in a deliberate way, eyes half-lidded and bored. Half of them were smoking. God—they reminded her of Henley's friends.

One stepped out of the group and sauntered down to the shore like he was doing her a favor. He outpaced her, then stopped and turned back. "You're really going to wear that?" The other boatmen laughed.

"I'm not going to take it off," she said acidly.

He shrugged and steadied the gondola while she boarded. "You must be new. Otherwise you'd have heard about the dress code."

"Silver?" She really wished he would stop talking.

"Silver for us every night. But yeah, silver's tonight's theme for the guests. They like themes. Helps to identify the out-siders."

He grinned at her as he started to row, and Viv turned her face away so he wouldn't see the burn in her cheeks.

Outsider—she'd never been an outsider. Not in any way that mattered. And she didn't like being made to feel like one now.

The silver forest bordered the lake on three sides. Globe-shaped lanterns hung from the trees and cast a golden glow on the water's slowly rippling surface.

The underworld was all shining and dark, bright metal and heavy shadow. On the far shore, hills of black rock repeated into the distance. There was no horizon, just a point at which everything turned to darkness, like the world around them had been rubbed out.

The palace stood on a rocky crag overlooking the lake. Below it, nearer to the lake, was the nightclub. There were no windows and, like the best nightclubs, no sign telling you what it was—but Viv's heart beat faster when she saw it. The gleaming black walls reflected the lake and the forest like mirrors made of obsidian.

When the boat bumped to a stop, the boatman held it steady so Viv could climb out. Her bare feet met rough stone and she winced, taking slow, careful steps as she made her way up the hill to the club. There had to be a smoother path—a ways off, other guests were approaching the club with far less difficulty—but the boatman had let her off *here* and she figured it would be just as much work to cut across the rocky hill as to go up it. So she went up.

When she rounded the top of the hill, she saw an old beggar woman standing outside the club, picking her teeth with a sliver of bone. Her face was withered but her eyes were sharp and bright.

A fairy, Viv thought. *Waiting to test me.*

Well, she wasn't going to walk into that trap.

"Took you long enough." The old woman flung her toothpick to the ground. "All this time and that's how you're dressed? I was told you'd need help, but I'm not a miracle worker."

Viv forced a tight smile. "It was kind of you to wait so long." Being rude to a fairy was one of the biggest mistakes you could make. They loved baiting people—then dealing out "just" punishments when you told them off.

"Damn right it was. Can't imagine why someone would want *you* all dressed up. You've got no figure to speak of—your ass is as flat as a squashed cockroach."

That was a new one. "Sorry. I don't know, either. Someone hired you?"

"You think I'd bother with you for free?" The old woman fished a thin gold wand out of her sleeve, and Viv stiffened as the fairy aimed it at her.

It wasn't like she'd never had magic used on her, but she'd been an infant then. It was different when you were old enough to know what was happening.

A flare of heat started at Viv's hips and moved up her chest. When she glanced down and saw that her pajamas were burning away, she let out a startled cry—but the fire didn't burn her. Her pajamas blackened, then crumbled to ash. And then the ashes swirled in the air like they'd been caught in a cyclone, and re-formed as a black velvet dress studded with pinpoints of light: blue-white diamonds whose glow faded and blazed, twinkled and winked out, like stars. It was as if someone had made a dress out of the night sky.

The stones she'd been walking on rolled up around her feet, coated her heels and her toes; then with a burst of heat, they transformed into high heels made of black glass.

The old woman came closer, scowling. "You couldn't be bothered to dry your hair?"

"I almost drowned."

The fairy touched her wand to Viv's forehead. Heat flared again, and Viv's wet hair unplastered itself from her head and neck and settled onto her shoulders in silky black waves. Cold metal teeth sank into her scalp. She glanced at the reflective black walls of the nightclub and saw that her now-dry hair was crowned with a tiara made of stars.

"That'll have to do," the fairy said. "Try not to embarrass yourself in there."

"Thank you," Viv said, managing an awkward curtsy on the stones.

The old woman groaned like that had *not* reassured her, then started down the hill toward the shore. *Thank god,* Viv thought. She'd made it through the trial unscathed.

There was no one guarding the entrance so Viv slipped into the shadowy alcove that led to the door. She wondered who had arranged for her to have the dress.

Wondering made her clumsy. She stumbled on her way in, one of her ankles almost twisting in the black glass heels, and she had to grab hold of a man's arm to keep from falling. He glared at her, dark gray brows furrowing—and she apologized and clunked away, every wobbly step making her nervous, every glance around the room making her feel less like she belonged.

Everyone else was wearing silver—it was the dress code, just like the boatman had said. And they all seemed to know one another. The dancers pressed close together, spun in unison, and traded partners like what happened tonight happened every night.

The floor was made of glossy black tiles and the walls were black mirrors. Silver disco balls spun light onto the dance floor, turning the room into a dizzying swirl of reflected light—like scattered moonbeams, or sped-up raindrops.

Plush black velvet benches lined the walls but Viv didn't want to sit down. She needed to find the person who'd invited her so she could find out what this was all about. The problem was she didn't know who she was looking for.

Viv grabbed a drink from a waiter and sipped it while she circled the room.

She recognized a few Cursed, but no one she knew very

well. A blonde princess stood with her arm raised like a falconer's, a long-tailed blue bird perched on her wrist—the two of them seemed to be carrying on a conversation. A ballerina was trying to coax a one-legged soldier off a bench. She would do a graceful leap, her feet propelling her as if she weighed no more than a paper doll—and then she'd hurry back to him, take his hands in hers, and urge him to join her.

At the center of the dance floor, eleven beautiful girls danced with eleven underworld princes. The girls wore slinky, silver dresses slit to midthigh or full skirts that puffed around their hips like storm clouds. The princes wore suits the color of cold steel, and silver sashes that signified their rank, in case their royal bearing wasn't enough.

At the edge of the eleven couples, a twelfth girl danced on her own, cutting a tango without a partner, her teeth biting her lip instead of a rose. She looked desperate—but all the girls looked desperate. Like they didn't want to dance, but something inside compelled them.

The girls wavered between laughter and sobs; they clung to their partners and then held them at arm's length. And their moods changed at different times, like the stars on Viv's dress—this one flaring brightly, this one winking out. . . . One would burst into tears just as another shouted a song request to the DJ. It made Viv feel sick. She didn't want to play audience to their torment. She wanted to get away from them.

Hurrying across the room, she downed her drink. The sweet liquid left a parched feeling in her throat.

So those were the Twelve Dancing Princesses. She'd seen them a few times, at a diner in the morning: their eyeliner smeared, their shoes broken, and their stockings torn. And

74

she'd always thought they were lazy, trashy party girls. They went dancing, they spent all night every night dancing, and they bought a lot of shoes. What a *hard* life. What a stupid curse.

She was rethinking it now.

Facing the wall, she could see the stars sparkling on her dress, the dancers shifting like shadows in the background. The fantasy of the underworld. But when she looked at herself, she saw an outsider—and she wondered what she was doing here. At home, she went through the motions. Every day was a twisted variation of the one before. She fought with Henley, or she clung to him. She hid from her stepmother. She went to the beach, a party, a club, a café. And every day she waited for her fate to be decided, while other people's lives changed.

Tonight was different—but she didn't know what to do with it. She was staring at her reflection, trying to decide, when she noticed a young man behind her, close and getting closer.

She whirled to face him and almost went skidding out on the glass shoes. He caught her before she fell, and one of the stars went floating off her dress like a snowflake.

"Careful," he said. "This floor isn't made for glass slippers."

He was her age, maybe a little older. Black hair, underworld-pale skin, dark gray eyes.

He held her like he was used to having a girl in his arms. He danced here often, maybe every night—she was sure. He had an ease about him, like he was a regular, but he was ignoring the dress code. He wore a black tuxedo, not silver like the rest of them.

"I don't think any floor is really made for glass slippers," Viv said. She felt short of breath from the shock of almost falling—and hot, like she was blushing all over, but she didn't know why.

His smile, which had started out smooth and welcoming, got wider. "No, you're probably right." He checked that she was steady on her feet, then let her go. The heat faded like a shiver.

When he stepped back she saw a silver sash peeking out of his pocket. A signet ring flashed on his finger, imprinted with a crown.

He was an underworld prince. And he was the only person, besides Viv, who was wearing black instead of silver.

"Did you invite me?"

The prince's smile broke free again. "I did. Do you mind?"

She wasn't sure what to say.

"I don't get it." She gestured to the crowd of dancing princesses and princes, and the twelfth princess in particular. "Don't you have a princess already?"

"The Twelve Dancing Princesses curse isn't mine."

"Then . . . what *is* your curse? Why am I here?"

"Why are you here?" He leaned in, so close she could see the silver flecks in his dark gray eyes. "You're here because I got tired of waiting for you to die."

CHAPTER TWELVE

VIV'S PULSE POUNDED IN HER SKULL. Her mouth felt dry and the words came out shaky. "You can keep waiting. Because I don't plan on dying anytime soon."

She started away from him and he followed, the two of them weaving through the crowd of dancers. Running was impossible when every step in the glass shoes threatened to send her sprawling. She finally stopped to pry the mini black glass coffins off her feet and flung them under one of the benches.

Barefoot, she kept going until she was out of the club, then at the edge of the hillside, her feet aching like every stone gave her another bruise.

There were no gondolas on this side of the lake. No way back, except—maybe through the forest? Who knew what was in there. But it was better than swimming back.

She started down the hill, picking her way carefully across the rocks—and the prince in the black tuxedo appeared, one of her black glass slippers in his hands. Guests crowded into the alcove behind him, eager to witness the drama, and the prince turned sharply and ordered them inside. He seemed agitated; he held the shoe awkwardly, like it was the wrong prop—an embarrassing fairy-tale symbol of *the girl who got away*.

Once they were alone, he said, "You didn't have to run out like that.".

"Stay away from me," she warned, backing down the hill.

He matched her step for step. "Vivian, please. Will you let me explain?"

"No. I'm leaving."

When she reached the lakeshore, she turned and saw that two of the gondolas were halfway across the lake, each carrying two passengers. The prince raised his arm and signaled to the boatmen, who then began to row the other way.

Viv tried to make another signal—a *get back here* wave—but the boatmen ignored her. The prince let the glass shoe fall to the ground, and sighed. It was too thick to shatter.

"All I said was—"

"What the hell was that?" She gestured to the retreating gondolas. "I want to go home, and you—"

She stumbled back as he came toward her, the silver water splashing her legs as she stepped into the lake. Something ribbony slithered around her ankle and she darted back onto the shore.

It felt like a snake had wound around her calf, but she looked and saw that it was a dirty necktie. She kicked to fling it off her, but the wet silk clung to her skin.

"Someone must have lost this." The prince crouched to untangle the wet tie, then threw it into the lake, like it was an all-purpose dumping ground. "Don't go in the lake if you can help it. It's deeper than it looks."

"I've already been in there. The door the horseman took me through lets out underwater. I thought I was going to drown."

Alarm flickered across the prince's face. "Well, if you come back—"

"I won't."

"If you come back, I'll make sure he doesn't bring you through that door again."

"Good," she said. "Not that it matters."

She glanced at the boatmen on the opposite shore—the escape he'd denied her. "Are we done? Will you summon a gondola for me now? Or are you still hoping I'll die?"

"I never said I wanted you to die. I said I was tired of waiting for it. And I didn't mean *real* death, I meant your enchantment. Your glass-coffin death. I thought you'd know that."

Her chest went tight with apprehension. "Why would you wait for that?"

"Because that's when I'm supposed to save you."

He took her cold hands in his and a shock of heat brushed through her. It flowed up her arms, through her chest, and then all through her body. It was like the sudden flush she'd felt when he'd held her in the club, only now she knew what it meant.

Recognition was what some people called it. The heat that burned between a prince and princess bound by the same curse. A cute little touch the fairies had added. A sign. *Magic.* Manipulative, definitely. But it had the desired effect. It made

79

her breathless, and a little scared, because this was her prince and he wasn't supposed to be here. This wasn't supposed to be real yet.

She pulled her hands free and the warmth receded like a tide. "I don't understand. We're not supposed to meet until—"

"I told you, I got tired of waiting."

Viv knew princes who were dreamy romantic types, who looked forward to the day they'd save their princess like it was the most important thing they'd ever do. But there were just as many princes who treated their single years like an extended bachelor party, a chance to have as much fun as they could before being tied down by happily ever after.

She'd always pictured her prince as belonging to the second group. Or maybe a subset of that group: a sick offshoot of princes who were biding their time until they found the dead-looking princess they'd been dreaming of.

"Are you disappointed?" he asked. "Were you hoping I'd be—"

"No. No, I just . . . didn't expect this. Yet." He was looking more and more nervous, so finally she said, "What's your name?"

"Jasper."

"Jasper . . . ?"

"Just Jasper. No surname."

"And you know that I'm—"

"Vivian. Vivian Deneuve." He smiled. "All those *v*'s."

"I go by Viv, actually."

"Viv." He said it like an apology. "I'll remember that."

She felt like they were on more neutral ground now—less emotionally fraught ground, anyway—and she wasn't likely to burst out with *I was afraid you'd be a necrophiliac,* or *To be honest, I'm not over my boyfriend-slash-ex-boyfriend-slash-boyfriend? And so your showing up like this just complicates things.*

She had to think, to be practical, not to start confessing things her prince didn't need to know.

"I'm going to need to see your mark," she said. "To be sure."

"Right. Um . . . best to do it over here."

Jasper led her away from the lakeshore and into the silver forest, where metal trunks sliced up through the powdery gray earth, as cold and smooth as pieces of jewelry, their shining branches covered with thin silver blossoms. They stopped in a dim, deserted part of the forest, where hints of lantern light made it just bright enough to see, and the icy music sounded like a winter wind whistling through. There were no strange creatures in the forest. No creatures at all.

Viv snapped a silver twig off one of the trees, as a souvenir.

"Would you like an entire tree? I could have one dug up and sent home with you."

"No, that's okay," she said, suddenly self-conscious. Breaking off a silver twig was a fairy-tale cliché and she tried to be above those. Like asking to touch Rapunzel's hair, or trying on Cinderella's shoes after the fact. She never wanted to seem overly impressed by other people's curses. That was for people who didn't have their own.

"It's all right," Jasper said. "Everyone does it. If someone's going to vandalize our forest, it might as well be my princess."

Then, before she could respond, he said: "There's no classy way to do this—sorry."

He started taking off his clothes—efficiently, as if he were at a doctor's office. He removed his jacket, bow tie, vest, and shirt, and hung them from the branches of the nearest tree. It still wasn't enough to expose his märchen mark. The mark was on the small of his back, so he had to undo his pants and push them below his hips to show her.

He turned, and there it was, dark red against his skin: the apple-shaped mark. The sign of their curse. Henley had one, Regina had one, and Viv was sure the old Huntsman had one, but Jasper was a prince, so that apple mark meant he was a Snow White prince.

Her prince.

The stars on her dress winked on and off, speckling his torso with fairy lights.

She kept blinking, waiting for the mark to prove to be a shadow or hallucination. But it stayed, and her heart felt like it was filling her chest, like her body didn't have the proper reaction for this. Her first sight of her prince was supposed to be when she opened her eyes, post-poisoning. After she'd almost died and lost everything. When his arms would seem like the only place to go.

"This is so weird. Surreal. Like I'm dreaming it."

"It does feel a little like that." Jasper lifted his shirt from where it hung, and slipped his arms into the sleeves. "I wanted to meet you sooner, but I'm not allowed to leave the underworld."

"Not at all?"

"Not until it's time to break your enchantment. I guess . . . the stars will align then, and I'll be able to go." He fastened his cuffs. "I didn't know who you were until recently. I was trying to be patient, let things happen naturally . . . but finally I broke down and paid a fairy for information. She told me your name, gave me your picture—a school photo, I think. Sketched in a little background. Where you live, your father's club, what you like, your animal blessing . . ."

Viv wondered if the fairy had told him about Henley. "That's . . ."

"Creepy?" He smiled. "Don't worry. She didn't tell me your secrets. A fairy isn't privy to everything. But it was a start. And once I knew who you were, I had to meet you. I needed to know you before it was too late."

"Too late?"

"Not every Snow White princess survives. You know that. And based on what I know about your situation, your chances are worse than most."

"My situation." She waited for him to elaborate, but he didn't. "What did the fairy tell you about *my situation?*"

"Well, you're not . . ." He looked away. "I don't want things to be awkward."

"Not telling me is what's going to make things awkward."

"Your Huntsman," Jasper said. "He's . . . volatile. You're not a child and he's not a kindhearted old man who'll be inclined to spare you. Your relationship is quite different. Can I leave it at that?"

"Please." She wished she'd never asked.

"All right. Then . . . listen. I have an idea. It's something I thought about a lot, before I invited you. So, hear me out before you decide it's crazy." He took a deep breath, then forged on. "Our fates are more or less decided for us. But we do have some choices to make in this curse. We can't control what anyone else does, but we can take away their opportunities. We can make it harder for them."

"What do you mean?"

"If you lived here, in the underworld—if you came to stay—I could protect you. I could keep your stepmother away from you. Make it so the Huntsman could never touch you. And your life wouldn't be in their hands anymore, it would be in ours, and I would guard your life as if it were my own."

"Jasper . . . that's . . . you don't even know me."

"You're my destiny. The person I'm meant to be happy with—forever. I don't need to know you to want to protect you."

He believed what he was saying, she could see that. And maybe if she were a different person she would have cried tears of joy and said *Yes!* If he had the power to protect her, if he really could keep Regina away from her, he was offering her life, and a possible happy ending. What more was there for someone with her curse?

But as much as she feared Henley would betray her, the idea of cutting ties with him *now*, of losing him before she absolutely had to, filled her with panic and a feeling that her life would be over no matter what she did.

"I don't expect you to give me an answer tonight," Jasper said. "But I hope you'll think about it. I want *us* to decide what happens to you. Not your stepmother. Not your Huntsman."

Viv hoped the panic was gone from her eyes. "Of course I'll think about it."

Jasper finished getting dressed, and they went back to the nightclub, where the guests who'd been eager to watch them fight now watched them dance among the Twelve Dancing Princesses and their partners. Viv tried not to be disturbed by the girls' outbursts—the sobbing, and sudden cries of *Don't touch me!*—or the abrupt switch to laughter and flirting, often while tears still ran down their faces.

Jasper did his best to lead, but Viv wasn't good at ballroom dancing and she lacked the grace to fake it. She'd taken a class when she was thirteen, when her father had decided it was embarrassing she couldn't waltz, but she'd skipped most of the lessons.

"You hate this, don't you?" Jasper said.

"I'm not a ballroom dancer. I like—"

"I know what kind of music you like. The fairy told me." He called out a request to the DJ, and the lovely, soaring ballad cut to a frantic pop song about dancing, drinking, and hating yourself.

"Much better!" She had to yell to be heard over the music.

The Twelve Dancing Princesses went on waltzing, or clinging to their partners and crying, but the guests did their best to adapt. Viv danced until her head was spinning and stars rained down from her dress and glittered at her feet. Heat pulsed at her wrists, in her chest; there was a surge of it, not every time they touched, but often enough to be a reminder: *This is your destiny.*

She stopped thinking, let the music fill her up, and every time she met his eyes he was looking at her like he wanted to know her. Not like she'd hurt him, or was about to. Here was a person she'd never abused, who wasn't destined to choose between killing her or losing her.

They were destined for happily ever after. He wasn't a sick prince with a thing for dead girls. He hadn't found her in a glass box and decided to take her home. What was there to be afraid of?

By the end of the night, Viv was downing water to ward off delirium, and then Jasper was carrying her on his back down the hill to the lakeshore, his arms hooked under her knees, hoisting her higher, saying, "You're choking me," because she had her arms around his neck and was hanging there like deadweight. She was laughing about nothing, giddy-tired, a few stray stars gleaming on her legs. The lakeshore was knotted with guests, all waiting for the boats that would take them home. The party was over.

Jasper set her down some distance away from where the crowd had gathered. The smooth wet stones were cool against her bare feet and the chill woke her up, made her feel less out of it.

Jasper put his arm around her and signaled to one of the boatmen, who began rowing toward them. "The horseman will meet you on the other side. He'll bring you back through a different door. You won't have to go into the lake."

"Good." She turned her head to watch the boat's progress, and Jasper spiraled his finger into her hair and twisted it playfully.

"Will you come again tomorrow night?"

"I don't know about tomorrow."

"Come for an hour, at least. That way I'll know you're okay." He took an invitation from his pocket and handed it to her. "The theme is *Inferno*."

Viv ran her fingers over the silver scrawl of *You're Invited*, the words as magical as the first time she'd seen them. "When will it do that thing, where it asks yes or no?"

"As soon as the underworld doors open tomorrow. Around eleven, your time. But you can give me your answer now, if it's yes." He smiled.

She took a chance. *Why not?*

"Okay," she said. "Yes."

CHAPTER THIRTEEN

VIV WOKE TO THE SOUND of the lawn mower at six thirty in the morning. *Henley. God.* She'd been asleep for maybe an hour, and her head felt like it was packed with mud. She hadn't even bothered to change. Once the horseman had dropped her at home, she'd collapsed into bed in her starry-night dress and passed out before her head hit the pillow.

My dress . . .

There was something troubling about that thought. And as the fuzziness cleared from her head she realized it was because she wasn't wearing one.

She was naked, and her sheets were covered with ashes.

The magic dress had disintegrated.

Last night, Viv had thought the fairy's ash-to-dress transformation was a cute trick. Now her skin was covered with sooty black smears, and her bed looked like someone had burned a bonfire's worth of stuff in it. She couldn't go back to sleep like this. She itched and her bed was disgusting.

She forced herself to get up. Pain shot through her feet when they touched the floor; they were so sore she could barely walk on them. She dropped to her knees and crawled to her en suite bathroom, then into the shower, where she turned on the water and tried to fall asleep for a few more minutes.

When the water turned cold she woke up and shut it off. She wrapped a towel around her body and then crawled back to her bedroom and lay down on a patch of carpet that didn't have ash all over it—and passed out.

"Viv. Viv! Are you drunk?"

Her eyes fluttered open. She *wished* she were hungover, instead of aching and exhausted because she'd spent the night in a place renowned for destroying people's shoes. It was too hot in her room. She felt sick. And Henley was there, kneeling over her, shaking her.

Oh, and she was naked. Except for the towel.

"Stop," she whined, closing her eyes and hoping he would be gone when she opened them.

"What's wrong with you? Did you try to burn your bed? Viv—*wake up!*" He jostled her shoulder and the towel slipped open. It wasn't anything he hadn't seen before, but she screamed at him, anyway. Something on the politeness scale between *go away* and *please die*.

"Don't yell at me! I thought you were poisoned. You weren't moving and—"

"And what? What were you going to do if I was? Call Regina and congratulate her?"

"Yeah, that's exactly what I would do," he snapped.

"I am not in the mood for this," she muttered, fixing her

towel and getting to her feet—which was a mistake, because her feet hurt like hell. She winced and doubled over, grabbing on to Henley to try to relieve some of the pressure. "Ow. Ow ow ow."

Henley's whole face changed. He went from snarling to being her best friend again. "What's wrong? What happened?"

"Is Regina home?"

"No, no one's here."

"Can you—" Her teeth clenched as pain shot through her legs. "Can you carry me downstairs?"

He picked her up and cradled her against him. Now that she was off her feet, they didn't hurt. She adjusted her towel so she wouldn't flash him, and he pressed his head against hers and said,

"You're scaring the shit out of me, Viv."

"I know. I'm sorry. Can you just take me downstairs?"

Henley set her up on a chair in the kitchen, with another chair in front of her so she could prop her feet. She felt worn-out and nauseated, but also relieved just to be there with him while he took care of her, or tried to. He got her a Coke and then rooted around in the cupboards, looking for breakfast. Viv could have told him not to bother. There was no food in the house except Regina's protein bars, some orange juice, Coke, vodka, and a bowl of red apples on the kitchen table.

Viv took an apple from the bowl and held it up. "*An apple a day*—she used to say that to me when I was in middle school. Like it was clever."

"Yeah, I remember you bitching about it."

"She also used to tell me not to let that dirty boy in the house."

Henley gave up on one barren cupboard and moved on to the next. "I know—she always made sure I could hear it. Your stepmom's not the most subtle person in the world."

"Doesn't it make you mad? I don't see why you don't hold that against her."

"I guess I'm too forgiving of people who treat me like crap," he said, holding her gaze.

"Touché." She bit down on the apple. The crunch was a satisfying coda to her statement—she thought so, anyway.

Henley's hand was almost to her mouth when she spit the bite onto the floor, unchewed. "What were you going to do?" she asked with a smile. "Reach in and pry it out of my throat?"

"If I had to." He looked embarrassed and a little annoyed. She tossed the apple into the bowl and flexed her sore feet against the chair. He turned away to continue searching through the cabinets, and she figured now was as good a time as any to confess. She focused on the broad expanse of his back and tried not to lose her nerve.

"So . . . I went somewhere last night," she said. "I got an invitation. To the nightclub in the underworld."

"The club where . . ."

She nodded. "Where the Twelve Dancing Princesses go to dance. That's why my feet hurt."

"What did you do there? You went by yourself?"

She could see him turning it over in his head, trying not to get nervous, to wait for all the facts. His muscles tensed and his eyebrows furrowed and he looked a hundred times more serious than he should ever have to. But Henley was always like that. Always wary, as emotionally jumpy as a rabbit. Physically, he was a rock, but inside, it was like he was burning up all the time.

"Did Jewel invite you? Who invited you?"

"Don't get mad," she said.

"Don't tell me not to get mad. Just tell me."

"I'm just saying, because—I know you'll get mad." She'd never been shy about pissing him off on purpose—but this was different. This was something he definitely didn't want to know, and she didn't want to tell him. But she didn't want to lie to him, either.

Her lips formed the words a couple times before her voice cooperated. "My prince invited me. He lives in the underworld."

"You're lying." The furrow between his eyebrows got deeper. "Why would you say that?"

"Because it's true. And I thought you should know."

Henley wasn't looking at her anymore—he was staring out the window at the massacred garden—but she could see him in profile. She'd always liked his face. He'd had that same frustrated expression when they were kids—except back then it had showed itself when he struck out playing baseball, or when Rafe Wilder said Viv looked like a boy and Henley was struggling not to punch him in the face. Although Rafe still said stuff like that.

"So is he twisted like you thought he would be? Or do you like him?"

"I don't know yet. I don't think he's turned on by dead girls or anything."

Henley's hands curled into fists. He probably didn't even realize he was doing it. "Do you want me to . . ."

She laughed. "What? Do I want you to kill him instead of me?"

"I wouldn't kill you, Viv." He closed his eyes and let his forehead touch the windowpane. "Although God knows you deserve it."

She laughed again. "Thanks."

She believed that he wouldn't do it right now. She didn't believe he would feel that way forever.

Henley let out a sigh and grumbled something about the garden while Viv poked at the bitten, slowly browning apple with her finger. Then he said, "You're not going back . . . are you?"

"Of course I'm going back."

"And what am I supposed to do? What am I supposed to do while you're figuring out if you want to date this guy?"

The sick feeling rose up in her again. Leaving Henley—choosing someone else—meant losing him.

"Whatever you want," she said. "I don't own you."

"Yes, you do, Viv. You know you do."

CHAPTER FOURTEEN

THERE WAS NO RIGHT THING to say after that.

Henley moved around the kitchen, rechecking the fridge and the cabinets, not meeting her eyes. He finally gave up with a frustrated "There's no food here."

"We could go out," Viv said.

"I guess."

She sent him upstairs to get her clothes—a summery red dress, sandals, underwear. The dress was new, and she cut the tags off with a knife she found in the cutlery drawer. Maybe it was more accurate to call it a dagger. It had a jeweled handle, like it should be used for fantasy role play.

"What is that?" Henley asked, coming up behind her.

"One of Regina's prized possessions, I guess. I don't know. Is it fancy enough to cut out a heart? I can't picture her cutting a lime with it."

"Give me that," he muttered. She gave it up gladly, and he took it and wrapped it in a dish towel.

"What are you going to do with it?"

"What do you mean, what am I going to do with it? I'm getting rid of it. Are you ready to go?"

"Yeah," she said. "Let's get out of here."

They took his truck. Henley tossed the dagger into the back, along with the loose mulch and gardening tools, and she didn't ask him how or when he'd dispose of it.

He was still wearing his grass-stained work clothes, but neither one of them felt like stopping at his house so he could change. They went through the drive-through at a burger place and then just rode around for a while.

The drive had a doomed, depressing feeling, even though they were just cruising the outskirts of Beau Rivage. It felt like he was taking her to the airport and they didn't know when, or if, they would see each other again.

"I'm sweating my ass off in here," Viv said, to break the silence.

"Tell me where you want to go."

She bit down on her plastic straw. "Drive us off a cliff."

Henley popped open the glove compartment and pulled out a road map. "Find a cliff. Maybe I will."

She didn't reach for it.

"That's what I thought."

In the end, they went to Jewel's place, because—although neither one of them said as much—they were afraid to be alone. Jewel was more Viv's friend than Henley's but, unlike most of Viv's friends, she didn't grate on his nerves. Jewel was the Kind Girl in a Diamonds and Toads curse. She'd been nice to the right fairy and now gems and flowers fell

95

from her lips when she spoke, sang, or even made out.

At nineteen, Jewel already had her own luxury condo with a view of the shore. She sang in Curses & Kisses with Blue, Freddie, and Rafe, and probably would have been living in a starving artist's garret if not for her curse. The nonstop supply of gems enabled her to do whatever she wanted, so long as she didn't take her freak show outside Beau Rivage.

Jewel came to the door barefoot, wearing a camisole and pajama shorts. Her dark brown skin was free of makeup, but all her jewelry was in: a row of colorful gemstone studs in each ear, and a diamond stud in her nose. The jewelry was her trademark; every stone had come from her curse. Her brown hair was pulled into a ponytail, and a single pink streak showed on one side.

"Surprise," Viv said. "Uninvited guests."

"You guys look like somebody died." Jewel's voice was throaty and had grit to it. She had a good *piss off* voice. That was why Viv loved her singing. When Jewel sang that you'd ruined her life and she'd make you sorry, she sounded like she meant it.

"Who died?" another girl called from inside the condo. Luxe. Jewel's girlfriend.

Luxe was a Kinder, meaning her curse had taken center stage when she was a kid, and she'd never stopped being the brat she'd been during her glory days. She had all the attributes that went along with her Goldilocks curse: butter-blonde curls, the charm of a sociopath, no regard for other people's property. And she complained about everything— but she was cute, and Jewel had this theory about artists and tumultuous relationships: that if she didn't have a frustrating girlfriend, she'd run out of things to write about.

Viv was not a fan. "I didn't know you had company," she said, wrinkling her nose.

Jewel gave her an amused half smile. "If you want to know that, you should call first."

"Do you want us to go?"

"No. Get in here."

Viv and Henley followed Jewel inside. The condo's floor plan was open—the living room and kitchen were right there when you walked in. Shot glasses filled with rubies, diamonds, and other precious stones decorated every flat surface.

"You guys want anything?" Jewel asked, heading toward the kitchen. The light from the wide back windows caught the gems in her ears and made them sparkle.

"A shower," Henley said.

Jewel pointed down the hall. "It's all yours." He headed to the bathroom and Viv went with Jewel into the kitchen, grateful to have a chance to talk to her alone. Her feet were still sore, so she sat down at the breakfast bar and let them dangle.

"What happened this time?" Jewel asked.

"I don't even know how to start talking about this."

"You never told me who died," Luxe called out.

Luxe was sprawled on the couch in front of the TV, her T-shirt pushed up to show her stomach, her skirt short enough to give all three bears a heart attack. Wet flower petals clung to Luxe's cheek and neck, and the couch cushions were littered with gems—a sure sign that Jewel and Luxe had been making out. They made out all the time.

Viv wasn't sure if Luxe was perpetually horny or just a gold digger, since Jewel let Luxe keep the gems that fell during their makeout sessions—but she tended to assume the worst about Luxe. The girl had been breaking and entering in grade school, after all.

"No one died," Jewel called back.

Luxe sighed dramatically and flopped into a new position on the couch. "Jewel, all your furniture is so lumpy."

"You're the only one who thinks so. Go hang out in the bedroom if you want."

"I would, but your mattress is too hard. You need a new bed."

"I'm not getting a new bed."

"Unnnnh, I guess I'll try this chair. . . ."

Viv rolled her eyes.

"So," Jewel said. "Tell me what the big crisis is today. Before he gets out of the shower."

"I met my prince," Viv said quietly. "The prince from my curse."

Jewel just stared. "Did I miss something? Like, your enchanted coma?"

"No, he hired a fairy to find me. He lives in the under-world."

"The *underworld*?" A pink rose blossom tumbled out of Jewel's mouth.

"Shh." This was information for Jewel's ears only. Viv didn't want to share it with Luxe. "His brothers have a Twelve Dancing Princesses curse, but he's a Snow White prince. His name is Jasper. He wants me to come back tonight. He asked me to stay there with him."

"Are you serious? Does Henley know?"

"He knows I met my prince. But . . . that's it."

"You're not really considering moving to the underworld."

"I told Jasper I'd think about it. He says he can keep Regina away from me. And . . . Henley."

Jewel snorted, and coughed up a few violets. "Yeah, I'm sure he'd *love* to keep Henley away from you. What's this prince like?"

"Uh . . . nice? I don't know. He wants to protect me, so I guess he falls somewhere on the hero scale. He doesn't strike me as the spoiled playboy type. Or the creepy pervert type."

"Too bad. I know you were looking forward to that."

Luxe had been sulkily flipping channels, her legs draped over the arm of the chair. Now she was digging around in a cereal box, dangling pieces over her mouth and then dropping them in like she was feeding a seal. "Jewel," she called, "these aren't sweet enough. Don't you have any good cereal?"

"I have cookies," Jewel said.

"I tried those," Luxe said. "The peanut butter was too sticky."

"Oh my god," Viv muttered. "When does it *end*?"

"She just needs attention," Jewel said, a note of understanding making it sound affectionate.

She's just annoying, Viv thought. But she supposed everyone made excuses for the people they loved. She wondered what kind of excuses Henley made for her.

Jewel coughed some rubies into her handkerchief, then tipped them into a shot glass. "I don't like the idea of you being in the underworld by yourself. You should bring me with you. Get another opinion."

Viv nodded. "I'll try to get you an invitation."

"Good."

Henley came back from the bathroom wearing the change of clothes he kept in his truck: a *Silva Landscaping* T-shirt and shorts. He sat down next to Viv at the breakfast bar, the wooden chair creaking as he dropped into it. He looked tired, like the shower had worn him out. Like it had given him too much time to think.

His hair and the back of his neck were wet, and Viv ran her fingers over his nape to wipe the water droplets off. He closed his eyes and leaned into her touch.

"You know what I find pretentious?" Luxe said. "Bears eating porridge. Bears are supposed to eat salmon. What the hell?"

Jewel went over and squished into the armchair next to Luxe, pulling her girlfriend against her like she was a big doll. "You're right. Those bears were totally obnoxious. They deserved it when you wrecked their house."

"Thank you," Luxe said.

"You guys want to watch a movie with us?" Jewel asked.

Viv weighed the annoyance of watching a movie with Luxe—who was bound to complain that the volume was too loud (or too quiet), the plot was too predictable (or too confusing)—against leaving, when leaving would mean being alone with Henley, awkwardly silent and haunted by their exchange:

I don't own you.

Yes, you do, Viv. You know you do.

Viv took her hand off his neck, touched his scarred knuckles instead. "Are you okay to stay for a while?"

He shrugged. "If you want."

Jewel and Luxe were curled up in the armchair, so Viv and

Henley took the couch. There was plenty of room to spread out, but Viv leaned her head on his shoulder, and Henley put his arm around her, and they didn't talk about it, didn't say a word about how reckless it was to be over but not over.

They were like a firecracker that had burned up. The pretty picture, the sparkling moment was gone; they were just smoke and ashes now.

In a few hours, Viv would be getting dressed in her *Inferno*-themed outfit, clutching her invitation, waiting to utter the word *yes* so the silver marks would appear on her arms. She'd wait for Night to summon her, and then she'd step through a door to the underworld and dance all night with the boy who was meant to be her future. Every turn on the dance floor would be like kissing Henley good-bye.

She curled up with him and pretended they were a normal couple, that they were their old selves. It was amazing what you could believe when you wanted to.

Viv closed her eyes, relaxed into the gentle sensation of his fingers against her hair, steady and calm, like a heartbeat when nothing was wrong. She wrapped her arm around his chest as if she could hold on to that feeling. He was precious to her in moments like this, and it made hurting him seem like something she would never do, instead of something she always did. She regretted so much. . . .

Just end it, she told herself. *Be good to him for once.*

But she didn't.

CHAPTER FIFTEEN

"IT'S ALL RIGHT. You can come in. She's gone."

Henley was surprised Regina was even awake at this hour. It was close to midnight, and the house was dark and still. She stood with her hip against the doorframe, her hair spilling over one shoulder.

The garden was restless with the hum of insects, the rustling of nocturnal animals making their way across the grass. He'd come to see Viv, and he'd been lurking below her balcony, trying to decide if he should call her or go home when Regina opened the back door.

He meant to tell her *no* and leave, but found himself moving toward the door, into the same kitchen where Viv had told him about her prince. A moth fluttered in after him and flew up to hover around the light above the sink. The rest of the kitchen was dark. The scent of jasmine blew in through the screens, and Henley could hear bats in the garden. He should have known Viv was gone—none of the bats had flown into her bedroom. They were always getting tangled up in her curtains when she was there.

"I'd offer to make coffee, but we don't have any," Regina said. "Vodka?"

He shook his head. "No thanks."

"That's right. You're health-conscious—except for that smoking habit."

"I'm not. If I cared about my health, I wouldn't be with Viv."

Regina laughed. "I'd always assumed you were because you take care of your body. But I guess you could have a different reason for doing that."

"It's just something to do." He shrugged, embarrassed to tell her the truth. He worked out when he was stressed, and because it had become a habit after years of doing it. But he had started because he wanted to be ready to protect Viv. So that no matter how big or tough her Huntsman was, he'd be able to stop him.

Oh, the irony, his friend Jack Tran would say.

"Sit down," Regina said. "You don't have to worry about Viv finding you here. She'll be gone all night."

Henley's eyes burned like someone had blown sand into them. "She went. She went, anyway."

Before they'd separated after spending the day at Jewel's, he'd held her close and whispered, *Don't go.* And she'd hugged him the way she did when she was sorry about something. He'd thought that had meant *okay.*

"You asked her not to?"

He nodded, not sure why he was confiding in Regina. Maybe because his mother would say *Forget her, you can do better.* His father would shrug and say *This is the way it works.*

Regina would offer a solution. It would be a solution he didn't like . . . but at least she would act like there was something he could do.

"And you're surprised?" she asked. "Or hurt?"

He didn't answer. He lit a cigarette and busied himself with smoking instead.

Regina reached for the pack he'd left on the table, and drew one out with her bloodred nails. She rolled it between her fingers.

"When I was your age, I thought I was a Snow White princess. I used to long for my prince to come the way a martyr longs for sacrifice. I was willing to suffer for it if I had to. Because I wanted to matter. And a princess always matters—especially if she suffers. That's not the case for all of us.

"I'm sure you can relate. You wanted to be her hero. You wanted to be something you were never meant to be. Cruel, cruel fate." She leaned her head on her hands. Smiled like they were in this together. "Do you mind if I get that vodka?"

"No, go ahead."

She moved through the kitchen like a boat rocking on water, hips swaying like a pendulum.

"The thing about this curse . . . is that it makes us not matter. We revolve around the princess. We play a role and then send her to her happily ever after. If she lives, I'll die. The queen always dies unless she wins. And you . . . your heart will be broken. Viv and her prince will send you a Christmas card every year to be nice: *Here's how we're doing. Look how big our kids are getting. Aren't they cute?* And you'll wonder, *What the hell did I do wrong? Why did she pick that idiot over me?* I know because I've been there. I get those cards. It sucks."

Henley closed his eyes and tried to picture the family photo Viv might send him in ten years. Smug prince in a reindeer sweater. Two prissy kids and a golden retriever. Viv sitting off to the side, her face retouched to give her a smile. It seemed impossible that she could be with someone else. Build a life with someone else.

Regina tipped some vodka into a glass. "That's our fate, Henley. We are *not* the chosen ones. Sure you don't want any?"

He shook his head, dragged on his cigarette. He was afraid his voice would come out broken if he said anything. Even a simple *I'm okay* would snap in his throat.

"I was always the wrong girl. I'd date a cursed guy, we'd get along great . . . but there was a princess waiting just around the corner. His perfect match. *Destiny.* And once he found her . . . I was the mistake. You're about to be the mistake, Henley. The first love who wasn't her real love. That's what she'll say to her prince, you know. When he asks her about your relationship. *I didn't know real love until I met you.*"

"Viv wouldn't say that. Even if—she'd probably tell him it was none of his business."

"Oh, you'd be surprised what a girl will say. She's tough with you, but that's because she doesn't want to impress you anymore. With her prince, it'll be different."

He thought of all the princes Viv had used to make him crazy. What would she be like with her prince?

"A lot can happen in a night," Regina said. "If you let things go on, if you don't step in and do something, she won't even be the girl you remember. You'll lose her. In every way."

105

Pain pierced his temples. "I can't kill her."

"Yes, you can. Look at those big hands. That body. You weren't built for playing the piano, Henley."

"I don't want to, then."

"Of course you do. You want it more than anything, or you wouldn't be here."

Henley had only killed once, and that had been an accident. He'd hit a deer with his truck when he was driving with Viv—it had leapt right at them, its love for Viv negating any sense of self-preservation. He'd had just enough time to throw his arm up in front of her in case the deer went through the windshield—but they were lucky, and it didn't. Viv had insisted on climbing out of the truck, dropping to her knees in the street, and putting her hands on the deer's chest as if she had some kind of healing power—which she didn't. Although it had seemed like she calmed it a little, like her presence put the deer at ease as it died.

Afterward, he'd wrapped his arms around her and she'd clung to him with bloody hands, her tiny body wracked by sobs. She was fragile in so many ways, but her emotions were fierce. She'd been devastated, so angry that her curse had done that. And he'd felt like it was his fault, too. Like he should have been able to save it for her.

He wasn't a killer. And yet, he would have to become one if he wanted to be the one to end this.

His hand shook, and he ground the cigarette out on the table. He didn't think Regina would care. She was asking him to murder her stepdaughter. A scorch mark was nothing compared to that.

"You matter, Henley. The curse might make you feel like

you don't, but you do. Ask yourself: Can you live without her? And if you can't, is it right that she can live without you?"

The pain came back, the pressure in his head expanding, and he stared at the table, at the fingerprints Viv's apple-sticky hand had left behind. A moth would batter itself against a light until it died. A deer would leap to its death for a chance to be close to Viv. And she would mourn them both. But she could walk away from him as if it were the most natural thing in the world. As if he should expect it and be okay with it, because that was fate.

The word caught in his throat like there were barbs attached to it.

"No."

"Good," Regina said. "There's someone I want you to meet."

CHAPTER SIXTEEN

THAT NIGHT, THE HORSEMAN didn't throw Viv down the well.

Instead, he swept her onto his horse, and they rode, inhumanly fast, until they came to a stop in an alley that was cleaner than any alley should be. Shards from a broken perfume bottle littered the ground, along with a misplaced tiara, but there was no other refuse, and the air smelled of roses, not overripe garbage. Guests in fire-colored evening attire waited in a line that led to an open manhole.

Viv turned to Night. "I have to jump into a sewer? I thought this was supposed to be a better option."

"You don't jump," the horseman said. "There's a ladder. And it doesn't lead to a sewer. It's a magic door. It leads to the underworld."

Night's horse stood beside them, heat radiating from its enormous body. The horse stretched its head forward to nuzzle the flame-shaped hair ornament of the woman in front of them. The horse's teeth seized the orange netting, along with some of the woman's hair. As she cried out, Night cautioned, "Don't move your head." But that was all the help he offered.

"You're so friendly," Viv told him.

Night regarded her with his unblinking black eyes, that smooth, dark face that could have been carved from jet. "I was not hired to be friendly."

After a few minutes the horse grew bored with the netting and settled on snorting and pawing the ground. The woman with the flame hair ornament fled the line, and Night grabbed the reins to keep the horse from stomping.

"What is it doing?" Viv asked.

"He wants to crack the earth open. Like in your story of Persephone and Hades. Bringing girls to the underworld. He doesn't understand that there are doors now."

Viv pictured Night, or someone like him, abducting a girl from a field of flowers and carrying her through a rift in the earth. She was almost glad for the sewer.

Standing in line with a bunch of strangers, Viv suddenly felt alone. She never went out by herself. It felt weird to be dressed up and going to a club without any of her friends, to be purposely leaving Henley behind so she could spend time with another guy.

She hadn't even told Henley she was definitely going to the underworld tonight. He'd asked her not to, and she hadn't answered.

You should have told him. You should have made sure he knew.

She reached for her phone—but she'd left it in her room. No reception in the underworld, no sense in bringing it. She hugged her arms to her chest, feeling edgy now.

As they approached the manhole, Viv watched the guests climb down, as if watching them might make her feel better about doing it. Some of the women needed help getting their voluminous skirts through the opening. Others wore dresses so tight they had to be lowered onto the ladder.

Viv's dress was somewhere between the two. It was short, with a strapless top and a puffy skirt, but it wouldn't give her the trouble a gown would. It was red enough to be devilish, and she'd paired it with a glittery devil-horn headband and sparkly red shoes.

When she made it to the front of the line, she hesitated before the open manhole.

"You'll know what to do from here," Night said. "Don't bypass the checkpoint."

"You're not coming with me?" He wasn't very helpful, but she didn't like the idea of being alone. She needed to ask Jasper for extra invitations.

"There's no need." Night closed his hands around her forearms, then lowered her through the manhole. Her shoes scraped the ladder once before finding purchase, and then she curled her fingers around an upper rung and Night let her go. She looked up to say something, but he was already gone.

The pain in her feet had eased since the morning. She still felt a tender discomfort each time one of the metal rungs dug into the sole of her shoe, but as she stepped off the ladder and joined the guests making their way down the wide stone staircase, the last of the pain disappeared. Maybe it was the atmosphere, the sudden excitement that came with being somewhere secret—or maybe it was the magic of the underworld.

As she continued down the staircase, several more stone staircases came into view, each leading from another door. As the groups from the different staircases merged, Viv caught snatches of foreign languages being spoken, and accents from the other cities around the world where Cursed gathered. Some of the guests were knocking snow from their boots. One woman was holding her torn skirt closed, complaining that she hated crawling through a fireplace to get here—her clothes were always getting ruined.

Viv followed the other guests along a path that wound through the silver trees, all the way to the checkpoint, where she presented her right arm to the guard. When he touched his ring to her silver mark, it vanished. The guard waved her through, and she headed toward the lakeshore.

She fit in tonight; she was dressed for the theme—and she wasn't the only one who'd taken it literally. She counted a handful of guests wearing devil horns—some of the cheap Halloween variety, others crafted from metal and precious stones. A few people sported devil tails. One woman wore a dress patterned with creatures from a Hieronymus Bosch painting; she was Viv's favorite. Her second favorite was the guy wearing a T-shirt that said HELL IS OTHER PEOPLE.

She estimated it was about eleven thirty, whereas the night before she'd arrived around two. The wait for the boats was a long one. There were fifteen gondolas, each with the ability to carry one or two passengers, and there were at least fifty guests ahead of her. Viv didn't like waiting in line, so she made her way over to the boathouse to see if there was something they could do.

She had a face that was easy to remember: her curse was

written all over it. If they'd seen her with Jasper last night, surely they'd know her now.

The boatman who'd rowed her to the club was there. He bowed at the waist.

"Princess," he said. "You're so much easier to recognize in clothes."

"Is there any way I can cut the line?"

"Normally we only give special treatment to princesses who have eleven sisters. But I guess I could make an exception . . . since you remembered not to wear your pajamas."

"Thanks," she said. "I'd hate to have to get you fired."

He waved his hand in a *let's go* motion. "You're misinformed if you think you can get me fired. There's not exactly an endless supply of cheap labor down here. Maybe you've noticed the lack of a bustling metropolis."

She had noticed, but hadn't given it much thought. There were no houses, no shops . . . nothing but the palace and the nightclub. And the boathouse on this side of the lake. But she'd figured the rest of the underworld denizens lived farther away. That there was a city or a village somewhere.

The boatman began to row and the lake rippled like silver satin.

"Where is everyone?" Viv asked.

"In the club. On the shore."

"No, I mean everyone else. The people who live here. Your family."

"I don't think I'm supposed to discuss that with you."

"Oh please." She thought he was joking.

The boatman stopped rowing for a moment, and the gondola drifted. A stagnant, wet-metal smell wafted up from the lake. "You're going to be our princess. That's the idea, isn't it?"

"Well—one of them. Maybe."

"No, you'll be the only one. Someone always breaks the Twelve Dancing Princesses curse. And you'd have to be running from something pretty awful to stay here by choice."

Viv made sure her face was composed before she said, "Why is that?"

"It's more fun if you find out on your own, isn't it?"

"No. Stop messing with me and tell me."

"Look around you. There's no life here. It's party-all-night and then it's a barren hole with some fancy buildings. Only one person lives here because he wants to. That alone should tell you something."

"So you don't want to be here?"

"No one wants to be here."

He started to row again. He waited until they were nearly across the lake before he said,

"Every underworld curse—that I know of—involves getting new people to come here. The Twelve Dancing Princesses curse, obviously. And then there's your curse. Prince Jasper is supposed to find you in a coffin, right? And in your curse, the prince doesn't kiss you to wake you up. His instinct is just to bring your body home. That's why Snow White is perfect for the underworld. They need new people here so badly they'd take a dead girl."

"Thanks for that disgusting comment," Viv said. "Why do they need new people?"

"If you stay here long enough, the magic of the underworld gets into your blood. It changes you."

"Changes you how?"

113

The gondola nudged the shore and the boatman braced the craft so Viv could get out. "I think that's enough for tonight."

"No. You don't get to do that." Viv stood, but didn't leave the gondola. "This place could be my destiny. It's not like I'm going home tomorrow and never coming back. I need to know what could happen to me."

"Nothing will happen to you. You're immune. That makes you quite the valuable commodity as far as the royal family's concerned. You should leverage that as best you can. See what you can get out of them before you agree to any proposals."

She didn't like being called a commodity. Just the idea of it was nauseating. "I still want to know what kind of place this is."

"And what will you give me that would make it worth my while to tell you? I don't think your prince would appreciate my sharing secrets he's still keeping from you."

"What do you want, money?"

"Bring me a carton of cigarettes. A nice lighter, if you have one." He took his own lighter out of his pocket. "This one's trashed."

"You know those things'll kill you, right?"

"I won't live to be twenty-five. Let them try to kill me before then."

"Why won't you live to be twenty-five?"

"I'm not special like you, Princess. My destiny doesn't give me a free pass. Or a clean bill of health."

"You're sick?"

"Is that a *yes* to my cigarettes?"

"Yes, I'll bring them. Just tell me what the hell you're talking about."

"It's a deal, then. A deal." He laughed. "Ah . . . anyway. Keep this information to yourself. If you do mention it, you didn't hear it from me. Understand?"

"Fine."

The boatman secured the gondola, then led her away from the shore, over to a group of boulders that looked like they'd been rolled into place by a giant. The boatman ducked behind them, out of sight, and Viv followed. There was a little inlet there where the lake water smelled stronger, more sharply metallic. A golden brooch lay in the shallow water on top of some stones.

"This realm is for Jasper's family," the boatman said. "The royal bloodline is immune to the underworld's effects, but everyone else gets sick from exposure. It's like the fairies who built this place wanted to make sure the underworld had limited use. I don't know the reasons. I just know that after enough time down here, parts of your body shut down. After ten years or so, you're totally infertile—that's why the princes need brides who didn't grow up here. After twenty-some years, your mind starts to go, until you lose it completely and you get the ax. You and the Twelve Dancing Princesses are protected by your curses. You could stay here and be all right. But anyone who's serving you a cocktail, checking you in at the checkpoint, sweeping up broken glass . . . they're in the same boat I'm in. Sick, stuck, and screwed."

"Everyone here?"

"All the workers."

"Wait." Viv held up her hands. "What about your family? If people are infertile after ten years, did your parents have you at nine? If you're . . . twenty—?"

"Eighteen."

"That means they've already lost their minds and they're dead now? And you're—"

"My parents are famous. Successful. I can't say whether they're alive or not. Probably alive." He rolled his head along the stone until he was facing her. There was a tightness around his eyes.

"Do they know you're here?"

"They know. They're the reason I'm here."

She stared at him, confused, and he smirked in a way that looked painful.

"They made a bad deal."

He moved away from the boulder. Took a fresh cigarette from a pack in his jacket and wedged it into the corner of his mouth. "Don't forget my cigarettes. Two cartons."

"You're leaving?"

"I have a job to do. I've already been gone too long."

"What's your name?" she called, too shaken by his story to keep thinking of him as *the boatman*. "I won't tell anyone about you. I just want to know."

"Owen," he said.

"I'm Viv."

"I know," he said.

"I—"

I'll free you, she'd started to say. *When I'm the princess— when I'm the queen of this place—I'll free you.* She was thinking impulsively, her blood burning with the injustice of it, ready to make promises she didn't know how to keep. When it was her own life at stake, she felt resigned—but this was someone else's life. Many lives, if what Owen said was true.

Maybe she could help them. Maybe she was the only one who could, and that was why she was here.

The thought was so grandiose it almost made her laugh. She couldn't even take charge of her own life. How was she supposed to save anyone else's?

And yet . . . she couldn't shake the feeling that maybe she could do something—and she hadn't wanted to fight for anything in a long time.

CHAPTER SEVENTEEN

RED LIGHTS CAST A FIERY GLOW on the dancers and made the black floor and walls shine like dark blood. The music was loud tonight, throbbing like a giant heart. The air smelled of charcoal and cinnamon, and Viv couldn't take more than a few steps without dodging a lurching devil, or waving a puff of smoke out of her face. She almost wished she had Henley there to carve a path through the crowd for her. But she could never bring him to the underworld. Henley would lose it if he met Jasper. And she still didn't know how much Jasper knew about Henley.

She wasn't sure what to tell him, either.

Viv made her way through the packed club to the middle of the dance floor, where the Twelve Dancing Princesses and their partners danced together in an endless display. The princesses wore ember-colored dresses with jagged hems, layers of chiffon that flicked the air when they twirled. The eleven underworld princes wore black suits shot through with veins of red, like lava flowing over rock.

It was still early, and the couples moved in perfect unison. The princesses and princes wore adoring smiles, pressed their noses together, kissed and laughed and never missed a step. All except for the princess who danced by herself, swaying like a candle flame, her eyes sad one moment, angry the next.

Viv lingered, caught up in their performance, until she felt hands on her shoulders and turned to find Jasper. He wore a parchment-colored suit covered with black calligraphy. Italian. Viv guessed it was from Dante's *Inferno.* Jasper looked so genuinely pleased to see her, she felt a surge of hopefulness. Like maybe there was something to this destiny thing.

He hugged her, warmth flooding her as he bent his head to speak into her ear. "I'm so glad you came. Do I have you for an hour or the whole night?"

"I don't know yet. It depends on how interesting you are."

He laughed. "Do you feel like dancing? Can I get you anything? A drink? A room?"

"A *room*?"

"A room in the palace," he said, shouting to be heard over the music. "In case you've decided to stay."

"I haven't decided anything."

"Then I guess I'll have to convince you!"

"You can try!"

He never fully let her go. His hug relaxed into more of a dance posture, and he spun her around the floor until their cheeks glowed and she was dizzy, laughing. More than once she bumped into one of the twelve princesses and the girl and her partner gracefully stepped out of the way, but when she bumped into the solo princess, the girl bared her teeth and shoved Viv away with a motion that was like a slap.

"What the hell?" Viv said.

"Ignore her," Jasper said. "She's bitter about the curse."

"What does that have to do with me?"

"We have the freedom to stop dancing. She doesn't. You're about to be rescued—and who knows how long she'll have to wait? She only thinks about her own pain. As if there aren't Cursed who have it worse than she does."

"You don't like her?"

"No, I don't!"

All the shout-talking was giving her a headache, so Viv pulled Jasper off the dance floor and out of the club, stopping just long enough to grab a gold drink from a tray on her way out. The liquid sloshed around in her martini glass and spilled over the side, staining her fingers a shimmering gold.

"What is this, nail polish?"

"Yes, Viv, our club serves nail polish to the guests."

"Well, I don't know. This place is weird. And I can't tell what this is."

"I know you're afraid of being poisoned, so let me ease your mind." Jasper raised the glass to his lips, tipped it back long enough to swallow a mouthful, and handed it back to her. "There. Wait ten minutes; we'll see what happens to me."

"So you'll be my taste tester? Check everything I eat for poison?"

"If that's what you need. Now tell me, why are we out here? Sick of dancing?"

"Sick of yelling. The music's great to get lost in, but if we want to talk it's better out here."

"I don't mind talking." He smiled.

"Is there anywhere we can go? Like . . ." She glanced around innocently, as if she didn't know that underworld civilization started and stopped with the nightclub and the palace. "A coffee shop?"

"Uh, no, we don't have anything like that. But we can go to . . ."

Guests flowed around them: tacky devils and Royals in red lace, a ballerina in a flame-blackened dress, a soldier in a suit that looked like melted tin. While Jasper tried to decide on a destination, Viv studied his face. She wondered when he would start confessing things, and when she would start telling him things he didn't want to hear. She wondered who would hold out longer.

One of the guests—a woman in a low-cut red evening gown, with an expression that said her dress was more ready for this night than she was—sidled up to Jasper. "Prince— you're one of the princes, aren't you?"

"Yes, but you'll have to excuse me. I'm busy right now."

"It'll only take a second," the woman said. Or was she just a girl? Her face was young, her makeup bold and clumsily applied. Flecks of mascara clung to her cheeks, and though her neckline exuded confidence, her nails were bitten down to the quick. "Is your father around? I thought—I hoped—I heard he came to the club sometimes."

"He never comes to the club anymore." Jasper's voice was tight, distinctly unfriendly. "And you don't want to meet with him. Trust me. Come, Viv, let's—"

"Oh, but I do!" The girl lunged and caught his arm before he could leave. "I do. I know you probably think I haven't thought it through, but I have. I just need his help with one

thing. It's not going to escalate. See, I brought this bracelet—"
She tugged it off her wrist to show him. "It's jade. It was my
mother's. It's the most valuable thing I own. Do you think he'll
take it?"

Jasper's tone was even colder than before. "I'm sorry, I can't
help you. You should go home." His fingers clamped around
Viv's and he pulled her through the crowd of guests, away from
the girl.

"Please!" the girl cried after them. "Do you know where I
can find him?"

Jasper ignored her and kept going, up the steep path that
led toward the palace. The path was empty, as if the guests
sensed it was off-limits. Viv turned to see if the girl would
follow them, but she was talking with someone else, showing
them the bracelet.

"Jasper," Viv said. "Who's your father?"

"He's someone who helps people with things."

"That's really vague."

He sighed. "He's just my father. What do you want me to
say?"

"His name and his curse would be a start."

"I was really looking forward to getting to know *you*
tonight. Not talking about him."

"It's a simple question."

"Well, maybe it's not a simple answer."

She stopped walking, and loosed her hand from his.
"That's not good enough."

Jasper reached out and grasped both her hands. He looked
sort of contrite, ready to start over. "You wanted to talk. Let's
talk. We can go to the palace."

"All right." Maybe his father would be there and she would find out for herself who he was. In any case, she'd learn more than what Jasper had told her so far.

The palace looked like a cathedral, or a wicked fairy's lair—not a home for Prince Charming. Gargoyles crouched on ledges and the windows were made of alternating diamonds of red and black glass. The front of the building was covered with glossy black ivy that turned out to be butterflies upon closer inspection. The butterflies weren't clustered there, resting; they were more like . . . glued, their wings shiny and stiff like they'd been coated in lacquer.

"Are those—?" Viv started, before she answered her own question. "That's disgusting."

"They're dead; it's just decoration. Come on. Don't look if it upsets you."

Inside, the darkness gave way to white marble floors and glittering gold. Gold trees grew up from cracks in the floor, their branches heavy with gold blossoms, gold birds, and gold beetles. Massive chandeliers hung from the ceiling, their hundreds of candles dripping hot wax onto the floor and causing everything in the hall to gleam.

"Someone likes gold," Viv said.

"My father."

"So he's . . . helpful and has a tacky sense of style. That's two things I know about him."

"Keep your voice down."

"Why? Is he here?"

"I don't know, but if we run into him he'll ruin our night."

"So he's a killjoy? Or just an asshole?"

"You sound like you like the idea of him bothering us, but I promise that you won't."

She stopped provoking Jasper then, and followed her reflection in the dozens of gold-framed mirrors that covered the walls. She watched for another person in the glass, and wondered what an underworld king would look like. In Beau Rivage, kings wore anything from suits to designer loungewear. But Jasper and his brothers wore signet rings and silver sashes; they took their royal blood seriously or, at least, wanted to ensure that their guests did. If Jasper's father appeared, would he stride into the hall wearing an ermine-trimmed cape and a bejeweled crown? If he liked gold, he probably liked gems, too.

Their steps rang out in the high-ceilinged hall, but no one appeared to greet them. It was eerie not to encounter a single living creature. "You don't have a dog or anything?" Viv asked.

"No. Animals don't do very well down here."

"*Don't do very well* meaning . . . ?"

"I don't know. We've never had a pet. But I've always gotten the impression that it isn't a good idea."

"And how do people do down here?" *Might as well start somewhere.*

"They do just fine."

Lie number one, on either Jasper's part or Owen's. She didn't want to think Jasper would lie. Owen seemed more the type to mess with her. But he'd also seemed upset when he talked about his parents.

"So, can we look around?" Viv said. "I've never been in a palace."

"Never?"

Her eyes wandered. Mirrors, mirrors, everywhere. A hundred reflected Vivs leaping from gold frame to gold frame. "Never one that wasn't a museum."

"I could show you around . . . but I was hoping to introduce you to someone. Someone very special to me. Are you interested?"

"It'd better not be a girl in a glass coffin. If you have a dead girl collection . . ."

"Viv . . . don't take this the wrong way, but you're disturbed. I don't have a dead girl collection. I don't have any kind of girl collection."

"Good."

"And I'm not sure why you thought I might."

"I know people who have them."

"If you say so. . . ."

They came to a wide, sweeping staircase. "It's upstairs," Jasper said. "The place I'm taking you to."

"So mysterious. Any other surprises?"

"Considering how little we know about each other, I'm sure there will be endless surprises. But I don't have any others in mind."

They climbed until they reached the second floor. The corridor there was carpeted with a red velvety material and covered with impressions of footsteps. Every ten feet there was a door with a gold Roman numeral on it—a I, then a II, then a III . . .

"All the way up to twelve?" Viv guessed.

"Thirteen, actually."

"Interesting. What number are you?"

"Seven. But we're going . . . here."

They stopped at the door marked VIII, and Jasper let himself in without knocking.

It was a bedroom, dark and gothic and yet somehow cozy: the furniture upholstered in red velvet, the unmade bed showing sheets of black silk. A black-haired girl in a long white dress sat on the window seat, her head bowed over a book. She was wearing bulky headphones, and saying something in . . . Italian? It sounded like she was repeating after someone. A pair of crutches leaned against the wall.

She was absorbed in what she was doing and didn't notice them come in. Jasper crept up to her and flopped down on the window seat. The girl's body jerked, startled, and she pulled off her headphones so they hung around her neck.

"Jasper! It's so early! Why are you home? Did something happen?" She leaned back to get a better look at him. "Oh, you're wearing the suit! I bet I can almost read it!"

"How much Italian have you learned?"

"*Grazie. Amore,*" she said, exaggerating the accent.

"You're missing something obvious," he said, poking her in the shoulder. "Either that or you're being rude."

"Why are you poking me? Honestly, just tell me why you're here—" Her head turned toward the door finally and her eyes met Viv's. "Oh! This must be Viv! Come and sit by me! We'll get rid of this creature." She shoved her book onto Jasper's lap and then pushed his shoulder as if to knock him off the seat.

"Hey!" Jasper said. But he got up and made room for Viv. "Viv, this is my sister, Garnet."

"Hi," Viv said. She sat down as she'd been told, and Garnet giggled.

"Those are very cute—your devil horns."

Viv touched her headband. "Oh, thanks."

"Did you know that in one of the dancing princess tales, the princesses spend the night dancing with devils? And they do more than dance—they go to bed with them, all except for one princess—and when their father finds out, he has his daughters executed. Isn't that atrocious?"

Viv had spent too much time fixating on her own curse to familiarize herself with every version of every fairy tale. "That does seem like overkill."

"Overkill, yes." Garnet laughed. "The dancing princesses' father loves killing people. Beheading the suitors who fail to break the curse, that's the best known. But there have been tales of the king beheading his daughters when they denied where they'd been, or burning them at the stake once he discovered they'd been dancing in the underworld."

"The curse was viewed differently in the past," Jasper said. "Ladies disappearing all night, going to another realm, consorting with devils . . ."

"Do you think we're devils, Viv? Oh, oh—this is where you tell me that Jasper's a handsome devil!"

Jasper shook his head. "You'll have to excuse Garnet. I usually give her a pass on her bad jokes, so she hasn't learned to make any good ones."

"Be nice to me or I won't let you hang out with us," Garnet told her brother. "I'll order you out the door with my imperious princess voice."

"And I'd have no choice but to go."

"That's right."

Viv wondered what Garnet's curse was, or whether she even had one. She was trying to decide if it would be rude to ask. Garnet seemed pretty chatty and welcoming, but people could be sensitive about their curses.

"Do you like chocolate, Viv? Marzipan? Jasper, get one of my candy boxes down, will you?" Garnet pointed at her bookshelves. "I make him put them up too high for me to reach so I don't eat them all at once and make myself sick. Am I talking too much? I am. Sorry. It's just, there's never anyone to talk to. Other than Jasper, I mean. Never anyone new."

Jasper opened a two-tiered candy box and held it out to them. "And aside from being her candy fetcher and an audience for her bad jokes, I'm next to worthless to this girl."

"That's not what I meant and you know it." Garnet sighed. "If only Minuet could be here. Then it would be perfect."

"Minuet?" Viv asked.

"Minuet is one of the Twelve Dancing Princesses," Jasper said. "The one without a partner."

"My princess," Garnet said. "Didn't Jasper introduce you?"

"We met," Viv said, wondering why Jasper had failed to mention it. "I must have missed her name. Um—" Viv hesitated.

"Yes?" Garnet said.

"You're not at the club. But you have a Twelve Dancing Princesses curse? How does that work?"

"I'll show you." Garnet lifted the skirt of her dress to reveal one pale leg ending in a satin slipper. "I had both legs when the fairy marked me, but I lost one to an accident when I was nine. And since losing a leg or a foot breaks a dancing curse, I'm no longer compelled to dance. But there's a princess who's meant for me, and I still believe we're destined to be together. I can't woo her on the dance floor, so Jasper keeps her company most nights. He'll have less time now that you're here, but I don't begrudge him that. He's been my hero long enough—haven't you, Jasper?"

Jasper gave a weary smile. "I suppose."

"So you've never met your princess?" Viv said. "You haven't gone to the club to talk to her?"

"No. I would like to. I have thought of doing that, but—I don't like to leave my room. I don't like to be out where my father might see me. I prefer to stay out of sight, out of mind. So he can't find anything else wrong with me, and—fix it."

Garnet looked away, and the pain on her face was clear enough that Viv knew better than to ask what she meant. But she wanted to. She was trying to put things together, figure out who Jasper's father was and whether he was a villain or just an overly critical parent. *Materialistic, bad relationship with kids, helps people . . .*

"I just have to wait and hope that Minuet and her sisters decide to stay in the underworld." Garnet hugged a red velvet pillow to her chest. "This curse is full of damsels in distress. The Twelve Dancing Princesses are waiting for someone to seal the door to the underworld and end this. And meanwhile my brothers and I are waiting for our princesses to choose *us*— so we don't have to spend our lives alone and unloved. You're so lucky. You and Jasper both. You'll have the fairy-tale ending everyone wants."

"We are lucky," Jasper said, taking Viv's hand.

Viv tried to smile. She didn't feel lucky; her curse had torn her life apart. But she knew she was luckier than some. Her prince was here, introducing her to his sister, trying to include her in his life. There were Snow Whites who had it much worse.

"Even if your princess doesn't decide to stay," Viv said, "that doesn't mean you'll be alone your whole life. There are other princesses. Other girls."

"Oh, but they couldn't stay. They wouldn't. Maybe they could come for six months and then go away for six months, lessen the toll, but . . . I wouldn't want them to."

Viv was about to ask what Garnet meant—she thought she knew—when Jasper cut in with:

"Do you want to hear about tonight? You might not be able to see Minuet, but she had plenty to say to you."

Garnet's gloom relented, and a smile returned to her face. "Tell me what she was wearing. Tell me everything."

Jasper spun an elaborate story about his night with Minuet, up to the time Viv had arrived at the club. It was full of inside jokes, sweet messages from Minuet to Garnet, a list of the songs Jasper and Minuet had danced to, a careful description of the twelve princesses' clothes . . . and Garnet listened, rapt, her laugh springing to life whenever Jasper relayed something particularly funny or cute.

Viv didn't interrupt. She let Jasper tell his story, and eventually the conversation moved to other things. It wasn't until they'd said their good-byes to Garnet and were descending the stairs that Viv asked, "Why do you lie to her?"

Jasper stopped midway down the staircase. He glanced up, as if to check that Garnet wasn't in the corridor, listening. Then he resumed his descent. "Because it's kinder than the truth."

"Does Minuet even like Garnet? Does she know about her?"

"She knows about her. She likes her about as much as she

likes you, or me, or anyone who isn't forced to dance. Maybe she likes Garnet less, because Garnet's supposed to share that misery with her. But it's hard to explain that Garnet's afraid to leave the palace. That she feels truly safe in one place and that's where she stays. It's not the kind of thing that would endear her to Minuet."

"Why is she so afraid? Is it because of her accident?"

"Yes."

"Okay. But even so—why would you create this fake love story for her?"

"Because I want Garnet to be happy. And telling her that her princess is an angry mess who hates her isn't going to do that."

"Jasper—"

"Please don't lecture me about this. You barely know us. You don't know what our lives are like."

At the bottom of the staircase, Viv's shoes made a final clack on the marble floor. "No, I don't."

They stood awkwardly in the gold-drenched hall, not meeting each other's eyes. The blazing candlelight made Viv feel like she was on a stage being watched by an audience of their reflections.

"Do you want to go back to the club?" Jasper asked.

"Let's just . . . go."

Viv was quiet as they started down the steep path. From this height, the silver trees looked like a forest of knives—less enchanting, and more like something you wouldn't want to fall into. The silver lake was a mirror blurred by ripples. Guests trickled from the shore to the club, faceless figures in red and orange, and boats cut through the water like insects.

Viv was tempted to give Jasper the silent treatment, but she wanted information more than she wanted that tiny victory.

"Jasper . . . why is Garnet afraid of your father?"

"Because of what he did. After her accident."

"What happened to her?"

Jasper motioned to the distant darkness that merely hinted at a landscape. "Beyond the trees, that way, there's a pit. We were forbidden to play there because it was dangerous. We did it, anyway. And one day a chunk of stone came loose and hit Garnet. It crushed her leg."

"Oh my god."

"It was awful. I thought she might die, or lose her leg, and I knew my father would punish us for disobeying him. But I thought if anything could help her, it was magic. So I brought her to my father, because he had magic."

"He's a—" *Not a fairy. Not a witch.* Viv tried to think—who else had magic?

But Jasper kept going. Either he hadn't heard her, or he didn't want to interrupt his story. A sigh punched out of him, like the next words were going to be painful to say.

"When I say *my father*, I don't want you to picture a man who teaches his children to play baseball and comforts them when they have nightmares. We saw him around the palace and at meals, but he was more like an overlord than anything else. We were afraid of displeasing him, of drawing his attention for any reason. I knew he would be angry, but I thought he could help her. I didn't understand then that his magic has limits.

"It turned out that he couldn't heal Garnet. And he was furious—both because we'd broken his rules and because his perfect daughter wasn't perfect anymore. He couldn't bear to see her like that, but it wasn't the anguish of a father who sees his child in pain. It was the reaction of a collector whose priceless piece of art has been ruined by a childish mistake.

"He wanted the offending part gone. So he summoned a doctor to amputate her leg. Not to examine her, or try to save her leg. No—that wouldn't be enough of a punishment. I was made to stay and watch. He said if I didn't stand there quietly and give the doctor room to work, he'd get the executioner to do it."

"Executioner?"

"That's my father for you. He has to call out for a doctor, but he keeps an executioner on staff."

"God." Viv shuddered.

"Afterward, he said it was a mercy. That if Garnet had kept her leg, it would never be useful to her, it would only bring her pain. The curse would force her to dance and she would suffer. But with her damaged leg gone, her curse was broken. It was like he wanted us to thank him. To acknowledge his foresight. And generosity."

Jasper's jaw was tight. Viv laid her hand on his arm and kept it there as they walked. They were nearing the club now. She could make out the details on people's costumes, but she didn't think anyone could hear their conversation.

"Why can't your sister just leave? Why is everyone who lives here trapped?"

"That's the way my father wants it. This is his kingdom; those are his rules. He's afraid no one will come back to him. He's not like the Beast. The Beast can let his Beauty go, and hope she'll return—because he loves her. My father never learned to love. He won't free anyone."

133

"He shouldn't treat you like prisoners."

"*Shouldn't?*" Jasper laughed. "He doesn't live according to rules like that. He doesn't have to."

Viv walked down to the lakeshore, far enough that the silver water lapped at the toes of her shoes, sparkling and ruby red, like a cruel joke: *there's no place like home.* Jasper had told her she'd be safe in the underworld—safe from Regina and Henley. But maybe true safety was impossible.

"So you're telling me that if I come here, I'll have to live under the thumb of your ruthless father. If everyone's powerless against him, that means I am and you are, too."

"No, that's not what I'm saying. Viv . . ." He turned her toward him. "My father wouldn't hurt you. The Huntsman, your stepmother—*they* will hurt you. But in the underworld, I can keep you safe. It's my destiny, and . . . my second chance. To protect you the way I couldn't protect my sister. I won't fail you."

"But how do you know? How do you know any of that? If your father would do that to his own daughter . . ."

"I'm different now. I'm not a child anymore. I would never let him hurt you. But I also know that he *wouldn't* hurt you. He wants you here as much as I do. You'll be my queen one day. The queen of this whole dark kingdom." He smiled, almost self-consciously. "It might not be what you dreamed of, but I think you'll find that it suits you. I know, even if my brothers don't believe it, that the twelve princesses are never going to stay here. *You* are destined to be queen. With your hair as black as night and your lips—almost—as red as blood . . ."

He touched her face. She could see he wasn't nervous now; he was warming up to the idea: the two of them side by side, ruling. Viv could almost imagine herself, not as a weak, pathetic princess, but as a queen, strong and finally in control. She thought back to what Owen had told her, and how she'd felt like maybe she could be the one to free him, free all the people who were trapped down here.

"Your father would give up his throne that easily? Power-mad control freaks don't usually step aside."

"Well, not right away. We'd want some time to ourselves first. But my father, as difficult as he can be, very much wants there to be a new generation here. New life. A larger family."

"I think your family is large enough."

"What I'm trying to say is—"

"I know what you're trying to say. He wants grandchildren. But I haven't even kissed you yet. So could we please not talk about babies?"

Jasper flushed—even in the underworld gloom it was obvious. "Sorry. I didn't mean to make you uncomfortable."

"Let's just not get ahead of ourselves." She took a deep breath. "Um. On that note. I'm going to go now. But I'll come back tomorrow."

Jasper reached into his jacket for an invitation. "Then I'll look forward to it. The theme is *Winter*, by the way."

"Can I have two? I want to bring my friend Jewel."

"Of course. You can bring anyone you want. I should have offered sooner." He gave her two invitations: black cards with silver script. "Although—when I said you could bring anyone, I meant anyone but the Huntsman."

"Oh. I wouldn't. He wouldn't want to come here, anyway."

Viv looked down, feeling awkward, and Jasper pulled her into his arms. It felt nice, but also poorly timed. The rush of heat came with a rush of sadness. She was already starting to feel lost at the mention of Henley, knowing he could never be a part of her life here—that if she chose the underworld and Jasper, Henley would never be hers again. So she was startled when Jasper said, "Can I kiss you before you go?"

She'd never kissed—*really* kissed—anyone besides Henley. And she didn't want to pretend.

"Not now," she said. "Not tonight."

"Oh . . . all right . . ."

She hugged him quickly. "I'll see you tomorrow." And then she stepped into a waiting gondola and let the boatman ferry her across the lake.

When she finally reached the surface, a warm, misty rain was coming down and there was no one to meet her. The alley was empty, quiet except for the hiss of rain and the splash of cars speeding across wet pavement. Viv had fifty dollars tucked inside her bra. She took it out and stepped into the street to hail a cab.

The cab pulled up to her house a little after three in the morning. She hadn't kissed Jasper, hadn't done anything really—so she didn't know why *guilt* was the first thing she felt when she tiptoed into her room, and found Henley sitting on her bed in the dark, Regina's jeweled knife in his hand.

CHAPTER EIGHTEEN

VIV WALKED TOWARD THE BED, slipping off her shoes as she went, like she had all the time in the world to be murdered.

Moonlight poured through the open French doors, framing Henley in silhouette—broad shoulders, a body solid with muscle. The curtains fluttered like doves' wings, and so did Viv's heart.

She'd felt guilty at first, because she'd let him believe she wasn't going to the underworld; but the longer he stayed silent, the less guilty she felt. Henley didn't need a knife to kill her. He could do it with his bare hands. So what was this? Was he trying to scare her?

She steeled herself to be as cold and sharp as the knife.

"You're going to make a mess if you do it here," she said. "And if you think I'm going into the woods with you, I'm not. I'm tired. I've been dancing with my prince all night. But I guess you knew that."

"Yeah, I bet you had a great time. Was he worth it?"

"More than worth it."

"You really don't give a shit, do you? You just go off and party. You don't tell me anything. I have to find out—"

"I don't have to tell you anything. I told you enough this morning. Clearly, that was a mistake."

"A mistake?" Henley dropped the knife. "Yeah, you're full of those."

She tensed, but didn't back away as he came near her; and when his fingers closed around her wrist she could feel the emotion in his touch. He lifted her closed hand to his face as if it were a rose, his lips brushing her knuckles as he said:

"Do you have a death wish? Why didn't you tell me there was another Huntsman?"

The question startled her.

"I—I don't know."

"Viv." He sighed against her hand. "You need to tell me stuff like this. I can't control him. I can't help you if I don't know what's going on."

The house was so quiet . . . Viv could hear their every breath, and the chorus of insects outside, the bellow of frogs, the slow creaking whir of the ceiling fan. Hot summer sweat glued their skin together. He bent his head to her hand like a prayer.

"I came here to see you. I didn't know you were gone. And Regina invited the other Huntsman over. He talked to me like I was his apprentice. . . . He brought a rabbit and gutted it on the kitchen table. He said that next time, he'd bring a doe. He said it would be more like killing you."

She put her hand over her heart instinctively, as if it were in her power to hold it there.

"You can't stay here. He'll always know where to find you if you do. I don't know if your stepmom believes in me. If she doesn't, and she orders him to kill you . . . I can't save you. I won't even know it's happening."

"Is that why you kept the knife? To save me?"

"I kept it because I need her to think I'm on board for this. That I"—he seemed to wrestle with the words—"want your heart . . . as much as she does."

"Don't you want it more?"

Henley didn't answer. He didn't have to. She was his life. They were each other's, or had been.

Viv sank down on the bed next to the dagger and pressed her fingertip to the blade. It was sharp enough to cut with the lightest touch, and a bead of blood blossomed on her skin. Out of habit, she squeezed three ruby drops into her palm. The same three drops that had inspired Snow White curses for generations.

Red as blood, white as lies.

"You can't stay here," Henley said.

"I'll go to Jewel's."

"What's Jewel going to do if the Huntsman kicks in her door and comes after you?"

"I don't know. Are you planning on kicking her door down?"

"I'm serious. What's she going to do for you? She can't protect you. You need to be somewhere safe."

"Like the underworld? My prince has a bedroom reserved for me."

"Yeah, I've got a coffin reserved for him. The glass one downstairs."

"No, that's mine. Didn't Regina tell you? I figured she would have covered that during one of your chats."

"Get up. We're leaving."

"I'm not going anywhere with you."

"Do you think I have a special murder spot picked out? If I wanted to kill you, why wouldn't I do it here? I'm not worried about traumatizing your stepmom. I don't think that's even possible."

"My chipmunks would bite the shit out of you. You might not want to risk it."

"Get. Up. Right now. Pack a bag if you want. If I have to carry you out, all you're going to have is the dress you're wearing."

"Where are we going?" she asked, getting up to pack, not wanting to call his bluff.

"Somewhere the Huntsman won't look for you. Somewhere he'll regret looking if he does."

CHAPTER NINETEEN

THE BARKING STARTED as soon as they pulled up in front of the farmhouse—a rapid-fire assault that cracked into Viv's skull like the start of a headache. Then one of Elliot's monstrous dogs, its eyes as big as dinner plates, came charging into the dusty glow created by the truck's headlights. It halted at a sharp whistle from Elliot, who was standing on the porch in jeans and a white tank top, holding his tinderbox as if he might strike the flint and make a wish any minute. His blond head was shaved and he had lines around his eyes. He was eighteen, but looked twenty-five. Murdering an old witch tended to carve the last bloom of youth off a person.

"I thought animals were supposed to like you," Elliot said as Viv got out of Henley's truck.

"Animals, yes," she said. "Enormous demon dogs, no."

"That's not very nice." Elliot leaned down to scratch the folds of skin at the back of the dog's neck. Then he nodded to Henley—"Jack said you were coming"—and went into the house, leaving the bug-eyed dog to stand guard.

The yard was pitted with holes, and here and there the knobby joint of a giant's bone stuck out of the earth. Anytime Jack killed a giant, something had to be done with the remains, and it was easier to let Elliot's dogs tear it apart and bury the bones than to dig a grave large enough to hold the corpse. Viv felt like she was walking through a cemetery with zombie limbs jutting up ready to grab her.

A boxy air-conditioning unit was wedged into the front window and over the churning noise she could hear a TV and loud voices.

"They're not having a party, are they?"

"Jack didn't say."

Viv could barely deal with Jack Tran and Elliot; if she went inside and found herself surrounded by Red Riding Hoods and Bandit Girls doing body shots she would walk right back out. "I should just go to Jewel's. I can't actually stay here."

"Tonight you can. It's the safest place for you. The Huntsman's not getting past those dogs—or Jack and Elliot."

"Maybe we should look harder for some dwarves. *Seven.* Seven dwarves. Power in numbers."

Henley sighed. "Come on."

Inside, there were about a dozen more people than Viv had expected, but it wasn't exactly a party.

Jack Tran was sprawled in an armchair like it was his throne, wearing shorts and a black shirt that showed the green vine tattoos twisting up his arms. Jack had that sinewy look common in guys who made a habit of climbing beanstalks, robbing giants, and then running like hell. Out of all the Giant Killers, he was the best. Lots of Giant Killers died; Jack Tran hadn't so much as broken an arm falling off a beanstalk. He'd stolen more treasure than any of them, but he never hung on to it. His golden-egg-laying hens had a habit of getting turned into fried chicken by vindictive ex-girlfriends. The money, he spent. He was a *live fast, die young* type, and he reigned over his ring of thieves like the Royals ruled Viv's social circle.

Beth Teal, who'd gone to school with Viv before her Wild Swans curse forced her to drop out, was sitting cross-legged on the couch, knitting nettles into jackets while a mixed martial arts match played on TV. Beth's phone rested on the coffee table in front of her; every once in a while she would pick it up and text something, since she wasn't allowed to speak. Her curse required seven years of silence. If she said one word before the curse was broken, her brothers would die.

Beth's hands, wrists, and forearms were covered with hives from the nettles, but she went on knitting like a little machine. She'd been doing it for a few years already, camping in the woods or sleeping on people's couches, occasionally texting friends to ask for a ride to a graveyard to gather more nettles.

The Teal brothers, with their dirty feather-colored hair and gloomy expressions, drifted between the living room and the kitchen, beer bottles or shot glasses in their hands. During the day they were cursed to live as swans, but by night they were human. Viv had seen them at parties before: they would show up anywhere there was free booze, wearing the swim trunks Beth kept for them in her backpack. And then by day they would angrily chase people away from whatever pond they were floating on. If normal swans were ill-tempered, swans with hangovers were that much worse—but there was

143

nothing like an alcohol-induced blackout to make you forget you'd transform into a bird in a few hours.

The more guilt-ridden brothers hung behind Beth like an entourage, drinking and mumbling apologies, sorry that their sister's every moment was spent knitting the jackets that would break their curse. The brothers who just wanted to forget were getting hammered in the kitchen, and two others were begging Jack to hook them up with a hot girl before daybreak.

"First off," Jack said, slurping the last dregs of a lime-green slushie, "I don't know any girls who like swans. Second, your sister's over there knitting, not talking so you don't die . . . and you can't be celibate a few more years?"

"You don't know what it's like," one brother whined.

"Beth doesn't mind," the other insisted.

The Teal brothers had names, but Viv didn't remember them. She refused to memorize all of the names of siblings in any family that had more than six kids. There was far too much of that going on in Beau Rivage and there was only so much room in her brain.

She sat down on the arm of the couch, since a partially finished nettle jacket was spread across the cushions. Beth nodded *hello*. Henley went to discuss the arrangements with Jack. They spoke in low voices; she couldn't hear what they were saying over the hum of the air conditioner, the loud TV, and the spontaneous vomiting noises in the kitchen.

"It's time for Swans, party of twelve, to go home!" Elliot shouted. "Clean that shit up or I'll feed your bird asses to my dogs!"

Beth stopped knitting long enough to type a message on her phone. Viv read it to Elliot. "She says they don't have a home. Also, she's tired of sleeping in the woods. *Sadface.*"

"You can stay," Elliot told Beth. "Although, the house is getting crowded." His eyes shifted to Viv.

"Sorry," Viv said.

Elliot headed to the kitchen to give the Teal brothers their last-call warning. Beth resumed knitting an itchy green sleeve. Viv watched a fighter on TV get punched in the face until blood gushed into his eyes, and wished she were at Jewel's—even if Jewel didn't know how to kill people. Finally, Jack got up, tossed his slushie cup on the table, and motioned for Viv and Henley to follow. "I'll show you your room," he said.

Viv checked out other rooms as they passed—she'd never been inside the farmhouse before. In the kitchen, Elliot stood with his arms crossed while the Teal brothers scrubbed regurgitated pond weed and booze off the floor. In Elliot's bedroom, a dog with eyes as large as saucers stood guard on top of a padlocked footlocker.

When they reached Jack's room, all three went inside. It was spare, whittled down to the essentials. There was a bed with a dark green bedspread, a hardwood floor worn down by decades of footsteps, a TV mounted on the wall, and a few shelves where Jack kept assorted treasures. Two windows faced the backyard.

"Don't worry, I changed the sheets," Jack said.

"I'm sure they needed it," Viv said, because thanking him felt too weird.

Jack's hand went to the knife at his belt. There was a leather pouch there, too—for magic beans, supposedly. "How old's that Huntsman? Fifty?"

"Forty, fifty," Henley estimated.

145

"Don't worry about it, then. I've got you covered."

Viv dumped her bag on the floor, and Jack circled around in front of her.

"If you want to stay here," he said, "I've got a few rules. You'll have to clean the house, get your animal friends to do the dishes, and bake some pies. Not apple—I'm not sadistic—but something all-American. Oh, and sing a song while you're at it."

"Sounds fun. Too bad this is only for one night." It was dark enough in the room for Viv to be able to see out the window, past the transparent mask of her reflection. She watched as the Teal brothers trooped across the lawn: eleven boys in swim trunks, drunk off their asses.

"We won't kick you out tomorrow if you need to stay longer," Jack said. "But you can't have my bed forever."

"I think tonight will be enough."

"Let's see how this goes," Henley said. Viv and Henley hadn't really talked about where she would go after tonight. She wasn't sure he should even be part of that decision.

"I'll be on the couch," Jack said. "Yell if you need something." He pulled the door shut after himself, leaving Viv and Henley alone.

Viv sat down on the bed, still gazing out the window. Henley sat next to her and she let herself sink against him, watching their reflections as his arm went around her. His hand traced a nervous path over her hair.

"I have to think about what to do," he said. "I know I used to tell you I would kill the Huntsman. That I would never let him hurt you. I promised you that. But if I killed him now, unprovoked . . . I don't know if I could get away with it.

I'd have to hide the body. The evidence. I think I could do it, but . . ."

"Regina would use it against you. You'd end up in prison. I'll hide somewhere."

The laws in Beau Rivage favored curses. If you were fated to kill someone, you wouldn't be prosecuted for the crime. But that was the extent of the amnesty.

"Do you think you'll go back to the underworld?"

"To hide? No . . . but I'm taking Jewel to the club tomorrow night. She wants to see it."

Henley was silent and Viv wondered if he was hoping for an invitation.

"I can't bring you," she said.

"Because I'm the Huntsman?"

"Because—"

Because I love you.

"That, and everything else."

In the window glass they looked hollow. Like ghosts. An unhappy couple who haunted each other, but couldn't let go. Henley's eyes were downcast, his mind occupied with thoughts of murder. Neither one of them smiled. Even during the good times, it felt like they were trying to hang on to something temporary before it slipped away. Always anticipating loss or betrayal.

Viv closed her eyes. She slid a hand across his chest, her fingers pushing at his shirt. "Do you want to stay with me?" She could feel his heart beating beneath her palm and her own beat a touch faster, anticipating something other than loss.

"I don't know if I should, Viv."

"Don't you want to?"

"It's not that. . . ."

"Then stay. We almost never get to stay the night together."

She knelt up on the bed, ran her fingers lightly across his neck and jaw, and his head tipped back, his eyes closed, and he sighed and wrapped his arms around her waist. She leaned her weight against him as if she could topple him, and kissed him, kissed the film of salt on his skin, the taste of summer, like so many summers before.

He lay back and pulled her down with him, the bed giving one righteous squeak, his eyes warm and dark and focused on hers. And suddenly she was aware of the limited time they had left—how many more moments like this would there be? And she felt like she needed to make the most of it, to give and take as much as they both had left.

She wanted to engrave her name on his heart, but she'd already done it; she wanted to press down harder, retrace all the lines. She wanted to be the one he loved the most, forever.

She pushed his T-shirt up; it snagged around his head for a second before he raised his shoulders so she could pull it off. And then she was unzipping her party dress, shedding it, the loss of the dress making her feel powerful, steady, like reverse armor. She lay against him, hot skin against skin, feeling the thrill of being near him, and also, the rightness of it. Sometimes they could be magic again. The curse ceased to exist, and there was just the two of them.

"Viv," he said, "what happens tomorrow?"

She traced a fingertip down his side. "Tomorrow? I could be poisoned tomorrow. Killed by—"

"No." He grabbed her hand and held it. She kissed his knuckle where their hands were joined.

"Let's not think about tomorrow. We're here. Together. We have to live for the moment." Her voice was playful, trying to keep this from getting serious, because serious for them was so often dark, the first step to ruining a good thing. But maybe if she'd let some emotion—her need for closeness—into her voice, he wouldn't have felt the need to say it. He would have understood.

"You never live for the moment," he said. "You've been living for the future since the day I was cursed."

"That's not true. I do—sometimes. If I couldn't do that, we wouldn't be together at all."

"So, are we together? What is this? You want me to stay. Does that mean . . . ?"

"What?" she whispered.

"Does it mean you've decided—"

She lowered her head to kiss him, but he wouldn't let her dodge the question. He caught her face in his hands.

"Do you know what you want, Viv?"

It hurt, the way he looked at her. This was her chance to make everything better. All she had to do was say *you*, and make him believe it. *I want* you—and seal it with a kiss.

She couldn't.

She couldn't even look at him. She let her gaze drift, focused on the curve of his shoulder, the seam of the bedspread, anything but the hope she was about to crush. His hands were warm against her cheeks, and she couldn't take it— that tender, patient feeling—so she pulled away, sat up, straddling his waist. Just a few feet of distance, but it was everything.

"Henley . . . it doesn't matter. I can't make any promises."

149

He rose up on his elbows. "Why? Why can't you? I would promise you anything."

"Yeah, and it would be a lie. Because you don't *know*. You don't know what you'll do. The fairies have a pretty good idea—"

He lifted her off him, and got up quickly, anger rippling through him as he stood.

"That again." He half turned toward the door, fists clenched, and then turned back, spreading his arms wide as if to gesture to everything, the entire mess. "What moment are we living in now? The one where I'm trying to protect you? The one where I love you? The one where I've never done a goddamn thing to make you think I would kill you?"

His voice got louder as he went on, and the dog across the hall started barking. Harsh, choppy barks, and Viv flinched with each one. Henley had never hit her, never hurt her, never broken anything she couldn't buy at the store—but an instinctive fear reared up in her when someone that big and loud was angry with her.

"This should be fun when your friends show up," she said, her voice calmer than her heart. "At least you know they'll be on your side."

Henley picked up his shirt and pulled it on. He didn't bother to respond.

"You're leaving?"

"I don't need to be here talking in circles, having the same fights with you. I need to think about what to do next."

"Henley—" She reached for him, but he eluded her grasp. "I don't want you to go."

"No, you want to be the one who leaves. That's how it

works, right? You go whenever you're ready. And to hell with what I'm ready for."

"You're making me feel like shit."

"Welcome to my life. You make me feel like shit all the time."

He slammed the door as he left and she hugged her knees to her chest and started crying, pressing her face against them so she wouldn't be loud. "Screw you, then," she said. But it didn't make her feel better. The time they had left together—that precious, fading time—maybe he didn't even want it anymore.

She changed into pajamas and then lay in bed with her back to the door, one tear after another sliding sideways down her cheek. She waited for the sound of Henley's truck starting up, but there was only the drone of the TV, late-night commercials and action-movie explosions. Jack's voice, Elliot's voice, definitely not Beth's. After a few minutes the bedroom door opened, and she listened to the heavy tread across the floor until she was sure Henley's shadow was falling over her, but she didn't open her eyes to see whether that shadow held a knife.

He laid his hand on her shoulder. Whispered, "Viv?"

She didn't answer. The bed sank as he sat down behind her, and she had to resist rolling over and clinging to him to keep him there.

"I don't want you to think I'm not going to help you. I will. I'll do everything I can. Okay?"

She shrugged, smushed her face into the pillow, furtively drying it.

"I'm not staying. I just wanted you to know that."

He stroked her hair back from her face. Let his fingertips linger on her cheek. Waiting for something? But she gave him nothing. She didn't know what to give.

"'Night, Viv," he said finally.

"Good night," she said.

His steps were softer as he left. He closed the door, and she touched her face where he'd touched it, knowing she wouldn't sleep for hours. Because he was gone.

CHAPTER TWENTY

THE DENEUVES' KITCHEN smelled like citrus instead of blood. In the clean light of early morning, it was hard to believe a Huntsman had gutted a rabbit on that table as a demonstration of how to kill a princess. Someone had washed the blood from the blond wood surface, and now there was a centerpiece where the carcass had been: a bowl of red apples, the same decoration that had been there for years.

Regina, dressed in workout clothes, her hair up in a ponytail that made her look younger, was juicing oranges by hand. A pair of white butterflies flurried through the garden, like white petals caught by the wind.

Last night's bloody scene was erased by the bright chirps of birds and the cool, misty air. Like the world had taken a deep breath, ready to begin again. Henley felt wide awake, tired but almost painfully alert. He hadn't slept well . . . he didn't think he would for a while. His window of opportunity was closing. He only had so much time to make this work, to make sure everything happened exactly how he wanted it to.

"You stayed late last night." Regina licked a dribble of juice off her finger. "Tying up loose ends?"

"I wanted to see where her head was at. If there was a chance for us."

"And?"

"I'm here, aren't I?" His eyes went to a groove in the table, where the wood was still dark with blood. "I used to think that if I could get her to trust me again, things would change. We'd go back to the way we were before. Now I know that won't happen. But I still need her to trust me."

"Oh?"

"I don't want this to be any uglier than it has to be. I don't want to hurt her. I want it to be a shock—so she barely feels it. That's why I brought her away from the house last night. I want her to feel safe with me. To trust me. I think it'll be less traumatic for both of us if she does."

"Well. No one wants you to be traumatized."

Regina carried the pitcher of orange juice to the table and set it down as carefully as if it were a vase of flowers. He rarely saw her do anything domestic and wondered if it was for his benefit or if she was a different person without Viv in the house.

"Help yourself," she said with a smile. He just stared at the pitcher, not in the mood to drink anything, and Regina turned to sort through her cupboards. Usually the cupboards were bare. Now they were stocked with jars and bottles, like Regina was preparing for a hurricane. He saw honey and grenadine. He wasn't sure what else.

"Also . . ." Henley cleared his throat. "There's something I need from you."

Her eyes were wide and attentive, like she would do whatever she could to help. "What is it?"

"I need your word that you won't turn this over to the other Huntsman. Taking care of Viv . . . that's my fate, not his. I need to know you can accept that."

"Of course. I wouldn't take that from you."

"All right. Then . . . I'm trying to work out how I want to do it. This is something I'll have to live with for the rest of my life. I don't want to regret the way it happens. If that's possible."

"You won't regret it," she said. "It's not like you didn't try. It's not like you didn't try everything to make people see you as something other than your curse. But you *are* your curse. For a long time I thought . . . if I could be a good mom, a loving wife, care about craft projects and bake sales and schmoozing with the Royal bitches at Seven Oaks, people would see that my destiny didn't fit me. But it does fit me. It just took me a while to realize that. My destiny is the only thing that gives me some semblance of power over my life.

"If I regret anything, it's waiting as long as I did. Giving in to false hope. Because the whole time I was doing that—taking Viv to the movies, playing dolls—my husband was having sex with the same women who sneered at me at the grocery store when I was buying Viv ice cream. It didn't matter how good I tried to be. Everyone knew what I was. I was the only one who didn't know. But . . . there's something freeing about finally giving in to your destiny. I know it's been hard on you; I can see it. It's been hard on me, too. You've probably thought of me as evil—maybe you still do—but there's nothing evil about being happy. You're doing what's best for you. I'm doing what's best for me. Viv's doing what's best for Viv. We can't all get what we want.

"Once this is over, you can really move forward. You'll find someone who's worthy of you. Maybe one of those long-suffering girls who has to perform a task for seven years. Or maybe a normal girl, without any cursed baggage at all."

"Maybe. It's hard to think like that right now."

"I know. Believe me. I can hardly imagine what it'll feel like after. Our whole lives have been building to this moment."

He stood up, rubbed his eyes. "I need to try to sleep. I was up all night. Waiting for her and then . . . thinking about this."

"Oh, before you go, look"—Regina took a black-lacquered box from the cupboard—"I had a box made."

Her eyes glittered like she was holding a treasure chest, and she flipped the hinged lid up to reveal an interior lined with bloodred velvet, just large enough to hold a girl's heart. "Beautiful, isn't it?"

"It's perfect."

CHAPTER TWENTY-ONE

SNOWFLAKES DRIFTED FROM THE DARKNESS overhead and frost glittered on the silver trees. The guests wore tiny bells on their shoes, diamonds on their cheeks. Their lips were painted white or silver; their peppermint breath fogged the air.

Viv hadn't realized the *Winter* theme would be so literal— she wore a thin white gown, more appropriate for a Greek goddess than a winter wonderland. But she wasn't the only one, and servants were busy passing out velvet cloaks to the underdressed guests. Jewel wore hers over a white bustier and tight white pants. Frosty white eyeliner shimmered on her dark brown skin.

Viv handed over two cartons of cigarettes—tied with a silver bow, topped with a sparkly snowflake—and finally got a real smile out of Owen.

Inside the nightclub, ice glazed the mirrored black walls. Part of the dance floor had been transformed into an ice rink. The black benches had been replaced by sleighs where guests could curl up with a mug of hot cocoa or cider. Bartenders mixed drinks at a bar made of solid ice.

The last time Viv had been here, the club had been hellish and loud—red lights glowing like an oven, sweat dripping off the dancers. Tonight, the guests hid beneath layers of fur and velvet, and the music was softer, floating under the conversations instead of preventing them.

A Snow Queen had wrapped a teenage boy in her cloak, and was kissing his face, leaving ice-blue lip prints on his cheeks. A man with white-blond hair and black eyes was dancing with a blindfolded girl. He was probably a polar bear by day, and the blindfold was there to keep the girl from seeing his true form—a loophole in the curse.

Viv pointed the couple out to Jewel. "Kink? Or East of the Sun, West of the Moon curse?"

"Both," Jewel said. "Definitely a curse, but any of those *lover is a monster by day, can't look at him at night* curses are inherently kinky. I mean, you don't know what you're sleeping with, but you do it, anyway, because the guy climbs in your bed at night?"

"She always looks at him eventually."

"Yeah, but then he wakes up because she's dripping hot candle wax on his body. That's kinky."

"Point."

Jewel pressed her handkerchief to her mouth, tears leaking from her eyes as she coughed up a string of white foxgloves. "Should we find your prince, or do you want to talk about kinky bears some more?"

"Nah, you probably hear enough of that from Luxe."

"Luxe didn't do anything with those bears!"

158

Viv did her best Luxe impression—"*It's too big! It's too fuzzy!*"—then ran away laughing before Jewel could smack her.

She dashed through the crowd, darting past Prince Charmings dressed for a trip to the Arctic and a Beauty who'd scooped snow into a champagne bucket and was throwing snowballs at the other guests. A clump of snow exploded against Viv's shoulder and she ducked to avoid the next one. As she came up, Jasper grabbed her cloak and spun her to face him.

"Who are you running from?" he asked. His cheeks were flushed.

"My friend Jewel. I insinuated some things about her girl-friend and the three bears."

"*None* of which were true," Jewel said as she caught up to them. Diamonds spilled from her handkerchief, sprinkling the floor like hail.

"Jewel," Jasper said. "You have a Diamonds and Toads curse."

"What gave it away? The reckless way I drop gems all over the floor?"

He laughed. "I'm Jasper. I'm so glad you came."

Another snowball arced over their heads.

"Should we get out of this war zone?" Viv asked.

They headed to the ice bar and ordered drinks that nearly froze their throats on the way down. A horseman dressed entirely in white, with skin, hair, and eyes the color of milk, stood there drinking a tall glass of vodka. On the bar stool next to him was an old woman Viv guessed was Baba Yaga. The old woman's white tiger-print dress didn't scream *witch*, but her wild white hair was pinned down by a tiara made of crystals and finger bones, and she was using a mortar and pestle to muddle fruit for her drink. The mortar and pestle were her trademark.

Next to Baba Yaga was an old man with a skeletal face, a tanning-booth tan, and scars on his arms in the shape of chains. He looked about seventy but wore a shirt that was unbuttoned to show his chest, leather pants, and a ring on every finger, including one that was topped with a Fabergé egg.

As they were leaving the bar, the old man whistled at Jewel. "Hey, sweetheart. You like older men?"

"*No,*" Jewel said, gagging on a winter rose.

"That's Koschei the Deathless," Jasper said. "He was chained up in a basement for a few years. He just got out."

"I guess he wants everyone to know he's available," Viv said.

Koschei wrote his phone number on a napkin and tried to give it to Jewel, then Viv, then Jasper, until finally Baba Yaga grabbed it and ground it up with her pestle.

After a while Jasper asked if they wanted to skate. Jewel declined, saying she didn't think falling gems played well with ice skates, but told them to go ahead.

Mounds of snow bordered the rink—smooth and rounded like perfect scoops of ice cream. Viv sat down on a bench to put on her skates, and Jasper knelt in front of her to make sure the laces were tight.

"Are you good at skating?" she asked, while he pressed on her toes to check the fit.

"I skate about once a month—whenever we do *Winter*. I'm good enough not to fall all the time."

"Sounds like you're better than I am."

"We'll help each other."

Jasper offered his arm and they chop-stepped onto the ice, then slowly worked their way up to gliding. It was a nice feeling to be side by side like that, strangely warm in the frigid air, cozy from the velvet and the heat that raced through her when they touched. Every time their eyes met, Jasper was smiling. "I'm so happy you're here," he said. "I can't wait to show you, every day, how lucky I am to have you."

"Every day? I think you'll get bored of that."

"No. I'll never get tired of showing you. I won't be able to help myself."

Once they'd finished skating, Viv excused herself to use the restroom. On the way there she passed the Twelve Dancing Princesses and eleven underworld princes—twining together like sparkling ice and untouched snow. Minuet was solo waltzing with a glass of wine in her hand. She tilted the glass backward, far enough that it should have spilled, but didn't.

And yet . . . some wine was definitely missing when she righted her glass. Two, maybe three swallows were gone. And Minuet was grinning like the Cheshire cat. Or like a cursed princess playing games with her invisible rescuer. Feeding him wine while he sidestepped the princes.

There was a suitor in the club, wearing an invisibility cloak, getting cocky. Viv had no idea who he might be—the fairies who bestowed the Twelve Dancing Princesses curse marked twelve princesses and their partners, but not the hero who'd eventually break the curse. Anyone could volunteer— but a suitor who failed to break the curse after three days was beheaded. And, unlike in the fairy tale, the suitor had to figure out how to seal the door that led the princesses to the underworld, so they could never return. Only then would he get his reward: marriage to one of the princesses and half her father's wealth.

Was the suitor's cockiness a celebration? Did he know how to end this?

Viv didn't say anything when she caught up with Jasper and Jewel, in case Jasper was obligated to inform on the invisible trespasser. She caught them mid-conversation.

"I understand changing your name to fit your curse," Jewel was saying. "I did; my birth certificate says Renee. But those are some odd choices."

"We're talking about the twelve princesses' names," Jasper said.

"Oh." Viv supposed it was a natural thing to be curious about, but she'd never asked. She'd never asked Jasper about his brothers' names, either. They fell into her category of *too many children in one family*, even though they might be her in-laws one day.

"They're named after dances," Jewel said.

Jasper pointed them out. "Minuet, Lindy, Mazurka. Chacha, Salsa, Rumba. Charleston, Calypso, Musette. And the inseparable trio of Waltz, Tango, and Foxtrot."

"Are you making that up?" Viv asked.

"I swear I'm not."

As the night stretched on, the lights that had kept the club white and shining dimmed to an icy blue, like the guests were on the cusp of night instead of deep inside it. Viv, Jasper, and Jewel sipped hot cocoa and danced to music that sounded like bells. When Viv began to get sleepy she leaned against Jasper, her arms wrapped loosely around his waist, and swayed with him like they were in the middle of a dream.

Toward the end of the night, the DJ played only love songs. The music seeped into her—familiar, comforting—and it wasn't until the third or fourth track that Viv realized they were all songs she used to listen to. They could have been pulled from one of her old playlists: Love circa age fifteen. Soft, sweet, familiar love. Us-against-the-world love. Nothing can tear us apart.

The songs were soothing in their certainty, their love-is-forever sentiment, their just-try-to-stop-us loyalty. And once she recognized them, once she realized they'd been *hers,* she couldn't stop the past from grabbing on to her. The songs stirred old memories—and the rush of tenderness they brought was painful.

Henley in her bedroom, freshman year. No one in the house but the two of them. A sheet hung over the mirror to keep it from purring out, *"Exquisite!"*

His body at sunset, ruddy light burnishing his face and chest, the hard muscle of his arms. A love song playing in the background like it was the soundtrack to their lives.

The way he looked at her and saw all of her. Not *the fairest.* Not the princess. Just the girl she was. He knew her like no one else did, and she'd thought she knew everything about him, too. Who he was. What he'd do.

Jasper was humming in her ear, content.

"Did the fairy give you one of my playlists?" Viv asked.

"She mentioned some songs that you liked. Was she wrong?"

"Not wrong. Just a few years out of date. I'd like to know how she even found them . . . but, then again, I don't. Stop paying her, though. Seriously. If you want to know something about me, just ask."

"I'm too polite to ask everything." She couldn't tell if he was wearing a smile or an expression of restraint.

By the time the DJ announced the last dance, Viv had relived her entire freshman-year date-night playlist, and Jewel had turned down another overture from Koschei the Deathless.

"He tried to give me his soul for safekeeping," Jewel said. "He keeps it in a Fabergé egg, apparently. I thought about taking it, for the good of the world, but . . . I think he was drunk when he offered. I didn't want to give him an excuse to show up at my place and ask for it back."

"A wise decision," Jasper said, taking three invitations from his jacket. "However, I hope you *will* accept these. There are three this time, in case you want to bring your girlfriend."

"These are for tomorrow night, or any time?" Jewel asked.

"Tomorrow night. They'll turn to dust after that."

"Got it."

"Good night," Jasper said, hugging them both. He hugged Viv until the heat burned between them, and then kissed her cheek.

Jasper summoned a boat for them, and Viv and Jewel dozed on the ride across, wrapped in their velvet cloaks, using each other's heads as pillows. The mood on the opposite shore was sleepy and subdued. The guards were on alert, but the guests were relaxed, drifting down the path like leaves on a stream, their steps soft in the powdery snow.

"That was fun," Jewel said. She yawned and plucked a red poppy from her mouth. "I'm exhausted, but that club is amazing. Deathless old dudes notwithstanding."

"What did you think of Jasper?"

"He seems like a decent guy. Friendly, cute. But . . ."

"But?"

"I wonder how emotionally involved you could get. I think you could have fun with him, but it's going to be hard to feel anything else while things are so unsettled with Henley."

"I know." Viv sighed. "Right now, when I think about being with Jasper, I think logistics: should I come to the underworld, and when? I don't think about . . . being in his arms, and falling in love."

"Well, yeah. Because you're already in love."

Viv swallowed. "But at the same time, Jasper and I are destined to be together. So maybe I'll love him eventually and it'll seem weird that I didn't. That's what I'm hoping. Because if I'm wrong about it—"

"You don't *have* to rush things," Jewel said. "You don't have to break up with Henley one day and move in with your prince the next. You know you're welcome to stay with me. If you end up being a messy houseguest we're going to have problems, but . . ."

"We're going to have problems," Viv said.

Jewel smiled. "Yeah, I figured. But compared to my sister, I'm sure I'll barely notice. As long as you're not puking up toads in my kitchen, we'll probably be fine."

Jewel stopped to cough up an orchid that seemed stuck in her throat. Tiny flecks of blood speckled the snow.

"You okay?" Viv said.

"Fine." Jewel wiped her watering eyes with her handkerchief. She spit out a few wet pearls, then took a deep breath and said,

"I don't think you need to make a decision about Jasper right now. I really don't. The decision you need to make is about Henley. He has a decision to make, too. And I'm not saying he would hurt you—but you don't want him to be reeling from your last fight when Regina calls him and asks for your heart."

"I know. I keep telling myself to just *do it,* let him go. But once I do, it'll be over. And I don't know how to let it be over. I know it is, in a sense—it has been—but for it to be completely gone . . . We can't be friends, there's no way we could just be friends. . . ."

Viv had let her gaze drop to the ground, and now she saw footprints appearing in the snow like magic. Viv stopped breathing, scared that someone else would notice—and then was shoved sideways as a trio of guards raced down the path in pursuit.

There was a scuffle, the guards grappling with the air, struggling with someone they couldn't see; and then one of them got his hands on the invisibility cloak, and ripped it from the shoulders of the twelve princesses' would-be rescuer—who was suddenly *there,* where no one had been before.

Viv barely had time to register the man's features—the stain of wine on his lips, dark curly hair—before the guards forced him to his knees and pushed his head down, exposing his neck, readying it for the blade.

One of the guards raised his sword—

Viv screamed as the head was severed from the body.

There was a sloppy wet sound, like someone had emptied a bucket of water. Gasps from the crowd. Jewel doubled over, retching cherry blossoms that broke apart like confetti.

The suitor's head lay at the edge of the path, a river of red streaming behind it. One guard knelt to examine the neck, and drew the guests' attention to the three black hash marks tattooed on the skin.

"See this? Volunteers get one mark for each night they spend trying to break the curse. This was his third night. His time was up either way."

"No use crying over spilled blood," another guard said under his breath. A third guard snorted, like this was a joke he'd heard before.

The two joking guards lifted the still-bleeding body off the ground. The guests shuffled out of the way, and the guards carried the corpse to the shore and flung it into the lake. Another guard grasped the suitor's head by a fistful of hair, and lifted it from the path so the blood could be mopped up. The stench of bleach filled the air as pink blood sluiced into the snow.

At last the guests were allowed to continue to the checkpoint. Viv had probably said "Are you okay?" to Jewel about twenty times, and now she took Jewel's arm and led her past the bloody slush, down the path, and back to the surface. She was trying to stay calm, but no matter where she looked, she saw the murder superimposed over everything: over the guests as they mounted the staircase, on the walls of the alley, and hovering in the street as they waited for a cab, while the snow in their hair melted and ran down their faces.

Viv had been afraid of death before, but her basis for comparison had been fairy-tale death. Words. Ink on paper. Final, but clean. She'd imagined it as a sort of darkness, an end to everything. Loss more than pain. Now . . . she realized what it would be like to die. Not just oblivion, but the agony of being butchered. There would be more than just *her death*; there would be all the slaughter that led up to it.

She couldn't play this game anymore.

She couldn't keep toying with Henley, pushing him away and then pulling him back, breaking his heart and then running into his arms. They both had their reasons for letting this go on, but none of that would matter if he killed her.

It had to end.

CHAPTER TWENTY-TWO

BLOOD STAINED THE HEM OF HER DRESS. Rose-red light streaked the horizon. The air was as hot and damp as an exhaled breath.

As Viv made her way from the cab to her front door, she rubbed her tired eyes and tried to hold on to her resolve.

Birds were greeting the morning. They flew down from the trees and hopped across the porch as Viv let herself in.

She knew it was stupid to come back. She had an overnight bag at Jewel's, so it wasn't like she desperately needed anything. But there were a few things she wanted to pick up—like her mother's fairy-tale book—and she wanted to clear the animals out of her room.

The house was quiet, still. There was a noxiously sweet smell in the air—like candy and overripe fruit. The floor creaked softly; the hall mirror slept. Viv hurried up the staircase, eager to get her things and leave. Regina usually woke around seven, and it was earlier than that—but Viv didn't trust things to work the way they always had.

She opened the door to her bedroom—and recoiled as the stench of rotting fruit stuffed her mouth like a gag. Regina must have left her a present, then shut the balcony doors so the odor would get worse. Viv wasn't sure what or where it was, and didn't feel like searching for it, so she just yanked the balcony doors open—and breathed the fresh air with relief.

"You guys can come out now," she said, figuring the animals had gone into hiding when Regina showed up. "I won't yell at you if you crapped on the carpet. It's okay just this once."

She picked up the receiver of her red princess phone, and listened to the tone for a few seconds before she dialed Henley's number. She rarely used this extension, but she'd left her cell phone at Jewel's, and she needed to do this before she lost her nerve.

It rang—but then his phone went to voice mail and she wasn't sure what to do. She hung up.

She wiggled her fingers near the floor, trying to attract some animal attention—for moral support—but none of the animals emerged from their hiding places. Sighing, she called Henley again, and this time when she got his voice mail, she left a message.

"Henley. I need to see you. To say good-bye. I'm at home, but—I'm leaving. For good. It's"—she glanced at the clock—"a little after five in the morning. Please come see me if you can. I won't be here long." Her eyes stopped on a shallow dish on her nightstand, about the size of a saucer you'd use to give a cat cream. She hung up the phone and went to see what it was.

The dish was filled with a sticky red substance—like lip gloss, or strawberry syrup. The smell, when it wafted up to her, was sweet and sort of metallic.

A line of tiny red paw prints led from the dish to the edge of the nightstand, then vanished into the black of Viv's bedspread. She dropped to her knees. "Mouse?" She checked the animals' hiding places—beneath the bed, the dresser . . . until her missing pets revealed themselves. They were curled up, or stretched out, and very, very still.

She touched one of the chipmunks with her finger, and it felt as stiff and fragile as an autumn leaf. Dead.

Poisoned.

All of them had red syrup on their faces. She found two more dishes of poison—one on the floor under her desk, and one beneath her bed.

In the space between her dresser and the floor, she found the mouse that was most fond of her—along with its stash of wildflowers: daisies bitten off at the stem. The mouse had gone to the place where it felt safest, and it had died there, alone. Viv hadn't been there to protect it or comfort it. She cupped the mouse's body in her hand, feeling how light it was, how precious and frail.

Regina's fight was with her. There'd been no reason to do this. Tears ran down Viv's face until she could smell the salt and the skin around her eyes burned with it.

"I'm so sorry," she whispered. She kept saying it as she took a shoe box from her closet and lined the bottom with a silk scarf. She laid the mouse and its flowers in a fold of the silk, then laid the rest of the animals beside it.

She wished she could see them breathing, feel their whiskers flicker against her palm. And apologize—for leaving them behind, for not realizing that they might be in danger, too.

She needed to get away—but she couldn't leave without seeing Regina. She'd avoided confronting her stepmother for so long. . . . Now she wanted to fling a dish of poison in her face and watch her choke on it.

Cradling the shoe box to her chest, she grabbed a dish of poison and headed downstairs. The kitchen sink was piled with pots and pans, all glistening with syrup—some red, some green, some burnt black. All Viv's life, Regina had never made more than a sandwich—and now she was brewing death.

Viv balanced the dish on top of the shoe box, and tried Regina's door. It was locked.

"Regina!" She pounded on the wood until the hinges rattled. The sweet candy smell was making her sick. A hiccuping sound escaped her throat and she started crying again. The dish of poison fell and splattered at her feet.

"Why did you do it? Why did you do that to them?"

She set the shoe box down to try to force the door open, jiggling the knob and jamming her shoulder into the wood—until she heard the lock slide free on the other side. She stumbled in, her momentum carrying her as far as the bed, where Regina sat, directly across from the mirror. Her makeup and hair looked freshly done, and her smile was baffling: smooth and slick, like the smile of a wax figure. She'd had hours to regret what she'd done, but she showed no sign that she even cared.

"Tell me. Tell me why," Viv said. "You used to love us. You used to want to be here."

"What does that have to do with the rats in your room?"

Viv grabbed a container of powder off the vanity and flung it in Regina's face. It exploded around her in a cloud of white, while Regina sat there calmly, watching. Viv knocked every container of blush, eye shadow, eyeliner, and perfume off the vanity, then twisted open Regina's favorite lipstick and crushed the creamy red cylinder in her hand. All the while Regina—and the mirror—stayed silent.

"*What* is the point of this?" Viv raged. "Is it really because you're getting older? Because the mirror says you're not as beautiful? Why don't you just throw acid in my face and be done with it?"

"Now there's an idea."

Viv's red hand was trembling, greasy with the smashed lipstick. She felt like someone had reached in and ripped out her heart. She wished there was some way to touch Regina's. "We're trapped in this curse, I know, but you didn't have to . . . they didn't *do anything* to you!"

Regina just sighed, like this was becoming tiresome. "In the grand scheme of things, does it really matter? They would have died of heartbreak when Henley killed you, anyway. Oh, and don't try kissing them awake—they're dead. It's not worth getting a disease over."

"Don't make a joke of this."

"The way they adored you . . ." Regina murmured. "What is there about you to adore? Who in this world do you care about, aside from yourself? You're a pretty face, but you're empty inside. You don't even know what you want. You're just waiting for someone to give it to you."

173

"*I'm* empty inside? You killed them! You killed them and they were innocent!"

She wanted to hurt Regina the way Regina had hurt her—but she didn't know how. Regina seemed invulnerable, whereas Viv had a hundred weaknesses and Regina knew them all.

Regina . . . Regina had one weakness.

"*Mirror*," Viv said. "Who's the fairest of them all?"

"*You are.*"

"And what about Regina?" she said, stepping aside so Regina was caught in the mirror's gaze. "What is she?"

Regina kept that same cool look on her face, but now that the mirror had her in its sights, she shifted her posture, sitting up straighter, raising a hand to brush some of the powder off her hair.

The mirror rippled, and when the glass cleared, the reflection of the bedroom was gone, and in its place was a garden. A teenage Regina and a boy with blond hair. Viv had never seen anything but reflections in the house's mirrors, but Regina whimpered as if she knew what was coming.

In the glass, teenage Regina held out her hands, pleading. The blond boy spoke fiercely, his body half turned as if he was about to walk away.

"*I told you, I was never in love with you. What we had—it didn't mean anything. So stop coming here. Stop calling me. You're upsetting my princess. And she's the one I'm meant to be with.*"

The mirror rippled a second time, and when the glass settled it showed a white cake topped with a black graduation cap, buffet tables, a bunch of teenagers at an outdoor party. She saw teenage Regina again. Pretty, but lacking the princess polish of the girls around her—girls who, Viv could see, were all paired off: a Cinderella on the arm of her Prince Charming, a drowsy Sleeping Beauty clinging to her prince, and a few other Royal couples practicing the obnoxious custom of wearing T-shirts emblazoned with their matching märchen marks: glass slippers, spinning wheels, golden braids.

Regina was the only girl alone, wearing the anxious expression of the late bloomer, the outcast. She held a paper plate piled with apple slices she probably hoped she'd choke on. She'd still believed she was Snow White back then.

"Wasn't your prince supposed to come?" Cinderella asked Regina.

"Some . . . day," Sleeping Beauty replied languidly. *"Who thought* she'd *be the one waiting a hundred years for her prince?"* The Regina in the mirror flushed with embarrassment. One of the princes, whom Viv recognized from the last scene the mirror had showed, looked away but didn't speak.

The princesses and princes began to laugh—and then their laughter grew louder, as if there were a hundred people laughing instead of ten.

As the glass rippled, the laughter faded. Now the mirror showed Regina and Viv's father lying in bed—but the bedroom was decorated the way Viv's mother had left it, as it had been in the early days of their marriage. Regina snuggled close to her husband, saying, *"You were worth waiting for. You're better than a prince. Our love is going to last. I just know—I can feel it. I'm so happy."*

The glass rippled once more and, finally, Viv saw her own reflection, her face drawn with shock; and she saw Regina, as still as a statue except for the tears rolling down her face.

"Everything you struggle for comes so easily to the fairest," the

mirror said. *"Love. Beauty. Admiration. No one has ever loved you the way she is loved. No one ever will."*

"Shut up!" Viv shouted. But the voice went on.

"Your beauty was never enough to make them stay. Beauty: the one thing you had. Now look at you. Look what you've become."

Viv regretted ever encouraging the mirror; this was so much worse than anything she'd imagined it might do. She picked up a heavy perfume bottle and bashed it against the mirror once, twice, again and again, until the glass broke up into fang-shaped shards and slivers. Some of the glass fell away; the rest clung stubbornly to the backing, reflecting dozens of tiny Vivs and broken, crouching Reginas.

It wouldn't change anything. Regina would hang another mirror in its place, like she did every time she destroyed one. She hated the mirror, but she needed it.

Regina crawled to the phone, and stayed on the floor while she dialed, trembling.

"Regina . . ." Viv took a few steps toward her, then stopped. She wanted to comfort her, but she couldn't forget the shoe-box coffin in the hall. She couldn't put her arms around her and say *I'm sorry you're hurting* after what Regina had done.

Viv picked up the shoe box and went upstairs to get her mother's book of fairy tales and a few other mementos. Now that her animals were dead, most of the things she'd come back for seemed unimportant.

As she packed, she remembered that Regina had been calling someone; she lifted the phone to listen in. But there was only a dial tone. So it had been a quick call, or no one had answered. It didn't matter, anyway; she was leaving.

Viv grabbed her car keys, her bag, and the shoe box, then

went downstairs and straight to the garage where her car was parked.

She piled her things on the passenger's seat and started to back down the long driveway. She went slowly, checking to make sure there weren't any animals about to dash under the car, and also watching the house, in case Regina came out. Viv almost wished she would—to show that she was okay, cold again instead of devastated. Not broken like the mirror.

As she backed down the last part of the driveway, she heard the roar of an engine—an angry, impatient sound that made her hands tense on the steering wheel.

She turned her head and saw a pickup truck speeding down the road. Not Henley's. She started to pull forward; and then the truck swerved into the driveway and rammed the rear of her car. Her body smacked the steering wheel; she felt like someone had wound up and smashed her with a plank. She blacked out for an instant—and came to as the passenger-side window exploded, pelting her with shattered glass. The old Huntsman reached his hand in to unlock the door, and then he grabbed her and dragged her out of the car while she kicked and screamed, the shards of glass digging into her skin, pricking her like a hundred thorns.

The Huntsman carried her across the road and into the thick woods that had always made the property feel private. Now Viv wished they had neighbors, or even a gas station across the street. Anything with people. Anything to make this harder for the Huntsman to get away with.

Blood dripped down her arms and she smeared them against the trees as they passed, hoping to mark their path— *just in case*—but Henley wasn't scheduled to do the lawn today, and he hadn't answered when she'd called. She knew, deep down, that he wasn't coming, and in a few minutes she was going to say good-bye to this world without saying good-bye to him.

This wasn't how she wanted to die—if she had to.

She didn't want it to be at this Huntsman's hands.

She wanted—

The old Huntsman took a thin rope from his belt and looped it around her neck, pulling it tight like a leash. When she tried to run he yanked the rope to cut off her air supply. While she was gasping and choking, he tied her to the trunk of a tree, winding the rope in a crisscrossing pattern around her throat, across her shoulders, behind the tree to bind her wrists, and then around her hips and thighs before securing it with a firm knot.

The way he looked at her let her know what was coming. He'd bound her tightly, but he'd left her chest and abdomen an open canvas for his blade.

"It's not supposed to be you," she said. "Henley's supposed to do this. You're retired."

"Looks like I'm back in business." The old Huntsman grinned. He looked even more savage in the daylight. "I must say it feels natural getting back to this. It's been a while since I used these blades on anything human. Last girl was little like you. Younger, though. Eleven. Little heart, little lungs. When I cut them out of her body it was like holding a doll's organs. I could've fit three of those hearts in that box. Men think women like diamonds. . . . I've never seen a woman happier than when you present her with the heart of her rival. She'll stroke it like a kitten. It's the sweetest thing."

"You're sick," she choked.

"No sicker than a fairy godmother. This whole world is sick. You've had seventeen good years. Never cold, never hungry. All those years and your only hardship is that you have to die today. And dying's not even hard."

He held her white dress by the neckline, pulled it taut, then slashed it open from throat to hem. "There," he said. "Nothing in the way now."

"You're not supposed to do this. You have to let Henley do it! This is his curse. Ours. You have to—"

"Sorry, Princess. Your stepmom called *me*. The woman knows what she wants."

He placed the blade against her collarbone and drew it down slowly, barely exerting any pressure. A hot line of pain opened on her chest—and a trickle of blood followed. She heard the squawking of crows as she cried out, the beating of wings as they took to the sky. Then quiet. The hush of a vast stretch of woods that would swallow every sound.

Viv cried as he cut her again—another surface cut, designed to hurt. By the third cut she was sobbing, her body jerking with emotion, chest rising toward the knife when she wanted to shrink away from it.

"Come on," the Huntsman said. "Beg me to spare you. Let's make this fun."

Viv gritted her teeth. Tried to make her body go rigid. If she had to die, she didn't want to be his entertainment.

Her head drooped, just enough for the rope to choke her, and as she lifted it she thought she heard someone running. Hard footsteps smashing through the underbrush.

The Huntsman was turned away from her, facing . . .

Henley, who was coming toward them.

She might have thought she'd imagined him, if his face hadn't been so coldly angry. Henley's anger had always been hot, burning under the surface, a struggle to contain. This looked closer to resolve. He wasn't fighting with himself; he'd made a decision. He had the jeweled knife in his hand.

"Henley—"

He barely looked at her. His focus was on the old Huntsman. "This is my curse. I don't need you stepping in for me."

"That's not what I hear," the Huntsman said.

"Then you heard wrong. Viv's mine. She's *been* mine. Regina promised me I could have this."

Standing there, watching them square off, it was clear that although the old Huntsman was an experienced killer, Henley posed a threat. He was taller, more muscular, and had youth on his side—and he was furious. The Huntsman gave him a curt nod. "Go on, then. I've already got her trussed for you."

"I don't need that. She won't run from me. Will you, Viv?"

She made a sound that was neither a *yes* nor a *no*, but a *help*, and Henley cut the rope with his jeweled knife, the blade scraping the tree as he slashed her bindings. Viv fell into his arms as the rope dropped away, her body trembling with fear and adrenaline.

Henley tipped her chin up to look into her eyes. There was no tenderness in his face. His gaze was hard, as if he barely saw her, as if that was what it took for him not to waver.

He turned her around and held her body against his, not roughly—almost like a caress. His right hand held the knife. His left arm was holding her body, keeping her close, and she gripped his arm as tightly as she could—the way she used to hold Regina's hand at the doctor's, for courage before a shot. Her fingers slid over veins and hard muscle. She imagined she could feel his heartbeat. As rapid as hers.

"This will be over fast," Henley told her. "Just listen to me and it won't hurt, okay?"

"Okay," she said. She took deep breaths, and closed her eyes so she wouldn't have to see the old Huntsman. She tried to focus on Henley's arm . . . tried to remember the first time he'd put his arms around her, surprising her—like a boyfriend, not a playmate.

She breathed in, out . . .

Henley folded Viv's fingers around the handle of his knife, then closed his hand around hers. He drew the knife up to her throat, gently, as if the blade were a bow and Viv a violin, and they were about to coax a single, fragile note from her—together.

"I made a promise," he said.

"I love you," she said.

Henley's whisper brushed her ear like a kiss. *"Run."*

The warmth of his body left her, but the knife was still in her hand.

She opened her eyes to see Henley lunge at the old Huntsman, to see them both hit the ground as Henley tackled him. Leaves flying up from the dirt. A smear of blood on the Huntsman's face.

Startled, she dropped the knife—then quickly snatched it up. "Henley!"

They were wrestling, fighting for control of the Huntsman's blade.

Viv hesitated. She still had the knife. Maybe she could help him. . . .

The two Huntsmen rolled over, faces flushed, tendons straining—and Henley saw her.

"Run, goddamn it!" he yelled.

So she ran.

CHAPTER TWENTY-THREE

VIV TORE THROUGH THE WOODS like there were beasts at her heels. She was less familiar with this stretch of forest, but she knew that if she kept running she'd reach a pond with a picnic area. Families used it during the day, teenagers hung out there at night. She didn't know who might be there this early, but she hoped there would be someone who could help.

When she stumbled into the clearing, the last of the morning mist was rising off the pond. Blood plastered her torn dress to her skin, and she clutched the dagger in a death grip. Her feet hurt like someone had burned them. Her chest was heaving, and she knew she looked like she'd committed a murder. Or escaped one.

She saw Beth Teal sitting on a picnic table on the far side of the pond, her head bent over the nettle jacket she was knitting. Viv gathered her breath to yell—and Beth's swan brothers swam toward her, honking aggressively. Beth glanced up at the commotion.

"I need your phone!" Viv shouted. "Henley's in trouble!"

They met halfway around the pond, Beth pushing her phone into Viv's hand before Viv had a chance to ask again. It was already calling Jack Tran's number.

Jack sounded worried when he answered—"Beth?"—and Viv realized it was because Beth never called people; her brothers would die if she spoke.

"It's not Beth, it's Viv. Henley got into a fight with the other Huntsman. The Huntsman has a knife and—"

"Where?"

She did her best to explain, but it was hard to describe their exact location. "I can take you there."

"No, you stay with Beth. I'll find them."

Viv paced while she waited; despite her injured feet, she couldn't sit still. The swans had stopped menacing her, and birds were chirping and sunlight glimmered on the water and it just seemed wrong that Henley could be dead in those woods. If he didn't get his hands on the knife fast enough. If he didn't strike first.

"I shouldn't have left him. God. What was I thinking?" She burst into tears and Beth rubbed her back with one blotchy red hand.

Two hours had passed by the time Jack showed up at the picnic area. The dirt on his clothes and skin hinted that things hadn't gone smoothly, and Viv ran to find out what he knew. Beth came with her, tossing a handful of crackers to her brothers to keep them busy.

"Did you find him?" Viv asked.

"Just this." Jack took Henley's cell phone from his pocket.

Dirt was caked in the grooves and the screen had been smashed. "This doesn't mean anything," Jack said. "He probably dropped it and stepped on it while they were fighting. But I think I found the place where they fought. I followed the blood trail, but . . . it just stopped."

"Blood trail? Whose blood was it? Why didn't you—?"

"I don't know whose blood it was. It probably belonged to both of them. But—it looked like someone was being dragged. I don't know who came out on the better end of that fight. I wish I did. We just have to hope we hear from Henley. And hope we don't see that other Huntsman again."

"We can't just *wait*! We have to look! I'll go with you this time. We have to find him. He could be hurt! He might be—"

Jack wrapped his arms around her and hugged her tight. He smelled like pine needles and earth. "Viv, I want to find him as much as you do. But there's no one in those woods anymore."

"Then we need to find a grave." She buried her face in Jack's chest, wiping her runny nose on his shirt, not caring how disgusting that was because she didn't have any pride left.

She'd always worried about whether Henley would kill her. She'd never considered that he might die because of her.

"I'm going to get Viv out of here," Jack murmured over her head. She felt Beth patting between her shoulder blades and then Jack was leading her to his car—an old Mustang painted the leafy-green color of a beanstalk. Viv felt like a zombie. Jack opened the door for her.

"I need to take you somewhere safe," he said. "At least until we know if that Huntsman's still out there. You can't stay at my place. . . . Is there somewhere you can go?"

"I can stay at Jewel's."

"Jewel the singer?"

Viv nodded.

"What's the address?"

CHAPTER TWENTY-FOUR

JACK HAD DRAPED A JACKET over Viv's shoulders so her bloodstained dress would be less panic-inducing. He walked her to Jewel's door, shooing away the feral cats and pigeons that swarmed them when Viv got out of the car.

"I don't know if she'll hear the bell," Viv said. "We were out all night. She's probably passed out."

"Someone's awake." Jack nodded at the door—it was opening. Viv hugged her jacket closed to spare Jewel the sight of her dress; but when the door swung fully open, it wasn't Jewel standing there, but Blue.

His spiky blue hair was crooked from sleep. He was wearing heart-print boxers and a Maleficent T-shirt, and past him, Viv could see a heap of blankets and a pillow on the couch.

Blue squinted sleepily. The barbell piercing above his left eyebrow glinted in the light. "Did Henley trade you to Jack Tran for some magic beans?"

Viv burst into tears.

Blue's lazy expression turned frantic. "What happened?"

"You might not want to make any jokes about Henley," Jack told him, ushering Viv inside. "Is Jewel here?"

"Yeah, yeah, I'll wake her up."

Viv sat down on the couch. Her feet hurt; her eyes burned from crying. She was covered with blood and her guilt was so intense she had the near-constant urge to throw up. *Why did you leave him? What the hell is wrong with you?*

She wiped her wet face. She wanted a shower. She wanted to go back and do this day over, or fall asleep and never wake up. Jack didn't seem nearly as troubled. He browsed around Jewel's living room like it was a showcase, lifted a shot glass full of gems, and held it to the light. "Are these real?"

"Don't steal those," Viv said. "You're not at a giant's house."

"Yeah, I know, but . . . she has so many. . . ."

"I'm serious."

Jack set the glass down and sighed.

Jewel came rushing into the room, her bright pink robe tied over a Curses & Kisses T-shirt. She was walking funny, as if every step hurt—and finally she dropped down on the couch next to Viv, pulled her into a hug, and said, "Tell us what happened."

Viv couldn't get the words out, so Jack told them: How the old Huntsman had come for Viv. How Henley had arrived to stop him. How they'd fought, and Viv had run, and now no one knew where Henley was.

"Viv needs to be somewhere safe," Jack said. "She wants to stay here. Is that all right with you?"

"Of course she can stay." Jewel's arms were still wrapped

around her. Viv felt the soft tumble of flowers down her back as Jewel breathed nervously in and out. "We'll look after her."

"Good," Jack said. "I'll let you know if there's any news."

"As *soon* as you hear something," Viv said, twisting around to face him. Her palm came down on a damp chrysanthemum. "You have to tell me right away. Good or bad."

Jack nodded. "I won't pull any punches." His eyes danced over the shot glasses full of gems. "I'll be in touch."

"Thanks for bringing her," Jewel said.

Jack stopped at the door on his way out. "Hey—Viv. Don't take any candy from strangers. You're not out of the woods yet."

"I know," she said.

The curse wasn't over. Once Regina knew that Viv had survived, she would try to kill Viv herself. That was Snow White's fate.

The door slammed as Jack left and, right away, Blue went over and locked it. He'd put on pants at some point, and now he was wearing ripped jeans with his Maleficent T-shirt. Someone had written *Property of Mira* in black marker on the butt of his jeans. Probably Blue since it didn't seem like Mira's style.

"That is so classy," Viv said.

He turned to look at her. "Locking the door?"

"The 'property of' on your ass."

"Does that mean you're feeling better?"

"No. It just needed to be said."

"Blue, can you make us some coffee?" Jewel asked. "I'd do it myself but I feel like I woke up with mermaid feet. Every step hurts. Wait—you do know how to use a coffeemaker, right?"

Blue lived at the Dream, the hotel and casino his father owned. He didn't actually have appliances. He got his coffee from cafés, his food from restaurants.

"Walk me through it," Blue said.

Viv got up to take a shower while the two of them worked it out. She stuffed her dress in the bathroom garbage, then stood under the hot water and scrubbed her skin clean of dirt, blood, sweat, and tears until she felt faint from the heat. After she'd shut off the water, she sat on the edge of the tub and took deep breaths, water dribbling from her hair and making puddles on the floor. She felt dizzy, and so full of regret she could hardly breathe. The cuts the Huntsman had made looked like three rusty zippers running down her chest.

There was a knock on the door. "Are you okay?" Jewel asked. "I mean, physically?"

"Go sit down, Mermaid Feet. I'm doing better than you are." Which wasn't true. But she wanted it to be.

"I brought your bag. In case you want to wear something that doesn't have blood on it."

"You know me so well." Viv opened the door and Jewel passed her the overnight bag.

"Hurry up. We miss you when you're traumatized." Jewel's smile was weak, worried, but she was trying. Viv was grateful for it. She didn't want her friends to tiptoe around her. If Jewel and Blue were too careful with her she wouldn't be able to think about anything except what had happened in the woods today. And she wanted to feel normal enough that she could feel something like hope . . . hope that Henley might be okay.

Viv pulled on a sundress patterned with ladybugs, then checked herself in the mirror. The cuts on her chest were visible—too disturbing—so she changed into a black T-shirt and a frayed denim skirt. Her face did not look nearly as broken as she felt. Her sadness was artful, too pretty. Like it wasn't real. Like *she* wasn't real.

She tried not to look.

In the living room there was a steaming cup of coffee waiting for her, a cheese Danish big enough for a giant, and a support group. Jewel was on the couch, and she'd been joined by Mira, Freddie, and Layla Phan.

Layla was a Beauty, destined to redeem the obnoxious, womanizing, so-far-unrepentant Rafe Wilder—once he turned into a Beast, anyway. She had long, silky black hair that was in a fishtail braid today, dark eyes, a warm sheen to her skin, and a smile that made you feel like everything could be okay. She and Freddie were both Honor-bound—they were destined to break curses. And like Freddie, Layla could be too good for her own good sometimes. She despised Rafe and claimed she'd leave him as a Beast once he transformed, but her friends suspected she was too compassionate to actually stick to that plan.

Layla, Freddie, and Mira were looking at Viv like they wanted to cry her tears for her. Viv tried to lighten the mood, but her voice was raw as she said, "What, the Beast doesn't care about my pain?"

"Did you want Rafe here?" Jewel asked. "We left him out to spare Layla."

"But if you want to see him," Layla added quickly, "and I don't know why you would, but if you do, we can call him."

"I don't. I don't think I can handle his brand of sensitivity."

"What should we do?" Mira asked. "Do you want us to look for Henley? Do you want us here?"

"I have a German shepherd in the car," Freddie announced. "He's not trained in search and rescue, but—we have a rapport. I think together we could—"

Layla put her hand on top of Freddie's and he stopped talking. "We'll do whatever you need. We're here for you, okay? And we're not giving up. No one's giving up on Henley."

"Thanks," Viv said. "I don't—I don't really know what I need right now. If you look, I should go look, too. . . ."

"No, you should stay here," Blue said. He was in the kitchen, unpacking large quantities of baked goods from a bunch of paper bags stamped with the Twin Roses Café logo. There was a swipe of frosting on his arm, just above his spiked leather bracelet. "If your stepmom thinks you're dead, you should let her keep thinking that. Don't venture into the open yet."

Viv sighed. "So just . . . stay here. Stay useless."

"Stay alive," Jewel said, as a ruby rolled off her tongue. "Freddie can go look for Henley. Freddie and Scruffy."

"His name is Lancelot," Freddie said.

"Of course it is."

Freddie and Layla stayed long enough to eat some of the pastries, and to tell Viv things like *It will be okay* and *I'm sure Henley's alive, he's strong, he had something to fight for.* Viv felt hopeful while they were saying it—their Honor-bound earnestness made it hard not to feel that way. But once the sunny optimism contingent had gone, Viv was left with her pessimistic self, Blue and Jewel, who were more cynical, and Mira, who seemed so desperate to say the right thing that she wasn't saying anything at all.

"What do you guys think?" Viv asked. "Do you think it's

possible he's just . . . hurt? Or can no one find him because—" She swallowed. "Because he was buried?"

"He could have a head injury," Jewel said slowly. "And not know where he is. He could be wandering somewhere. I don't think we can just . . . rule out something like that."

Blue was sitting next to Mira now. He had his arm around her, and she was leaning into him, her legs pulled up on the couch. It reminded Viv of the last time Mira had been in trouble—when they weren't sure whether she was asleep or dead. Viv had tucked herself into Henley's arms and he'd held her as they waited to learn the truth. Viv closed her eyes, remembering how good it had felt to turn to him. For so long, she'd felt like she had no one to turn to, but she'd had Henley—she'd had him there all that time. She fought not to let any more tears fall, but she didn't have the power to stop them.

"Don't lose hope," Jewel said softly. "If your positions were reversed, Henley wouldn't give up on you."

"I wish he'd given up on me a long time ago."

"You don't," Jewel said. "You wish this hadn't happened. We all wish that. But no matter where Henley is, you're alive right now because of him. Don't wish yourself dead. He didn't."

Viv bent forward in her chair and let the tears flood her until she was choking and shaking. Jewel was stroking her hair and Mira was squeezing her hand. She could hear Blue on the phone with Freddie, and then with Jack. When he hung up, the condo was silent except for Viv's gasps. She stopped herself long enough to say, "Did they find him?"

"Not yet. They haven't found anything."

* * *

There was no news. No word from Henley.

Nothing all day.

By evening Viv was curled up on Jewel's couch, sinking deeper into depression.

She'd called Jack Tran six times. She'd called Freddie and Layla so many times she was starting to feel guilty because she could tell they felt bad saying, *No, we haven't found him, we're so sorry. . . .*

And then it was too dark to search.

Blue and Mira were spending the night. They gave Viv the couch and spread out on the floor, but offered to stay up with her if she couldn't sleep. Eventually Jewel went to bed. She told Viv to try to do the same—*you haven't slept in two days.* But Viv didn't want to sleep. She was used to nightmares, but they'd just been about her own death. If she dreamed about Henley's death . . . No. She couldn't handle that.

She curled up on the couch in the dark and left the TV on mute; let the light from the screen wash over her and keep her awake. She'd told Mira and Blue they could sleep, but she could hear them whispering together, worried about her. At some point Viv passed out—the phone in her lap, her head resting crookedly on the arm of the couch.

She woke to the sound of a newspaper hitting the door— and ran outside before she knew what she had heard, as if she might find Henley waiting there. The sky was dim, the air was wet. Birds flocked to her side, but Henley was still missing. It was a new day, but nothing had changed.

CHAPTER TWENTY-FIVE

EVERY DAY WENT LIKE THIS:

Hey, Jack, I thought maybe by now you might have—

Sorry, Viv, wish I had better news. We just have to keep hoping, you know?

You'll call me if—

Yeah, of course. Of course I will.

And her hope deflated. Her heart sank. Every day.

CHAPTER TWENTY-SIX

TEN DAYS OF SITTING BY THE PHONE, desperate for news. Ten days of night sweats, of dreams that were snatched away the moment she woke, leaving only the vague impression that Henley had been there for a little while.

It was the longest she had ever gone without seeing him.

Viv slept on Jewel's couch, barely showered, and didn't leave the condo.

No one had seen Henley or the old Huntsman. Viv didn't know what to think. If the old Huntsman was alive, he might have left town, or he might be living in a cabin in the woods; it wasn't like people had really seen him around before.

But if Henley was alive, he would have contacted her. He would have met up with Jack, or gone home to his parents.

There would be some sign of him. He wouldn't just disappear.

On the eleventh day, Viv decided that she needed to reach out to Jasper. If she had been poisoned and was lying in her glass coffin, fate would have arranged for him to come to her. So if he was still trapped in the underworld, and no one he talked to at the club had seen her, he probably thought the Huntsman had killed her, as he'd feared. It wasn't fair to let him believe that.

She would go to the underworld, just for the night. She told Jewel what she wanted to do.

"How are you going to get in? The invitations Jasper gave us turned to dust."

"I'll have to get another one. Find someone who's been invited and beg, buy, or steal it from them."

Viv tried to remember who she had seen at the club. Guests came to the underworld from all over the world, but there had to be someone she knew who was a regular. Still, her mind was blanking. Every night except the first, she'd been focused on Jasper and the underworld itself, not the other Cursed on the dance floor.

"Do you think Rafe knows anybody who has one?" she asked Jewel.

"Maybe. He does throw a lot of parties . . . and he knows a lot of people. I'll call him and find out. You should call Blue. They give out so many perks at that hotel . . . they might have someone who can get invitations for guests."

Blue was a bust—the Dream did not have an underworld connection. But Rafe said he could definitely get his hands on some, and he wouldn't even ask for compensation, out of respect for Viv's tragedy.

"Definitely? He guaranteed it?" Viv asked.

Jewel shrugged. "Keep in mind this is Rafe—the guy

who also guarantees that he can get any girl he meets to sleep with him. But I think there's a good chance he'll come through."

Viv nodded, trying to prepare herself to leave the couch and enter the underworld. She hadn't been out in over a week. She felt safe at Jewel's, sort of, but she was afraid to set foot outside the door. "Do you think he can get two? I don't want to go by myself."

"He acted like he could get a whole handful. I'll try to remind him to make good on that. Okay, so . . . you need something to wear. I'd offer to take you shopping, but it's probably best if no one sees you. Luxe and I can pick something out. She's been complaining that we haven't spent enough time together, anyway."

"I doubt she'll want to spend the day shopping for me."

"No, she loves giving her opinion. And casing the store, figuring out what she'd shoplift. Not that she does that anymore. You'll be okay on your own?"

"I'll be fine."

"Call me if you need anything."

Viv took a long, hot shower, then wrapped herself in one of Jewel's robes and spent half an hour teasing a week's worth of tangles from her hair. She poked around the kitchen in an aimless way before finally making coffee and eating some yogurt and an orange that she hoped she could keep down. She was about to call Jewel and ask how things were going when there was a knock at the door. Her heart jumped, even though the knock was too soft to be Henley's.

Luxe was by herself, holding a black bag overflowing with white tissue paper.

"Where's Jewel?" Viv asked.

"Busy. With band stuff." Luxe thrust the bag at her. "Here. We bought this for you. I think it'll fit. It was hard finding something slutty in the children's department."

Viv rolled her eyes. "Thanks."

She reached into the bag and pulled out a strapless black dress with a lace-up back. It wasn't really her style, but maybe it was the only dress Jewel and Luxe could agree on. She looked for the tags to see what she owed Jewel, but there weren't any. "Did you steal this?"

"Don't act suspicious when someone gives you a present. It's rude."

"You better not have stolen this," Viv said, shedding her robe and stepping into the dress. Luxe was watching her in a too-intent, creepy way. Viv angled her body so there was less to see. Luxe had never ogled her before, so this was weird. She'd even announced once that Viv wasn't her type—then gone on to list all the things that were wrong with Viv's body.

Whatever, it's not like she doesn't have the same parts.

Viv did her best to cinch the laces by herself, but it was hard to do, especially since the dress was designed for someone who had a little more up top. "Luxe—can you help me tighten these so the dress doesn't fall off?"

"I guess," Luxe said. "Or you could try eating lard and just grow some boobs."

"Lard? Is that what bears put in their porridge? I thought they were supposed to eat salmon," Viv said, since Luxe had been complaining about that recently.

"The three bears eat porridge, dummy."

Viv sighed. Of course she wouldn't remember.

Luxe yanked the laces with surprising force and skill, like maybe she'd done this for Jewel before.

"Okay, I'd like to breathe still," Viv said. "You're pulling it too tight."

"Do you want to show the whole world the boobs you don't have? I don't think so." Luxe pulled the laces tighter, and Viv gasped—she felt like her lungs had sealed shut. She went to pull away, and stars popped in front of her eyes. Her thoughts slipped; her chest fought to expand.

"—tight—"

"Stop complaining," Luxe said viciously.

Another jerk of the laces. Viv felt like her lungs were being tied closed. She opened her mouth to breathe—and darkness swept in.

CHAPTER TWENTY-SEVEN

WHEN VIV OPENED HER EYES, she was lying on her side, staring at a spill of gems on the floor in front of her. Her mind was muddy with confusion and her back was cold—someone was peeling the dress off her body. She heard the soft sound of more gems falling, along with a rush of breath.

"God!" Jewel said. "Why did you let her in? And how badly did you want this dress, to let her put it on you? Are you sick in the head?"

"What?" Viv said. "You're the one dating a psychopath."

"Excuse me?"

"Luxe brought me this dress. *She* laced me up. And when I told her it was too tight—"

Jewel shook her fist in front of Viv's face—a tangle of black laces swung from her fingers. "Viv—why would you let someone lace you up? The stay laces in the fairy tale?"

Viv's cheeks grew hot. She hadn't thought of it, but obviously she knew that the evil queen disguises herself as an old woman and tempts Snow White with stay laces for her corset—then laces her up so tightly that she falls into a swoon.

"I'm not an idiot. I wouldn't let Regina or some sketchy old lady in here. It was Luxe. She brought me a dress, like you guys were supposed to. Why don't you ask her what the hell she was doing?"

"Luxe was with me all day. Shopping for you. Buying this." Jewel lifted a dress out of a shopping bag. It had a strapless white top and a knee-length black skirt with a red-ribbon belt at the waist. "She didn't come back here."

"But I *saw* Luxe. It was her."

"I'm telling you, it wasn't. Maybe it looked like her, but . . . Viv, just how much witchcraft can Regina do? Can she change her appearance?"

"I don't know. I didn't know she could do any witchcraft. I thought her witch friends were just teaching her how to cook a human heart, and . . . brew poison, maybe. I didn't know they were teaching her to use magic."

"Well, she definitely knows you're here. She's still trying to kill you. And apparently she can disguise herself as my girlfriend, which I am really not okay with."

Viv sighed—and as her breath slipped out she recalled the feeling of her lungs being crushed by the tightening stay laces. Regina would try again, and her next attempt might be fatal.

What kept her here? Henley was dead because of her. She could hardly remember a world without him, and that's all Beau Rivage would be now: the city where Henley was murdered. Every place she went would remind her of him and would be like a fresh accusation. If she'd let him go sooner, if she'd trusted him instead of putting them through all this misery . . .

He'd died so that she could live. And if she stayed here Regina would kill her. Jasper had promised he could keep Regina out of the underworld. Maybe he could, maybe he couldn't—but she had a better chance to survive there than she did here.

"I think I need to go to the underworld for a while. Not just tonight."

"Are you sure you want to do that?"

"If Regina poisons me, I'll either die or end up in the underworld, anyway."

Jewel sighed. "I just don't want you to regret—"

"I regret *everything*," Viv said savagely. Tears burned in her eyes, then rolled down her cheeks when she blinked, leaving hot streaks in their wake. "Sorry. I don't mean to take it out on you. I just—regretting staying with Jasper? That's the last thing I'm worried about. I don't even care about regretting that."

"Okay," Jewel said softly. "Okay." Her eyes said *I don't agree with you, but I don't want to fight with you.* That was all Viv could ask for, really.

They met Rafe at his house. Blue, Mira, Freddie, and even Layla—who had never been to Rafe's house before—were just getting out of Freddie's car when Viv arrived with Jewel. She'd told them Viv was going to the underworld indefinitely, and they should meet here if they wanted to see her off. Viv had a feeling Jewel hoped they could talk her out of her decision, but she wasn't going to be swayed.

It was both too dangerous and too painful to stay in Beau Rivage. Just being at Rafe's house reminded Viv of the last time she'd been there with Henley. At a party. It wasn't even a good memory. She'd been drunk and flirting hard with someone she couldn't even remember now—and Henley had thrown an antique chair through a window, and Rafe had kicked them both out. She remembered being so pissed, stumbling down the driveway on her red espadrilles with the stacked heels . . . and Henley having to catch her and then yelling something like, could she at least stay sober so she could drive her own ass home? Then he took her keys, and they argued the whole way to her house, and all she wanted that night was for him to leave her alone.

Tonight, Rafe had left the gate to his enchanted rose garden open, and that was where they found him, drinking a Red Bull and watching something on his phone. He was a big guy with shaggy, dark gold hair and an affinity for Hawaiian shirts. He lived alone in his mansion, which looked like a museum that had been co-opted by a fraternity: ornate furniture, priceless paintings, kegs, random girls' thongs hidden everywhere like Easter eggs.

Rafe gave Viv an awkward hug. Weirdly tentative, the way a cat person pets a dog—like he was trying not to grope her. She appreciated the gesture. With Rafe, you had to be impressed by the little things.

"Sucks about Henley," he said. "That guy was always kind of a jerk-off, but he died doing a good thing."

"Way to be sensitive, Wilder." A ruby rolled down Jewel's lip.

"I'm expressing my condolences. And . . ." He took five

black-and-silver invitations from the pocket of his shorts, fanned them out like a poker hand. "I came through for you. You can bring the whole gang. Well, except for Layla. I promised the guy who gave me these she'd pay him back with a lap dance."

"You repulsive piece of—" Layla started.

Freddie drew his sword and pointed it at Rafe. The tip of the blade hovered about an inch from his nose. "Do not speak to her that way."

"Whoa, simmer down, Knight." Rafe took a step back. "We're all friends here."

Either Rafe hadn't noticed that Freddie was now equipped with a sword all the time, or he was so used to Freddie's polite requests that it never occurred to him to expect anything else. Although, to be fair, none of them had expected that. Certainly not Layla.

"Apologize," Freddie said.

Rafe cleared his throat. "All right. Sorry. It was a joke. No one has to gyrate if they don't want to. Satisfied?"

Freddie sheathed his sword but still looked like he was waiting for Rafe to slip up.

Rafe took a moment to recover—they were all a little dazed—then said, "There's a theme. Some kind of angel thing. I bet there'll be a million chicks wearing underwear and wings. . . . Too bad I'm banned or I'd take one of these invites for myself."

"Banned?" Viv said.

"Yup. Check this out." Rafe held up one of the invitations. Light glimmered across the silver *Yes or No?* "Yes," Rafe said. "Yes, mofo, I accept." But nothing happened. The invitation remained intact. Rafe showed her his forearms. "See? No silver diddlies."

"What did you do to get banned?" Viv asked. "I didn't even realize you'd been there."

"Eh, it was no big deal. I was pretty drunk—open bar all night—and I think I pissed in the punch bowl or something. I pissed *somewhere* I wasn't supposed to. Nothing worth banning a man over, but they're kind of prissy down there."

"That's disgusting," Layla said.

"That's nature. You think I won't piss wherever I want when I'm a Beast? Get used to it, 'cause you're gonna be seeing it all the time."

"I hope you enjoy that perk," Layla said, "because you're going to be a Beast for the rest of your life. And I'm not going to be anywhere near you."

"Yeah, yeah. You're gonna be all over me," Rafe said. "Just as soon as—"

The sword slid out again and this time Freddie's jaw was clenched. "Blood is going to be all over you if you don't start being respectful."

"Jesus, Knight! Does this kid need medication?"

Viv stepped between them. "Could you stop before Freddie decides to use you for decapitation practice?"

"I don't remember him being this high-strung. This is because of Mira, right? The thwarted happily ever after? You need to get laid, son."

"When I said stop, I meant *now*." Viv took the invitations from him. "Anyway . . . thanks for these."

"No problem. People were happy to give them up when they heard it was for you."

"You told people it was for Viv?" Jewel asked.

"Uh . . . was I not supposed to? They needed a motivating factor to part with those suckers. And kissing up to the new underworld princess was a pretty good one."

"We didn't want anyone to know whether or not she was alive," Jewel said, wiping petals from her lips. "We didn't want word getting back to her stepmom."

"You think her stepmom doesn't know everything that goes on here? She's got that mirror to tell her Viv's alive. 'Hey, am I the fairest? Nope, still old and ugly compared to Viv.'"

"Well, Regina tried to kill her today, not yesterday, so maybe, if you'd kept your mouth shut—"

"Maybe a witch who works retail heard you asking if they had any black-white-and-red dresses in stock—ever think of that?"

"Guys, it's fine," Viv said. "It doesn't matter how Regina found out. I just want to go to the underworld and . . . get out of here."

"That's right, Viv," Rafe said. "Your life is not over. It's just beginning. Go get it."

"Uh, thanks." She sighed and looked at her friends. "Are you guys coming with me? What's going on?"

"*Can* we go like this?" Mira asked.

Her friends were dressed for a picnic, not a nightclub: Mira in a T-shirt and shorts, Blue in a T-shirt and ripped jeans, Freddie in khakis and an Oxford shirt with the sleeves rolled up, Layla in a sundress.

"You'll stick out, but they'll let you in," Viv said.

Rafe grinned. "Ladies and gents, I've got tons of formal wear in the house. Smells like mothballs, 'cause some of it was Granny's, but a very classy array. You are welcome to any of it."

Mira and Blue exchanged glances. "There's no way your brother would be at that club, right?" Mira asked.

"No, that's one place we definitely won't run into Felix."

"There are only five invitations," Freddie said. "I'll excuse myself."

"No, I'll bow out," Jewel said. "I've already been there. You four should go. Just take care of Viv and make sure she absolutely, one hundred percent wants to stay before you leave—okay?"

"I've made my decision," Viv said.

"Just make sure," Jewel repeated.

Mira, Blue, Freddie, and Layla went into the house with Rafe. Layla seemed reluctant to enter the house that might be her prison one day, but Mira coaxed her inside.

Jewel paced back and forth on the driveway. "Are you sure? You're really sure?"

"I don't want to be here anymore. I don't want to remember every—everything I did with him. To him."

"Going to the underworld isn't going to make you forget Henley. Or forgive yourself. What if he's alive and—"

"He's *not*. We both know that if he were alive, he would have come for me right away. Or let me know, somehow. I have to accept that I won't see him again. It'll be easier to do that if I'm not here."

Jewel sighed. She pulled a string of bleeding hearts from her mouth and crushed it in her fist. "You'll send invitations so we can come visit?"

"Of course."

"And you'll come back eventually? Or are you not going to come to any more of our shows?"

"Eventually," Viv said. "Maybe you guys can play a gig in the underworld."

"With our banned bass player?"

"I'll vouch for him. Maybe I can get him unbanned."

"I'm going to miss you."

Viv nodded. She didn't want to get choked up. It was too easy lately to cry over everything. She took a moment, breathing until the tightness in her throat relaxed. "I won't be that far away."

CHAPTER TWENTY-EIGHT

IT TURNED OUT THAT THE THEME that night was *Paradise,* not *Angels,* and though girls in lingerie were few and far between, plenty of guests wore wings, halos, and other ethereal attire. Lots of white and gold, sheer and shimmery fabrics, gladiator sandals, and flower crowns.

Viv was dressed for a cocktail party, Mira had found a sky-blue dress from the 1950s, and Layla shimmered in a violet beaded evening gown. Blue and Freddie wore vintage tuxes. Freddie had been forced to leave his sword in the car.

"So I guess we picked the wrong outfits," Blue said. "We should have gone with bedsheet togas."

"I like you in that," Mira said, touching his sleeve.

"Oh, you do, do you?"

Viv led them to the lakeshore where they waited their turn for the gondolas. As anxious as she'd been to get here, she wasn't in a hurry to reunite with Jasper. She knew she wasn't here as his guest or friend—not if she wanted to stay. That wasn't their story and never would be. She was supposed to come here as a lovestruck rescued princess, a future bride.

When Viv's group reached the front of the line, Owen was just rowing back with an empty gondola. Viv waited until he'd made it to the shore and then climbed into his boat, leaving her friends to travel in pairs—Blue and Mira in one gondola, Layla and Freddie in another.

"You're back," Owen said with genuine surprise. "We didn't know if we'd see you again. In fact, I distinctly remember your prince crying after the horseman returned alone for the third time. There was some fighting in the palace, too. A rare argument between father and son. Your prince wanted to go up, find out whether you were still alive. But that was a *no*. It wasn't time, apparently. At least, that's how the maids reported it."

"I was in hiding. My stepmother sent a Huntsman after me."

"Congratulations on getting him to spare you."

"He didn't. He—I got away. I don't know if he's still out there."

"He won't find you here. They have a way of keeping people out. If the king doesn't want you in the underworld, forget about an invitation—you can't even pass through the door."

"Oh?" That was the first truly good thing she'd heard about the underworld king.

"Uh-huh. So who are your guests?"

As she gave Owen the rundown, half of her mind was floating forward into the future, trying to rehearse the conversation she would have with Jasper. She'd never really talked to him about Henley and now she'd at least have to say that he was dead. She'd probably cry and if she did she wasn't sure she'd be able to stop. Then Jasper would know how much she loved Henley, and how much she wasn't ready to love someone else.

Viv had to do her best to hide that. Things wouldn't be right between them—might always be tainted—if he knew her heart was gone. She had to heal privately, and when she was with Jasper she would have to play the part. If she wanted the safety her prince could offer her, then she needed to give him the romance he wanted. Pretend, until it became real.

At the club, guests were lounging on white divans shaped like clouds, feeding one another grapes, pretending to play minia-ture golden harps. They drank wine from glasses shaped like lilies and ate cakes cut and iced to resemble roses, narcissi, forget-me-nots. A shallow stream curved along the edge of the dance floor, its waters shining with gold and silver fish. The decor was a mishmash of heaven and Mount Olympus and the fairy tale "The Garden of Paradise." As if no one, not even their hosts, could decide what the theme truly meant.

"If we eat something, do we have to stay here forever?" Mira asked.

"Different underworld," Viv told her.

Layla sniffed a flower-shaped goblet and set it down. "Do they have anything besides wine?"

"I'll find out," Viv said.

She could tell by the way people were looking at her that she'd been recognized. That her story had traveled—Jasper's inability to find her, the rumor that a Huntsman had struck in

Beau Rivage. Dancers gathered close together, grabbed their partners, and pointed her out, but they kept their distance, as if no one wanted to be blamed for delaying her reunion with Jasper. Their whispers rippled outward, from the people she passed to the far edges of the club, and maybe all the way to the palace, if that was where Jasper was.

From the bar she could see the Twelve Dancing Princesses and eleven underworld princes, waltzing and weeping, twirling so their skirts spread out like petals. She wondered how they felt about the suitor they'd lost. She supposed they were used to it by now. Having their hopes dashed. Striking up a friendship only to have the guy be killed after three nights.

Viv had found two goblets filled with pomegranate juice and was carrying them back for Layla when someone grabbed her from behind and pulled her close, too close, his face buried in her neck—

Both goblets went crashing to the floor. A reddish-pink pool spread around her feet.

And though she knew that no one here but Jasper would dare to touch her like that, the memory of being tied to the tree was too strong. She went rigid, only relaxing when he said, "You're alive. You're all right. Viv, I was so—"

His lips brushed her neck: quick kisses of relief. "I heard there was blood all over your car. I sent a horseman for you every night, but you never came. And now you're here. Tell me you'll stay. Please . . ."

He held her so tightly that her heels lifted off the ground. Viv grasped his hands, gently prying his fingers away from her. "I'll stay."

By then they had drawn a crowd. Cursed loved a fairy-tale

213

romance, particularly at one of its high (or low) points. Her friends emerged from the crush of angelic onlookers. Viv knew it seemed strange—as long as they'd known her, they'd seen her with Henley. And now Jasper was standing beside her with one hand on the small of her back—protectively, where her märchen mark was—in a quintessential boyfriend pose.

Just like that, in a room full of witnesses, it was real. Or had to look real from now on. It occurred to her that so much of happily ever after was about making sure it *looked* like happily ever after to everyone else.

"Jasper, this is Blue Valentine, Mira Lively, Layla Phan, and Freddie Knight. You guys, this is Jasper. My prince."

Jasper shook everyone's hand; they all exchanged hellos, nice-to-meet-yous. She could sense that Jasper was trying to make a good impression, while also being a bit guarded. And her friends were trying to be friendly, but they seemed as wary of Jasper as they were of Viv's decision to stay. Viv just stood there, smiling blandly, Jasper's hand getting heavier, more and more like a promise she wasn't ready to make.

"Is your hair naturally that color?" Jasper asked Blue.

"No, I dyed it. So people would think I had a villain's curse and hate me and fear me. Like the X-Men."

"It's natural," Mira said. "He's just being . . . himself."

"It was probably a rude question," Jasper said. "I should have assumed it went along with your curse. Well, you won't find yourself ostracized here. Our club is open to all manner of guests."

"Koschei the Deathless comes here," Viv told them.

"I am definitely a step above that guy," Blue said. "Although not nearly as stylish."

"Who's . . . ?" Mira started, and Blue stopped to explain the fairy tale to her.

"Why haven't we met you before, Jasper?" Layla asked. "Do you not like Beau Rivage?"

"It isn't that," Jasper said. "I just . . . haven't had the opportunity."

"Well, I hope we'll see you and Viv soon. There's a lot to do up there. It's not just beaches and casinos, if that's what you've heard."

"I'd like that," Jasper said. "Once it's safe for Viv, especially."

"You should get a sword," Freddie said. "Every hero needs one."

"Do I need one?" Layla asked.

Freddie flushed. "Yes. You especially should have one. It may be the only thing that gets Rafe to shut up."

It seemed rude to bring her friends all the way to the underworld and not let them have fun. So even though she didn't feel like dancing, Viv took Jasper's hand and led him onto the floor. She wanted her friends to enjoy themselves. They didn't have to hover around her, worried they would miss some sign of her distress.

You're happy to be here, she told herself as she whirled around and around with Jasper. *Remember that.*

Viv couldn't make herself dance for more than an hour. Too many people were watching, storing up the memory so they could tell their friends. She wondered what Regina would hear about tonight—and whether it would make her give up, or plot harder.

215

When Viv told her friends she was going to the palace, but they should enjoy the club until they were ready to leave, they insisted on coming with her.

She could tell that Jasper wasn't happy; she could sense him drawing in on himself, closing conversational doors. There were things he'd shared with Viv that he didn't want to share with her friends. Things about his family or their life-style. He gave half-answers and evasions, and when Mira spun around in the palace's golden hall, and Blue grabbed her and hugged her and her laugh pierced the quiet, Jasper muttered, "Thank god my father isn't here."

"He isn't?" Viv said.

"No, not tonight, he . . . had an appointment. He'll be gone a while. Till dawn, probably."

Layla stepped up behind them. She was looking above her at the chandeliers. "It's strange . . . this is how I used to imagine my curse starting. In a place like this. Everything magical and . . . a little dark. But Rafe's house is just a house. The front hall smells stale. Like beer and Doritos."

"Not very fairy tale," Viv said.

Layla laughed. "No, not very fairy tale at all."

Jasper led them up the wide staircase, then down the corridor where his siblings lived, until they reached a door that was bare of any markings. "This is it," Jasper said. He hesitated, then opened the door.

It was decorated similarly to Garnet's room—dark colors, red velvet armchairs, a window seat—but it had been specially prepared for Viv. There was a tall, four-poster bed with a white coverlet embroidered with forest scenes. The floor was dark wood, the fireplace unlit. A pair of satin slippers waited on the floor beside the bed, and there was a wardrobe full of gowns in every color, from plum purple to autumn gold. Stuffed animals had been arranged around the room: rabbits, foxes, squirrels, bears. The shelves were stocked with music boxes, windup songbirds, and a whole menagerie of glass animals. There were loads of books, candy boxes tied with ribbon, perfumed soaps, stationery. And, of course, there was a gilt-framed mirror on the wall. A silent one.

"I know you like animals," Jasper said. "I didn't know how else to give them to you, without . . ."

"Thanks," Viv said. "They're cute."

Freddie opened a dresser drawer and then slammed it shut. Viv went over to see what he'd found. It was filled to the top with fancy underwear. Lace and ribbons and . . . Viv wondered who had chosen it, and felt almost as embarrassed as Freddie.

It was a relief to have her friends there, but also a strain. Jasper obviously wanted to be alone with her and was just waiting for them to leave.

Finally, she told her friends that she was tired. She hugged them good-bye, thanked them for coming, promised to send invitations. Jasper saw them out, and Viv, finally alone, made a tour of the room, touching the new dresses, the tiny glass animals, the lock on the window. She picked out a few stuffed animals—a chipmunk, a rabbit, a blue jay—and placed them on her bed. It didn't cheer up the room or make it feel like home; it just reminded her of all the deaths that had led her to this place.

She opened a narrow pane of the stained-glass window and watched her friends head down the path. They kept stopping and looking back, reluctant to abandon her to her fate. She loved them for it, but wished they would just leave, the faster the better, and stop thinking about her. Stop thinking there was a choice.

Blue was holding Mira's hand. Layla was wearing Freddie's tuxedo jacket over her shoulders, and Freddie was telling some kind of story and making sword-fighting motions.

When Viv heard Jasper enter, she closed the window and turned. His smile looked tired, like her friends had worn him out.

"Finally," he said.

"You didn't like them?"

"It's not that. I've been mourning you for a week. I wasn't in the mood to share you, and I don't think they were in the mood to give you up."

"They're just worried."

"Are you worried?"

She shook her head. She didn't think *worried* was what she felt, so it wasn't really a lie. She was grateful he didn't ask whether she was happy. That would have been harder to fake.

"Are you hungry?" Jasper asked. "Can I get you anything?"

"No."

"Do you want to tell me what happened? Or do you want to try to forget it?"

"I—I'll tell you."

The bed was so high she had to climb onto it. She sat with her legs hanging over the edge, feet not touching the floor. Her hand found its way to the rabbit she'd placed there and she pulled it into her lap, playing with its ears while she spoke.

"Henley. He . . . died."

"How?" Jasper asked quietly.

"Another Huntsman found me. Older—a guy Regina knew when she was young. He dragged me into the woods, and—you can see where he cut me." She pushed the neckline of her dress down to expose the scars. "He was . . . toying with me. Making it hurt before he killed me."

She took a deep breath. "But he didn't have the chance. Henley showed up, and . . . told me to run. The last time I saw them, they were fighting for the Huntsman's knife. No one knows how it ended. There was blood, but no one's found their bodies. It's not impossible that the old Huntsman would disappear, but Henley—if he was alive, he wouldn't. That's how I know he's—that's how I know."

Jasper touched the scars on her chest. "It's over now. You don't have to be afraid anymore."

He kissed her. It was slow, soft, but it was a real kiss—a *relationship* kiss—and it was a shock to her system. She'd come here because she was heartbroken, scared, full of loathing for herself and her old dreams. But to Jasper her arrival was cause for celebration. Day one of their happy ending.

All the sick games she'd played with Henley, and this was the kiss that felt like betrayal. Now, when there was no one left to betray.

She kissed Jasper back. She didn't want to sit there and *be* kissed like a dead girl. She didn't know how long she'd need to grieve—maybe the pain would never go away. But she couldn't expect Jasper to sit by for a year consoling her while she talked about Henley. She needed to be safe, and Jasper could keep her safe. . . .

Kissing him felt like trying on a glass slipper that didn't fit. *But I can make it fit.* It would feel natural eventually.

When she said she was tired, Jasper offered to stay with her so she wouldn't wake up alone. He went to his room to change, and Viv slipped into a white nightgown that looked like it had been designed for a virgin sacrifice. Sheer, puffed sleeves. Lace neckline. Pink scars standing out against the white of her chest.

That night, Jasper slept beside her, his hand on hers, his voice the last thing she heard before she fell asleep. The first night of the rest of their lives.

CHAPTER TWENTY-NINE

VIV OPENED HER EYES, not to sunlight, but to the faint glow of the lanterns in the silver forest, filtered through the colored glass of her window. Instead of birds singing and the growl of a lawn mower, there was a vast quiet that gave the impression of an extreme emptiness.

She didn't know if it was night or morning—there was no discernible difference in the underworld—but she couldn't sleep. She pushed aside the covers and slid down from the bed. When Jasper didn't stir, she opened the door and stepped out into the corridor.

The velvety carpet was littered with post-party debris: grape leaves, silver sashes, shoes the princes had kicked off. The silence was as heavy as the darkness.

Viv took the stairs slowly, alert for the sound of footsteps or creaking doors. Did anyone other than Jasper know she was here? She hadn't met his parents, hadn't spoken a word to his brothers, and now she was living in their home. She wondered whether Jasper had even gotten permission for her to stay. If he hadn't and she was discovered, would they send her back to the surface? And would Regina be waiting for her? She'd known Viv was going to the underworld, known Viv needed a dress. She'd known . . . too much. Did Regina think that all she had to do was wait for Viv to climb up through the manhole and then . . .

Barefoot, Viv crept deeper into the palace than she'd ever been. The marble floor was cold against her skin and the candles on the chandelier had melted down to squat stubs. Only about a third of the candles were still burning. Shadows crowded the hall and her own shadow joined them. The Viv in the mirrors looked solemn, ghostlike. More flames guttered and were swallowed by wax.

She peered into dark rooms, feeling around for light switches, flipping them on if she could find them, continuing forward if she couldn't. She found a ballroom, and a dining room with a table with sixteen chairs. There were pitch-black corridors she avoided, not wanting to smack into something and wake whoever lived there. There was a narrow stone staircase that led below the palace; the air that wafted up was cold and damp—she avoided that, too. She kept going until she found herself in another wing, where the floor shifted from marble to polished wood. The doors on either side of the corridor had been left open and lamplight flowed out into the hall from a room here and there, enough for Viv to find her way, and to see that the color scheme had changed from white and gold to dusky purple and dark brown. There was a smell like an old man's cologne, and also . . . something like apple juice and gingerbread.

Viv sniffed—baby powder, too. She stopped at the door where the odor was strongest and tried the knob.

The door opened into a nursery. Infants and toddlers in cribs or in small beds with guardrails on the sides. A teenage girl sat in a rocking chair, her head pillowed on her arm. She sprang up when Viv came in, shuffled forward in slippers that had half fallen off her feet.

"What is this place?" Viv asked. "Whose kids are these?"

"You're not allowed in here. No guests in the palace."

"I'm not a guest. I live here." She wondered if it was a mistake to say it. Looking around, she saw that the nursery held nine children, ranging from one or two years old to about six.

"If you lived here, I would know," the girl said. "I've worked here my whole life."

"Your whole life?"

"Since I was one of these." The girl pointed at the nearest crib.

"Well, I live here now. I'm Jasper's princess."

The girl bit her lip. "Come into the hall. Where it's brighter."

Viv stepped out and stood in a wash of light that spilled from one of the rooms. The girl followed her.

"You do look like a Snow White princess. Maybe you are. But—how long have you been here?"

"Just since last night. Those kids . . . Who do they belong to?"

"They belong to the king."

"He has twenty-two children?"

"They're not his by blood. He brings them here after their parents give them up."

"What do you mean, *give them up*? This place is an orphanage?" Her head was spinning. Owen had said that after twenty years here people lost their minds or something; this was about the worst location for an orphanage, aside from a cannibalistic witch's candy house.

"I have to watch over them," the girl said. "I can't stay out here with you. When the king comes back . . . he won't like that you're here. You should go. I'll pretend I never saw you. Good night." The girl let herself back into the nursery, and this time she locked the door to keep Viv out.

Orphanage . . . babies . . . think, stupid, think.

The king was still gone; that was all she needed to know to keep exploring.

The door at the end of the corridor was shut, but light showed at the base. Viv took a chance and opened it.

The first thing she saw was a king-size bed with a gold canopy and gold curtains. She stepped inside, closing the door behind her. The old-man cologne smell was worse here. Notes of bergamot and . . . decay. Viv saw a sliver of bathtub through an open doorway; through another she caught a glimpse of gold. She thought of fabled dragons' hoards, of King Midas. She thought of all the Royals she knew with their family heirlooms, their jewels and gold, art and antiques, on display throughout the house or packed away in attics.

She peered into the room with the gold and saw what looked like a museum exhibit: plain white walls hung with paintings, the center of the room taken up by sculptures, every piece labeled with an artist's name.

She stood there staring, her eyes raking over the artwork, convincing herself she wasn't having a nightmare.

The paintings showed women tearing out their own hearts.

There was an unnerving Warhol-style portrait series of a grinning man with long black hair and a widow's peak: the same face ten times, in garish colors.

There was a collage—hundreds of pictures of men and women, cut from snapshots and wallet-sized photos. And hanging all around it, fastened to the wall like more dead butterflies, was an assortment of baby booties, pacifiers, necklaces, rings.

In the middle of the room were three shining metal sculptures—one gold, one silver, one bronze—their shapes distorted to show that they were art, not functional objects. All spinning wheels.

He's someone who helps people with things.

Gold . . . babies . . . deals.

The king of the underworld had a Rumpelstiltskin curse.

CHAPTER THIRTY

JASPER WAS STILL ASLEEP, lying on his back, every princely feature at ease. He didn't look the way she'd expect a troll's son to look. But that was who he was. Rumpelstiltskin curses were rare and, based on gossip Viv had heard back home—Rumpelstiltskin's latest victims, et cetera—the current and only bearer of the curse was a troll.

She turned on the light and sat down heavily on the bed. Jasper rolled over, sleepily content. "Good morning."

"What's your father's name?"

"What?"

"Your father. Now that I'm here, I'm going to meet him. What do I call him?"

Jasper's smile faded. He sat up against the headboard. "I suppose you can call him Father if you like. No one uses his name."

"Why? Is it a secret?" Viv knew she wasn't being subtle. Rumpelstiltskin took advantage of people who were desperate, locked them into horrible deals—and the only way to defeat him was to speak his true name.

When Jasper didn't respond right away, she said, "I'm tempted to go home."

"Please don't." He threw off the covers and took her hands, pleading with her again. She noticed that her silver exit mark had worn off sometime during the night. "It isn't safe for you there. That's just what your stepmother wants."

"Why didn't you tell me about your father's curse?"

"I intended to. There wasn't time. I didn't want to over-whelm you."

"You didn't want to scare me. You didn't want to give me a reason *not* to come."

"Of course I didn't want to *scare* you. I needed you to know me first, so you would trust me—and feel safe with me—despite that."

"And what if I don't, Jasper? He did something horrible to your sister; she's so scared of him that she won't leave her room. Do you make *her* feel safe? Your father has a palace staffed by people that he . . . stole. . . ."

"He didn't steal them. He performed a service and col-lected on his deals. It's no different than . . . than a prince marrying his princess after he saves her."

"This is a *deal* to you?" She went to the wardrobe to get her dress. "I don't think I can stay here."

"Viv—" He jumped up after her. "That wasn't what I meant. I want to be with you. I want to make you happy. I'm just saying that what my father does, as despicable as it may seem, is not that different from other fairy-tale arrangements. It isn't a crime."

"Jasper—people are getting sick down here. *That* is a crime."

"No. It's an unfortunate side effect of where we live. One I don't remember telling you about."

"You conveniently left that out."

"Because it doesn't affect you. Your curse renders you as immune as I am."

"You think what happens to the people who work here doesn't affect me?"

"Why would it? You're a princess. You were born luckier than everyone else. That's your fate."

"I'm lucky? My best friend is *dead*." The tears came before she could stop them.

Jasper wrapped his arms around her, pulling her against his chest. "Don't cry. Every Cursed goes through an ordeal. But you're where you're meant to be now. This is the place where you'll find happiness. Where we will, together. But you have to want it, too. I can't be the only one who wants us to be happy."

She gripped his shirt in her fists, her words muffled. "Of course I want to be happy."

"Then don't worry about what my father does in his spare time. You're safe here. I'm going to take care of you like no one has ever cared for you. I promise you that."

Jasper arranged for breakfast, lunch, and dinner to be brought to Viv in her room. For three days she didn't venture out into the palace. She was still a little uncertain about staying, but she felt that as long as her presence remained a secret—from Jasper's father, in particular—she could leave at a moment's notice. No one but Jasper, Garnet, and a handful of servants would know that she'd ever planned to stay.

During the day she heard Jasper's brothers coming and going, talking to one another about their princesses and other random topics. In the evenings there was a flurry of activity, the corridor filled with voices. *It's almost time. Hurry up! Your tie is crooked. How do I look? Brush your teeth! You'll knock her out with breath like that. Tonight's the night they'll decide to stay. Last night I swear Charlie almost said she loved me. Charleston? You wish.*

Viv and Jasper never went to the club, although Jasper promised they would go again soon. For now, Viv was content to stay hidden. They spent some evenings with Garnet. Talking, listening to music. Viv answered Garnet's questions about Beau Rivage, and Jasper apologized for not having tales of Minuet. Viv would try to drag out the conversation until Garnet was too exhausted to keep them there, and then she'd retire to her room with Jasper, where they'd lie down on her bed to talk. At some point, he would kiss her, and she'd kiss back, making an effort, like it was something everyone raved about but she just didn't like and kept trying to acquire a taste for.

True love's kiss was supposed to be natural between a cursed prince and princess. You were supposed to feel like you'd known each other a lifetime. But Viv knew what it felt like to know someone your whole life, and to love him, and it didn't feel like this.

Fate and magic were supposed to bind them together, but she felt like her heart had been cut from her chest. She tried to counter the numbness with action: she pretended she was an actress, playing the part of in-love princess; she pushed Jasper down and kissed him, held him so close she could feel the blood pulsing in his veins.

They were destined to be together. She had no future with anyone else. But every night, when his hands moved under her dress, she whispered *not yet,* as if there were a ghost in the room.

Not yet, as if there were a beast beside her.

She moved away in the enormous bed, far enough that Jasper's hand lay in the space between them, her body hot with Recognition, her heart cold. Every night she waited for something to change. She *hoped* she would want him—but she didn't.

CHAPTER THIRTY-ONE

ON VIV'S FOURTH DAY in the underworld, the king summoned her to dinner.

Jasper's eldest brother delivered the message and emphasized that it was not a request. Jasper had already gone down to dinner, as he did every night, to allay suspicion. Viv dressed hurriedly, rehearsing what she would do. She needed to make a good impression—that was the only option if she wanted to get along with the king. He had to approve of her and like her enough that giving his throne to Jasper and Viv would seem like a good idea.

She'd dreaded this meeting, but it was as inevitable as every other part of her curse. The sooner she got it out of the way, the better.

She followed Jasper's brother to the dining room. He didn't attempt to speak with her, just looked her over when she appeared in the corridor in a dark purple gown. His eyes held a trace of bitterness—a sort of, *Why should Jasper's princess be here, when the twelve princesses leave every night?*

Viv tried to remind herself how to behave. All the times she'd bitten her tongue with Regina, or laughed politely with some lecherous old club member, or faked an attraction to a prince she had no interest in—all those times were practice for this moment. The most important performance of her life.

Jasper's brother pushed open the door to the dining room and they stepped inside. Seated at a long table, dressed in suits and ascots, were Jasper and the rest of his brothers. The queen—a harshly beautiful, black-haired woman wearing a dark blue gown and a tiara—sat at the foot of the table. At the head of the table was Jasper's father, the king of the underworld.

Viv's gaze skittered over the troll quickly, nervously, so she encountered him in pieces. Thick, sharp nails. Stone-gray eyes. His limbs were long and gangly, his hands far too large for his body. Unlike the little man in the fairy tale, Jasper's father was extremely tall. His black hair was slicked back from his forehead, revealing a steep widow's peak. He wore a gold brocade suit, a powder-blue shirt, a tie with a gold-and-white diamond pattern, and gold cuff links shaped like spinning wheels. The stench of bergamot and cabbage wafted off him and killed any appetite Viv might have had.

When the troll spoke, he licked his pale lips.

"Vivian," he said, as if her name were delicious. He made it sound almost dirty.

"I prefer Viv."

"I prefer Vivian," the troll replied. "*Viv* sounds like a tart. Not the pie, dear."

Jasper stayed silent. He was going to let his father insult her. Fine. She could take a few insults.

"So," the troll said, "it seems you've been here for a while.

Sit down, dine with us. We're not savages. I'm hurt you didn't join us sooner."

"I didn't want to intrude."

"How considerate." The troll smiled. "Please, take your seat." Jasper pulled out her chair for her, and she eased into it, trying to maneuver the full-skirted purple gown into place without knocking something off the table. The queen was seated to her right. She was eyeing Viv with distaste, as if Viv were a disgusting Frog Prince ruining her meal.

The queen blinked repeatedly while she stared, twisted her napkin in her hands, and cleared her throat until the troll called out,

"What seems to be the matter down there?"

"I can't eat with her staring at me!" the queen said.

"I wasn't staring—"

"Is there something wrong with my face?" the queen demanded. "Oh! I'd forgotten! *This one's* the fairest of them all. No wonder she doesn't like what she sees!"

"I didn't—" Viv wasn't sure what she'd done to provoke this. She was stuttering out replies, trying to defend herself, but the queen talked right over her, and finally smashed a champagne flute with her palm.

"Ahhh," the queen cried, clutching her injured hand. "I'm bleeding."

"Of course you are, dear," the troll said pleasantly. "That's what happens when we break glass with our hands."

The queen moaned. "It hurts."

Jasper took Viv's hand beneath the table. "It's not your fault," he murmured. "She's not herself."

"Eat your dinner before it gets cold," the troll said. "Go

on. Yes, Vivian, my lovely queen wasn't fated for the under-world, so the magic has spoiled her mind. But you needn't be concerned that will happen to you. If you go mad, it will be for other reasons."

Only the troll ate with gusto. The princes picked at their food, as did Viv. They sat and suffered through seven courses and a trifle for dessert. All through dinner the queen kissed her bloody hand, murmuring, "There, there. It will be all right." By dessert Viv felt sick and stuffed, like the food had risen as far as her throat, but she kept spooning cream and cake into her mouth until the troll was done with his own meal. She tried to think of some way to ingratiate herself, to endear herself to this monster, but all she could do was eat and wait for someone else to break the silence, to alter the tense mood and make it easier for her to say something friendly. No one did.

When everyone was finished and the troll had tossed his napkin onto his plate, Viv pushed her chair back. "Thank you. For the lovely dinner. I—"

"Wait," the troll said. "I know you're eager to return to your quarters. But I believe my son has something special planned."

The room went quiet. The servants stopped moving. Only the crackle of the fire continued.

"Rise, both of you," the troll said, gesturing as if they were his puppets. Jasper did as he was told; Viv followed a second after.

Don't, she wanted to say. *Whatever it is, don't.* But she was afraid to challenge the troll. He held all the power here and she couldn't afford to make him her enemy.

"Viv," Jasper began.

"Call her Vivian," the troll prodded.

"Vivian," Jasper began again. "I—you mean everything to me, and—it would make me—you would make me the happiest man in the world if—"

Jasper went down on one knee.

Viv recoiled in dizzy horror. She started to tip back on her heels, unwilling to believe this was happening.

"If you would be my wife." The hinge on the ring box made a loud snapping sound as it opened. "Will you marry me?"

Dessert and all seven courses reared up. She couldn't breathe.

"Give the boy an answer," the troll said.

Her hands were trembling. Jasper stared up at her with a desperate message in his eyes. A warning not to offend his father?

She made a choking sound and Jasper slid the ring onto her finger. It was cold and heavy and felt like a lead spider clinging to her hand.

"She said *yes!*" the troll exclaimed. He threw his long arms into the air and whooped and called for drinks. Not champagne—they would drink pomegranate brandy in honor of her decision. Pomegranate—the fruit that bound Persephone to the Greek Underworld.

"I'm sorry," Jasper whispered. He wrapped his arms tightly around her and she collapsed against him in shock.

Music began to play. Something loud and celebratory. The troll grabbed one of the female servants and whirled her around. The other princes stayed mutely in their seats. The queen was nursing her fingers. Viv closed her eyes and pressed her face to Jasper's shoulder so she wouldn't have to see any of it.

* * *

Alone in her room, Viv examined the ring. It was a large, heart-shaped diamond surrounded by smaller pieces of ruby and onyx, set on a platinum band that curled around her finger like a claw. She kept turning her hand to look at it, appalled that it was there.

Jasper had gone to give Garnet the news. Viv had stayed behind so as not to be congratulated.

Restless, she pushed open the stained-glass window. Boats streamed across the silver lake. Another night of dancing for the twelve princesses. She lifted a music box from a shelf and was winding the crank, waiting for the ballerina on top to start twirling, when Jasper came in.

"Garnet sends her love," he said. "She's dying to see your ring."

"She'll see it tomorrow."

The music box played a fragile lullaby. The ballerina was turning, turning on her bright red toe shoes, her arms frozen in the air above her head.

"I would have liked to do that differently," Jasper said. "I hope you know that."

"Why did you do it at all?"

"My father . . ."

"Rules this place. I know. But this is serious. This is about us. You have to take a stand *now*, or it's always going to be like this. Your father is going to think he controls us as long as you let him."

Jasper sighed. "I know. But I think it's important to be smart about when we defy him. We were going to get engaged, anyway. There's no sense in pissing him off when the thing he wants is something we want, too."

"Jasper . . . I'm not ready to be engaged. I just—"

"You just what?"

I just lost the boy I love.

"We should do something fun," Jasper said. "Do you want to go to the club? Or we could spend a little time together. . . ."

He wrapped his arms around her, kissed her neck, and she jerked away.

"Save it for our wedding night."

Jasper sighed. "What was I supposed to do?"

"I don't know. *Anything* other than what you did? You have more power here than I do!"

"I don't have any power here!"

Viv bristled. "That wasn't your story when you were begging me to come live here. What happened to *I can protect you?*"

"This is different. My father isn't hurting you. He's just . . . eager to make it official."

"Well, I'm not!"

"Then why are you here?" Jasper snapped. "Is it just because your Huntsman's dead, and you didn't know what to do with yourself?"

Her mouth dropped open. "Don't talk to me like that."

"Answer me. I've tried to pretend that nothing ever happened between you two, despite what I've heard. But that's not working. So let's get it out in the open. He was your first love, wasn't he? You had sex with him. Go ahead, admit it. I might as well know."

She laughed, bitter disbelief staining her voice. "Oh. My god. This is unreal. You think you get to make demands? You and your messed-up father forced me into accepting a proposal, what—two hours ago? So let me be helpful now and reveal my dirty, dirty past, because *yes,* I loved Henley, and I *still* do. Even if he *is* dead—his corpse would make a better husband than you. At least he had the balls to stand up for me."

Jasper slapped her hard across the face. The pain spread in a stinging wave across her cheek, and she gaped at him, eyes watering—and then she laughed. That's what she was good at. Being cold. Walling herself off. Not letting anyone see her feel anything.

"Well," she said. "I guess you'll stand up to someone."

"I *was* going to apologize." He'd looked almost shocked after he hit her, but his face turned fierce when she mocked him. He felt the slap was justified now. She could see it in his eyes, the anger that flashed there before he stormed out of the room.

She locked the door after he left. As she lifted her hand to her burning cheek, she caught sight of herself in the mirror, and she wasn't sure who she was looking at: the fairest, or the most foolish.

The troll's words repeated in her head.

If you go mad, it will be for other reasons.

This was her happy ending.

CHAPTER THIRTY-TWO

"NO," VIV MURMURED to herself, "I'm not staying."

She waited until the eleven princes had left the palace for the night, then went to Jasper's room. She'd guessed he wouldn't be there—that he'd be sulking with Garnet, or at the club—and she was right. She was looking for invitations, and it didn't take her long to find them. Resting on a small table, on a silver tray, was a stack of black-and-silver cards. *You're Invited.* She picked up the top invitation and more words appeared. *Yes or No?*

Hell no, she thought. But that wasn't the question it was asking.

"Yes," she said. But nothing happened. Maybe these were for tomorrow night?

She searched the room, opening drawers, flipping through the books on Jasper's desk, and finally found a handful of invitations in one of his jacket pockets. She picked one up, tried again.

"Yes."

This time the card crumbled instantly, leaving a pair of silver swirls on her forearms and a pile of dust at her feet. Viv kicked the dust under Jasper's desk—or tried to—and quickly left the palace. She hurried down the path, resisting the urge to look over her shoulder, crossing her fingers that no one was watching out the window at that moment. She didn't stop until she'd merged with the thirty or so guests who were mingling outside the club.

Viv spotted a woman with purple lips and asked her, "Can I borrow your lipstick?"

"What?"

"Your lipstick. Do you have it in your purse? Can I use it?"

"I don't even know you," the woman said, drawing back.

Another guest whispered in the woman's ear—*underworld princess* was all Viv heard—and the woman gave her another look and said, "Uh—yes. All right. But I don't know why you'd want to cover up your trademark."

"Right," Viv said, taking the tube the woman offered. "Sometimes you feel like a change."

It was a weak plan—but she needed to do something to be less immediately recognizable to the guards. She ran the lipstick over her lips twice to make sure her red-as-blood feature was covered, then gave it back and made her way down the hillside, avoiding the part of the shore where the boats docked, and continuing into the silver forest. Very few guests cut through the forest—the storybook allure of the gondolas was too great, and the powdery gray soil would ruin a pair of shoes or the hem of a dress—so Viv had a few minutes to think about what she would do once she'd escaped.

If Regina was counting on Viv's stay in the underworld being brief, she might be waiting for her—in the alley, even. It wasn't as if she had other obligations. She could devote every waking moment to ending Viv's life. Maybe she'd be there with the old Huntsman. Or maybe one of her witch friends would hold Viv down while Regina crammed a poison apple down her throat. Maybe Regina would enlist some other cursed villain to help her. Or just some bored, unethical guy who wanted to sleep with her.

Viv knew she could be walking into a trap. Maybe it was stupid to leave, but she had to take that chance.

She exited the forest and came out onto one of the paths. All the guests were moving toward the lakeshore. She was the only one who was trying to leave, and she worried that alone would be suspicious. Would they even let her out? She made sure her sleeve covered the entry mark on her right arm, and stepped up to the checkpoint. She waited until one of the guards turned to her, then pushed up her left sleeve so he could see her exit mark.

She didn't say a word. She kept her head down, which meant, unfortunately, that she was looking at his sword.

"Leaving already?" the guard said. "You'll have a hard time getting up there. It's a nonstop flow of people coming in through the doors. You're likely to get shoved back a few times. Kicked in the head, depending on the door you use. Or we could avoid all that," he said as another guard grabbed her arms and twisted them behind her back, "and bring you back to the palace."

"What are you talking about?" Viv said, struggling to free herself. "I've never been to the palace. No one goes there."

241

"I'll let the king tell me if I have the wrong girl," the guard said. "I have orders that you're not to leave. The prince's fiancée needs to be protected at all costs."

The guard called for someone else to relieve him. Then he and the other guard took Viv through the silver forest, and though she kept up a barrage of lies and excuses—everything from *I'm not your prince's fiancée* to *Why are you following the troll's orders? He stole you. He's making you sick. Why are you doing what he says?*—nothing had any effect, except maybe to piss them off.

"Why would I do what you say?" the guard asked. "You're not going to kill me if I disobey you; he will."

"Isn't that reason enough to disobey him?" she asked, struggling anew. Her wrists were so raw it felt like she was about to twist the skin off.

The guard laughed. "Yeah, let me risk death so you're happy. Sorry, Princess, not gonna happen."

They dragged her past the crowd outside the nightclub and every head swiveled to watch. The woman with the purple lipstick opened her mouth, scandalized, and smacked her companion on the arm. Viv hated them all right now. She hated everyone so much.

The guard brought her to her room, shoved her in, and locked the door from the outside. "I don't recommend climbing out the window," he told her. "If you fall and break your leg, the king might cut it off."

Viv slid down against the door. She bit her purple lips in frustration, banged her fists on the floor. She'd just blown her best chance to escape.

She sat there until the silver marks disappeared from her

arms, trying to figure out how to get out of this. Pounding on the door woke her. She sprang away from it, holding her head.

"The king expects you at breakfast," a man's voice said. "Hurry up. You're making everyone wait."

The troll, his queen, and all twelve princes were already seated in the dining room. A few of the princes glanced up at her arrival. Most—including Jasper—stared at their empty plates, or at the profusion of breads and muffins piled in baskets and arranged just so. A rainbow of fruit was scattered decadently across the table, as if the troll planned to paint a still life later: plump grapes lounging on top of apples, which bumped up against bananas, pomegranates, and oranges. The servants had begun pouring the drinks: coffee for the troll, orange juice for everyone else.

"We have our meals at regular times," the troll informed her. "You're late. I suppose your escape attempt caused you to oversleep."

Viv ignored the last comment. "I didn't know the schedule."

"Breakfast at ten, lunch at one, dinner at seven," the troll said. "Perhaps now you can arrive on time."

Viv went to the empty seat beside Jasper, and put her hands on the chair back but didn't sit down.

"I want to go to Beau Rivage," she said. "To announce my engagement. Today."

She thought she detected a twitch in Jasper's posture. The troll steepled his fingers and sighed as if he was sorry to have to say this, but . . .

"I'm afraid I can't allow that, Vivian. It would be irresponsible of me to let you go. You're still in danger, and what

243

would it look like if I put my future daughter-in-law in harm's way?"

"Then send me with someone. A guard." She was certain she could lose a bodyguard in the city. "You're a father. Don't you think I should tell my dad I'm engaged?"

"I'd send him a postcard if I thought he cared. But you're a Snow White princess, so we know that's not the case. Now sit, Vivian. Eat something. We don't want you to waste away."

She took her seat finally, her nails digging into her palms. There was a lusciousness to every piece of fruit, a golden warmth to every pastry, but she looked at all of it and imagined it sticking in her throat, as repellant as a chunk of poison apple.

"I'm not opposed to a little display of affection," the troll prodded, smearing butter onto a roll. His gaze hovered on Jasper until he leaned over and kissed Viv's cheek, to which the troll replied, "Ah, young love."

The princes took tiny, decorous bites, sipped their juice in such small doses the drinks might as well have been props. No one initiated conversation but the troll, and he seemed to wield that power deliberately, using either silence or talk to ensure they were all constantly uncomfortable.

Viv tried again. "I would come right back. I came here by choice; I obviously want to be here. I just think it's important to share the news myself, in person—"

The troll held up a long finger to silence her. He took his time chewing, then said,

"Vivian. Do you know what I've learned over the years? Generosity is never rewarded. It's an old saying that if you give a man an inch, he'll take a mile, and it's true. Do you know how I know this?"

"Natural-born cynicism?"

"Because I've experienced it. So many times, I've lost count. The quickest way to lose faith in humanity—even cursed humanity—is to see them all following the same greedy patterns."

Viv thought he was done—he'd made his point—but he'd only begun. He had a captive audience and intended to make use of it, like a sea captain lecturing a prisoner he had tied to the mast.

"I believe that giving your word—such as, *Yes, I will marry you* or *Yes, I will give you my child*—has meaning. But for most people, those words are only words. They'll claim they agreed under duress, they didn't know what they were saying. But they knew *exactly* what they were saying.

"They knew that by saying *yes* to my deal, they would get what they wanted most: riches, fame, love. They could not look beyond that desire to see the consequences of their decision—which, may I remind you, were spelled out in advance. A child seemed to them—at the time the deal was struck—to be well worth the exchange.

"I usually give my clients a year with their children. I don't have to, but I am generous enough to do it. Yet, each time I return and ask for the debt to be paid, do they thank me for that bonus? No. They cry, and scream, and beg me to reconsider. Until the day I come to collect, they are enjoying my labors for free—and it seems natural to them. I am merely a tool, a magical monster who does their bidding. An ox exists to pull a plow, and I and my magic exist to enhance their lives.

"People are expected to pay for their groceries, are they not? Car repairs? Admission to your father's country club?

245

None of these things are free. And yet, something as powerful and rare as magic is supposed to be *gratis*? Because I see a mommy kissing her baby?"

He cast a look at the queen—affectionate? smug?—but her eyes were focused elsewhere.

"I remain generous, even now. I give the crying mothers a chance to cancel their debts—*if* they can guess my name. So, who is the unfair one? My only crime is being clever. It pains you that you can't outwit me. It's *unfair* not to be able to steal from a monster like me.

"You see, Vivian, I know your promises are good only as long as you don't have what you want. Once you have it, those promises disappear because you never meant to keep them."

He settled back, pleased with himself, and popped a handful of grapes in his mouth to chew while his audience reflected on the insight he'd so *generously* shared.

His little monologue had worn on Viv's patience. "So what should I call you?" she asked. "You still haven't told me your name."

The troll laughed and licked a scrap of grape skin off his tooth. "You're a brazen one." He dropped his napkin onto his plate, signaling that breakfast was over.

"One more thing," the troll said. "In case you intend to try to leave again: don't. My guards have important work to do, and if you persist in distracting them, I'll be forced to show you just how much I value your safety."

CHAPTER THIRTY-THREE

VIV'S SANCTUARY, her so-called happy ending, was closing around her like a crypt. She lay on her bed with her hands covering her face, buried deeper than any grave, and spoke to Henley's ghost. "Are you watching me? Can you see what I've done? Do you think I deserve it?"

She didn't know if she believed in ghosts or spirits. She wasn't sure if it would be more painful if Henley could witness her misery or if he were simply gone forever. Just flesh and bone in a hole she would never find. Clothes stiff with dried blood, slowly dissolving into the ground.

Viv sat up and wiped her eyes on her sleeve. How dare she cry for herself. She was alive. She was alive thanks to Henley, and no matter how awful she felt, she still had tomorrow. Still had to live through the next day, and the next, and figure out, as best she could, how to do it without him. How to get herself out of this.

From those first few days of conversation with Jasper and

Garnet, Viv knew that the lower level of the palace was where the kitchen, laundry, and dormitories were located. When the troll's slaves weren't working elsewhere, that's where they could be found. Viv wasn't sure she could count Jasper as an ally, so she went in search of Owen. He'd been willing to trade information for cigarettes; maybe the promise of freedom would tempt him to share more secrets.

It was an hour before dinner, and the upper floors were mostly deserted. The royal family had retired to their rooms, as if they needed to rebuild their stamina to endure another torturous banquet. Downstairs, the air was full of steam and the smell of onions frying. Servants hurried through the narrow corridors, dodging silver puddles and stepping around Viv. Most averted their eyes, as if they didn't want to see her. She didn't blame them. It was hard to know what the troll would deem worthy of punishment, and she supposed it was safer to go about their work as if she didn't exist.

She continued down the corridor until it dead-ended in a cell block. The cells were empty, the barred doors unlocked. The floors were black with grime and flecked with bits of straw. Straw. Viv wondered if that was the troll's little joke.

She turned to go back the way she'd come and saw Owen standing in the doorway. The boatmen didn't report for duty until ten, and he wasn't wearing his uniform yet, just a pair of gray pants that looked like they had been washed too many times and a flannel shirt with a hole in the shoulder.

"Taking the tour?" he asked.

"Looking for you, actually."

"I'd ask if you were enjoying your stay, but I heard you tried to run away last night. So I guess not."

"I just . . . wanted to share my news," Viv said.

"Congratulations."

"You can tell your friends I wasn't trying to escape. And they should let me go next time."

Owen laughed. "Yeah. Nice try."

Viv sighed. "Why are the guards such assholes?"

"What did you expect? That they'd be falling all over themselves to help you?"

"I was hoping that they were as unenthusiastic about their jobs as you are."

"No, they're the king's favorites. The ones he pampered growing up. They know they'll die early, but their lives are pretty good right now. They're not going to risk that to win your eternal gratitude. That's pretty useless down here, I'm sorry to say."

"Yeah, I'm starting to realize that."

"Uh-huh. So, you were looking for me? That must mean you need something."

"I need to know what names people have already guessed."

Owen looked at her like she'd just told him a joke that was more sick than funny. "I have no idea. I was a year old the last time I was present for that."

"Does anyone know?"

"Isn't that something you should ask your prince?"

"Yes. And I will. I was just hoping someone else would be able to tell me. Someone I can stand to talk to right now."

Owen raised his eyebrows. "I've never heard anyone call the king by a personal name. Even his kids rarely address him directly. When they do, they might call him Father, or sir. His wife usually sticks to endearments. We mostly bow our heads and do what we're told."

"All right, then . . . When's the best time to search his rooms?"

"Never. You might be his son's fiancée but a troll is still a troll. You don't want to make him angry."

"Yes, I do. I want to make him so angry that he rips his body in half—because I just spoke his true name."

Owen sighed. "I don't want it to be my fault if something happens to you."

Viv flashed her engagement ring. "*Something* is going to happen to me whether I look for his name or not."

"Princess, marriage to a guy you don't like is not the worst thing that can happen to you down here. Don't give the king an excuse to show you."

"Can you just tell me when he's likely to be out? He has a fixed schedule for meals. Is there a certain time when he leaves the underworld, to go make deals, or . . . go to strip clubs, or something?"

"I forgot about Strip Club Saturday. That'll give you a good six hours to search."

"Seriously, Owen. Is there any kind of schedule? It might take me a long time to figure this out. I need to start as soon as possible."

"He's not there during meals, but the maids do their housekeeping then. . . . They'd notice if you were snooping around. When he leaves to do a deal, he's usually gone all night, but you can't really anticipate that. You just have to notice and take advantage of it. He might announce his plans at dinner. I really don't know."

"Thank you," she said. "I mean it."

"Yeah, well, try not to get caught."

"That's the plan."

She heard an intake of breath, like he'd been about to speak but stopped himself.

"What is it?"

Owen was quiet. Finally, he said, "You look so sad. I hate that. You look like one of us. I hope you can be happy again . . . like when I first met you."

"I seemed happy then?"

"Well, maybe not the *first* time I met you. But the second time you came here, yeah. I thought so."

She tried to remember. "I don't know if I was happy. Maybe excited. I thought this place might mean something good for me. I still thought—*ugh*."

She closed her eyes, angry at herself.

"I used to think my prince would be a freak. A sicko who liked dead girls. But then I met Jasper, and he was different. He told me he could protect me and I believed him. I wanted to believe there was *someone* who could keep me safe.

"But *I* have to keep me safe. My prince already came. There's not going to be a second prince riding up on a white horse to save me from this one. Finding that name . . . that's the only control I have."

Three nights went by before the troll left the palace.

He announced his departure at dinner, spinning a jade bracelet around his finger. It had been another uncomfortable meal, everyone eating until the serving platters were empty, just to keep from drawing attention to themselves. Although,

251

since Viv had joined them, the troll seemed to have lost interest in harassing his family. Viv was the novelty, a blank canvas on which to inflict fresh emotional wounds. It didn't take her long to abandon her plan to win him over. He didn't want her to kiss up to him. He wanted to watch her squirm.

"Dreams will come true tonight," the troll said. "What do you think of that, Vivian? Am I ruining lives?"

"You mean, besides ours?"

One of Jasper's brothers started choking. He held a napkin to his mouth and coughed until he was red in the face.

The troll's mouth stretched in a thin smile. "Ah, yes. A seven-course banquet. A luxurious palace. Clothes made of the finest silk. How cruel of me."

The prince's coughing fit made Viv think of Jewel—the constant flow of flowers and gems, the handkerchief she caught them in. Homesickness hit her when she least expected it. She missed Henley constantly, and that pain was lodged in her chest, hard and tense like a fist clenched around her heart. But her longing for her old life was something she fought to push down, so she could focus on escape. She told herself not to miss her friends—she would see them again. She would find the troll's name. She would get out of here.

"I wonder what else she'll need," the troll mused. "The young lady I'm meeting tonight claims she only needs my help this once, but that's rarely the case. Hunger intensifies the more you feed it. Like in the old tale. A room full of straw spun into gold? Not good enough. Once that feat is proven possible, one room is insufficient; the king requires another. And then another. Although we're hardly dealing with straw-to-gold these days. What father would make that boast about his

252

daughter? Spinning has gone out of fashion. But greed hasn't."

The troll directed his attention to the queen. "Do you remember that worthless lout you married before me? Do you remember how important his dreams were to you?"

"I wish Malcolm could dine with us," the queen said.

"My dear queen stumbled upon her 'madly ever after' in a roundabout way. I won't get into the details of our bargain—they're about as interesting as her first husband—but it started with a simple request and quickly escalated. In the end she had nothing to offer but her firstborn."

Viv's gaze flitted to Jasper's eldest brother.

"Oh, no," the troll said. "The princes you see at this table are my sons. That unfortunate savage is someone I own, not someone I would ever share a table with. He's useful in his way, but his bloodstained clothes would ruin our appetites. Well, not my queen's. The atrocities he commits don't faze her. She's come a long way since she first came crying to my bed."

"Do you mind if I vomit?" Viv said.

"Vivian." The troll clicked his tongue disapprovingly. "So squeamish. Do you know why I had to break my queen's firstborn son? Why I kept him in my dungeon for the first few years of his life, taught him that his only respite would come if he pleased me, if he did exactly as I commanded? Pay attention. This should be edifying for you. You see, I'm a jealous man. What's mine is mine, and what's mine I keep forever. Perhaps you've noticed. I couldn't have my wife favoring her firstborn son over the children we would have together. I couldn't have her gazing at him adoringly, remembering the boy's father, using those memories to keep her hope alive."

Viv could see where this was going.

"It's very juvenile and impolite to cling to the past. There's no sense in longing for a life you chose to leave. Once you've made a commitment, you try to make it work. If you can't try—like an adult, not a spoiled child—I'll be forced to help you. It's in my power to break people. You may think it's in your power, too, but I assure you, that's a delusion on your part.

"Now." The troll treated the table to a toothy grin. "Who's ready for dessert?"

Viv responded to the troll's threats with a blank stare. She knew he liked upsetting her, and she wasn't going to give him evidence that he had.

Instead, she thought of names, running through them like a song in her head. All the names she could guess.

After dinner there were preparations for the troll's departure—more cologne, a new obnoxious suit. Viv slipped inside the deserted dining room, sat with her back against the wall just to the left of the door, and listened. The dining room was near the troll's chambers; he'd have to pass by it to leave. And once he had, she'd wait a few minutes more, and then slip down the corridor to his rooms. If she was lucky, no one would even notice.

The click of his shoes preceded him. Then a cloud of scent—that special blend of bergamot and rancid troll—floated under the door. He lingered there—adjusting his tie? Grooming his hairline with a just-licked finger?—and called for a servant to clean up a scuff he'd seen on the floor. Then he left, humming as he went. Viv waited until the squeaking of the cleanup was over, before slipping out into the corridor.

First stop: the troll's bedroom.

* * *

The lights were on. Everything was neat: most of the belongings put away in closets or drawers, only the furniture and a few pieces of art on display. Viv's hope was that the troll's name was hidden somewhere in his lair, that he wouldn't have been able to resist writing it down. Scribbled onto the wall behind a dresser, carved into the wood of a table, or finger-painted into the steam on the bathroom mirror, only to reveal itself when the glass fogged up. Or maybe he had a notebook where, camouflaged by to-do lists and daily journal entries, he practiced his autograph. A man that full of himself had to have left his name somewhere.

If it was anywhere in this room, Viv would find it.

She searched under his mattress—feeling around for a scrap of paper, a secret journal—and after a few minutes, deciding she was going about this the wrong way, she decided to strip the bed entirely and push the mattress onto the floor. If she left a single piece of the room unexamined it would keep her up at night, imagining the name there, hidden in the one place she hadn't looked.

It took a lot of heaving and straining, but eventually she shoved the mattress off the bed and was able to check it for the faintest trace of the troll's handwriting. She examined the box spring; wriggled under the bed—glad for once that she was small enough to fit there—and felt around for a fold of paper wedged into the frame. Next time she would bring a flashlight. Assuming they had flashlights in the underworld.

She crawled out, dust-covered and sweating, and pawed through the sheets, in case they'd been embroidered with a name. Even a monogram would give her something to go on.

She opened all the drawers and sorted through the objects inside—carefully, because she wanted to put them back in the right places. The maids might rearrange his pillows, but she figured the troll would be pissed if he thought anyone had been messing with his stuff. He had so much jewelry—cheap and expensive, much of it the kind that came with sentimental value: engagement rings, lockets, heirloom tiaras. Pieces his victims had traded away before the troll upped his demands. More wallet-sized photos—ones that hadn't made it into the collage in his gallery. A stash of fountain pens, none engraved with a name. A few journals where the troll recorded his deals: his victims, what they wanted, the high and then higher prices they paid, plus musings in his typical self-congratulatory fashion. Viv skimmed the troll's nauseating observations in the hope that she'd stumble across a *Luckily she didn't guess my true name, Grimbletoes!* But there was nothing like that.

She kept checking the clock, careful not to overstay. The troll wasn't due back until morning—or so he'd said—but she didn't want to cut it that close. Three hours had passed. She'd searched the bed and still needed to put it back together. She'd gone through all the drawers, and was midway through a third journal, pinching herself to keep her eyes from glazing over, when the door opened behind her. She turned—

It was Jasper. He shut the door behind him. Then his eyes flicked to the bed. "How in the world were you going to explain that?"

"You've picked an unfortunate time to start talking to me again." She resumed skimming the journal. "I'm busy searching for the key to your father's destruction."

"Yes, I see that. And you're the one who's been avoiding me."

"I guess I didn't feel like getting hit in the face again. For being such a slut."

"I didn't say you were—I never said that."

"No, you just made it very clear that it was wrong of me to have a boyfriend before you."

"That's not—" He sighed and came over. "What are you looking at?"

"*The Rumpelstiltskin Diaries*. Your father keeps track of the people he's scammed. I thought his name might be in here somewhere. So far, I haven't found anything."

"You won't. Do you think you're the first who's tried?"

"Do you know something? Names that have already been guessed? Has he ever told you? Do you know his name?"

Jasper laughed bitterly. "Why would he tell me? Don't I have plenty of motivation to use it against him?"

"I don't know. You guys seem pretty tight, despite the sadistic shit he's put you through. He threatened me on your behalf tonight. That must have made you feel loved."

"I didn't ask him to do that. I don't want him to threaten you."

"And yet, he seemed to know the crux of our problems."

"I didn't go to him. I would never do that. But he knows everything that happens here. The servants are his eyes and ears—the ones who want his favor, anyway. Anyone could have heard us arguing, or noticed that we weren't together. Anyone could have told him about your past. It's hardly a secret."

"Hmm," Viv said disinterestedly.

257

"Would you put that book down for a minute and listen to me?"

"Fine, but help me fix this bed while you talk."

Viv set down journal number three. Together they wrestled the mattress back into place.

"I want to apologize," Jasper said. "I would have done it sooner but I didn't think you wanted to speak to me."

"I didn't."

"I never should have hit you. I'm not trying to excuse what I did, but I was jealous. Hideously jealous from the moment I found out about your relationship with your Huntsman. I hated thinking that you might still be in love with him. That you might want him more than you wanted me. I was—I was happy when you told me he was dead. I'm sorry, but I was. It meant I didn't have to compete with him anymore. And then, when you said he was better than me, because he'd protected you—I snapped. I'm sorry. I promise you, if you give me another chance, I'll never lay a finger on you without your permission."

The worst thing that's ever happened to me makes you happy.

It hurt Viv worse than the slap. If you cared about someone, weren't you supposed to hurt when they hurt? If Jasper loved her at all, it was a selfish love, more about himself and what he wanted than it was about her.

Was that the way she'd loved Henley? She bit her lip, sorry all over again for everything she could never take back.

"So, next time, you'll ask first before you slap me in the face?"

"If you like."

She glanced up at him, alarmed.

"I'm joking! Sorry. It's just—it's so tense with you. I thought a joke would help."

"Your sister's not the only one whose jokes are bad. Maybe you should stop trying."

"Maybe. Will you forgive me?"

"What choice do I have? I need your help. You know I do. And I don't want your father locking me in a cell when I forget to bat my eyelashes at you."

They took a moment to fight with the sheets. Neither one of them was skilled at making a bed. "I'll call one of the maids," Jasper said.

"No. I don't want them to know we were in here."

It took them twenty minutes to get the bed looking good enough to pass the troll's inspection. Viv took stock of the room. There was still the closet, the bathroom, the gallery to go through. More journals. And that was just the bedroom suite.

"Do you think I have time to check the bathroom?" Viv asked. "I want to fog up the mirrors and see if he ever wrote his name there."

"If you insist on doing that, better to do it right after he's left. The last thing we want is him coming in and wondering why his bathroom is steamed up. Plus, we wouldn't hear him come in."

"We? So you'll help me find his name?"

"I'd rather you gave up on this idea. My father's not stupid enough to have written his name on a wall or a mirror. If he were, someone would have found it a long time ago. My mother spent years searching before she changed."

"How did your mother end up here, anyway? What was

your father talking about, about her firstborn being covered in blood?"

Jasper sighed. "Malcolm. He's . . . the child she was supposed to give up when she couldn't guess my father's name. But she couldn't part with him. So she offered to stay in the underworld—she thought she could keep Malcolm, in a sense. It didn't work out as she'd intended. My father decided to marry her, so she assumed Malcolm would be raised as a prince. He was locked up like an animal. And then my father trained him to be the executioner. The only time my mother gets to see him now is when someone's sentenced to be killed."

"God . . . your father's such a monster. We have to stop him."

"We can't. Think of how many names there are in the world. How many possibilities."

"But . . . people with Rumpelstiltskin curses reveal their names. That's how the curse gets broken."

"Some of them do. In the past, supposedly, there were trolls who'd get drunk at the club, start dancing, and shout out their names. They couldn't help themselves. But my father doesn't lose control. Everything he does is calculated. He's very fond of himself and his continued existence."

"I still have to keep looking. There's no other option, Jasper. There's no other way to be free of him. You let me believe that it wouldn't be like this."

"I—hoped," he said, bowing his head. "I may have been a little too optimistic. I still think he'd ease off if you acted happier to be here. Right now he doesn't trust you. He wants you here, and he knows I want you here, and he thinks you want to leave. Maybe if he thought you were more amenable to staying . . ."

"He doesn't trust anyone. You told me that from the start. *That* I should have paid more attention to. He won't let any of you leave the underworld because he's afraid you won't come back. It's not just me he doesn't trust. If his own family hasn't been able to win him over, how am I supposed to?"

"I understand you want to do this. You think it's worth it. But I want to keep you safe. And antagonizing my father by searching for his name . . . that goes against what I'm trying to do to protect you."

"I let fear dictate everything I did before, and it didn't make me safe. It just led to another trap. And this one's harder to get out of."

"Life with me is a trap?"

"Jasper . . . your life is a trap. Me being here doesn't negate that. It just means we're in the trap together. If you want to look at me instead of the cage, and convince yourself you're happy, that's your business. But I can't do it. I won't do it. Not anymore."

CHAPTER THIRTY-FOUR

NAMES BECAME HER ESCAPE. Viv found herself longing for the troll's absence like it was a favorite holiday. But since he only left to do deals, getting her wish came with a catch. For her, it was an opportunity to search the troll's chambers. For others, it was one step closer to losing something they could never get back.

When she couldn't search the troll's rooms, she flipped through books and copied names into a notebook. She didn't read for content, but stayed alert for capital letters: people, places. And the more she searched, the more hopeless she felt. In the beginning the hunt had given her a sense of purpose, a way to gain power over her situation. But as the scope of the project began to reveal itself, it started to seem as impossible as finding one specific grain of sand on a beach that stretched for miles. She could dig and dig, but the truth would likely stay buried.

If you go mad, it will be for other reasons.

Had that hastened the queen's split with reality? The search she realized was futile, the trap she realized was permanent? Was it a blessing to be broken inside, divorced from what went on around you? Was that the only escape Viv would ever have?

The troll could be called Tom or Horace or Yoda or Gravyface. Maybe he was Rumpelstiltskin2x16&#5. Maybe his name was a song or a dirty limerick. She wouldn't know until she guessed something and he told her whether or not she was wrong.

Maybe life would be easier if she could just accept her fate, learn to ignore the troll's taunts, and take comfort in Jasper's arms. But she couldn't. She felt like she was giving in to his dreams, not her own. And though the heat of Recognition still burned on her skin when he held her, it was an empty warmth.

She thought of Henley when Jasper lay in bed beside her. She thought of all the times she'd refused to believe they could have anything more than what their curse dictated because she was afraid to hope. She'd been like Jasper then, unwilling to try. What was the point? She'd thought she could never, ever have what she wanted. Never be happy. All she'd hoped for, in the end, was to be safe.

She'd let herself be carried along, swept from one danger to the next, as helpless as a princess who was already dead.

It was unfair of her to resent Jasper for doing the same thing, but she couldn't help it. She barely felt capable of accomplishing this task, and knowing she had to do it alone made it that much harder.

A week had passed since Jasper's apology in the troll's

bedroom. In that time, she'd managed to sneak into the troll's library once, when he was off collecting a second token and performing a second favor for the girl with the jade bracelet. Viv had pulled old books down from the shelves, checked for bookplates signed in the troll's spidery handwriting, or for words that had been underlined, even faintly. The desire to reveal his name, his illicit secret, had to be so great . . . surely he would have written his name somewhere, or drawn a thin pencil line around it when he saw it in a book. Wouldn't he feel safe doing that? Underlining his true name in one book out of hundreds was the Rumpelstiltskin equivalent of hiding a needle in a haystack. Wouldn't he feel safe enough to take that small risk?

Viv intended to go through every book in the library, tracing her fingertip over the lines as she read so her attention wouldn't drift.

When the task seemed impossible, she told herself that he would do the work for her. She had to believe that, because the other option was to give up and drown herself in the silver lake.

She didn't talk to Jasper about her efforts. Not anymore. He knew she was still searching, but talking about it made him anxious. They'd argue and he'd try to convince her how stupid she was being. Sometimes, though, those arguments were preferable to his attempts to reconcile.

Tonight he lay next to her while she stretched out on her stomach and copied names from a volume of Shakespeare. Shakespeare, at least, was easy: the characters' names were listed at the beginning of each play.

"You might enjoy that more if you read it," Jasper said, running his fingers along the arch of her back.

"I have read some of them."

"Did you like them?"

"Not any more than I do now."

His hand came to rest on her märchen mark. She felt the warmth of his palm against that symbol of their destiny, and then the heat of Recognition slipped down along her legs, and up her chest.

"Viv," he said. "Why don't you take a break for a while? You're going to burn out if that's all you ever do."

"Think how much faster this would be if two people were working on it."

"We should both waste our time?"

She sighed and put down her pen. "You're welcome to go back to your room."

"I don't want to go to my room. I want to spend some time with my princess. Appreciate her a little."

"Feel her up a little."

"Do you have to be so crude?"

"If I let you, would it matter how crude I was being?"

"I just want to know how long things are going to stay like this. We were close when you first came here."

Viv didn't say anything. Jasper was insecure, and vain in some ways, and the last thing she needed to tell him was: *That was only real for you.*

Their uneasy alliance was still vulnerable. He was a lousy ally, but having him on her side was better than having no one at all.

"I miss my friends," she said. "It's lonely down here."

"I miss *you*," he said, scooting closer. He laid his head down on her book. It reminded her of the times the animals in her room would sit smack in the middle of her textbook until she paid attention to them. It annoyed her and made her sad all at once.

"Jasper, I'm trying to work."

"How do you expect to enjoy yourself down here if you never try? You make it out to be this endless suffering, and it doesn't have to be. We have each other. And you liked being with me at first."

She pressed her lips together. How long could she keep this up?

He took her silence as indecision. "We don't have to talk about the past. But I know this isn't new for you. Why can't you give me a chance?"

"I hope you're not talking about what I think you're talking about."

"I'm just saying, what is there to be afraid of? What are you waiting for? I could understand if you hadn't before, and you were scared, but . . ."

"Shouldn't you be scared, then?" They'd never talked about his personal life. She'd gotten the impression he'd never had a girlfriend, but that didn't mean nothing had ever happened.

"I don't think either of us should be scared. I'm not going to hurt you. I'm not . . . some ruffian, who—"

"Don't," she said.

He sat up. "Unless that's what you like. Someone who's fated to cut your heart from your chest. Is it a bad-boy thing? Is that what you find attractive?"

"Open this door or don't, Jasper. If you want to know, fine. If you don't, then shut up."

He was quiet, his nail scratching against his signet ring.

Brooding. She tensed, waiting for his decision. She knew that no matter what he chose, once she told him, he would change his mind, and she would be the one to pay for it. He claimed he didn't go running to his father, but she wasn't sure she believed him.

"I want to see my friends," she said again. "It's been two weeks since I came here. I promised we'd send invitations. They're going to think I forgot about them—or they're going to think you hate them."

"Tell me where they can be reached. I'll send them invitations."

"You'll do it tonight?"

"Tomorrow. It's already late."

He lay down next to her again, and pulled her to him, away from her book. Her elbow bent against his side and she laid her head on his shoulder. Otherwise he would kiss her. He'd made an effort to mend things between them, and now she was supposed to do the same. With a kiss, a worthless kiss that meant nothing. But it was a nothingness that would go on, and on.

Viv felt like she'd run out of smiles, and she didn't have enough breath in her chest to fake all the lovely sighs that would keep him from turning on her. The paranoia she'd lived with in Beau Rivage had never left her. She wasn't safe in the underworld; she wasn't even safe from that.

Jasper turned off the light, and once it was dark, he whispered, "Give me a chance to be what he wasn't."

"You already are."

Alive, she thought, as he held her tighter, as if she'd finally told him what he needed to hear. She let him believe what he wanted.

"We'll see your friends tomorrow night. We'll dance. It will be like it was in the beginning. I can hire a fairy to make you a dress. Something no one's ever seen before. Would you like that?"

"Mm-hmm."

In the darkness, as he held her, all she could think about was her dead boyfriend.

CHAPTER THIRTY-FIVE

INVITATIONS WERE SENT to Jewel, Luxe, Freddie, Layla, Mira, Blue, and even Jack Tran.

Jasper hired a fairy to create Viv's dress—a living embodiment of spring, fragrant with blooming flowers and pink clouds of cherry blossom. And though he said they should wait for her friends at the club, Viv insisted on waiting at the checkpoint.

They went down early, at the same time that Jasper's brothers went to meet the twelve princesses—an hour before the rest of the underworld doors opened.

Viv knew the brothers' names now—she'd made it her business to learn everyone's name—but their personalities were less distinct. It was that way with most multi-sibling curses. There might be one sibling who was better known, and who functioned like the front man of a band—but the rest got grouped together.

She watched as the first door opened—the one that joined the underworld with the Twelve Dancing Princesses' bedroom.

A rectangle of light formed in the darkness, and then the first sister appeared in silhouette. One by one the princesses descended the staircase—gracefully, taking beauty pageant steps—and then they hurried to the shore to greet their princes. Lindy and Jet embraced. Calder grabbed Musette and spun her around, her satin slippers lifting off the ground, her laugh all sweetness and light. Calypso, the youngest sister, had brought a present for her prince: a book they proceeded to look through together. Sard and Charleston didn't even say hello; they went straight to making out.

They all lit up like a holiday. There were no tears, no arguments. Even Minuet looked happy to be in the under-world, smiling in wonder at the sparkle of the trees. It was an enchanting place, all lit up by lanterns, with the forest whispering music and the promise of good things in the air. They all looked so sure that nothing could go wrong. Nothing could change the way they felt right now.

Viv watched them board the boats and begin the journey across, fragments of talk and laughter carrying over to where she waited with Jasper. Soon the rest of the doors would open and more Cursed would enter the underworld, bringing the mood up just as the princesses started on their downward spirals.

Viv bounced on her heels—eager, edgy. The first flowers on her dress were wilting, and others were sprouting to take their place. The faint halo of mist that had surrounded her skirt was burning away as the fresh green of her dress turned golden, like grass singed by the summer sun.

"You really won't wait at the club?" Jasper said. "It'll be another hour, at least."

"I don't care. I want to see them as soon as they get here."

When the rest of the doors opened and the guests began streaming down, Viv stood on tiptoe to try to see past the crowd.

"Do you want a step stool?" Jasper asked.

"Very funny."

After twenty minutes, Jasper said, "I don't want to stand here all night."

"It won't be all night."

Viv waited there for another hour, checking every face, desperate for a glimpse of someone familiar. If not one of her friends, then *someone* she recognized. A classmate, a member from Seven Oaks, someone she'd met at a party. But there was no one. All the guests seemed to be coming from somewhere other than Beau Rivage.

"Let's go see if there's something wrong with the door," Viv said. "If they're having trouble getting through."

"The guards won't let me take you up there."

"The guards won't *let you*? You're the prince."

"You know whose orders they follow."

"I'm going up there," Viv said.

She stepped around the checkpoint and as she moved past it, one of the guards grabbed her arm and yanked her back. "Testing my reflexes or my resolve?" he asked.

"Let *go* of me. I'm Jasper's princess. I'm not some uninvited guest you can manhandle."

"Princess, we don't manhandle uninvited guests, we cut their heads off."

"Jasper," she said. "Tell them—"

"Bring her to the shore," Jasper said. "We'll go to the club. We're done waiting here."

The guard kept a tight grip on her arm and marched her to the lake. Jasper signaled to a boatman whose gondola was already occupied and the boatman ordered his passengers out. Jasper stepped into the gondola then, gracefully, so that it barely rocked, and held out his hand to Viv. The guard released her and she whipped around, searching the distance for Blue's hair or Jewel's falling gems.

"Come on, Viv."

"Tell my friends—when you see them, tell them to go right to the front. I don't want them waiting in line. All right? You saw them before. You'll tell them."

The guard gave a mock bow. "Sounds easy enough."

"Make sure you tell them. If I find out they were waiting in line for an hour . . ."

"He'll tell them, Viv. Stop worrying. Let's enjoy ourselves until then."

At the club she paced around with a drink in her hand. Her dress was doing all sorts of amazing things—going from summer to autumn to winter and then back to spring again—but she kept her eyes on the door. She only noticed her dress when a guest remarked on it, or Jasper told her how beautiful she looked in a gown of snowdrifts.

"Can we dance a little?" Jasper said. "Maybe they were busy tonight. Your friends are in a band together, aren't they? Maybe they had to perform."

"Some of them would have come. Mira. Layla. Jack Tran."

"I don't know what to say, Viv. Maybe they were tired. Maybe they're not as good friends as you think they are."

"You promised you'd invite them!"

"I did invite them!"

"If you don't want them here, why don't you just tell me? Why are you lying?"

Guests were beginning to gather around them, sipping cocktails, pushing closer so they could hear every word. Jasper took her by the arm the way the guard had—as if he were escorting her, but squeezing hard enough that she knew he was serious—and dragged her out of the club. He didn't even let her stop on the hillside to squint across the lake. He just hauled her toward the palace.

"If you want to fight with me," he said under his breath, "don't do it in public."

"Don't lie to me and I won't have to!"

"I didn't lie to you. I can't help it if your friends chose to come late, or to do something else tonight. If you don't believe I sent the invitations, I'll send them again. Now. In front of you."

Viv waited in the palace's front hall while Jasper summoned a horseman, put a stack of invitations and a list of addresses into his hand, and paid him off with a fistful of gold branches. Then they returned to the club. Viv circled the room, looking for her friends. Crocuses sprouted on her dress and cherry blossoms fell from her skirt. Green grass and cattails smothered the flowers until they, too, were buried under a tapestry of red and gold leaves. Eventually a soft layer of snow blanketed her dress and melted on her shoes as she paced.

Season flowed into season, and Jasper sighed, and the night passed. Viv stayed until the club had emptied out completely. Even the Twelve Dancing Princesses were gone.

Debris littered the floor; the servants were sweeping up when she left. Her friends never came. Not even Jack Tran, who she'd thought would show just to steal some silver branches.

"I'll send more invitations tomorrow, all right?" Jasper said. "I'm exhausted. What a waste of a night."

"I want to know what happened."

"So do I. But I don't think we're going to. Not until they show up and tell you."

Jasper sent new invitations every afternoon. And every evening, before the doors to the surface opened, Viv went and sat on a rocky hill overlooking the lake. She stayed there for hours, eyeing each new group of guests, searching for a face she recognized, and never seeing one.

Her friends had been worried about her; she knew they would come if they could. So why hadn't they?

CHAPTER THIRTY-SIX

THE THEME TONIGHT WAS TREASURE, and the dance floor glittered like a dragon's hoard. Dresses dribbled down bodies like liquid metal. Royals came wearing their heirloom jewelry: pearls that had been cried by their ancestors, gold chains that had been spun from straw. Bright silks blazed against the black backdrop: ruby and sapphire, bronze and silver, emerald and amethyst.

Viv's only piece of jewelry was her engagement ring. Her treasure was the notebook she carried in her black clutch purse: her storehouse of names. Jasper had stopped accompanying her to the club because she refused to dance, and she spent the nights having conversations like:

I don't think we've met. I'm Viv. Right—the Snow White princess. And you are? Great name. I'll remember that one.

After an hour of introductions Viv went to the VIP ladies' room—which was usually empty because it was reserved for her and the twelve princesses—and sat down on the fainting couch and added the names to her notebook. She did that every hour. It gave her something to think about besides how alone she was.

On her third trip to the ladies' room, she went to the mirror and studied her reflection—that dark-eyed, cold girl who'd grown darker and colder in the underworld. She was still watching herself when she heard a male voice say her name.

She jumped, startled. The mirror spanned the length of the wall, and yet she didn't see any reflection but her own. The stalls were open, empty. She glanced up, looking for a speaker or an intercom or something.

"Jasper?" she said.

And then . . . she looked at her reflection again. And stumbled backward, away from it.

It had been weeks since a mirror had talked to her. She'd left the magic mirror up *there*, on the surface. And though the magic mirror could pull other mirrors into its network, she hadn't thought it could reach her in the underworld. The thought of being watched by that thing for the rest of her life . . .

"Do I sound like that piece of shit?"

"Wh-what?" The voice was right next to her, and now she was panicking, because—she shouldn't be hearing his voice. Her hands were trembling and her clutch clattered to the floor. "I'm finally going crazy. . . ."

She felt strong arms wrap around her, a broad chest pressed to hers, a safety she hadn't felt in so long. And then that mouth—his mouth—lips she would know anywhere. She closed her eyes so her mind wouldn't feel so breakable, and gave in to the sensation she'd longed to feel.

With her eyes closed, lost in darkness, he was here beneath her hands. She found his face, his shoulders; threaded her fingers into his hair and pulled so he'd kiss her harder, until she found herself on the fainting couch, with the taste of Henley in her mouth.

"Are you a ghost?" she whispered. "Or am I losing it?"

"Are there cameras in here?"

"What?"

"Security cameras. Are there—?"

"Oh my god." Delusions didn't ask practical questions. Neither did ghosts. She started crying before he pulled off the invisibility cloak—a gray cape that appeared just as he came into view. Henley. He was here.

CHAPTER THIRTY-SEVEN

SHE PULLED AWAY SO SHE COULD LOOK at him. Held his face in her hands and just absorbed him for a moment. He was someone different now that she'd almost lost him: miraculous. She wanted to say a million things. She wanted to kiss him again; she wanted to work herself back into that space where no words were necessary. It just felt . . . so *powerful,* being with him again, when she'd thought he was gone forever. She could sense it was that way for him, too. He looked at her with the same awe and longing she felt coursing through her own body.

He was wearing a tuxedo. He almost never dressed like that.

"How did you—? What happened?" she asked. "I thought you were—"

"I was afraid you'd push me away. That you'd replaced me already."

"No, never."

"Never?"

"Never."

"That doesn't sound like you." His hands were gentle on her face. He watched her like every flick of her eyes, every breath, every quiver of her throat, was something he wanted to remember.

"It should sound like me," she said, watching him just as carefully. "That's who I am. That's how I feel."

He smiled, almost surprised, and it was such a soft look on him. So different from the pain and frustration she usually provoked. His surprise nearly broke her heart. The month they'd been apart felt like a year. Now, she felt as distant from the Viv who'd stopped trusting him as she'd once felt from the Viv who'd trusted him implicitly.

"Everyone thought you were dead," she said. "What happened? Where were you?"

"I was at the farmhouse. With Jack and Elliot."

"You . . . no." She shook her head. "That's impossible. Unless Jack Tran is a sadistic asshole."

"Will you let me explain?" he asked quietly.

"Because I called him. I called him *every day.* He told me no one knew where you were. I needed to know you were okay, and he—" Her anger broke like a wave. Tears ran down her face and she couldn't speak.

Finally, she choked out, "I thought I killed you. I thought you died because of me."

"I'm so sorry, Viv."

She crawled into his lap and held on to him. She needed to feel his heartbeat, his breathing, the vibration in his chest as he spoke. He kept his arms around her and told her what had happened, his voice low and reluctant, like it wasn't a story he wanted to tell.

"I killed him—I guess you know that now. Jack helped me dispose of the body. We went to the farmhouse and . . . the dogs . . . took care of the evidence. I stayed there because I didn't want anyone to know what had happened. Whether I was dead or alive. I didn't want Regina to be sure. I thought if she knew, she'd sic the police on me and that would be the end of us. I'd be locked up, you'd marry your prince, and I'd never know if we could make this work. If we were still . . . if you even wanted to."

"You don't think I would've waited for you?"

"Viv . . . you didn't even want to be with me. We were as good as broken up. You were all about your prince."

"I'm sorry," she said. "I was stupid. I . . ."

"You were scared. I don't think I knew *how* scared until I saw you with the Huntsman that day."

The old Huntsman was dead. She'd been so thrilled to see Henley that she hadn't thought about what else his presence meant: the man who had tried to kill her would never hurt her again.

"Thank you," she whispered. "Thank you."

"Don't thank me. I just keep thinking, if I hadn't been there . . . I thought I'd convinced your stepmom to leave him out of it. And then I got your message, and I came over and I saw his truck smashed into your car, and I had this pain in my chest like I was going to have a heart attack. I've never been more scared in my life. It was like my mind went blank, and I was just following your trail through the woods, and then when I saw you I was so relieved . . . and so full of hate for him. I didn't know if I could kill him until I saw you, and then I knew."

He was trembling and she put her arms around his neck and hugged him as if to say: *I'm here. We're alive.* His hand slid up her back, pressing her closer. It felt so good to be with him. *This* was what it was supposed to feel like.

"Every time I heard Jack on the phone with you I felt like shit. But I needed him to lie. I needed there to be doubt. I thought that if you believed I was dead, Regina might believe it, too. I was still trying to decide how to tell you when Jack found out you'd gone to the underworld. No one knew when you were coming back. I thought that meant you'd made your decision. And—"

A burst of music broke up their embrace as the door opened and all twelve princesses swept in. Henley threw on his cloak and Viv fell over onto the fainting couch, her heart racing, hoping none of them had seen him. Fortunately, the princesses had other things on their minds. They'd been dancing and drinking for hours; they were sweaty, tearstained, and desperate to pee. In five seconds the stalls were full, the mirror reflected a row of primping princesses, and Waltz, Tango, and Foxtrot—holding hands like a chain of paper dolls—stepped up to Viv and said:

"You're on our couch."

"Yeah, it belongs—"

"To us."

Viv got up. "Take it," she said. They could have their couch. She just wanted them to hurry up and leave before one of the sisters bumped into Henley. The bathroom was much more crowded when you added twelve princesses.

Flush. Flush. Flush. Flush. Flush.

Five princesses emerged from the stalls and five more replaced them. The girls at the sinks checked their makeup, their teeth, their cleavage, while they washed their hands. Viv stood in the corner, trying to stay out of their way.

"What are you doing in here?" Calypso asked her.

"Um—taking a break." Viv realized how weird it must seem to be standing in the bathroom, just kind of . . . hanging out.

"Were you crying?"

"She looks like she was crying."

"Are you depressed? I think you can get depressed from not being in sunlight."

"If you're depressed," Rumba said, "you should ask Jasper to get you some Xanax."

"Or chocolate!"

"Or sex."

The girls started laughing. Charleston clapped her hands over Calypso's ears—she was already giggling with the rest of them. They went on like that until Calypso's feet started tapping. When she twirled, the other girls groaned and began to move, as if dancing was an itch they had to scratch, a pain that needed to be soothed.

"Break time's over," Charleston said. "Come on, girls."

The sisters danced out in a halfhearted conga line. Charleston was the last one to leave. She stood in the doorway, slippers tracing a box step, her eyes roving over the empty spaces in the room.

"Silva," she finally said. "Door closes at four. Don't be left behind."

She let those words sink in—then minced out onto the dance floor.

Viv spun, searching for Henley, only letting out her breath when she saw that swirl of gray cloak and then—him. Tall and striking in his black tuxedo. His face more troubled than before.

"She knows . . . you're here?" Viv said.

Wordlessly, Henley pushed down the collar of his shirt so it dipped to the base of his throat, and showed the single black hash mark that had been tattooed there.

"No . . ." Viv choked on the word, and her protests were lost as a sob filled her throat.

"I had to. I had to see you."

"*Why*? Why did you have to?"

He was holding her now, trying to calm her down. "No one could get to you. None of the people you invited could enter the underworld. There was some kind of magic keeping them out. Keeping me out, too—I tried to get through; I couldn't. And then even the invitations stopped. I knew something was wrong. They were isolating you, and I didn't know why they would do that—unless you didn't want to be here. I couldn't abandon you.

"Jack told me that if I wanted to do something crazy, there was a way. There's one door that can't be blocked by magic: the door the Twelve Dancing Princesses use. Anyone who volunteers to break the curse has to be able to follow them to the underworld. So I volunteered."

Viv leaned her head against his chest and closed her eyes. This was a nightmare. He couldn't come back to her, couldn't be *alive* just so she could lose him three days later.

"I don't want you to worry about me. I didn't come here to break the curse—I came to get you out of here. I want you to take my cloak—"

"No."

"I want you to take my cloak—"

Henley was touching her hand, running his fingers along her wrist, and then he stopped. "Is that an engagement ring?"

She'd forgotten she was wearing it. "It doesn't mean anything."

"It means you're engaged."

"It doesn't mean anything to *me*! It's like an arranged marriage. That I didn't agree to. You don't know what it's like here. . . ."

"He's forcing you to wear it?"

"Not Jasper. His father."

"You're engaged to his father?"

"God, no!" Viv shuddered at the thought. "No, his father makes all the decisions. He decided he wanted Jasper and me to be engaged—then he made it happen. I don't want to marry Jasper. I don't even want to talk to him half the time."

"All right. Let's make a trade." Henley balled up the invisibility cloak and put it in her hands. "You give me your ring so I can cram it down his throat, and I'll give you my cloak so you can get out of here."

"*No.*" She shoved the cloak back at him. "I'm not doing that to you. I won't be responsible for your death twice. I can't go through that again. I hate myself enough."

"Viv—"

"We'll figure out how to break the Twelve Dancing Princesses curse. We'll save you. And when we do—"

It hit her, like water dousing fire.

"You'll get married. To one of the princesses."

"Now you're the only one who can get married?"

"Don't say that to me!" Tears sprang to her eyes. "It's not funny. I'm not like you. I don't want you to be happy if it means you're happy with someone else."

He kissed her again. "Do you think I could be happy with anyone else? Do you think I could ever be happy, if you're not in my life?"

He wiped her tears with the cloak. He kept offering it to her, holding it up, raising his eyebrows—*please?*—but she wouldn't take it. Finally, she stopped crying and her breathing went back to normal. She wiped her face roughly and forced herself to get it together, at least a little.

"We can't stay in here all night," she said. "We have to look for a way to break the curse. Three days will be over so fast. . . ."

"What if three nights are all we get? Don't we get one more night together, before . . . ?"

She knew what he was saying. "Before we don't have each other. Ever again." She sighed. "I know. I want us to have more time together . . . but you can't risk getting caught. The guards will kill you if they find you. They don't even ask questions. They just . . ." She made a slicing motion with her hand. "And if Charleston knows you're here with me, she could tell someone. She might not, but . . . I don't think we should count on that. We have another chance. I don't want to throw that away."

"Okay," he said with a heavy sigh. "If that's what you want."

Before he could leave, she grabbed his arm. "Henley . . . I'm different now. I mean . . . I'm a little different. Still a coward, but . . . to you, I want to be—"

"You're already everything to me."

"You're going to make me cry."

"Again?" He touched his cloak to her cheek, ready to catch her tears, and she laughed and brushed it away.

"I'll be back tomorrow night," he said. "And the night after that. And after that . . ."

"After that you'll be rich and married."

"Viv—" She kissed him quiet. His eyes fluttered closed.

"Be careful," she said. "Now go."

CHAPTER THIRTY-EIGHT

"HE'S NOT ON THE COUCH."

"I told you he followed us."

"Someone figure out where he is before we start taking our clothes off."

"He'll be dead in two more days. I don't care if he sees me naked. He can take it to his grave."

"Noooo! I like this one!"

"You like *every*one."

"Not true . . ."

"My feet hurt."

"My feet hurt more."

"Okay—shoe pile." The girls flung their tattered dancing shoes onto the floor, as if they were about to be burned. All twelve girls slept in the same cavernous bedroom, the beds lined up six on each side. "We live like the girls in *Madeline*," Rumba had told him when he'd first arrived and been given the tour.

Most of the sisters shuffled into the dorm-sized bathroom. Others crawled into bed, eyes still crusted with glitter and mascara. The sounds of water splashing into sinks and tired bodies hitting mattresses followed Henley to the couch he was meant to keep watch from.

The princesses' father knew his daughters went to the underworld to dance—everyone knew that—but the couch was tradition, as was the goblet of drugged wine the sisters had given him before they left. It was tradition to pretend to drink it and feign sleep, but Henley had just poured it into a vase of dying flowers—a gift from the last guy who'd tried to break the curse. Brittle, crumbling roses that had outlasted the suitor who'd brought them.

"He was handsome," Chacha had told Henley. "And confident. I really thought he'd break the curse."

"Would you like to see his head?" Salsa had asked. "We have it in a box."

Henley had declined.

Now he lay down on the couch, one leg stretched out to rest on the floor, the other propped and extending past the armrest. The couch was too small to be comfortable and the tuxedo he wore had about as much give as a straitjacket, but he had three, maybe four hours before the girls' father would summon him to find out how the night had gone. He'd make do.

Most of the sisters were related only through their father, who'd had twelve daughters with ten different women, so there wasn't much of a family resemblance. They looked more like sorority sisters than blood sisters. Black hair, brown hair, red hair, blonde hair. Dark skin and light skin. The one thing they had in common was that their legs were really toned and they walked like they had thorns stuck in their feet.

He heard them slamming doors, dropping things, yelling at one another to shut up, they were trying to sleep. Several toilet flushes. Loud talking. Giggling. Muffled sobs. He was in the room just outside their bedroom suite—a kind of antechamber, with just the uncomfortable couch and a few chairs and the flowers. There was another door that led to the rest of the mansion, but it was locked from the outside, and would stay locked until morning.

Henley closed his eyes.

The princesses had gone mostly quiet—just the occasional sound of someone turning over in bed, or a loud sniff—when he felt the brush of a feather across his lips. He opened his eyes and saw Lindy hovering over him, holding the offending feather, brown curls framing her bowed head. She wore a pink nightgown that was tight around her breasts and flowed loose to her hips. She was sixteen but seemed younger.

He kept his voice just above a whisper. "Aren't you tired?"

"No. Stay up with me?"

He shifted into a sitting position and she tucked her body into the space he'd left behind. "I can't sleep on this couch, anyway. Lindy, right?"

She nodded, pleased. "And you're Henley. Henley . . . what was your last name?"

"Silva."

"That's right." She smiled, then ducked her head and started tracing something on her leg. Loops. Like cursive handwriting. Her smile turned to embarrassment as she traced the last part of whatever it was. "I like it," she said.

"My name? It's all right."

"Do you think you'll break the curse?"

"I hope so."

"Well . . . I think you'll do it. I just have a good feeling." She took a deep breath, then burst out, "Do you know which one of us you'll want to marry, if you do?"

"Uh . . . I need to figure out how to break the curse before I can think about that."

"Is that a nice way of saying it's not me?" She bit her lip.

"Go to bed, Lindy," a voice called from behind them. Charleston stood in the doorway, her arms crossed over the football jersey she slept in. She was one of the more assertive sisters, the kind who ordered the younger ones around. She stood and stared at Lindy until her sister obeyed the order, then settled in the chair near Henley. Her bare feet were covered in bruises and Disney Princess Band-Aids.

"Don't get the wrong idea about her. She's not desperate, just desperate for this to be over."

"I didn't get any ideas about your sister. Don't worry."

"Hmm, true. You have another agenda." She leaned her chin on her hand, and watched him like he was a secret to uncover. "I wondered at first why you were doing this. Like, did you want to be a hero, instead of a Huntsman? Oh yeah—I know who you are. But then I saw you in the bathroom with Snow White. I'd forgotten Vivian Deneuve was your princess. Well, your ex. I guess she was never your princess, but you know what I mean."

Never your princess. It felt weird to have it stated so bluntly by someone who barely knew him.

"Are you going to tell anyone about me?" he asked.

"Like who? The princes?"

He shrugged. "I don't know. Anyone."

He was wary of saying more—if she wanted to screw him over he didn't want to give her ideas. The other princes, Jasper, her sisters—any of them would have reasons to punish him if they knew he was meeting Viv.

"I'm not going to tell anyone. It's not like I want to see you die."

He nodded, relieved. "I don't suppose you know how to break the curse."

"No . . . none of us knows. We only go to the club and back. We spend all night dancing; there's no time to play detective. Does Viv know?"

"Not yet. She's going to try to find out."

"That would be amazing. That would be huge." Charleston looked at him again, like she'd thought one thing about him and now she was reconsidering. Although her first impression had probably been closer to the truth. "Is that why you volunteered? You figured you could break the curse if you had some inside help?"

He bowed his head, hand reaching for a cigarette, then curling up when he remembered he didn't have any. Stress was pounding through him like a hammer. "Maybe it'll help."

He was lying, but it wouldn't do him any good to let the twelve princesses know he didn't care about their curse. They might blow his cover just for fun, then. Royals were messed-up people. They had a taste for torture, and they viewed their own actions through a different moral lens.

A lower-born Cursed like Jack Tran killed a giant, or a girl with a Hansel and Gretel curse flambéed a witch, and that was evidence that they were depraved. A princess told a suitor *Solve this riddle or it's off with your head*, and that was okay because she was supposed to be worth it.

When the twelve princesses' father chopped off his hundredth head, they'd probably serve cake to commemorate the milestone.

"So you *do* want the fame and the money—and the girl," Charleston mused. "I thought you were pulling some Romeo and Juliet act, like—*I* have *to see you, I'd rather* die *than be without you!*—but you have a plan. Interesting."

The way she said it—like only a fool would die for love—irritated him. Especially because risking his life for a chance to get rich and marry one of the twelve princesses, that made sense to her.

Royals.

He let her mockery slide in one ear and out the other. He'd gotten worse from his friends. Jack had helped him arrange this, had even helped him find an invisibility cloak, but Elliot had tried to talk him out of it. *The underworld did you a favor. Move on. Don't trade your life for a girl who doesn't give a shit about you.*

Jack had tried to be positive. *Henley's going to break the curse. That witch I got the cloak from—she's got money riding on this. My ass is frogged if he dies, so I know he's coming back.*

He shook his head now, remembering. He had no doubt that Jack would weasel out of whatever trouble he got into. There were always people (or giants) gunning for him, but he went through life as if his biggest problem was what to eat for breakfast.

Charleston's eyes were faraway, daydreaming. "It would be

amazing to be able to sleep at night. See some different people. Travel. I need a vacation so bad."

"Where would you go?" Henley asked. Not that he cared.

"Hmm, maybe London? Why, do you want to come?" She winked. "I don't know if I could marry a guy who's in love with another girl. But I'd consider it if he broke my curse. Uhhh, it's late."

She got up, making a face like her heels were grinding out hot cigarettes. "The pain's kicking in. Post-underworld soreness. You'll feel it, too, soon enough. Try to get some sleep. I want you to be alert tomorrow so you can break my curse." She smiled and he did his best to smile back, like her faith in him was warranted.

"Yeah, good night," he said.

"Good night."

He lay back down, his hand covering his face to block out the light that was always on. His skin smelled like the stone in the underworld. He could feel it closing in on him already.

He couldn't break the curse. He'd gone into this knowing that. Jack had given him a fifty-fifty chance, but Jack had pulled that number out of the air, trying to be encouraging so Henley would actually *try* instead of just wrapping Viv in his cloak, hustling her out of the underworld, and then—well, either the underworld guards would kill him or the princesses' father would.

He was afraid of dying, of not having a future, but he could go to his grave with no regrets if Viv was safe.

Why?

Because he was crazy? No.

Because of hours and days and months and years that all added up to Viv.

Because of baseball games he'd skipped, friends he'd ditched, chores he'd abandoned to hang out with this princess who, when they'd first met, had acted like Henley was an animal she didn't know what to do with; but who'd gradually opened up to him, and taken root in him.

Because of lazy summer afternoons in the cottage, when she'd asked questions like, *What do you think you'll be in the future?* And he'd said, *I'll be your bodyguard,* when what he'd meant was *I'll be your boyfriend.*

Because of seventh grade: that time he'd drifted closer and closer to her mouth, both of them awkward, pretending they didn't know what was going on, until her breath slid across his lips, and then—

That first kiss like an electric shock.

The smell of her hair—like shampoo and fox fur.

That first heartfelt *I love you more than my whole family* when they were ten.

The first *I love you* when she'd really meant it. And actually, it had been *I love you, too.* He'd said it first, his heart speeding toward a collision.

The first time.

Because of all of that.

Because that was still who she was—who they were. No matter what had happened. He knew because he felt it. Because that *I love you* was still there, still strong—if anything, stronger—and that girl he'd wanted to protect, whose boyfriend/bodyguard he would have died to be . . . she was still there, too.

CHAPTER THIRTY-NINE

"I'D RATHER GO ALONE," Viv said, fidgeting with the string of pearls that went along with her *Film Noir* outfit.

"Don't want to be seen with me?" Jasper teased. He was wearing a pin-striped suit and a fedora, which had startled her when she saw him. She hadn't expected Jasper to come to the club tonight. It would make meeting up with Henley much more difficult.

"I'm not going to dance. I have names to collect."

"Come on, I'm all dressed up like a gangster. You have to dance with me." He tipped his hat playfully. She didn't give him the reaction he wanted—no smile, nothing.

"Do what you want."

"Do you not want me there?"

"I told you, I have things to do. But, whatever. Obviously you don't care."

"Well, I'm going. I want to go."

"Fine."

"And I'm a little annoyed that you don't want me there."

Viv kept her eyes on her reflection, her face as smooth as glass. "Be annoyed, then." She kept adjusting her outfit, fixing things that didn't need to be fixed, until Jasper left. Then her shoulders finally slumped. Her hand shook.

Two more chances to see you. How am I supposed to see you?

Tonight, the women were gun molls, femmes fatales, and lounge singers. Dangerous dames dressed for breaking the law and breaking hearts. The men were gangsters and private investigators, world-weary in loud ties and suspenders. A tiger in a three-piece suit blew a stream of cigarette smoke into the air. A fairy fixed a run in her stockings with a tap of her wand.

Viv wore a black forties-style dress with wide shoulders and a white belt. Her hair had been styled so that it fell in waves over one eye, giving her a seductive, can't-be-trusted look, and she was sure Jasper noticed, because he'd taken her arm as soon as they'd entered the club.

Now that she knew he'd prevented her friends from seeing her—or that his father had, which amounted to the same thing—she didn't want to stroll around the club with him. She hadn't had a chance to confront him, and she wouldn't until Henley was safe. She shifted her body, hoping to pull away without making it obvious that she didn't want to be near him.

"Why are you being so moody?" Jasper asked.

"I'm getting into the noir spirit," she said, unable to stop herself from searching the crowd for Henley. He was invisible—*he* would have to find *her*—but he couldn't approach her while Jasper was around.

Finally, she said, "I'm going to get a drink."

"I'll come with you."

"I don't need a chaperone to go to the bar."

"Maybe I want a drink, too. Did you think of that? But go. Drink by yourself if that's what you need to feel independent." He shoved off into the crowd and she sighed with relief.

Finally.

The bar was crowded so she picked a seat at the end, hoping Henley would see her. He could put his hand on her shoulder or her waist, whisper a message in her ear. Where they should meet. How much he missed her.

Or maybe he won't come to me at all.

Maybe the guards found him.

"Waiting for someone?" the bartender asked. He started to mix her a drink without asking what she wanted.

"What? Oh. No. Just looking around."

"We're doing a special drink in your honor. Red apple martini."

"Seriously?"

"Yep." The bartender set the drink in front of her. It was a gorgeous ruby-red color and smelled like fruit juice. A golden glaze of caramel dripped from the apple wedge garnish.

"I think I'll skip this," she said, taking the apple wedge off her glass.

The bartender laughed. "Let me know if you need anything else."

Viv had finished her first red apple martini and was halfway through her second when Jasper showed up again. She'd hoped the alcohol would settle her nerves but it was just agitating her and making things worse.

"Getting drunk?" he asked.

"If I want to."

"You're a princess," he said. "It wouldn't kill you to act like it."

"I guess I'm not as good at my role as you are at yours. Because you are *so charming* right now. Isn't he charming?"

"Cut her off," Jasper told the bartender. "Or I'll have your hands cut off."

She didn't even turn to watch him walk away. Just raised her finger to the bartender—making a point. "Ignore him," she said. "He doesn't back up anything he says. He's all talk. Trust me, I would know."

She downed her second drink—and hoped it would help. It didn't. It just stirred up more fear. There was no whisper from Henley. No brush of his hand—just people bumping into her from behind.

He could have been caught. A wrong step, a snapped branch, too much weight in the boat. All it took was one person to notice, one to grab the cloak, another to draw his sword. . . .

Or maybe he hadn't seen her. Maybe he was hanging around the Twelve Dancing Princesses because he assumed she'd be over there.

"One for the road," she told the bartender. "That's a Royal order."

"You got it."

He mixed her a third red apple martini and she took it with her, sipping it as she made her way across the dance floor. The apple wedge brushed the corner of her mouth, and she pulled it off, fingers sliding through the glaze.

The glaze was different this time—not caramel, but sticky

red candy, as bright and shiny as lip gloss. Impulsively, Viv pressed her lips to the glaze. The honeyed, tart taste melted on her tongue. Sour apple. Sweet sugar.

It was apple season on the surface. The time for fallen leaves and parties where kids bobbed for apples. When Viv was younger, kids would harass her at Halloween parties, crowding around her with apples, trying to get her to take a bite—as if she had a fatal apple allergy and could be killed by any Red Delicious. She'd eaten one and pretended to die once—then had gotten a serious scolding at home after the adults hosting the party told her father what she'd done.

Most people assumed she hated apples, but Viv actually liked them. She liked the smell, and the taste. She liked the way they filled her palm, the way they looked hanging from a tree or sitting on a teacher's desk. The way they were a symbol of temptation.

She ate them sometimes when the mood struck her. She just didn't take them from witches.

She wanted this one.

The red glaze shined like a new pair of patent leather shoes. She bit the wedge in half, and felt the candy cling to her teeth. The cool flesh of the apple slid across her tongue. It tasted so sweet it brought tears to her eyes. And it brought back a memory—a time she and Regina had gone to an orchard. Viv must have been about six. They had matching baskets and went down the rows of trees, picking the biggest, brightest apples to take home.

Afterward, they'd sat in the grass outside the gift shop and eaten apples until their stomachs soured, giggling like they were doing something forbidden. When they were finished

Regina used her sleeve to wipe the juice from their faces, then kissed the rest of it off Viv's chin.

"We can make a pie," Viv said.

"No." Regina took both baskets and tipped them over into the grass. "We can't bring these home. Your dad wouldn't like it. We shouldn't tell him about coming here, either."

"It will be our secret. We can have all kinds of secrets from him!"

Regina had laughed at that. She had been so beautiful, and Viv had beamed with pleasure, certain that nothing could spoil this, nothing could ever go wrong between them.

The apple in Viv's mouth tasted exactly like that memory: pain and happiness with an aftertaste of lost innocence. She made a sobbing noise, gasped, and the piece of apple slid down her throat and stuck there.

She was conscious long enough to notice the blood-tinged tartness of the poison, the blur of the crowd, the way the world shrank to nothing as her eyes closed, and then the floor hit her so hard she stopped feeling it.

CHAPTER FORTY

VIV WOKE UP SPRAWLED on the ground outside the palace, coughing up poison, bright red flecks spattering the stones like blood. She could feel the poisoned wedge scraping down her throat and into her stomach, hard as a gem. A circle of legs surrounded her. Jasper and his entourage.

"Did it come up?"

"No, she swallowed it."

Her bones ached from crashing onto the rocky ground. There was a stretcher behind her; she must have fallen off when they dropped her. That was the way it was supposed to happen, but the servants all looked like they were sorry about it.

Jasper knelt and gathered her in his arms, wiped the syrup from her face with a handkerchief. The poison burned her stomach and she shuddered.

"We have to get the apple out," he said. "You'll feel better after that."

"I want to go back to the club. I have to—" She couldn't finish. She couldn't tell him about Henley.

"We can go back tomorrow," he said gently.

Jasper's entourage accompanied them all the way to Viv's room. Jasper laid her down on the bed, then sent servants to fetch hot water, towels, salt. He sent guards to round up the bartenders for questioning, and to remind the other guards to be extra vigilant at the checkpoint.

"The bartender I saw talking to you—he's the one who served you the drink?"

"Yes. But I doubt he works for you. It was probably my stepmother in disguise."

Jasper leaned over her and brushed her hair back from her face. "Impossible. The doors are blocked to her. She must have hired him. Don't worry, we'll find him. He won't get away with doing this to you."

He stayed near her, his hand warming her cold fingers. "Go and break some diamond leaves off the tree in my father's study," he told a maid, "and pay a horseman to bring a doctor from the surface."

"A doctor?" Viv said.

"Just in case."

The first group of servants returned with a solution of warm salt water. They poured it down her throat until she vomited into a bowl: the cursed apple chunk floating in a foamy swirl of liquor, brine, and blood. They whisked away the poison apple, combed her hair and washed her face, removed her pearls and her dress, and by then she was tired of the hands tugging at her and she ordered them away. Everyone except Jasper.

He covered her with three layers of blankets. Tucked her

in. She took a sip of water from the glass beside her bed and felt the cold liquid coil inside her stomach.

"Do you feel better?" Jasper asked.

"I think so."

She'd missed her chance to meet Henley. They were supposed to have two more nights together, and now half that time was gone. The twelve princesses hadn't left the underworld and she'd already lost tonight.

"I tried shaking you at the club. Turning you over, pounding your back. It didn't help. It wasn't until I started to bring you home, and one of the servants tripped, that . . ."

She looked toward the window. She wished she knew if Henley was all right. If he was out there, waiting. Or if the guards had found him. She wondered if Jasper would tell her if they had.

"Do you think it's over? The curse? Now that you've eaten the poison apple?"

"Maybe. There's usually another attempt, but the apple is kind of the coup de grâce."

Jasper sat down next to her, his hand resting on the blanket over her arm. "Let's hope that's the end of it. I'd be wrecked if I lost you. I don't want us to fight over stupid things. At the club, when I said—"

A knock at the door sent Jasper sliding off the bed to answer it. It was the doctor they'd summoned—accompanied by the troll, who wore a bright gold smoking jacket over a pea-green suit.

"Get him out of here," Viv said.

The troll smiled. "Vivian, is that any way to speak to your future father-in-law? A little respect, please. I'm here to make sure you're all right."

"I don't want him here," Viv told Jasper, hoping that now, of all times, he'd stick up for her.

"Just let the doctor examine you," Jasper said.

"Yes. Let the doctor do his job," the troll said. His presence made her feel worse than the poison had.

Viv allowed the doctor to look down her throat, listen to her heart, et cetera, just to get rid of him, and finally he made her drink something that was supposedly an antidote—although Viv doubted there was a ready-made antidote to Regina's poison.

When the doctor left, the troll took his place at Viv's bedside. His scent was overpowering. He smelled like he bathed in Earl Grey tea, and also like there was garbage inside his clothes.

"Now that the prince has saved his princess from the poison apple, it's time to move forward with the wedding preparations," the troll said.

Viv started to protest and the troll muzzled her with a hand that reeked of rotting vegetables.

"Vivian, ever the firecracker. I'm sure you were about to give me a reason why we ought to delay the wedding. Maybe you'd rather find my name before you and my son exchange vows. That would be nice for you—a wedding and a coronation on the same day! But that's not going to happen. You will marry my son, bear his children, and rest assured, I will outlive you both."

He smiled again and held it as if the expression were carved onto his face.

"Now, I don't want you to worry that your dream wedding will be a rushed affair. We'll make it a night you'll always remember. No one in the world throws a better party than I do. I'll leave it up to you to make it a night your husband always remembers.

"Good night," the troll said as he left. "And congratulations."

Jasper seemed stunned, but not unhappy. Maybe he was feigning shock so she wouldn't be pissed at him.

"So, how can I make it a night you'll always remember?" she asked tartly.

"Viv . . ."

"No, I'm serious. You might as well tell me your preferences since you always get what you want, anyway."

Now he gaped at her. "You think I had something to do with this?"

"I know you didn't do anything to stop him. And his disgusting hand wasn't covering *your* mouth. Which, by the way—"

She grabbed the glass of water by her bed, swished some water around in her mouth, and spit it on the floor.

"I can't believe you think I'm in league with my father."

"When you just go along with whatever he wants, it's the same thing!"

"Why don't *you* want it? Why are you so against being married to me? This is our destiny. We're meant to be together. *We* are. Not you and your Huntsman—he's dead!"

"Do you *listen to yourself*?"

"Do *you*? You haven't thanked me once. I saved your life. I've done so much for you. And you don't even appreciate it. You just expect it."

"Of course I expect it," she said coldly. "I'm the princess."

"I'm leaving," he muttered.

"*Thank you!*" she screamed as he slammed the door behind him.

Her whole body felt wrenched between sped-up and sloweddown. Racing heart, sluggish limbs. She was tired and cold from being poisoned, and full of terror for Henley. They had one more night to figure out how to break the Twelve Dancing Princesses curse—if Henley was still alive—and she doubted he was any closer to the answer than he'd been before. If Henley had been at the club, and he'd seen her collapse, then he was probably worrying about her right now, instead of thinking about how he could save himself.

I won't let you die, she thought. *I'll protect you. I'll be the one who saves you this time.*

Earlier, when Jasper had given orders to summon the doctor, he'd told a maid to take some diamond leaves from a tree in the troll's study.

Viv had already seen trees made of silver, and of gold . . . and she'd associated the silver with the underworld and, eventually, the gold with Rumpelstiltskin. But the mention of a diamond tree got her thinking about the Twelve Dancing Princesses, and the way the soldier in the fairy tale had won their father's challenge.

Once he reached the underworld, the soldier followed the princesses through three different forests: one with silver trees, one with gold trees, and one with diamond trees. He broke a twig off each type of tree as evidence, and on the morning after the third night, when he was supposed to solve the mystery or be executed, he presented the three twigs to the king, and the twelve princesses confessed to everything and never returned to the underworld.

The actual curse couldn't be broken that easily. But if there really were silver, gold, and diamond trees in the underworld, maybe they were part of the solution. It was worth a try. She didn't have anything else to go on.

Gold and silver twigs would be easy enough to get. But if the diamond tree was in the troll's study, Viv would have to sneak in there without getting caught.

And she'd have to do it tonight. Tomorrow was Henley's last night in the underworld.

CHAPTER FORTY-ONE

THE TROLL WASN'T DOING A DEAL tonight. He was in his chambers somewhere, asleep or awake, dreaming of ruining lives, or counting his treasures, or planning a wedding.

Viv had never snuck into the troll's chambers while he was there—hadn't even set foot in the corridor—but tonight she had no other choice. If she didn't try, Henley would be executed. If she was caught . . . well, she supposed she'd know exactly how far she could push the troll.

A few of the doors were open and lamplight filtered out into the corridor. The library was lit, and so was a room Viv had taken to thinking of as the troll's treasure room. It was full of glass cabinets that held the mementos he'd taken from his victims. The nursery door was closed, but Viv could smell baby powder, could hear a baby fussing and the creak of the floor as someone paced. The bedroom door was shut. The study door was open, but the room was dark.

Viv quickly slipped inside the study, closed the door behind her, and turned on the light.

She left it on just long enough to switch on the smaller, weaker, and hopefully less noticeable desk lamp, then started her search for the diamond tree, or a tree with diamond leaves, or whatever it was.

She'd never searched the study. It contained some bookshelves, and also a desk, and cabinets—but all the drawers and cabinet doors were locked. Viv had always planned to go back once she'd gotten her hands on the keys, or stumbled across a book on lock-picking. Wherever the diamond tree was, it wasn't out in the open. So where to break in first?

Viv went to the desk. She felt around for a key—taped underneath, maybe?—and finally ended up unfolding a paper clip and trying to pick the lock on the top drawer. She felt completely inept—she was sure Jack Tran or Luxe would be able to do this with ease. Jack had stolen from giants. Luxe mainly broke things. But still. How would they get these locks open? Would they bother with a paper clip?

While Viv was kneeling in front of the desk, a speck of sparkle caught her eye, lying on the floor below one of the cabinets. She abandoned the lock to examine it, and saw that it was a tiny diamond leaf, about the size of a fingernail clipping.

The diamond tree had to be in the cabinet. The maid must have dropped the leaf in her hurry to summon a doctor for Viv. Slowly, Viv stood up. She tried the cabinet door.

It was open.

The tree sat on a shelf inside, growing out of a small porcelain tray. It looked like a bonsai tree, but its warped trunk and branches were made of shining, angular diamond.

Diamond-sliver leaves stuck out from the branches like tiny fangs. Glittering dust sprinkled the soil where some of the leaves had been snapped off.

Viv felt around for a weak point on the longest branch. All the trees in the underworld had points where they were meant to be broken, and the diamond tree was no exception. The branch sounded like a candy cane cracking as Viv snapped it off. She closed the cabinet—then heard the click of toenails on the floor in the hall, like a large dog was moving slowly toward her.

She switched off the desk lamp and dropped to a crouch.

The door opened. Viv cringed, eyes squeezing shut in anticipation of the light, but the room stayed dark. She heard breathing and the soft scuff of large feet on the carpet.

"Vivian," the troll said, "you make things so interesting. It's been a long time since a young girl searched the palace for my name. You're like a pretty little rat, sinking its teeth in everywhere. So what have you found out?"

She didn't answer.

"Do you want to hazard a few guesses? Should I dance around a fire and sing it to you? Wouldn't that be nice. The way it is in storybooks." She could almost see the dry curve of his mouth.

"'Call me Ishmael,'" he said—and her heart jumped, thinking he was revealing the answer, until he said, "'What's in a name? That which we call a rose by any other name would smell as sweet.'" *Moby-Dick. Romeo and Juliet.* He went on reciting name quotes, some she recognized and some she didn't, until her hands were clenching from nerves and her heart felt like it was about to stop. The three branches were just a hope, a long shot, but if this plan was taken from her she had nothing to replace it.

"You know, dear . . . if you're going to guess my name, you might as well get something for it. We could make a wager. I give you something you desperately need and, in exchange, you give me something you can't bear to lose. And then, if you can guess my name within three days, you get to keep everything. What do you say, Vivian?"

Quick breaths rushed in and out of her chest. *You could save Henley . . . you could save him and still guess the name.*

No. He wouldn't want that for her.

"Maybe some other time," the troll said. She heard his footsteps moving away, and she trembled with relief. "Now go get your beauty sleep. You want to be the fairest on your wedding day, don't you?"

She heard the click of his long toenails on the wooden floor of the corridor . . . heard them fade as he walked away. She waited a few more minutes, her body still curled into a crouch, her fingers frozen around the diamond branch, before she unfolded her shaky limbs and ran to her room.

CHAPTER FORTY-TWO

VIV STOOD IN FRONT OF THE MIRROR, eyes locked with the evil queen who stared back at her. White as frost, black as kohl, red as poison.

Tonight's theme at the nightclub was *Fairy Tale*. It came up every few months, a more loaded, self-aware costume party, where Cursed discarded their roles and dressed their fantasies to the hilt. It was fun for princesses to slum it as the Little Match Girl, for older, experienced ladies to take on the innocence of Cinderella at her first ball, for Beauties to pretend to be Beasts.

Viv wasn't in the mood to wear glass slippers, or to tiptoe around yawning, showing off the spindle prick on her finger and giving everyone bedroom eyes. And dressing up in a donkey's skin or a coat made from the furs of a thousand animals was just disgusting. She didn't want to be any kind of princess or prey. When the underworld seamstress had asked her what kind of costume she wanted, she'd told her to make her an evil queen.

Her dress was long and black with a high, stiff collar, the skirt slashed at the bottom to reveal ribbons of red silk that tangled around her legs when she walked. The wide sleeves extended past her knuckles, in jagged edges that resembled the webbed feet of a frog.

Last night, on her way back from the troll's study, she'd broken a twig off one of the gold trees in the main hall. Now, while everyone else was getting ready, she slipped the diamond branch and the gold twig into a velvet pouch and bound it to the underside of her forearm—easy to conceal beneath her long, wide sleeves, and easy to release.

Jasper escorted her to the club. He was still angry with her, but they had to appear together as a triumphant couple now that he'd saved her from a public poisoning attempt. They danced mechanically for a few songs before Viv excused herself to go to the ladies' room—the safest rendezvous spot. Jasper wasn't likely to follow her.

She felt sick. She was afraid for so many reasons. Henley could be dead already. If he'd been at the club last night and had seen her bite into the poison apple, and he'd tried to get to her—tried to save her—and the guards had found him . . .

She waded through a sea of interpretations, passing a fairy-kei Gretel with tiny plastic cupcakes glued to her fingernails; a prince dressed as a wolf, delicately waltzing with a white cat in a Red Riding Hood costume; and an old man holding a blue satin pillow with a glass slipper on top of it, who kept exclaiming, "Still haven't found her!" as if he'd planned it to be his catchphrase for the night.

Viv lingered near the Twelve Dancing Princesses to give

313

Henley a chance to notice her. Already she was sweating through her dress, but she was cold, too. She hugged her arms to her chest, feeling the crush of the velvet pouch and the sharp edges of the branches. Either way, this was the end. The end of Henley would be the end of her. And if he lived, and broke the curse, their relationship would be over. Henley claimed he couldn't be happy without her, and once she would have hated the idea of him being with someone else. But standing there, feeling the cold sweat of fear roll down her sides, all she wanted was for him to live, and be happy like he deserved.

She went into the empty bathroom, witch heels loud on the tile floor, wondering if the door had stayed open a few extra seconds before it swung shut—and got her answer when Henley shed the invisibility cloak. He appeared all at once, one eye-blink *not there* and then suddenly towering over her in the same tux he'd worn the first night. She barely had time to look before he was pulling her to him, and she felt his hands in her hair, tilting her head back, and then his mouth was on hers, like it all needed to happen now, because they wouldn't be together very long.

He didn't have a solution. He didn't know how to break the curse, and he thought—

Viv wanted to tell him, but she was too busy kissing him. She threw her arms around his neck, and when she did he lifted her up; he grabbed her hips and pressed her back against the wall and one of her legs scissored up out of the slit in her dress. They went on kissing, his body pressing against hers. It would be so easy to lose herself, to forget everything else . . . but her kiss wouldn't keep him safe.

Viv turned her head, the only way she knew to stop

314

herself. His breath was heavy in her ear. "I thought you might be dead," Henley said.

"I thought the same thing about you."

"Jesus, Viv. Stay the hell away from poison apples."

"I didn't think Regina could get to me down here."

"Your future in-laws don't think I can get to you down here. But there are work-arounds."

"Speaking of that . . ."

"This is our last night together."

"I know," she said. "But I think—I have an idea. Get invisible, and come with me."

He looked unsure, but set her down and pulled the cloak across his shoulders. "Lead the way," he said as he vanished.

She heard him laugh as she fixed her dress—straightened the skirt where it had twisted around her hips. "Some of us aren't invisible," she said.

She held the door open so Henley had a chance to slip through, then picked a path across the crowded dance floor, trusting him to follow. Tonight, more than ever, walking through the club was like passing through a dreamscape: pastel princesses, James Bond–style princes, a girl covered in honey and feathers, a gothic Sleeping Beauty holding a baby doll in each arm, a man whose upper body bristled with bloody hedgehog spines, and more than one Snow White blithely admiring an apple, her red lipstick gleaming under the lights, her face powdered as white as a slice of Wonder Bread.

By the time Viv got out of the club she felt like she'd run a fairy-tale gauntlet. The train of her evil queen dress swept over dark stone now, instead of a floor sprinkled with gold glitter and rose petals. She reached behind her and felt Henley's fingers close around hers. Secure that he was with her, she started down the path that cleaved the rocky hillside.

A few latecomers straggled by, passing on Viv's left while Henley kept to her right; she saw a couple small stones get dislodged by his footsteps and go skittering down the hill. The latecomers didn't notice. They were busy talking, praising one another's costumes and fishing for compliments about their own.

At the lakeshore, Viv turned and headed into the silver forest, walking until the shadows and bladelike trunks were thick enough to shield them from view. She reached up and snapped a silver twig from one of the trees.

"Hold this," she said.

Henley took the twig, and the silver was swallowed up by the magic of the cloak.

"I wish I could see you," she said. "But don't!—don't take that off."

Viv freed the velvet pouch from her forearm. "I was thinking about how you could break the curse," she said, opening the pouch and taking out the twigs, "and I was thinking about the fairy tale, the three twigs the soldier brings back to the princesses' father. You have a silver one. There's a diamond and gold one here. I don't know what we can do with them, but I thought . . . maybe they're involved in breaking the curse somehow."

"I can't see anything I'm holding with this on," Henley muttered. He reappeared as he pulled the cloak from his shoulders and draped it over the crook of his arm. "Can I see those?"

"Here, take them."

He held all three in his hand, spread out on his palm like they might reveal their secrets to him. "I'd like to think there's something to this. I don't have any other leads. The princesses seem like they want the curse to be over, but they don't know anything about breaking it. And the princes, they don't know anything, either?"

"They've never said. Once you were here, I was afraid to ask. I didn't want them to start looking for someone. I know what they'd do if they found you. Put your cloak back on."

"Wait a minute. No one can see us back here."

She glanced in the direction of the club. "You'd better hope not."

Henley closed his hand around the branches and sighed. "I don't know, Viv. I don't know what to do with these. I think I might just—"

"*No*," she said. "There has to be a way. We still have all of tonight."

"You can't be gone all night. Your prince will look for you."

"Well, I'll make it so he doesn't find me."

"I want you to take my cloak. Get out of here. If this is it for me, then you might as well—" He stopped and looked at his closed hand. "Something's happening."

Henley uncurled his fingers. The three twigs had rolled together in his fist, and now they stayed that way, melded. Viv leaned closer and saw that the gold, silver, and diamond twigs were intertwined, and the metal and diamond leaves were re-forming into the teeth of a key.

A delicate gold-diamond-and-silver key, so fine it looked like it would snap inside a lock if you tried to use it, the same way the branches had snapped off the trees.

But magic objects—like Cinderella's glass slippers, and Rapunzel's braid—were never as fragile as they appeared.

"Damn," Henley said, still staring at the key in his hand. "Should we try it?"

"Not until the princesses are back in their bedroom. You have to lock them out of the underworld, not into it, and I doubt that key will hold up to multiple uses."

"No . . . probably not. So I'll leave it till the last minute—"

"And see if it works. Yeah."

They both breathed heavy sighs. Viv felt jittery.

"Put it away," she said. "Don't lose it."

Henley tucked the key into an inside pocket of his tux. "I just want to try it already."

"I know."

They stood watching each other, both nervous.

Viv bit her lip. "So . . . congratulations. This is big for you."

"If this works, I get to keep my head."

"That's not what I meant. But yeah, that, too. Priorities, I guess. Heads before hos."

Henley sighed. "Viv . . ."

"When you pick your princess . . . just don't pick a stupid one. And don't call her Viv when you're making out. Girls hate that."

"Remember that heart someone drew on my hand? That you hated?" He took her left hand in his. "I hate this more." She felt a tug on her engagement ring—a small jerk that pulled it over her knuckle, then one more light scrape before he got it off her finger. Her hand felt suddenly naked without the heavy clawlike band.

"Henley—" She reached for it instinctively, but he was

taller, faster—and had a better throwing arm. She was still jumping for it when Henley sent her ring sailing over the tree-tops, toward the lake. She pictured it hitting the silver water, sinking to the bottom, and coming to rest inside the rib cage of some long-dead suitor.

She held out her ringless hand. "Like that won't be suspicious."

"I have something better for you to wear." He moved to drape the cloak over her shoulders—and she darted out from under it.

"Are you crazy?"

"If that key breaks the curse, I don't have to worry about showing my face on the surface. I can go back. And I want you to go with me."

"We don't know that it'll work. And anyway—"

She felt like a six-year-old trying to run away from a boy who wanted to drop a frog down her shirt. He wouldn't let up with the cloak. He was determined to make her wear it. And she was determined not to.

"Stop!" she said. "I'm not taking it!"

"Why? Do you want to stay here? Do you want to be miserable? If this is about punishing yourself—"

"It's not. Why don't you think about yourself for once? Even if the key does work, right now you're still in the underworld—you still have to get out. And if anyone sees you—the guards, Jasper, his brothers . . . They. Will. Kill. You. So you need to wear that cloak until you're back in the princesses' bedroom. I don't care how much you want to protect me. You don't get to do that. *I* get to protect *you*."

"You are so difficult," he muttered.

"Excuse me if I don't want you dead. Anyway . . . there's still something I need to do here."

"Swim to the bottom of the lake and get your engagement ring back?"

"No." She made a face at him. "I need to find Jasper's father's name. And destroy him."

"Uh—*why?*"

"He has a Rumpelstiltskin curse. He rules this place with an iron fist. No one will stand up to him. He steals babies and raises them to be his slaves—"

"What kind of place is this?"

"Exactly. I need to find his name and put an end to it all. I think maybe I can do it. He's afraid of me. He wouldn't threaten me if he wasn't afraid."

"He's threatening you? You are *not* staying here."

There was no compromise in her expression. She needed him to know she was serious. "We can't both get out of here tonight. The difference is: If the guards see *me* in the underworld, they'll go about their business. If they see *you*, they'll cut off your head. It's not that hard to decide which one of us should use your cloak."

He sighed, brow furrowing in that frustrated way that made her think he was giving in. "How much time do you need to find this guy's name?"

"I don't know. I guess . . . I'll be able to let you know . . . when I get it right."

She watched him fight with himself: his hands in fists, head bowed, feet rooted to the ground. He didn't want to die, and what she'd said made sense. But it didn't change the fact that he didn't like it.

When he finally looked at her, his dark eyes were full of

loss. "I don't know how to walk away from this. I don't know how to walk away and leave you here."

"Henley—"

"I came here to make sure you were safe. But you're *not* safe. So how can I leave you?"

She didn't know what to tell him. Nothing she could say would make it hurt less, or make him doubt himself less. She put her arms around his waist and hugged him with all her strength. A hug so tight it said, *I'm with you. I'm here. Nothing can tear us apart.*

"I love you," she said, he said—laced together. They held each other, and they were one person against the world for a little while longer.

She could hear the rhythm of his heart, his breathing, the wind-chime whisper of the trees, and then—the crunch of shoes on sand.

"Cloak," she whispered. "Someone's coming."

They broke apart, Henley donning his invisibility cloak as Viv turned to see who'd crept up on them. She narrowed her eyes; the lanterns that lit the forest were sparse this far from the lake, and shadows filled the spaces between the trees. She didn't see anyone. Maybe her eyes passed right over them. It was hard to say.

"Hello?" she said. "Is someone there?"

She took a step in the direction of the club—in pursuit of the witness, at first—and then another, and another, until she was firm in her decision not to turn back—not to run and throw herself into Henley's arms one last time. Neither one of them wanted to leave the other; that had been their strength and their weakness, always.

321

But she couldn't risk exposing him. Couldn't keep arguing, giving him a chance to convince her, making it more likely that he would be caught.

She had to let him go. Had to *make* him go.

Even though walking away, keeping him safe, seemed crueler than anything she'd done to him before. Because they hadn't really said good-bye. They were supposed to see each other again. But that hinged on the hope that the key would work, that Henley would still be in love with her, and not his princess, a month from now, a year from now—if that was how long it took her to find the troll's name.

And if not, then it had ended when she walked away. Without warning, or last words.

Everything depended on the key.

CHAPTER FORTY-THREE

VIV HAD GONE TO THE KITCHEN in the hours between partying and dawn, and made herself coffee with the intention of staying awake until the following night—when the princesses' door either opened, or proved itself sealed forever.

Until then, she couldn't sleep, wouldn't sleep, didn't want to sleep. She sat surrounded by books, hunting names on every page, coffee carafe listing on her bedspread as she wrote. Caffeine rattled in her veins like turbulence. The pen was jumpy in her hand, and gave every word wings and jutting peaks.

She wasn't sure what time it was when she heard the key turning in her lock. But she knew she didn't want to see anyone. She definitely didn't want to see Jasper.

He sauntered in with his hands behind his back. "Did you enjoy yourself tonight?"

"That was locked," she said, going back to her books. "Don't open the door when I lock it."

"I asked if you enjoyed yourself."

"I'm asking you to leave."

"Not yet. I brought you a present."

His hands had been clasped behind his back. Now he threw something in her face: a jagged rectangle of gray cloth, slippery to the touch, stained with blood.

One half of an invisibility cloak.

"Don't try to use it," Jasper said. "We cut it up so it doesn't work anymore."

Viv pushed it aside, to keep her hands from holding it too tenderly, fearfully. . . .

"I don't know what this is," she said.

"You told me he was dead. And I believed you."

The footsteps she'd heard. Whoever it had been . . . they'd told Jasper.

Or it had been Jasper standing there. Watching them through the I-love-yous and the long embrace.

"Surprised?" he said. "I know I was."

He got away, she told herself.

They got his cloak, but he ran.

"I thought we were both trying to make this work. I thought, at least, that I didn't have to compete with your Huntsman anymore. So to find out your dead lover's alive and you're only staying here because you want to destroy my father, well—*that* was eye-opening. I guess you fancy yourself a hero, and not just a spoiled bitch."

She flung the coffee carafe. It hit the wardrobe instead of Jasper, bounced, and barely splashed him. He wiped the drops away with the back of his hand.

"Throw your tantrum," he said. "I don't care if you're pissed at me."

"Get out!"

"Would you say it means I loved you if I gave him a head start? Not that it mattered in the end. The guards are good at catching intruders. They enjoy meting out punishment. It's probably the only release they get."

Viv held the cloak to her face and inhaled—afraid she'd catch a hint of cigarette smoke, or Henley's skin. Something that would tell her it was his. But there was only the smell of the underworld. Wet stone. Blood and silver.

"You're lying," she said. "This could be anyone's."

It could be Henley's—but it wasn't. She wouldn't let it be.

"And I'm *not* staying. You can't keep me here."

"Can't I? Where are you going to go? The bottom of the lake for one last kiss?"

She pushed past Jasper out of the room and he didn't try to stop her. He shouted: "You, kissing a dead boy—how ironic! But you can't revive him. You can't do anything!"

His taunts followed her as she ran from the palace, and as she stumbled through the forest she kept hearing him—*you . . . can't . . . do anything. . . .* All the way around the lake, until she was panting so hard her breaths drowned out that inner voice. Her throat felt like it had been scraped with a dull knife and there was a pain in her side like someone had stabbed her.

She'd known, when she ran, that there would be no escape. The doors to the surface were closed at this hour. But she'd let a desperate hope drive her. As if her defiance and anger could create a way out, the way Rapunzel's tears could heal her prince's blindness. But Viv wasn't pure of heart like that, and the tears that poured down her cheeks didn't have magical powers.

"I hate this place!" she screamed. "Let me out!"

. . . out . . .

. . . out . . .

She felt like the underworld was mocking her with each echo.

You . . . can't . . . do . . . anything.

The shadows didn't shift to reveal a secret door. No kindly fairy appeared to dry her tears and make her dreams come true. But she wasn't alone.

"Why are you crying?"

Viv turned to see who had spoken, and found a woman sitting in the forest, facing away from her. She was dressed in a blue-and-yellow Snow White costume—the Disney-inspired dress found in countless costume shops, complete with curled black hair and a red headband. The woman was dressed for the *Fairy Tale* theme night, but the club had closed hours ago.

"Are you lost?" Viv asked. It wasn't the kind of thing you said to an adult, but something about the woman struck her as childish. Maybe it was the props scattered around her: a stuffed fawn, a hand mirror and comb, a fake apple covered with red glitter.

"Lost? Always." The voice seemed darker, tragic somehow, and Viv took a second look. She remembered those glittery apples. As light as puff pastry. Dusting her hand with red sparkles when she held them. Her stepmother had used them as Christmas ornaments once.

"Regina?" she whispered.

The girlish Snow White turned around, and Regina's face smiled back at her. Berry-red lipstick. Porcelain foundation.

Her pupils as wide as if she'd dripped poison into them.

"What are you doing here?" Viv asked.

"Waiting for you. Come sit with me."

Viv was wary, but overwhelmingly lonely, and Regina was smiling at her in a way she hadn't in so long. . . .

Cautiously, Viv came closer, and sat down just outside Regina's circle of princess accessories.

"How have you been?" Regina asked.

"You should know. You poisoned me yesterday."

Regina laughed. "I mean beyond that. Your Prince Charming. Your regrettably loyal Huntsman. How's that working out?"

"You probably know that, too. You keep pretty good tabs on me." She didn't think for a second that Regina wanted to have a heart-to-heart. If anything, she probably wanted to rub Viv's face in the mess she'd made of her life. "How did you get here? The doors are supposed to be blocked to you."

"They are. They're blocked to your friends, too. Well—that's what I've heard. It's powerful magic. More than I can undo with witchcraft. But there are some rather, well, you'd call them *evil* fairies who think the fairest is being a little unfair. Skipping out on her curse and going straight to happily ever after. Although if they think you're happy, they don't know you very well."

Viv looked away. "They gave you a way in. Did they give you a way out, too? Could you . . . take me with you?"

Regina smiled. "You want to continue the show for our fairy friends back in Beau Rivage? An interesting proposal." She extended a pale hand, and her fingertips grazed Viv's hair, her ear, before Viv pulled away.

"Your hair's a mess," Regina said. "You still don't know how to fix it."

"It's the middle of the night."

"Yes, but you never have. You're like a boy, except a boy has the sense to put on a baseball cap. Come here. Let me do it."

When Viv hesitated, Regina cleared the toys away and pulled Viv in front of her, almost into her lap, as if Viv were five years old again. She picked up the comb—a beauty tool, but also one of the poisoned items from the fairy tale—and Viv grabbed her wrist.

"No," Viv said. "No comb. If you want the rest of this curse to play out, you have to take me back to Beau Rivage with you."

"Fine." Regina released the comb, and Viv picked it up and flung it away from them. "I can fix your hair with my fingers. Remember how I used to do it? Braid it when we were at Seven Oaks and it was hot and you wanted it out of your face?"

"I remember," Viv said. "Yours was braided, and I wanted to look like you."

"Come here. Let me do it for old times' sake. I have to wait for the fairy to open the door for me, anyway."

"You'll take me with you?"

"I might as well. Otherwise your dad will complain about the money I wasted on that glass coffin."

"Has he . . . asked about me?"

"I haven't seen him. He's been hearing some vile things about me lately, most of them true. He knows enough to keep his distance."

Viv sighed and settled into the space in front of her stepmother, the way she had when Regina had first come to live with them. She knew nostalgia was dangerous—it had made her prey to the apple—but right then she didn't care.

Regina finger-combed Viv's hair, teasing apart the tangles. "I know you probably hate me. But I did you a favor when I took your heart. I don't mean that business with the Huntsman; I took it from you long before that. Little by little I was carving away at your weakness, making you colder, killing that naïve, innocent part of you. I wish someone had done that for me. Well, *life* did that for me, but it took its sweet time.

"If your heart is too big, everyone can see it. They know exactly what will hurt you, and they'll do it, because it gives them power over you. Power. That's what you need. Not love. Love depends on somebody else. Power you can get by yourself."

Regina's nimble fingers tugged Viv's hair this way and that, lifting it above her ear, twisting, braiding.

"I knew how to hurt you . . . and it felt good to do it. You wouldn't believe how good. I hated how easily everything came to you. How adored you were. That love you had—as a *child*— why did you get a love like that? I would have given anything to be loved that way. But you, you just . . ."

Viv closed her eyes, sick with regret. "Why do you act like no one ever loved you? I loved you."

For a second Regina's fingers were softer, almost caressing, at the nape of Viv's neck. "Hmm. Maybe you did. But it's funny . . . how we want love from certain people, and if we don't get it from them, it'll never be enough coming from someone else."

"Coming from me."

"It's not your fault, Viv. It's just the way things are."

A few last twists, and then Regina tucked the loose strands behind Viv's ears. "There. Do you want to check the mirror?"

Viv reached for the hand mirror, nervous to admire her reflection in front of her stepmother. And as she leaned forward, she felt the stab of a hairpin, deep into her scalp.

A fierce burning pain, and then—

Body oozing down, her muscles useless. Regina's hands guiding her to the ground, where she lay on her back, lovely coiled hair flat against the earth, eyes gaping, lungs frozen.

It felt like the instant you took a deep breath, and held it, no air moving in or out, your body stiff, full, anticipating. A moment that went on and on with no change. She wanted to exhale, to move—but her body was paralyzed by the poison. Her eyes stayed open like those of a doll.

Regina circled her, slipping in and out of view.

"Only one of us can survive this. I didn't choose this curse. I wanted to be you. I wanted to be the beautiful girl the prince wants to save. But it wasn't meant to be. I have to ensure my own survival."

Regina bent down and kissed her, once, on the lips.

"Good-bye, Viv. I hope death comes for you soon."

Regina fluttered out of sight. Butter-yellow satin and tiny black shoes.

The silver branches sprawled across the sky, as stiff and still as bones. Viv could hear Regina's footsteps, crunching, fading, until they were drowned out by the music of the trees, the heartless, shivering laughter of the underworld.

She felt her breath catch, her chest strain with pressure—but it was all in her mind, a memory of what panic felt like, because she couldn't breathe, couldn't move, couldn't do anything.

Like a true princess, all she could do was wait.

CHAPTER FORTY-FOUR

A GUARD FOUND VIV'S BODY, and an eternity passed before he returned with Jasper. Together they carried Viv back to the palace; they even dropped her, as if she'd choked on another apple and they only needed to jolt it free, but her body just tumbled to the stones. The hairpin didn't come loose. She felt every burst of pain, but couldn't cry out, couldn't even prove she wasn't dead. Jasper had listened at her chest and found no heartbeat, and muttered, "But that doesn't mean anything; she has no heart." They brought her to her room in the palace and laid her on the bed. The guard left, and Jasper sat down somewhere, out of sight.

She didn't want him to touch her, but she thought he would kiss her, check her body for poisoned jewelry, at least *try* to revive her. He didn't. He sighed; she could hear the tap of his shoes on the floorboards as he paced.

And then he turned out the light and left her there.

* * *

Viv couldn't sleep. She remained painfully alert, but unable to twitch her finger or shift her eyes or signal to anyone that she was awake inside her body.

Hours passed. The door opened. The glow of the lamp drew a circle of light on the ceiling. She heard the sigh of springs in an armchair, then scattered footsteps on the floor.

"Did you kiss her?" Garnet's voice. "Did you look to see if she's wearing anything new? A cursed ring, perhaps?"

"No." Jasper.

"Aren't you going to?"

"I haven't decided. I don't particularly want to."

"Jasper! You can't just leave her like this."

"Can't I? Who would know?"

"You're being cruel. . . ."

"*I'm* cruel? She was using me. Letting me believe—"

"Yes, I know—and I don't think she was right—but still. You can't leave her to waste away as a . . . statue."

"I think I'd like her better as a statue."

"Jasper!"

"I really thought it was meant to be, Garnet. From the first night I met her, I thought we could be something together. That it would last. But we were *nothing*. She never had any intention of trying to love me. She was so angry when we got engaged—well, now I know why. Her Huntsman. And I owe her something? As a *thank-you* for playing with me like that?"

"You do it because it's the right thing to do."

"I already saved her once. I don't have to keep saving her unless I want to. And I *don't* want to."

"Jasper . . ."

"If I wake her, I'll have to marry her. Father's already

making the preparations. I'd rather be alone and lonely than married to a girl like her. Maybe I'll change my mind in a few years," he muttered. "I could always store her in a closet until then. It's not like she's going anywhere."

"You're just angry right now. You have to calm down, and then . . ."

"I'm tired of looking at her. Let's get out of here."

The light clicked off. Darkness descended. Viv was alone.

Torture. The worst tension she had ever felt. Her insides rigid with panic, her lungs tight with trapped breath. She wanted to run, cry, scream to release some of her fear, but it just kept building. There was nothing she could do. She couldn't break her own curse. She was a princess who depended on her beauty . . . and that was enough to attract a stranger's attention and get him to save her, but she and Jasper weren't strangers. The curiosity of the prince who stumbles upon the lovely maiden in the forest was gone. He knew her well enough to despise her, to want to punish her. And that was what he would do.

Who knew how long she could survive in this state? A Sleeping Beauty enchantment could last for a hundred years, but this was different. Would she die after one year? Five? Twenty? She'd go mad after a month of this: trapped in her own mind, as helpless as a mannequin. They could store her in a closet, leave her on the bed to gather dust, use her as a toy . . .

She'd rather be dead. But death wasn't hers to choose anymore.

I hate you, she thought.

And: *Save me.*

And: *Please let this end.* When she thought anything at all.

The door opened and light from the hall trickled in. It touched her face, and she drank up the sensation, that glow that proved she did exist.

Footsteps. More than one person—she wasn't sure how many.

And then the troll's face, leering over her, teeth bared as curiosity turned to glee. He was gloating, pleased to see her like this: immobile, silenced.

"Our dear Vivian . . . she doesn't look like herself, does she? There's a bit of terror in her eyes. It makes her prettier."

The troll moved out of sight. "You don't want to wake her . . . because you don't want her, is that it? You'll have her. And she'll have you."

"She doesn't want to stay here," Jasper said. "She never did."

"Well." The queen's voice now. "We'll tell her she can live here and be your bride, or we can bury her. She'll learn to want it."

"Very good, my dear," the troll said. "Young girls don't know what they want. That's why they have fate and their elders to guide them. Send the servants in. We need them to dress her. The guests will be arriving soon."

Viv didn't know if it was a dream or really happening; she was too afraid to hold out any hope. *Help . . . please . . . I hate you all but please just break the curse. . . .*

Soon there was the sound of silk rustling; the low voices of girls giving one another instructions. They pulled Viv upright,

335

jerking her by the arms, then wrestled her body this way and that to get her into the enormous white wedding dress. They pushed her arms into narrow lace sleeves, buttoned her into tight silk brocade, slid a garter up her cold, limp thigh.

"Shouldn't she have a bath?" one of the maids murmured.

"Just blow the dust off."

The maids wiped Viv's face and hands with a warm cloth, spritzed her with perfume, and began to loosen her braids and comb the dust from her hair. They did the job quickly, as if they were eager to be done with it, and she felt a jarring stab of pain as the comb collided with the poisoned hairpin. The pin was sunk so deeply that it stayed where it was, moving only enough to hurt. "There's something in her hair," the maid said. Steady fingers found the pin and pried it loose.

Viv felt her body come out of stasis as if it had been put on pause and all of a sudden thrust forward: air punched into her lungs; she sputtered and choked and almost started hyper-ventilating, she felt so desperate for air, and so afraid that the ability to breathe would be taken from her again. One of the maids pounded her back while she coughed; another held her upright. The rest jumped back as if a corpse had just revived.

"Excellent job waking the bride, girls," the troll said. "Now we don't have to worry about the groom seeing her in her wedding dress before the ceremony. It's bad luck, you know."

"I'm not marrying him!" Viv said.

The queen pinched the hairpin between two fingers, and pointed the bloodstained tip at Viv. "I can stab this back into your pretty little head and knock you out again. I don't care if my son takes you to bed like that—it's not unheard of in fairy tales. So play nice, won't you?"

CHAPTER FORTY-FIVE

THE TROLL ESCORTED VIV DOWN an aisle littered with rose petals, a sea of guests on either side: fairies, trolls, and Royals dressed in black. Eleven princes, but no sign of Garnet. Jasper waited at the altar, his face as cold as if it were made of stone. A tall, dark-haired man stood beside Jasper, bearing a wicked-looking executioner's ax instead of the wedding bands. There was no priest.

"Vivian . . . the fairest bride of all," the troll murmured. "You'll make my son a very happy man . . . eventually."

The queen followed behind them like a flower girl out of sequence, her mad giggles cutting through the wedding march.

The main hall had been transformed into a chapel. Every chandelier burned bright, and the gold trees shined like tangles of fire. Viv looked for a friendly face in the crowd, someone who might stand up and stop this, but she'd run out of saviors. She was on her own.

When they reached Jasper, the troll released her arm—
"Excuse me, Vivian"—and took his place at the altar. The
organ hushed.

The queen stayed behind her, poison hairpin in hand. Viv
had the urge to tear the pin from the queen's grasp and stab her
with it. But she knew it would be futile; even if she managed
to disarm the queen, there were other threats. She doubted the
executioner was up there because Jasper had asked him to be
his best man.

"Dearly beloved," the troll began.

"Is this a joke?" Viv said. "*You're* going to officiate?"

The troll smiled down at her from his place of honor.
"Whose deals are more binding than mine?"

The guests chuckled appreciatively.

"We are gathered here this day to join these two fated
individuals . . ."

The troll didn't waste time waxing poetic about love and
forever, sickness and health; he didn't even present the vows as
a question. "You will take Vivian to be your wife," he said to
Jasper. "Now give her the ring."

Viv kept her hands in fists at her sides.

"Malcolm, help her find her fingers," the troll instructed—
and Viv quickly held out her left hand to Jasper.

"Vivian, you will take my son Jasper to be your husband.
Put the ring on his finger. That's it; no shyness." Viv did as she
was told, and the troll's eyes flicked between them, his gaze
like the dart of a snake's tongue.

"Wonderful. I now pronounce you man and wife. Kiss the
bride, son. It's the part we've all been waiting for."

With grudging obedience, Jasper lifted Viv's veil and

touched her lips with a single perfunctory kiss. Viv turned her head away afterward, tempted to spit on the floor, but Malcolm's presence persuaded her not to. Petulance wouldn't earn her freedom. She needed to bide her time, and find the troll's name. None of them would have any power over her then.

Till death do us part, she thought. *No: Till* your name *do us part.*

The organist resumed playing—a dark song more suited to a haunted opera house than a wedding—and the queen began directing guests to the ballroom. Jasper led Viv down the aisle. The thought that he was her husband and they would have some sort of compulsory wedding night at the end of this made her want to throw herself in the lake.

Banquet tables had been arranged around the ballroom's perimeter, leaving a large area for dancing in the center. A dais had been set up at the head of the room. The wedding party's table was there, so that Viv and Jasper could hold court like the Royal couple they now were.

Endless platters of food and drink were brought out: white and red wine, black tea that smelled like smoke, bloody steak, blackened chicken, mermaid sashimi. The newlyweds had been seated at the center of the table, flanked by the king and queen and Jasper's brothers. Garnet had been excluded, as she was from every family event.

When the king and queen got up to mingle with their guests, Viv let a steak knife fall into her lap, folded her full white skirt over it, and tried to work out how to slip it into her narrow sleeve without accidentally opening a vein.

"Who are you going to use that on?" Jasper asked. "Me?"

He went on sullenly picking at his dinner like he didn't care in the least if she tried.

"I like to have options."

"I think you ran out of those when my father pronounced us husband and wife."

She went on trying to fit the knife inside her sleeve, the serrated edge snagging the lace. "That's only temporary."

"You still think you can find his name?"

"Yes. And when I do, it's going to be the best thing that ever happened to you."

"This certainly wasn't," he muttered.

"Cry me a river, Jasper." Viv went back to fiddling with the knife. If he expected her to feel sorry for him because he hadn't gotten his happily ever after, he was talking to the wrong person. She was only "awake" and mobile because his parents had wanted to see her walk down the aisle.

The shriek of feedback pierced her ears, followed by the irritating sound of the troll tapping his clawed fingertip against the microphone.

"Attention, everyone. I hope you're all enjoying yourselves tonight. Normally this is the time when I'd give a speech—but I think you're all more interested in the first dance. Vivian?"

Viv looked up, queasy with repulsion. She didn't want to waltz with Jasper. She was done with that.

"Don't get up," the troll said. "Traditionally the first dance features the bride and groom. But I have a different tradition in mind for tonight. Something very special. We don't get to do this often."

"What is he talking about?" Viv asked Jasper.

"Damned if I know."

"Guards!" the troll bellowed. "Let the show begin!"

The doors to the ballroom opened and four guards and a woman entered.

The woman wore a festive black party dress, all taffeta and sparkles, but that was the only cheerful thing about her.

Lank, dark hair hung in her face. She stood like an attack might come from any side. Bruises showed on her bare arms; red gouges on her wrists glistened where her skin had rubbed against chains or shackles. And she was barefoot.

"There wasn't room for many of your family members on the guest list," the troll said in his master-of-ceremonies tone, "but we managed to find this very special lady hiding in our silver forest, waiting for a way home—after she'd poisoned you, I believe. What a lucky coincidence for us."

Viv looked harder at the woman. She'd been beaten and held prisoner. Her face was hidden, her posture broken, but it was definitely Regina.

The first thing Viv wondered was: *Why? Why keep her here?*

Then her mind moved to the Snow White story, which ended with a wedding reception where the evil queen was forced to dance to death in red-hot iron shoes.

They wouldn't. They were twisted here, but no one followed the Snow White curse to the letter anymore.

Viv scrambled off the dais; the knife went clattering to the floor. "Okay, I get it—you can do anything to anyone! I'll regret it if I don't obey! Now stop!" she shouted. "Stop!"—as the troll said, "Someone, please control the bride."

In an instant Jasper's arms were around her. "Calm down," he said. "She's a murderess, not your mother." Viv kicked to get free and her feet met silk and petticoat instead of Jasper's shins. The wedding dress was too heavy, too bulky; it stopped her as surely as a rope would.

The troll strutted forward with his microphone, hamming it up like a game show host. "You've been such an important part of our Vivian's life, madam. . . . It's fitting that you're here to help us celebrate. Thank you so much for coming—and for failing to escape. Really. We couldn't do this without you.

"Bring out the dancing shoes!"

The ballroom doors opened again, and this time the executioner entered. He was carrying a pair of tongs in each hand, and each pair gripped a red-hot iron shoe, glowing and steaming in the cool air—and the crowd roared as if for a gladiator.

"Stop! *Stop!*" Viv felt like her voice was one long scream that no one could hear.

Only one of us can survive, Regina had told her. No, no, she didn't believe that. . . .

Sweat dripped down the executioner's face—that was how long he'd stood in front of the fire, heating the metal until it took on that ruby glow. He placed the iron shoes on the floor. There was a sizzle and hiss and the smell of burning varnish smoked into the air.

Regina looked up. She caught Viv's eyes and gave her a trembly smile. "You look so pretty, Viv. Don't cry. You're supposed to be happy on your wedding day."

It was Regina's resignation, more than her fear, that made Viv want to cry. Regina, who'd always fought against the certainty that she would lose, had finally given up. It was as painful a reversal as the day she'd turned from loving stepmom to Evil Queen. There was something about her now that reminded Viv of those sad, early days when she'd stroked

Regina's hair while her stepmother cried over Viv's father: that in-between time when they'd no longer had everything, but hadn't yet lost it all, either.

This was the end of the curse for both of them. Viv couldn't escape Jasper's grasp, and the troll had never shown mercy to anyone. She couldn't stop this, no matter how much she begged.

Viv's throat constricted as she struggled to speak instead of scream. She couldn't save Regina, but she wanted her to know.

"Regina! You're not alone. I'm with you; I won't leave you. Even if you didn't want it—you were my mother. You'll always be my mother."

She thought maybe Regina smiled then; just a twitch of her lips before she pressed her hand to her mouth and blew Viv a kiss.

"Music!" the troll commanded.

The band began to play.

The guards nudged Regina toward the shoes. They lifted her by the arms and carried her forward, like backup dancers supporting a starlet—then crammed her feet into the hot iron, the shoes that were melting the floor. There was a scream like all the pain in the world, and then Regina went limp, fainted from the shock, before being roused by the intensity of the pain. The smell of roasting flesh filled the ballroom, and the guards were jabbing her with their swords to make her move, shouting *Dance!* until the whole crowd joined in, screaming *Dance! Dance! Dance!* with a bloodlust that belonged in the Colosseum.

The iron shoes were so heavy, and the agony so great, Regina could barely move. She stumped forward one step, then another, growing clumsier as her feet became lumps of iron and bone. The guards hit her with their swords, spinning her as the smell of burning flesh grew stronger. Blood poured from her nose and darkened her teeth. The screams of the guests were so loud that Regina's own screams seemed silent—just a gaping mouth, a plea that would never be heard.

When Regina collapsed, the crowd surged forward, pressing in to see every gory detail. Viv joined them, to be near her, to see her stepmother one last time.

Regina lay on her side, face tipped to the ceiling, her hair in Medusa tangles around her head. Jasper's mother bent down to dab at the blood running from Regina's nose, then traced her finger over Regina's lips, like she was painting on lipstick.

"Red as blood!" the queen cried. The other guests cackled their approval. Even the troll laughed—his queen's madness had amused him for once.

"Very good, darling!"

Viv stared straight ahead and tried to make her face like stone, to keep her fury and despair in check so she wouldn't fall apart, wouldn't seem weak in this room full of enemies. Tears crawled down her neck like spiders.

"There's nothing like death at a wedding!" the troll cheered. Champagne flutes clinked—a toast, not to happiness, but to suffering. The Cursed and their schadenfreude. Bloodlust masked by the reasoning *She deserved it.* Torture as happy ending. Cinderella's stepsisters had their eyes pecked out by birds. The stepmother in "The Juniper Tree" was crushed and killed by a millstone. The false princess in "The Goose Girl" was stuffed naked into a barrel studded with nails, then dragged through the streets by horses. It wasn't anything new; Viv had read the stories a hundred times.

But living it was different.

The corpse was carried out and the cake was brought in: a towering white monstrosity decorated with sugared butterflies instead of fondant. The troll held out the knife to Jasper and Viv, so they could cut their own cake—then chuckled and said, "Maybe not."

He cut two slices for the bride and groom, opening a vanilla-and-raspberry wound. Viv's piece was topped with a broken butterfly wing—angled like a fancy chocolate sliver.

"You haven't smiled all night," the troll said to her. "I know you weren't keen on getting married—girls your age prefer freedom to wedded bliss—but I thought your stepmother's performance would cheer you up."

"Did you." Her tone was flat.

"Snow White princesses have thrilled to it for centuries. But you're impossible to please, aren't you, Vivian? Well. You'll have plenty of time to hone your misery here."

CHAPTER FORTY-SIX

"THEY MADE THE BED with white sheets," Jasper said as he pulled the covers back. "They'll check for blood. As proof that we . . ."

Viv cut him off. "There won't be any blood. So slice your hand or something. I'm getting out of this dress."

She locked herself into the bathroom to change. Once her wedding gown was off—in a pile on the floor, so enormous you could have hidden seven dwarves under it—she slid down against the door and covered her eyes. *Lips as red as blood*—she couldn't stop seeing it.

Regina.

The corpse hadn't even looked like her.

The bitch, the sexpot, the wicked queen was gone. Only the broken heart had remained.

Black as burnt flesh. White as bone.

She'd said that love was worthless, that power was everything. Love required an ally. Power you could claim on your own.

As long as Viv was breathing, as long as she had a voice to speak the troll's true name, she had a chance to take control of this hell she'd walked into.

She slipped on the nightgown the maids had left for her and heard a gasp from the other room. A grunt. Then nothing.

"Jasper?" Maybe he'd taken her advice and cut his hand. "Are you okay?"

When he didn't respond, she opened the door.

And met Jasper's bulging eyes, hands scrabbling at the rope wrapped around his throat.

Henley stood behind him, pulling the rope taut. Still in that same tux, grubby as a miner, black stone dust griming his collar.

Henley gave her a grim smile. "You want a divorce, or do you want to be a widow?"

"Jesus. Just . . . tie him up or something!"

Henley loosed the rope from around Jasper's neck and Jasper stumbled forward, gasping and clutching at his throat. He backed into a corner, as far from them as he could get.

"Get over here," Henley said. He opened his arms and she ran to him, leaping so he had to catch her.

"What are you doing here? How did you—?"

"You're happy to see me?" he asked.

"I'm happy to see you." She kissed his dirty face, his neck. His skin had taken on the wet stone smell of the underworld. His invisibility cloak lay in a pool at his feet. Whole, not slashed up like the one Jasper had showed her.

"I don't want to let you go," Henley said, "but we need to get out of here while the king's distracted. I don't know how long this party's going to last. And we still have to deal with your ex-husband."

"No, you're right. . . ." She parted from Henley reluctantly.

He picked up the rope. "On your knees," he told Jasper. "Hands behind your back."

Jasper didn't struggle as Henley bound his wrists and ankles, but he couldn't resist adding, "You're both insane. You know that, don't you? You'll be lucky to survive the night."

"Who told you to talk?" Henley stuffed the royal silver sash into Jasper's mouth.

"Wait." Viv pulled the sash back out so Jasper could speak. "Jasper, if you know *anything* about your father's name, you have to tell me."

"Do you have amnesia? Did you not see what happened in the ballroom? If you cross my father—"

Henley crammed the sash back into Jasper's mouth. "All right. Thanks for your advice."

Viv sighed. She caught sight of herself in the mirror, a bride in her frilly white nightgown. There was no way she could sneak out wearing that.

"Just give me a minute to change and we can go."

"Sure. I'll keep an eye on your ex-husband."

"Stop saying that," she warned him.

"What? *Husband?*" Henley put his shoe on Jasper's shoulder and shoved him over.

Viv dug through the wardrobe until she found the black-and-white cocktail dress Jewel had bought her. It looked like something a wedding guest would wear. She hurried into the bathroom, threw on the dress, and dashed back out.

"Ready," she said, stepping into a pair of black satin slippers.

"One more thing." Henley took hold of Viv's left hand, his fingers settling on her gold wedding band. He worked it over her knuckle and then pinged it at the wall.

"All right," he said. "Let's get the hell out of here."

The corridor outside Viv's room was empty, but it wouldn't stay that way. Jasper's brothers might return to their rooms, or the troll might drop by to make sure Viv was fulfilling her end of the marital contract. Viv urged Henley to put on his cloak, then led him through the first open doorway they passed. The room was dark, and when she pulled Henley close, her ears filled with the sound of his breathing. She kept her hands on his wrists so she wouldn't lose him and kept her eyes on the doorway. Any minute now they could be found.

It was dangerous for Henley to be here at all, but especially tonight when the troll had an audience and his son's pride was at stake. She wondered what he was doing here. Saving her—that was obvious—but why? If the key had worked the way it was supposed to, and broken the curse, Henley should have been on the surface, engaged to one of the twelve princesses, not in the underworld, risking his life.

If the key had failed, then . . . he'd been condemned to death, and dodged it somehow. But once they returned to the surface, he'd be a marked man.

"Did the key not work?" she asked, afraid of the answer.

"It worked. The door closed up like it never existed, and the key broke right after that. The princesses haven't come back. The curse is broken."

"But . . . you're still here."

"I didn't know if I'd be able to get back here once the door was sealed. So I locked the door from the underworld side. I've been hiding. Waiting for my opportunity to save you. I couldn't walk away from you. I just . . . I couldn't do it."

"Then how are you supposed to leave? The one door you could get through is gone. Are you stuck here?"

She felt the muscles in his arms tense. "Don't worry about that."

"Don't *worry* about it?" she hissed. "Are you serious?"

"Look, we don't have another choice right now. If I'm stuck here, I'm stuck. But you can still get out. You'll take my cloak, sneak past the guards, and climb through the door to Beau Rivage. Or hell, any of them. The first door you find."

"Unless the magic keeps me from leaving," Viv said as it dawned on her. "Everyone I invited was blocked from entering. The troll already told me I can't leave. Why wouldn't he have a little magical insurance?"

Henley swore under his breath. His hands curled into fists, like he wanted to break something, but that would make noise, and they were trying not to get caught. Viv pried his fists open and wove her fingers between his; making him hold her hands instead, trying to reassure him with her touch.

"What do we do?" he said finally.

"We try, anyway. And if we fail, we fail together. I'm not leaving you again."

"No. If you have a chance—"

"Henley." She pulled his face down to hers. Kissed him once, hard. "I am never leaving you again."

The blood-and-cake reception had given way to a debauched after-party. Nothing made Cursed want to live it up like death.

The red-hot iron shoes, the twisted end—it was a reminder that their own ends could come unexpectedly.

The chairs that had turned the main hall into a chapel had been cleared away, and now it looked more like an out-of-control house party. Half-naked fairies intertwined on the staircase. Couples danced to the music spilling from the ball-room, and drank champagne out of glass slippers or straight from the bottle.

A young girl ran barefoot through a stream of liquor, kicking at clumps of white rice and rose petals.

A group of Royals had cornered a fragile-looking teenage girl and harassed her to the point of tears. They watched in delight as pearls squeezed from the corners of her eyes and rolled down her cheeks.

Viv quick-stepped through the chaos, her hand tight around Henley's invisible one, and prayed she'd go unnoticed.

The seven ravens on the chandelier started cawing when she passed beneath it, but only got a bottle hurled at them for their troubles. No one grabbed Viv's arm and asked, *Princess, where are you going?* A few guests bumped into Henley, but must have been too drunk to care. No one called for the guards; Viv and Henley made it through the palace unscathed.

They made it all the way to the surface doors.

And that was where their luck ran out.

The doors would not open for them.

They tried all of them: the doors that looked out through mirrors, through fireplaces and wardrobes and hollow trees. Viv could see the alley in Beau Rivage, a moonlit garden, a fancy parlor, but couldn't reach through to touch any of those places. She was stopped by a barrier every time. She and Henley tried forcing their way through—throwing their bodies against the doors—but it was no use. The magic held.

"There might be another way," Viv said.

"Another door?" Henley had shed his invisibility cloak, as if he wanted to be ready to throw it across her shoulders, and she could see him: his forehead damp, the nervous way he kept biting his lip.

Viv started toward the lake, trusting him to follow.

"When I first came to the underworld, a horseman brought me through the well in my backyard. I ended up here." She pointed to the lake.

"It's underwater?"

"I don't know exactly where the door is. I thought I was drowning at the time. But I think it was somewhere around here. By the shore."

"So . . . what, we swim down? Look for a hole and hope we come out on the other side?"

"We can't get through the other doors, Henley."

"Yeah, but this—"

She knew why he didn't want to do it. They'd probably drown before they found a way out. But what choice did they have?

Viv waded knee-deep into the water. "I'm not scared of dying. If that's what you're worried about."

"Don't say shit like that. *I'll* look for it. You go hide."

"Those lights . . ." She squinted. There were lights dancing in the forest. No, not dancing: swaying in time with the steps of the men who held them. It was a search party. Light swept the forest and soon enough it would reach the lakeshore.

"We have to find the door. We have to find it now!"

Viv plunged into the lake, bitter cold up to her chest. She heard Henley splash in after her and she felt around for a hole, a depression, anything that might be the door. She found silt and gritty pebbles, tattered cloth that clung to her like algae. A shard of bone cut her foot and filled the water with a tuft of warm blood.

Henley grabbed her arm. "You okay?"

"Fine."

She tried to stay calm when the shouts started but the chill of the water and fear of capture made her shake. As the lanterns drew closer her foot found a dent, like a place an eel might live, and she dove down to pry at the sand, as if there might be a door or she might be able to make one. Fingers slipped and scraped at nothing. She dug until she had no breath. Under again. Under. And then she was swimming farther out, driven by shouts, the pounding of boots on the shore, the splashes that followed, until she was yanked up by her hair, gasping and choking.

The guards already had Henley. There was blood on his face and hands. One of the guards was cutting up his cloak with a pair of scissors.

The troll stood at the head of the search party, Jasper by his side.

"Hog-tying my son and running away," the troll mused. "This was not what I meant when I told you to give him a night he'd always remember."

"Let Henley go," Viv said. "I'll stay. I won't try to leave again. Just let him go."

"No, I don't think I will. In fact, considering how he's

shamed my son, I think a public beheading would make an excellent wedding gift. Well—for one of you. Would you like that?" he asked Jasper.

Jasper didn't answer. She was sure he was tempted to say *yes*, and the only thing that stopped him was knowing she would never forgive him if he did.

"What will it take to save him?" Viv shouted. "Tell me! Let's make a deal. What do you want? Henley lives, in exchange for—"

"Your firstborn child? That will be mine, anyway. No, it will have to be something better." The troll stroked his chin, as if he was thinking it over, but Viv had a feeling he knew exactly what he wanted.

"Your tongue," he finally said.

"My—what?"

"I will cut your tongue from your mouth. That is my price for your Huntsman's life. He will be free to go—though *not* to return—and you, my dear, will be blessedly silent. No more smart remarks. No more adulterous kissing. And no more guessing." He smiled. "It's not the same if you just write the name down. If that were enough, this little book"—he produced her notebook of names, and made sure she recognized it before he threw it into the lake—"might have some power. Alas."

She watched it sink. "I get a chance to guess your name first. If I guess your name, I get everything."

"Yes. Yes, you do. Bravo. An informed customer! However . . . three days is a bit much. I don't want your Huntsman in my underworld that long. I'll give you three hours to guess my name."

354

"Three *hours*?"

The troll shrugged. "If you don't like my terms, I can cut off his head. It's up to you."

"No." She took a deep breath. "I'll do it."

CHAPTER FORTY-SEVEN

"IS IT RUMPELSTILTSKIN?"

"That is not my name."

The troll lounged on his throne, one leg dangling over the armrest, like a joker pretending to be king. He wore his crown—solid gold and topped with spikes—and he'd dressed up for the occasion in an ivory suit dusted with gold, and a reddish-pink shirt the color of a human tongue. At the edges of the room, lined up like parade watchers, were the troll's guards, the queen, the executioner, and Jasper and his brothers. Ten feet away from Viv, a bound-and-gagged Henley knelt on the floor, with guards on either side of him to ensure that he stayed there.

The second hand of the clock ticked like a finger tapping her skull, reminding her that three hours was nothing.

"Is your name Balthazar? Melchior? Is it Blake? Byron?"

"No, no, no, and no, Princess."

"Is it James? Jamal? Evan? Edwin? Darwin? Andrew?"

"Those are not my name."

Viv tried to remind herself that, no matter what, Henley would live. She kept licking her lips, starting to speak and then feeling her tongue move in her mouth, feeling the air slip around it, aware that it would soon be gone. Every part of her trembled in fear of the moment the troll would grasp it by the tip and slice it from her mouth. There would be a hot gush of blood she wouldn't taste. And then her mouth would be a silent place, a carved-out shell.

But he'll live.

Henley would live, and so would she—though what kind of life it would be was something she couldn't bear to think about.

"Is your name Iago?"

The troll's grin stretched wider till she thought the corners of his mouth might split. "No."

Every time she looked at Henley she tried to say *I love you* with her eyes. *I love you* and *Believe in me*, but she barely believed in herself. Henley looked as broken as she felt. He'd been the one who'd believed they could fight fate. But they couldn't fight this.

"Is it Carl? Caleb? Ming? Mason? Alex? Lee? Dante? Dmitri?"

"No, those are not my name."

The task before her was nearly impossible. Maybe once upon a time, when a person had one culture of names to choose from, and some gibberish like Rumpelstiltskin and Tom Tit Tot, it was easier to guess the right name. But even then, success usually came when the troll screwed up and let the secret slip.

Malcolm was ready with his ax. The queen sat by his side, curled up on a cushion like a cat, clearly thrilled to have three hours with her firstborn son. From time to time she would shout a suggestion, but it was often a name Viv had already guessed. The troll didn't seem worried about the queen's "help," and Viv found his confidence as distracting as the queen's cries.

The night the troll had caught her in his study, he'd quoted a few books; she guessed the names from those, just in case. "Is your name Ishmael? Melville? Herman? Ahab? Romeo? Shakespeare? William?"

"I love the way your mouth looks when you're wrong. No, those are not my name."

The minute hand on the clock slid forward as if it had been greased. One hour, and then two, and nothing she'd said had unsettled the troll. She felt her courage breaking down. She wanted to give up. She wanted to spend the last hour with Henley—holding him for the last time, kissing him for the last time, and just talking to him, just saying his name and saying *I love you* before they cut out her tongue. If this was hopeless, was it better to admit defeat and make the most of that last hour? They'd been in such a rush each time they'd met in the underworld—worried they'd be caught, needing to break a curse, to escape—that there had been no time to just be together.

What would she regret more?

She'd been quiet a few moments and now the troll shifted in his throne, leaning back, relaxed. "Are you out of names, Vivian? Shall we call it a night?"

"No. No, I—" She closed her eyes, feeling almost dizzy.

If she gave up now, she would have an hour to spend with Henley—but she would be handing victory to the troll. This final hour of guessing . . . it was all she could do to give them a future. And if she squandered that chance, she would never be able to forgive herself.

Her voice, when it emerged again, was weak. It no longer had the strength of hope behind it. Only fear, and desperation, and the knowledge that each word she spoke was one of her last. "Is it Midas?"

"No, it is not Midas."

"Is your name John?"—*no*—"Juan?"—*no*—"Hans?"—*no*—"Ivan?"

No.

Fifteen minutes slid by, then twenty, thirty. The pressure on her heart increased.

"Edgar? Edward? Edison? Edwin?"

"You guessed Edwin already—the answer is still no." That smile—as if he couldn't be more pleased.

She felt like she was running to a destination she would never reach. Pushing a boulder up a hill, and then, just before she reached the top, watching it roll back down.

"Sisyphus?" she guessed.

The troll laughed. "No," he said, wiping tears from his eyes. "That is not my name."

Viv followed the clock. She could see the block of time that was left to her—ten minutes that the second hand was swiftly carving down.

"*Victor*?" she snapped out. Because he always won.

The troll's lips curled back to show his teeth. "No. But I like that one."

Every time Henley had tried to get up, the guards beat him back down. Whenever he'd tried to break free, he ended up with more blood on his face. He made a last, desperate attempt now that her time was running out—lunging at one of the guards, throwing his full weight against him, though Henley could barely stand, bound as he was.

He was doing it so they would kill him—so the deal would be broken. So Viv could keep her voice and guess another day, and still have that chance to be free.

She went to him before he could become a sacrifice, threw her arms around his neck, and held him, as tightly as she could, because he couldn't hold her. He was on his knees, and she was kissing his tears away faster than they could fall. Tasting salt and misery. She could feel the anger shaking through him—the helplessness.

"It doesn't matter," she whispered. "It doesn't matter. We still have everything."

By which she meant: the past. Memories. They were about to lose everything else.

Henley couldn't speak with the gag silencing him and she knew there were things he was desperate to say—she was desperate, too. . . .

But when she started to untie the gag the troll ordered her to stop. Sword blades crossed at the edge of her vision—a second warning, in case she'd missed the first.

She kissed Henley's mouth through the gag. She held his face in her hands, cheeks and chin wet with tears and blood. "I'm sorry," she whispered. "I want to say a million things, but I want to say that most of all. There will never be enough time to say all the things I need to say to you."

Viv glanced at the clock. Five minutes. She could spend that time kissing him, holding him, whispering words that would never be enough. Or—she could keep guessing while the troll laughed at her attempts.

She got up off her knees and forced herself to walk away from Henley.

"Done with your good-byes?" the troll asked.

"I'm not finished with you," she said.

"Five more minutes if you want to speak to him. After that, you'll have to wave."

Viv took a deep breath—and started to cry. Her mind was blank, a minefield of possibilities, like there were a million answers and also none. How had she let this happen?

"Oh, Vivian, poor Vivian," the troll crooned. "Will it really be so bad? Living with us? Wait. Don't answer that. Of course it will."

She felt like something had been jarred loose in her. Like the bite of poison apple, knocked free from her throat.

She looked at his mouth, the way his lips wormed and puckered as they shaped her name, like he wanted to make out with it. And no wonder. Of course he did. Of course.

"Vivian," she said.

"Talking to yourself? Is that really the best use of your time?" But she saw him twitch. She saw that ugly smile creep up and down.

"Your name is Vivian," she said—louder, sure this time.

Because he always said it. Excessively. He threw it in her face like a slap. She'd thought he was taunting her, using her full name, knowing she didn't like it, because it was one more thing he could do to her, one more thing she couldn't stop. But no. He'd loved saying it because it was his dirty secret. A secret he'd revealed himself, like every other troll.

Vivian. It had been a boy's name before it was a girl's. And it had been with her all this time.

He didn't have to tell her she was right.

His body said it for him.

It started at his hairline—a dribble of blood, a crack that began at his widow's peak, as if his frustration required a physical release. The crack ran between his eyes, continued down the length of his nose, sliced straight through his lips. His eyes bulged with rage and disbelief . . . and then his long fingernails scratched wildly at his scalp, as if it were infested with fleas. He grabbed two greasy handfuls of his hair—and pulled, hard.

His scalp split.

His face tore in half—

—not just his skin, *all of it.*

And he howled.

The queen howled along with him. And then she began to laugh and hop up and down. "Malcolm, look!"

There was a sound like paper tearing, like gas bubbling in a swamp, as the troll split down the middle—his body opening like a locket, revealing two gleaming slabs of meat and cracked white bone. His last scream poured into the room like blood . . . and echoed after he was dead.

The crown dropped from the riven corpse and cracked the marble floor.

They all watched it for a second—this last symbol of the troll's power—and then Viv picked it up. She placed the crown on her head carefully so it wouldn't fall.

Jasper had gone white with fear. One of the guards

shrieked with delight, then fell to the floor and began to laugh. Malcolm laid down his ax. The mad queen clapped her hands, giggling like a little girl on her birthday. And Henley . . . Henley's eyes conveyed the shock his mouth couldn't.

"Free him," Viv told the guards, pointing at Henley. "And bring everyone here. Everyone the troll imprisoned. Tell them their new queen has something to say."

CHAPTER FORTY-EIGHT

SHE KEPT THE CROWN.

Two weeks later, it was on her desk at home, in the room that had once been Regina's office. Viv spent her days there making phone calls, trying to track down the parents who'd traded their children for success. She didn't want to rule the underworld—Jasper and his family could fight over that job—but she did want to make things right, so she'd taken on the responsibility of reuniting the stolen children with their families.

And since they needed a place to live in the meantime, she'd moved them into her house in Beau Rivage. The first floor went to the boatmen, the second floor to the maids. Some kindly fairies volunteered to foster the younger children. The guards were on their own. Viv would help them find their families, but after the way they'd tormented Regina and beaten Henley, they weren't welcome in her home.

Her father protested this arrangement; apparently he

wanted to move back in. But it had been so long since he'd really lived there, Viv couldn't muster the energy to care. She resented that he'd stayed away because he didn't want to deal with the curse, and now that Regina was dead he expected to return and go on with his life, as if a storm had finally blown over, when Viv was forever changed.

The underworld had turned into a ghost town. The troll was dead, the nightclub deserted. The very-important-Cursed found new places to dance and be seen. Some of the underworld princes set out for the surface; some stayed in the palace, more reclusive than ever. The queen, as far as Viv knew, was hosting tea parties in Malcolm's honor, drinking from unwashed teacups and eating stale wedding cake.

Jasper was one of the princes who had moved to the surface. He and Garnet were renting a house near the beach. He'd been forced to tell Garnet the truth about Minuet, and Garnet had been more bewildered than heartbroken. Upset and a little offended: *I'm not that fragile that you have to lie to me and tell me someone loves me when they don't.*

Still, they'd made up quickly. They were planning a trip to Italy. Garnet had gone to her first party—ever—and met more people in one night than she'd encountered in her whole life. She seemed happier, brighter, more energetic now that her horizons had opened up.

Jasper's happiness was harder to gauge since he never seemed happy when Viv was around. He'd been different since she'd defeated his father. Awkward and ashamed, instead of angry and bitter. He'd used the troll and the impossibility of stopping him as justification for not helping her—and all the while he'd thought of himself as her protector. But when

Viv had defeated the troll, Jasper's rationalization had unraveled. It was like he realized he'd been lying to himself: that heroic Prince Jasper was no more real than pining-for-Garnet Minuet.

Viv could sort of understand his unwillingness to act against the troll, but understanding him and liking him weren't the same thing. She couldn't look at Jasper without seeing the prince who'd let her suffer in that poison stasis, who'd restrained her while Regina was being murdered, who'd thrown a torn cloak at her and claimed that Henley was dead. She didn't think they would ever be friends.

And that was fine. The curse had decided they were meant to be—but the curse was broken. Their marriage had been nullified with the death of the troll, as had all the troll's deals. The curse, the troll, Regina, Jasper—they no longer had power over her. And if she ever needed a reminder, all she had to do was pick up that crown.

Henley had officially declined his reward for breaking the Twelve Dancing Princesses curse: the package deal of marriage to the dancing princess of his choice and half her father's wealth. The twelve princesses had been shocked, insulted, relieved, and delighted by his decision. The ones who'd hoped for the fairy-tale ending—chosen by the hero, followed by happily ever after—were disappointed. The rest had rushed headlong into freedom as soon as the curse was broken and were pleased to know that freedom would continue.

Henley still had the triple hash mark tattoo on his neck. He'd said no to the prize, but the hero reputation was his to keep. And Viv was glad, because in Beau Rivage, a hero and a murderer were rarely the same thing. A hero's murders were always just, and if Henley's murder of the old Huntsman ever came to light, chances were a judge would rule in Henley's favor.

Henley's parents were proud of his success and his new role—a hero in the family was a big deal. Instead of being angry that he'd disappeared and let them believe he was dead, they threw a party to celebrate his return, and basically indulged his every whim for a few days—before they made him go back to school and back to work.

Of course, his parents weren't thrilled with all his decisions. There had been an awkward moment during the party when Viv had been looking for Henley, and had come across him just as his mother asked, "You couldn't find *one* girl you liked—out of twelve?"

She was sure a lot of people felt that way: that Henley had missed an opportunity, that he was stupid for staying with her. That he would wake up one day and regret it. How many men had died in pursuit of that prize? And yet Henley had put himself in danger, not for a chance at the reward, but for Viv. Because he thought she was worth the risk.

People would always have opinions about her.

You're the fairest.

She's a bitch.

How pathetic.

What kind of princess—?

Powerless.

Gorgeous.

You don't deserve to be loved like that. You don't deserve—

But it didn't matter what they thought.

* * *

367

The crown stayed in her office, but the magic mirror she hung in the cottage—her new home. It had been in her life longer than Regina, longer than Henley, and it would probably outlast Viv, too.

The mirror was quieter than it had been when Regina was alive, but every once in a while it purred out a meaningless compliment:

"You're stunning, beautiful, the fairest in the land."

She wondered if it would do that for the rest of her life. And how she would feel if it stopped.

That mirror-voice, and the glassy stare, were the last remnants of the curse she'd shared with Regina. The poison apple had shriveled, the hairpin had been lost, the stay laces had been clipped and thrown away. The glass coffin had been broken at a recent party when a drunk girl climbed inside it to see what it would be like. The house felt empty without Regina, and Viv couldn't help but look for her there, to flinch when she turned a corner or passed another mirror—and she couldn't help feeling sad when she relaxed and remembered she would never see Regina again. The threat was gone, but the possibility that they might reconcile, might come to understand each other . . . that was gone, too.

Viv couldn't bear to sleep under that roof again. She could work there, but not live there. She surrendered the house to her guests and made the forest her home.

Now, every morning she woke to the sound of birds chirping. Sun peeking through thin curtains. The smell of an autumn forest all around her. Chipmunks sitting on the clothes she'd laid out the night before. Shivering, she poured cold water into a basin and washed her face and brushed her teeth and tried to keep the birds from bathing in it, but they always ended up in there, anyway.

Henley had helped her make the cottage habitable. They'd scrubbed it from top to bottom, hung curtains, stocked the cabinets, replaced the bed, added a table-and-chair set—the table just large enough to hold two teacups or a dinner plate. There was a woodstove she hadn't quite mastered yet. A few hurricane lamps for light. A braided rug that the animals thought was their playground.

The windows were drafty, the roof leaked, and the floor was partly rotted through, but after being trapped in the dead landscape of the underworld, Viv wanted to be as close to nature as possible. The chill breeze creeping under her quilt, the mice bickering in the dark, the smack of raindrops on her cheek, all made it easier to breathe, less likely she would wake up and think she was still in the palace.

When she had nightmares about the wedding she could pull an armload of rabbits into bed and hold them until she calmed down. Or she could step outside and pace barefoot on the trail, the grass and earth promising *You're home, not there. Safe.* Breathing deeply, she could prove it to herself: the smell of the forest was nothing like that of the underworld. Here the air seethed with life and death. The threat of rain, a distant smell of smoke. Musk, pine, earth. A living, changing world, not a coffin of silver and stone.

Some nights she walked to Henley's house and knocked on his window, then waited for him to push up the screen and pull her through. His hair damp from a shower. The muscles of his chest tight against a cheap white undershirt. Her fingers would graze his arm, wanting to touch him, because there had been a time when she'd thought she would never touch him again.

Tonight, she said, "Ignore me, do your homework," not meaning a word of it, and he pulled her onto his bed and kissed her until autumn felt like summer, on the same sheets he'd had when they were fourteen. And when they lay tangled together later, she trailed a lazy finger along the photos on the wall, pictures of the two of them that he'd torn in half and then mended with Scotch tape. She touched the ragged fault lines of the photos, the paper scars that ran between them, and said, "We look good taped back together."

She had never been able to imagine a life without him— but she'd never been able to imagine a life *with* him. The curse had denied them a future. Now she could finally see it—in little bursts, daydreams of next summer and beyond. A ring she'd actually say *yes* to. A wedding where their friends threw birdseed and the smaller, furrier guests scampered after it. A home shared with the person who knew her best, who truly saw her, who had never tried to take her heart by force.

Henley.

She'd known him forever.

And she would keep him forever, if he'd let her.